Vanessa studied English and Australian literature at the University of Sydney and dreamed of one day writing fiction. She then went on to immerse herself completely in writing about real people, working as a journalist for 18 years. Vanessa has been a news, medical, entertainment and arts reporter for *The Daily Telegraph* and her writing has appeared in numerous other publications. She's happy to now, finally, be creating fictional characters. She lives in Sydney with her husband and daughter.

Also by Vanessa McCausland

The Lost Summers of Driftwood

The Valley of Lost Stories

VANESSA McCAUSLAND

HarperCollins*Publishers*

HarperCollinsPublishers
Australia • Brazil • Canada • France • Germany • Holland • Hungary
India • Italy • Japan • Mexico • New Zealand • Poland • Spain • Sweden
Switzerland • United Kingdom • United States of America

First published in Australia in 2020
by HarperCollins*Publishers* Australia Pty Limited
ABN 36 009 913 517
harpercollins.com.au

Copyright © Vanessa McCausland 2020

The right of Vanessa McCausland to be identified as the author of this work has been asserted by her in accordance with the *Copyright Amendment (Moral Rights) Act 2000*.

This work is copyright. Apart from any use as permitted under the *Copyright Act 1968*, no part may be reproduced, copied, scanned, stored in a retrieval system, recorded, or transmitted, in any form or by any means, without the prior written permission of the publisher.

A catalogue record for this book is available from the National Library of Australia

ISBN 978 1 4607 5956 1 (paperback)
ISBN 978 1 4607 1317 4 (ebook)

Cover design by Amy Daoud, HarperCollins Design Studio
Cover images by shutterstock.com
Typeset in Bembo Std by Kelli Lonergan
Author photograph by Sally Flegg Photography
Printed and bound in Australia by McPherson's Printing Group
The papers used by HarperCollins in the manufacture of this book are a natural, recyclable product made from wood grown in sustainable plantation forests. The fibre source and manufacturing processes meet recognised international environmental standards, and carry certification.

*For my daughter and
my mother*

PROLOGUE

Mummy is lost. She never came down in the morning like the other mums came. All the adults had worried faces but happy voices. It's a trick grown-ups always play but children can't be tricked as easily as they think. They kept on saying she'll be back, and she's probably taken a little morning walk and got lost in the bush, but I could see by their faces that they weren't sure. Police ladies even came. They were nice. They told all the kids not to be scared but they looked like I feel when there's a thunderstorm and I can feel the thunder grumbling in my tummy, like I'm sick but not sick. What if there's another thunderstorm? It was the worst one I've ever been in. Mummy said it was because we were in a valley and the thunder was echoing off the cliffs. I called out to her in the night because I was scared being in this big old, strange house, with the thunder so loud I could still hear it under the covers. And she came and did that thing where she pats my head but now there's no one to come and pat my head when I'm scared. And now that she's gone, I'm always scared.

PART I

CHAPTER 1

Nathalie

March

The lights caught her eye, drew her gaze like a lure, like a charm. A strange feeling came over her and her fingers flicked the indicator before she'd had time to think, to doubt. The hotel was luminous, its windows aglow, as though the world inside held something enchanting. Something she hadn't felt for so long – hope, peace, *rest*. And then Nathalie was turning into the drive, leaving the rain-slicked city street behind. There were white-gloved hands ushering her in, and she was sliding down her window, acutely aware of the state of her car; the debris of life with small children. The snowfield of cracker crumbs, and apple cores browned and shrivelled like small dried hearts. She put the car in reverse. *What am I doing?* she thought. And then the door was opening for her and her legs were moving, and she was getting out.

'Good evening, madam. Will you be staying for the evening?'

Nathalie found herself nodding, even as her heart raced and her breasts throbbed, rock-hard with unexpressed milk.

I could be a businesswoman, she thought. *Just back from a late meeting in the city with clients. No one is going to know I'm a mother running from her life for the night.*

'Will there be luggage to accompany you?' The gentleman had his head cocked politely.

The tone of his voice suggested the man had somehow intuited that there would be no luggage. Nathalie knew she probably looked stunned. Even she couldn't believe she was doing this. She glanced at her phone in her hand. It was 11 pm. On a Tuesday night. There were several missed calls from her husband. She wondered if the girls were asleep, but she knew Richie wouldn't be. Her breasts told her that. *You have left your newborn son. How could you?*

Guilt hit her in the chest like a punch. 'Oh, I should—' she turned back towards her car. What? Go home? Have to face him? Have to watch him try to lie? How would she even get the words out of her mouth? Her head throbbed. She needed another drink. The single glass of wine she'd had with her former colleagues had hardly even touched the edges.

I have dreamt of this, she wanted to tell the man with the white gloves. *I never thought I was capable of actually doing it.*

Instead she smiled at him as he took her keys and led her into the foyer. Stepping inside reminded her of opening a jewellery box she'd had as a child. When you lifted the lid soft tinkling music came out and a ballerina began to twirl before a tiny mirror. A sense that there was magic in the world, even for a moment. It smelled like freshly cut flowers and sweet, like vanilla bean ice cream. This was a place of order and quiet. There were solutions to problems with the flick of an elegant wrist. It was just as she'd imagined it on so many sleepless nights.

I could have driven to the Gap, Nathalie wanted to tell the woman as she handed over her credit card. She watched her neat efficiency and was comforted by it. *I could have ended it all and left them motherless. Instead I am taking one night. Just one night. To work out what to do.*

'Just one night please.' Her voice sounded foreign to her, too high pitched. Not the businesswoman she was pretending to be. It sounded like the voice of a mother who had reached the point of hysteria. To calm herself she reached out and touched the petals of the pale roses in the vase next to her, their heads distended, obscenely beautiful. The flesh was soft between her fingers.

'Check-out will be 10 am,' the woman said. 'Please sign here.' The surety of the process of checking in reassured her. People did this all the time. There were women who had three children and jobs, who travelled. She had just forgotten because she hardly left the house. Even orchestrating for her husband to be home in time to feed and bath the kids so that she could go to dinner in the city had been almost impossible. And the only reason he'd agreed was that he thought maybe she'd get some useful 'contacts' out of it. He was deluded in thinking that she could work from home while raising three children, two under five. She laughed under her breath and took the key card. The woman gave her an odd look. *I'm not even drunk yet, lady,* she thought.

Nathalie gripped the plastic card and headed over the plush carpet towards the lifts. Her phone had one bar left on it. She had no charger. As the lift ascended to the fourth floor, she considered whether she should text him and tell him where she was. So he wouldn't worry. She thought about all the times she'd asked him to come home at a reasonable hour – begged him, really – to help her at witching hour when the girls were screaming to be fed and Richie was inconsolable. And he routinely had a meeting, or an important function to attend, and sometimes he'd allude to her being the one who wanted three children, as though he played no part in it. Even though she had never wanted three. It had just happened. As life just happens and you live with it. As though he was removed in some essential way from the way their life was.

Now she knew why. He'd been meeting this woman. In expensive city hotels just like this. The pain stretched freshly in her chest and the lift door pinged open. She switched her phone off. No. He could be a father for one night, feel the full weight of responsibility.

She closed the heavy door behind her. Silence, pure and thick enveloped her like a hug. She kicked off her heels and lay on the king-sized bed. The bedding was clean and crisp against her skin. If she closed her eyes she could go to sleep right now and not wake for ten hours straight. It was so tempting. The tiredness was bone-deep. Instead she peeled herself off the bed and went into the bathroom to run the bath. While the water roared, she opened the bar cupboard and found a bottle of pinot noir. She poured herself a generous glass and took a sip. As soon as she swallowed the wine, she knew she'd made the right decision. She reached for her phone and switched it back on. She really should tell him she was here. He'd worry. Part of her said 'let him' but the other part ached for her children. For their uncertainty. She tapped out a message. *I'm staying in a hotel tonight. I know about your lover. You forwarded the concert tickets to me instead of her.* She thought about saying something vindictive, but found she didn't have the energy. *I might be back tomorrow.* She pressed send and pressed her palms into her eye sockets.

The bath was warm, and the wine had made her sleepy. Milk leaked from her breasts into the water in fine white lines, as though she were a sea creature. Tears squeezed from her eyes. Relief and guilt poured out of her and mingled so that she couldn't tell where one ended and the other began. It would be so easy to go to sleep and never have to wake up. Never have to face everything. She hadn't thought about ending her life before. But right now, it would be possible. The sadness felt like a whole sea, swelling inside her, taking up all the space.

Hey Ruby girl, can't wait to spend this special night with you. I've booked a hotel room for after. Her husband's words – so full of an energy she hadn't sensed in him for years – floated into her consciousness and she drained her wine glass.

She turned the hot water up until her skin scalded, until the bathroom bloated with steam. In the white haze another life opened up in her mind. She was an academic about to travel to Paris on a 6 am flight. She could almost see it, this imaginary life, shimmering in her mind. Maybe it could have been her life if she'd chosen a different path. If she'd chosen a different man. If she hadn't had three children. She could be heading to France for a conference at the Sorbonne, a small suitcase by her bed filled with chic business attire. This could have been her. She had been an academic seven years ago, in the Sydney University French department. Her desk had overlooked the city in the distance. She'd had time to read Camus and Sartre and discuss with her students their use of imagery and language.

That language was almost lost to her now, like a dream. *Un rêve bizarre.* She spoke the words under her breath. They didn't sound like her own. She turned off the taps and pulled herself up to sitting, pressed her forehead to her knees. Her skin glowed, the same swollen pink as those rose petals in the foyer, and the room spun. Why the hell couldn't that be her life? She could book a plane ticket online right now, before her phone battery ran out. She could disappear. Start a new life. It was better than having to face him. It was better than dying.

She stood and her equilibrium was gone. She found herself on the cold tiles without knowledge of having fallen. As she retched into the toilet bowl cool tears ran down her face. The lid of the enchanted jewellery box slammed shut. And she realised with equal parts relief and dread, that she could never, ever abandon her children.

Jean
1948

The hotel glowed against the cliffs like a trick of the light. Music echoed through the still night air. They called it the grandest hotel west of the Blue Mountains. The staircase in the foyer was built from the finest marble. It was rumoured to have taken a hundred men to transport the slabs into the valley. At dusk white statues shone in the gardens and Jean would wonder about what life was like inside its halls, where the mining officials, the wealthy and the important stayed when they visited.

The music called to her like a siren song. She would feel its stirrings in her belly, her body swaying unconsciously. That old muscle memory. She'd wonder which dance everyone was dancing. The Lindy Hop? The Balboa? The West Coast Swing? She used to know such things. She used to instigate such things. She used to be one of the women swirling in their full skirts, the filmy fabric catching the candlelight. The champagne, the delicacies, the fragrant haze of cigar smoke. She had known it all. And then she would shake her head and turn back to the task at hand. That wasn't her life anymore. She wasn't that person anymore. She'd tell herself the music had no purchase. She'd shut the windows and the doors against it, keeping her feet planted firmly on the ground. There was wood to chop and fires to light before the dusk ushered in the cold night and Robert would be hungry for dinner.

But tonight was different. Tonight she could not resist the beat in her blood. The music had been louder, more insistent than usual. It had felt like a twin heartbeat in her chest all evening as they ate their meal and she read Liv a story before bed. She knew that she must glimpse inside that life, even just for a moment. Just a sliver, a taste would be enough to fill her up.

By the time Jean reached the hotel by foot it was well after midnight. She could smell the chalky dust from the road on her dress. The music coming from inside was beautiful; mournful and slow. The kind of music to rest one's head on a man's shoulder. She had dressed in her best dress. Black because it was always elegant. Now it would just be dusty. As she looked through the window, she saw the women inside dancing and her heart sank. They were officers' and town officials' wives. Their hats were from Sydney's top milliners. Their dresses had not been sewn by hand at machines on the kitchen table, they'd been purchased in department stores and wrapped in delicate tissue. The only way valley women could purchase a new frock was from a hawker who – rumour had it – sold clothing taken from a Sydney morgue. These women wore gloves that extended past their elbows and their lips were stained with expensive lipstick. Had she been so stupid to think she'd somehow steal into this place? She slept under a blanket sewn from sugar bags and wore the second-hand clothing of dead people.

The hotel doors flung open and a woman tripped out. Her blonde hair was pinned into fashionable curls with exquisite red clips and she wobbled on matching red heels. She swung around, as though sensing Jean's presence under the tall arched window.

'Oh, I didn't see you there.' The woman's gaze was hazy, as though she needed spectacles but wasn't wearing them.

'Oh,' said Jean, feeling her face warm in the dark as the woman moved towards her. Her body swayed a little, but whether from languor or wine, she couldn't tell. Jean herself had taken a glass of sherry for courage before sneaking out of the house.

'Let's sit out here and smoke, shall we? It's so hot in there.' The woman adjusted her long red satin gloves and perched on a garden seat, placed a cigarette between her lips.

Jean looked around. The only other beings were the nymph statues in the garden, gleaming in the bright moonlight. Was this woman talking to her?

The woman held out cigarettes. Jean moved towards her and took one tentatively from a beautiful silver case. She sat down next to her, acutely aware of her plain dress and cheap rouge. The woman's nails were the exact same shade of red as the rest of her ensemble.

'Oh, these parties are such a bore sometimes, aren't they?' The woman took a long drag and sighed out the smoke. 'I just needed to get some air. You know, it's so beautiful out here. So quiet. Look at those stars. Those cliffs.'

They both looked up at the stars salting the sky.

'Oh, I feel rather ill doing that. I'm afraid I've had a little champagne. Sorry, I've been so rude, I'm Clara. Clara Black.'

Jean took her hand and nodded politely. Should she give another name? Her mind was racing. 'Jean,' she said, wondering if the woman had even guessed that she was an interloper, with her poor dress and dusty shoes. She took a drag from the cigarette, which was much smoother than the ones she sometimes pinched from Robert.

Clara looked at her. 'So, how do you like life out here, Jean?'

Jean paused, unsure of how to answer the question, unsure of whether Clara had pegged her as an intruder. 'You mean in the valley?'

'Yes, I mean, we're so far from civilisation out here. It's kind of an amazing place, don't you think?'

Jean was silent. Only an official's wife could think this. Jean lived in a roughly constructed fibro house that sweltered in the heat, froze in the cold and had rats, and she was considered one of the lucky ones because she wasn't still in a tent. Robert came home black with oil from the mines each night. She took a guess about Clara Black. 'Do you live in the hotel?'

Clara nodded. 'Yes, they tell us there'll be fabulous new housing built, but we just have to make do with living in a hotel for now.'

Jean cleared her throat. The hotel had a winding marble staircase, long, cool corridors and food that came via wait staff out of an industrial kitchen, or at least that's what she'd heard. 'What's it like?'

'Oh, well, it's a nice enough hotel, for these parts, you'd have to agree. But the rooms are very small, and we all have to share bathrooms, so it's far from ideal. Where have they put you?' Clara took a lipstick out of her purse and pressed it to her bottom lip.

'Oh, I love that shade of red,' said Jean, keen to steer the conversation away from living quarters.

Clara passed her the lipstick. 'Here, try it. It would suit your skin tone, too.'

Jean took the delicate gold case in her fingers. It was an Elizabeth Arden lipstick. She painted her top lip and then pressed her lips together. The movement was fluid. Her body remembered. All those times she had applied her lipstick this way, without a mirror, when her life had necessitated the painting of lips.

Clara stood and stretched her arms. 'I can't bear to go back in there. I might take a walk around the grounds. I hear the whole valley is haunted. The massacres of the Aborigines here at first settlement. It was a long time ago but still it's terrible. That's what the other wives whisper about anyway. But I don't find it frightening here. Well, it's not the bush that I'm frightened of.' Clara removed the red hairclips and let her long hair fall down her back. It made her appear younger. 'But I don't believe in ghosts, do you?'

Jean shook her head. If there were ghosts anywhere, they would be here. She too had heard about the Black people being killed by the whites in this area. Women and children, too. She hugged her arms close.

'Here. These would look pretty in your beautiful dark hair.' She pinned one of the red clips behind Jean's left ear. Clara stretched her hands to the sky, slipped off her heels and walked barefoot away from the hotel.

'Are you sure you should go walking by yourself? And barefoot? You could step on a snake.' Jean was about to tell Clara about the snake Robert had found curled under their front step a few days ago, but that would have given herself away. 'I could come,' Jean said.

'Oh, no, I want to go by myself.' Clara waved a hand and slipped off one of her long red gloves and then the other and flung them behind her. Jean had to stop herself from gasping.

'Don't you ever just want to be alone? The cool night air on your skin, no one knowing where you are? Sometimes it can be like a prison in this valley. So far from everyone and everything.'

Jean nodded. *I know that feeling*, she thought. She picked up the gloves from the ground. She ran her fingers over the smooth silky fabric. She did know that feeling of wanting to be alone. That's what had brought her here, to the hotel, late in the evening while her child and husband slept. She could never tell Clara this. It was one thing getting some air by yourself slightly giddy at a party, it was another sneaking away from your family for a glimpse into another life.

'I shall be back. You keep a watch out for devastatingly dashing men. But don't send them my way.' Clara laughed.

Jean laughed too and watched the night claim her, the luminous white of her hair fading into the shadows. Jean's heart was beating fast. Maybe she shouldn't have let her go off alone. She seemed a little dreamy with wine. But she'd be back. She slipped her foot out of her dusty black pump and into one of Clara's beautiful red shoes. It was a little too big, but it fit. She admired the way the shoes shone, even in the low light. She would never own a pair of shoes this beautiful. She put both on and stood up, wobbling as she did. She looked around self-consciously as she slipped the gloves up to her elbows. They felt right. Like a second skin. Suddenly this life, the valley felt like the ill-fitting costume. She felt so glamorous. No longer did she have on only a boring black dress. She caught the reflection of herself in a dark window. She was about to peel off the gloves when the heavy door to the hotel swung open and two men and a woman stumbled out, bringing with them the sound of loud, upbeat music and the smell of cigarettes and perfume.

'Oh my, it's deliciously cool out here.' The woman fanned herself with her hands. 'Hello. You have the right idea. Oh, can we pinch a cigarette?'

Jean realised that Clara had left her beautiful silver cigarette case on the seat. She looked around, feeling guilt tighten her throat. She glanced in the direction she'd seen Clara go but there was nothing but the glowing nymphs, the dark garden.

'Of course,' she said and offered the woman a cigarette. One of the men produced a box of matches and lit it. The woman's eyes were made up with dark kohl, lending her an exotic and mysterious air. None of the women Jean was around in the township wore eye make-up. She wished immediately to make this effect on her own eyes.

'What are you doing out here all by yourself?' One of the men was looking at Jean in a way that made her breath shallow. She was still wearing Clara's shoes and gloves, her own shoes lying suspiciously at her feet. She was going to be found out. Here she was wearing another woman's things.

'Just catching my breath.'

The man stuck out his arm for her to take. 'Well, these two will no doubt be kissing soon, so will you join me back on the dance floor? The band is rather good, even for these parts.'

Jean looked around wildly. 'Well, I'm just … my friend …' She peered once again into the night.

The man continued to hold out his arm. 'I'm Magnus Varesso. And you are?'

Jean was completely taken aback by this man's name, so foreign and famous sounding.

'Serpentine Rose.' The name slid from her mouth before her mind caught up and she pressed her fingers to her lips. The lipstick, the gloves, the shoes. They had tricked her into imagining she was Serpentine Rose again, about to take to the stage, about to surrender her body to the music.

'Well, it's lovely to meet you, Miss Rose.'

Jean was shocked he had believed her. She felt a flush of shame rise to colour her cheeks. Serpentine Rose had died a long time ago. She was Jean Peters, married to Robert Peters. But she let Magnus lead her inside the hotel with her red gloves and red shoes and the sparkling clasp behind her ear.

CHAPTER 2

Emmie

November

The mothers stood in cosy groups, their necks bent in understanding, smiles playing on their lips. Occasionally a laugh would bloom, rising brightly above the din like a flower in a hothouse. The school hall was too warm. It smelled like nostalgia; lunchboxes left in the sun too long. But the smell of the mothers, their hair conditioner and perfume overlayed the subtle scent of rotting fruit and sandwich bread.

Emmie watched these women. The sheen of their skin, their soft glances as they touched each other's arms. She wondered how she had got four years into primary school without a posse to stand with. A group of mums to incline her head towards in mutual understanding. She didn't mean to feel sorry for herself and she had acquaintances, yes, and there was one mum whose son was in Seraphine's class who she'd bonded with a bit. But somehow in one of those imaginary dreams of motherhood she had seen cups of tea at other mums' houses, weekends away together and minding each other's kids during school holidays. A network. A support group, as so many school mums seemed to have acquired as easily as their glowing skin and svelte bodies. The groups seemed to have formed and solidified early on when everyone was new, but somehow she'd missed out on that. Instead she had women whose names were interchangeable with their children's. There was no one here, for example, to whom she could confide that she'd just got her period this morning and wept into the toilet paper for ten minutes because it was another month closer to 40 without a second child.

They were all mothers. Why had it been so hard for Emmie to connect? She'd tried to get involved in school stuff – she was there at drop-off and pick-up ... maybe she was expecting too much. She'd learned that this was one of her weaknesses. The images in her head were idealised versions of some life she must have once seen on TV, or Instagram. It had taken her to almost middle age to realise that she needed to adjust her expectations.

She was observing a group over near the morning tea table – no one was eating the baked goods. They lived by the beach – strictly a sugar-free zone. Emmie longed for the comfort of carbs, but she wasn't about to be the overweight woman feasting on muffins in a sea of slim blondes. The coffee queue, in comparison, snaked back five or six.

Emmie saw all of the women's heads turn in unison, like flowers moving towards light. She followed their gaze. A woman had just entered the hall. She was dressed in flowing peach silk, her hair loose; a blonde halo around her head. A feathered white and gold fascinator was pinned above her left ear, lending her the air of a Pre-Raphaelite goddess. This woman looked as though she was ready for a fashion shoot, not a kids' concert. It was Melbourne Cup day; she was probably dropping into the concert on the way to some lavish event at a city bar. The woman took her little girl's hand and glided into the room. It was only then that Emmie noticed there was a baby strung to her front. Chubby kicking legs. About eight months old, she guessed. A mixture of desire and shame moved inside her. Desire to be like this woman; the hair, the dress, the elegance, but mostly the baby. And shame at her own lame jeans and T-shirt.

Emmie couldn't tear her eyes away. She had seen her in the playground. Nathalie. That was her name. She had that thing; that elusive something that life seemingly conferred on some people naturally. One could just call it beauty, but it was more than that. Like the cool girls at school with their easy way of being in the world, their breezy laughter, as though they knew they were cosseted against life's cruelties. She had long admired these types from afar with a mixture of trepidation, admiration and jealousy. How the hell did you have several kids, including a baby and still look like that?

The spell was broken as the microphone squeaked loudly and hands went to ears. The headmistress asked everyone to take a seat. Emmie always felt uncomfortable in these kinds of situations – who to talk to, where to sit? How to not look like the awkward person she was. Why did it have to be so difficult? She told herself not to overthink things and moved towards a bank of seats to her right.

She realised she was standing next to the woman.

'Oh, you take these,' Emmie said, gesturing towards the empty seats, noticing the woman's painted nails, her luminous skin.

It took Emmie a second to register that the woman was looking around her, her eyes glazed with panic.

'Oh my God,' she said. 'Where's Sim? I was holding her hand a second ago.'

The baby began to cry.

'Oh, shit. Oh, God.' The woman's chin began to tremble, and she looked around wildly, pressing her hands to her cheeks.

Emmie felt her own jolt of upset at the other woman's distress. 'Are you okay? Can I help? Have you lost someone?'

The woman reached out and grabbed her arm. Emmie felt the other woman's desperation rush through her like an electric shock. 'I've just lost my daughter. She has a habit of disappearing on me lately. I don't know why she's acting up so much at the moment.' She shook her head and gestured to her body. 'And I'm meant to be going to this Melbourne Cup thing today after the concert. I'm so mortified to be this overdressed.' She worried one of the sparkly rings on her fingers and shook her head.

Emmie blinked for a second, shocked that this incredible-looking woman was embarrassed. She wanted to tell her that every woman in the room thought she looked dazzling, but there was a more pressing situation at hand.

'What does your little girl look like?' Emmie asked, her eyes already scanning the crowd.

'Hair in braids, four years old. Pink dress. I feel sick. I'm such a terrible mother. Here for one second and I've already lost a child.'

Emmie smiled. 'This room is filled with mothers. It's the best possible place on earth to lose a child. You wait here and I'll have a scout.'

The woman's eyes softened with gratitude. She rocked back

and forth, and the baby began to settle. 'Her name is Sim, short for Simone.'

It seemed the room was filled with four-year-olds with hair in various plaits and braids and wearing pink. But Emmie found the likely runaway next to the morning tea table with a chocolate biscuit in her hand.

Emmie crouched down next to the little girl. 'Hi there, is your name Sim?'

The child nodded, obviously unwilling to stop eating to engage in conversation with a stranger.

'Well, I'm glad someone's eating the treats. I don't blame you. Those biscuits look aaa-mazing.'

Sim inspected her cookie.

'Now, your mum's looking for you. She's a bit worried,' Emmie said, holding out her hand. 'Come with me and we'll find her.' The little girl thrust her sticky hand into Emmie's. It broke Emmie's heart how trusting children were.

'If you'd all like to take a seat now, we have our first dance act raring to go,' the principal said over the loud-speaker, her voice infused with a practised patience.

The room began to shift, the huddles of mothers breaking apart and moving towards the seats. 'Here she is,' whispered Emmie, handing Sim over.

'Oh my God, you are an angel. Sim, you can't just run off from Mummy like that. Thank you so much. Sorry, I don't think we've properly met.'

'I'm Emmie. My little girl, Seraphine, is in Year 3.'

'What a beautiful name. My daughter Findlay is too. I'm Nathalie. It's such a big school. I'm still meeting mums I feel like I've never seen before.'

Maybe I'm invisible, Emmie thought, then admonished herself, replying brightly: 'Findlay and Seraphine. It could be a designer fashion label, couldn't it?'

Nathalie laughed. 'I think it's our modern names. Combine the names of any eight-year-old children and you've got a fashion label or a hipster bar. We'd better copyright ours and buy the website domain.'

Emmie nodded, feeling a flush of emotion at the intimacy implicit in Nathalie's comment. 'I feel a bit self-indulgent calling my child Seraphine, I've sworn that the next will be something like Bob.' She cringed internally. She rarely admitted that she wanted another child. It was just easier to make it seem like it was a choice. But Nathalie made her feel surprisingly comfortable.

'Seraphine and Bob. Yep, I could see that doing well in Bondi,' said Nathalie, settling into a seat, her hand cradling her baby's head.

'We're definitely onto something.'

Nathalie looked longingly towards the coffee queue. 'If I creep around the back, do you reckon I could score some of those scones and muffins? I've already had two coffees but I'm dying for sugar and carbs. Preferably both.'

Emmie smiled. A woman after her own soul. 'I've been thinking that for the past ten minutes but no one's eating all that lovely food.'

'I don't care if it's about to start, we are eating the food,' Nathalie said. 'Could you mind Sim for a sec? There'll be a muffin in it for you.'

Emmie nodded and watched Nathalie tiptoe around the seats, her baby still strung to her front.

An expectant hush finally fell over the crowd and the room

darkened. The booming beat of The Jackson 5's 'Blame It on the Boogie' filled the hall. Little bodies poured onto the stage in colourful fedora hats to hoots and whistles from the audience. The music was cut short and there was a sudden scrambling of kids off the stage. Someone accidentally started and then paused the next song.

The principal was back. 'It appears we're experiencing some technical difficulties, if you'll just bear with us.'

'It's going to be a long hour,' said Nathalie, returning with a plastic plate full of pastries and muffins and offering it to Emmie. 'I'm probably going to have to breastfeed Richie the whole time to stop him crying.'

Emmie's heart melted at the sight of the little boy. 'He's beautiful,' she said, taking a bite out of the muffin.

'Believe me, he's no angel. You should have heard him in the car on the way. I nearly ran into a tree just to make it all stop.' Nathalie shot Emmie a sheepish look. 'Too much information, sorry. I promise, I'm not really going to kill my baby.'

Emmie laughed. There would have been a time before having children when such a statement would have shocked her. 'Oh, I get it. I didn't sleep more than two hours in a row for about three years. Once I left the house and went for a walk and left her for 20 minutes crying in her cot.'

'Oh, you have to for your sanity,' said Nathalie. 'Every mum has done something like that. Most just don't admit it.'

The lights went down and the music swelled. 'Oh, it looks like we're back in business,' Emmie said.

Seraphine suddenly pranced onto the stage with much more zest than she'd demonstrated in the lounge room. Emmie felt her heart squeeze with a secret pride.

'That's Seraphine,' she whispered.

'Oh, beautiful red hair,' said Nathalie.

'It only took an hour to tame this morning,' said Emmie.

Modern motherhood was all about keeping up a ruse of cool indifference. But deep down, no mother was really indifferent to her child. She'd have to note that one down for her next blog-post topic.

She felt a cool hand on her arm.

'Is this seat taken?'

Emmie shook her head. A woman with startlingly blonde hair and woody perfume put her designer bag on the floor and crossed her long, tanned legs. Alexandra Maxwell. She leaned forward and waved to Nathalie, who pointed to the plate of pastries and gave an enthusiastic thumbs up.

'Oh, God, give them to me now,' the woman hissed. Emmie leaned over and passed the plate.

Emmie had seen these two in the playground together. It was impossible to miss them. Everyone knew Alexandra. Her husband was a popular morning TV presenter. He was known simply by his surname – Maxwell – as though he were a pop star, not a perma-tanned man with gleaming TV teeth. And although Emmie had no idea what Alexandra did for her own work, his glamour was somehow transferred onto her. She realised that she'd always sort of assumed that Alexandra worked in television, too. She also had those glowy white teeth, and something professional and gritty about her that suggested that she may be an investigative journalist or something equally powerful.

These women were the mother equivalent of the enigmatic high school girls. Long hair trailing down their backs, their eyes shining with secrets that everyone else wanted to know.

Those insouciant smiles. Even the uniforms could not hide their lustre; they shone and glittered in the dirt and squabble of the playground. It was impossible for Emmie to tell if they were aware of their allure – if it was an affectation or natural. But the last place Emmie expected to be was between them eating muffins.

The lights dimmed and the music got quiet, suddenly.

'What are you wearing on your head?' Alexandra whisper-shouted to Nathalie, leaning over Emmie.

Nathalie groaned.

'Is it a bird?' Alexandra cocked her head, squinting. 'A squirrel?'

Emmie laughed and then shot Nathalie an apologetic look.

'It's nothing. Not an animal.' She rolled her eyes, but she was laughing. 'I'm dressed for your bloody Melbourne Cup thing. I thought other mums would be dressed up for parties, wearing fascinators but it looks like I'm the only one. I'm mortified. I'm wearing freaking support underwear to fit into this dress, for God's sake.'

Alexandra raised one carefully manicured eyebrow. 'Well, you look a million bucks. Every lady in her mum jeans is worshipping you right now.' She shot a look at Emmie. 'Sorry, no offence.'

'None taken. Love my mum jeans.' Emmie smoothed her best pair of jeans over her thighs and lamented that she'd always be one of the worshippers, but she couldn't help smiling at Alexandra's dry wit.

'Oh my God, kid, pull your pants up. His pants are too small,' Alexandra whispered, pointing at a boy on the stage. 'I can't watch. And look at this kid. He thinks he's the next Justin Bieber. Are those tattoos on his arms? Who are these parents?'

'That's my kid,' said Emmie, shooting her a disapproving look. Alexandra's eyes widened in horror.

'Kidding.'

Alexandra slapped her on the wrist playfully. 'Sorry, I'm Alexandra. My eldest, Thomas, is in Year 3. I've seen you around. Your kid is stunning. She's that one with the incredible curly red hair, isn't she?'

Emmie nodded. As a parent of a redhead, she was used to people noticing Seraphine. She wondered what such renown would feel like. But she had boring brown hair. And a boring name – it was actually plain old Emma, but somewhere along the line, she'd attached the slightly more exotic 'ie' on the end. Even the fact that she thought that was exotic was plain sad.

She was about to reply when they were cut off by the crowd erupting as all the kids poured onto the stage, pride shining on their little moonfaces.

'Oh God, thank Christ that's over,' Alexandra muttered. 'No one ever tells you just how many of these you've got to sit through when you decide to procreate.'

Emmie laughed. It was refreshing to hear someone so searing about motherhood. Sometimes she felt like everyone else was in a silent competition that nobody acknowledged but everyone felt. She needed to get off Instagram.

The principal was back on stage. Emmie had to admire the woman. She was always perfectly turned out, with her curled hair, pointy heels and red lipstick, as though she was from another era where children had more respect for authority. She was probably hoping it was so.

Her voice was clipped, with a slight English accent. 'Now we're going to announce the winners of the lucky door prize,' she said, and a hush fell over the audience. 'The money raised this morning is going towards building a sailcloth over our asphalt play area.

'And, Amanda O'Neil has kindly donated her family's beautiful beach house for a week-long getaway. Now, I'm told that the house will fit three or four families and has a pool overlooking the beach. It's a shame staff can't enter.'

Amusement washed over the audience. A little boy came onto the stage holding a cardboard box.

'That house has got to be incredible,' said Nathalie. 'Amanda is the richest woman I know. She's on the board of one of the big banks. Okay, if one of us wins, we're all going, right? And we're hiring a nanny to look after the kids. Pinky promise.'

'Oh, Seraphine makes me do those. You do realise a pinky promise is serious shit,' said Emmie, raising an eyebrow.

'Bring it,' said Nathalie.

'Deal,' said Alexandra, extending her hand, so it hovered just over Emmie's lap. Their little fingers intertwined.

'Where's yours?' asked Nathalie, gesturing towards Emmie. 'Come on.'

Emmie placed her pinky carefully over both of theirs, unsure if she was really allowed to be included in this little pact. Her heart was beating fast.

CHAPTER 3

Alexandra

Alexandra realised she was holding her breath as the principal rummaged around in the box. *Just pick one, woman,* she thought, *so we can all get out of this sweat box.* She needed this. If she won a raffle holiday Maxwell couldn't possibly deny her that. She wouldn't have to pay for much, except the groceries and maybe she could rope the nanny in for a day or two, although realistically the nanny was about as reliable as a child herself.

Alexandra did have an uncanny knack for winning things though. She thought of herself as an exceptionally lucky person. She had the famous, handsome husband, the two kids, both of whom slept through the night at six months. Neither had learning difficulties or a terrible illness and she was an interior stylist even though she had never really earned any kind of formal qualification. She had straight teeth and skin that tanned. Both her parents were still alive and apart from her elderly grandparents, no one she knew and loved had ever died. Oh, and she won a lot of meat trays. She once even won a washing machine.

But despite, or perhaps because of all this good fortune Alexandra often felt like an impostor in her own life. On the surface everything was perfect, and she did gratitude meditations to try to find a way to confer the happiness she was meant to feel into her body. But there was always an unease leaking into her, like a dripping tap that couldn't be screwed tight. On long nights, when she couldn't sleep and she lay there studying the shadows playing on the cornices in her lovely ceiling, she saw ghosts of another life. There were no celebrity husbands, there were no husbands at all. But that life seemed impossible, a night-time dream that would never find its way into waking hours. She was living a perfectly normal, successful life, but it didn't feel like her own to live. Maybe that was the reason she'd given the washing machine she'd won away to the woman in the wheelchair that night. Maxwell had tugged her elbow so emphatically that she'd yelped. He would have sold it on eBay, of course. And so, to keep away the echo of that slow steady drip, to avoid a flood, she never stopped moving. She worked late into the night and checked her emails constantly during her one day off. She organised people and places, and sat on event committees, so that every spare second was filled up. She ran on her treadmill in the evening when the boys were in bed until everything went quiet and finally, finally she could sleep.

'And the number is blue, 312.'

Alexandra looked down at her number and her shoulders slumped. Her ticket was green. *Oh well, first-world problems*, she told herself. Wealthy, stingy husbands were better than poor, stingy husbands. An unreliable nanny was better than no nanny at all. And she certainly didn't have a monopoly on modern discontent.

She heard a little shout next to her. Emmie was holding her ticket up in front of her. 'I think ... yes, I think that's me,' she said in a small voice.

Emmie was short and plump, with an air of innocence and shiny hair and eyes. She was the sort of person who Alexandra assumed made cookies for her kids after school and volunteered at the canteen. She was the archetypal mum, something Alexandra had made a concerted effort to avoid in her own demeanour.

'Let me look at that.' She leaned over to inspect the ticket. Blue 312. Shit. 'It's us. It's us!' She realised she was yelling. She tugged at Emmie's sleeve. 'Go on! Go up!'

Emmie seemed to be in a state of shock. She stood, wobbled uncertainly for a second, shook her head and made her way towards the stage.

Alexandra looked over at Nathalie, who was shaking.

'You okay hon? Oh no, you're crying.'

Nathalie was wiping under her eyes. 'I'm just so freaking excited. Tell me we can sip champagne by a pool for a week?'

'A pool, a pool,' said Sim, clapping her hands.

'Oh my God, I'm roping in my nanny,' said Alexandra, extending her pinky finger and then pulling Nathalie into a hug. 'Remember, he won't be this little forever.' She could see her friend was struggling but felt hopeless. There would be no way in hell she'd go back for a third, even though a tiny part of her longed for a girl.

Emmie was heading back through the audience with an A4 envelope in her hands. Her eyes looked glazed. The poor love was in shock. She was breathless by the time she sat down between them.

'Shit, we won!' She shook her head. 'I don't understand. I've never won anything in my life.'

'I always win. I mean, I don't mean to sound boastful, it's just that I do,' Alexandra said.

'She does. It's crazy. Remember that holiday you won to Vanuatu?' said Nathalie.

'It's obviously your luck rubbing off on me.' Emmie was looking between them, her eyes wide.

'Open the envelope,' said Nathalie, clapping her hands together. Then she straightened and pressed her hand against her heart. 'Oh my God, we've totally crashed your prize. Of course, you can take anyone you want, you don't have to take us.'

Alexandra shot Nathalie a look, which said, *What the hell?*

But Emmie held up her little finger. 'Seraphine would kill me if I went back on a pinky promise.'

'That's our girl,' said Alexandra, craning to see the advertisement photos of the property in Emmie's lap. It was not to her taste – a bit too modern and predictable, with lots of harsh angles, but there was no denying the house was beautiful. It had seven bedrooms and a dedicated movie room. Alexandra loved the north coast with its blinding white sand and aqua water.

So, who was this woman, Amanda O'Neil, and why wasn't she friends with her? Of course, Nathalie already knew her. Everyone gravitated towards Nathalie, like a suburban mum towards activewear. It was inevitable. Alexandra's job was all about symmetry – the arrangement of a room to look just so. And the symmetry of Nathalie's face was like a beacon. Everyone was seduced by perfection, whether they knew it or not.

'We *have* to celebrate, girls. Nathalie and I are heading to a Melbourne Cup party at my work now. Hence the reason for the squirrel on her head.' She looked at her watch. 'Like now. Emmie, you must come. We can discuss dates for our getaway.' She picked up her handbag.

Nathalie looked doubtful, stroking Richie's head. 'I should really get them home for naps. It's going to be 40 degrees today. That's what a good mother would do, right?'

Alexandra cocked her head. 'Girl, you're dressed to slay. You nearly killed yourself getting into your support wear, there's no way in hell you're taking it off yet. You deserve something nice. You're coming. Put Sim in the corner with my iPad. We'll all keep an eye on her.'

Nathalie laughed. 'What could go wrong?'

Alexandra nudged Emmie. 'What about you?' She had become surprisingly fond of this chick in a short amount of time and it wasn't just because she was taking them away from their lives for a week. There was something about Emmie that seemed comfortably familiar. It was as though she'd known her for ten years, not ten minutes.

'I've only got writing planned for today and I don't have air con.'

'Oh, you're a writer?' asked Alexandra, her interest piqued. Creative people were so lucky. They had a certain 'flair' that she always found intriguing. Alexandra had tried it all – art, writing, graphic design, but she just didn't have it. She was good at organising, which was about the least creative thing you could do. And so, she managed Interiors Studio, which was really just an excessively expensive furniture shop in a posh suburb. She did a job that could be reasonably construed as an interior designer at parties, but was in actual fact, not much more than a glorified sales assistant.

'I'm writing a book, but I'm not professional or anything, and I just blog a bit,' Emmie said.

'Oh, I've always wanted to write a book,' said Alexandra. 'I don't think I'd have the patience, so I admire people who can sit still for that long.'

'I'd love you to teach me this blogging stuff. I'm hopeless,' Nathalie said. 'Everyone's always telling me to start a blog or go on Instagram, but I have no idea where to start.'

'That's just because we all want to stare at photos of you making smoothies and throwing your kids birthday parties, hon, 'cause you're so gorgeous,' said Alexandra.

Emmie shook her head. 'You wouldn't even need to use a filter.'

'It's true, right? Oh, it makes me sick,' said Alexandra. 'If you weren't my friend, I'd hate you.'

'Stop it,' said Nathalie. 'I feel hideous. You don't understand how tight this thing around my stomach is. You never truly recover from three C-sections.'

Alexandra shook her head. 'No sympathy, sorry.' They all stood and stepped out into the sweltering day.

CHAPTER 4

Nathalie

Alexandra's interiors shop was like a portal into another world. Nathalie had forgotten that there was this much beauty still. The space was filled with gilded mirrors, sunlit and bright as though there was nothing to fear in life. Ornate carved wooden doors promised luxurious and fragrant places behind them. And it was cool. They could have been in crisp New York, not Sydney on the cusp of summer.

Beautifully groomed people mingled among these stunning objects, as though their world was always this textured with promise. They sipped from delicate champagne flutes and it all smelled like exotic spice. She closed her eyes. Nathalie wished she could cocoon herself in the soft cream and white woollen throw in front of her and sleep. She envied Alexandra her job. She imagined coming to work here every day. Advising people on what type of timber to get their table made in, choosing pretty throw cushions to complement a lounge. Anything other than cleaning up spilled food, poo and doing the laundry three times a day.

A beautiful young man with mahogany skin offered Nathalie a glass of champagne from a silver tray. She took it and drank the cool, crisp wine. Alexandra was right; she really needed this. She watched gratefully while her friend arranged Sim in the corner of the room, an iPad propped up on what was probably a $200 cushion. She just hoped Sim wouldn't wipe snot on it. She was just beginning to feel the sweet ease of the wine hitting her bloodstream when Richie began to stir on her front. Would it be bad to down this glass and then breastfeed him? She shook her head. God, what was *wrong* with her? Where were these thoughts coming from? She patted the soft fur of his hair and felt a bolt of love. No one told you that motherhood would be like this – the love, intense and infinite and the exhaustion and the boredom and how they all fitted together into a strange, uneasy puzzle that became your whole narrow little life. She stroked his head, suddenly aware of the new smell of him, her annoyance overtaken by his physical pull on her body. She put the champagne down and went to the least populated corner of the room to feed him.

She was just beginning to feel relief in her throbbing left breast when she felt the eyes. Quick, sidelong glances. Whispers. She squirmed and Richie let out a wail, as though sensing her resistance. More people looked over. *Please, just leave me alone*, she thought.

A woman in a suit began to walk towards her. She bent at the waist and rested a perfectly manicured hand on Nathalie's shoulder. 'I'm the studio owner and I just wanted to let you know that while we fully support breastfeeding,' her voice lowered to a whisper, 'I think you'd be more comfortable in the back office.'

Nathalie felt her face turning pink. She pulled Richie off her breast and he began to scream. She wanted to let him scream; show this woman how ridiculous her demand was, but instead she shoved a dummy into his mouth and struggled clumsily to her feet.

What was she thinking, trying to look perfectly put-together, look like she was coping and strong and able to leave the house? Like she belonged in a place like this. That she was totally fine with having three small kids and a cheating husband, who she'd taken back the moment he'd apologised. She could feel her eyes filling with tears. Now she was going to be the crazy *crying* breastfeeding woman. She should just go home and let her breasts leak uninterrupted on the couch, who was she kidding?

Alexandra and Emmie emerged out of the crowd holding champagne flutes, sparkling water and a plate of mini quiches.

The woman's bright lips twitched into a smile. 'Hello, Alexandra. I was just telling this lovely lady that she might be more comfortable in the office.'

'Hello, Elizabeth. I see you've met my fabulous friend, Nathalie.'

The lips twitched again, as if the smile was painful to hold. 'Oh, wonderful,' she said, and Nathalie saw the tension between the woman and Alexandra.

'Since she had to feed her baby, we thought she deserved some food as well,' Alexandra said, straightening to her full height.

The woman clasped her hands in front of her, as though strangling something invisible. 'I just thought she might be more comfortable feeding without all the … attention.'

Nathalie wished she had the guts to tell this woman to bugger off, but she hated conflict. 'No, I understand, I'm making people uncomfortable,' she said, her voice small.

She saw Alexandra's eyes flare with what she recognised as suppressed rage. She opened her mouth to speak but another woman stepped into the tense little circle.

'I'm really sorry to interrupt. I just heard what was going on and I'm pretty sure this woman is within her full rights to feed her baby on this couch.' She gave Nathalie a knowing smile. She unwound a cream scarf from her neck and handed it over. 'You're welcome to use this if it makes you feel more comfortable, though you really shouldn't have to.' She shot a look at the owner, who backed away and then feigned sudden interest in something on the other side of the room.

'Thank you, that was so awkward,' Nathalie said, her heart beating fast as she took the scarf.

'He's beautiful,' the woman said, and Nathalie shot her a smile as she covered Richie's head and started feeding him again. 'I'm Macie by the way.'

'I'm Nathalie. Thank you again.'

'Was that rude woman your boss?' Emmie asked Alexandra. But she didn't respond. Her eyes were glassy, her gaze distant.

'I hope I didn't jeopardise your job,' said Nathalie, suddenly feeling terrible.

Alexandra shook her head vigorously, as though to wake herself up. She took a deep breath and put her hands on her hips. 'Yes, unfortunately, she's the owner. And no, Elizabeth is always like that. She just needs a good shag.'

'Keep the scarf. It's my gift to you so you'll never have to encounter another Elizabeth,' Macie said.

'Thank you, that's very kind,' said Nathalie, still burning with awkwardness.

'I think your table will be ready next week,' Alexandra said to Macie.

'Thanks, that's great news. Well, I'll leave you ladies to it, and Alexandra, I'll hear from you soon.'

'Do you know her?' asked Nathalie, watching Macie disappear into the crowd.

'She's one of our biggest clients. Hence Elizabeth's reaction. In no way would she want to jeopardise *that* account. For a while I thought she was stalking me she buys so much.'

'A lot of women have a throw cushion problem,' said Emmie. 'Dave calls them my pets.' She patted a plump blue and white one beside her.

Nathalie laughed.

'Yeah, she's loaded,' Alexandra said. She pointed to a huge mirror with gold gilding around the edges. 'She's bought that. She has quite the home in Mosman.'

'Lucky her,' said Emmie. 'God, I'd love to see *her* throw cushion collection. So, you help people style their homes?'

While Emmie and Alexandra talked, Nathalie took Richie off her boob and reached for her glass of champagne. The cool liquid had an almost-instant effect on her body, and she leaned back into the lounge, letting Richie's sweaty little milk-drunk body relax on her lap. She had counselled herself not to drink too much today, not to embarrass herself, especially with the kids here, but she'd already felt the humiliation of every eye on her exposed breasts. She drank the champagne down while Alexandra and Emmie had their backs turned. She reached for another glass and felt the sweet buzz take everything away.

CHAPTER 5

Pen

The mums were crowding into the playground for pick-up like industrious little ants scouting for crumbs. Pen marvelled at the effort so many of them made. Their shiny hair, their slim limbs, their pretty dresses, or the off-duty skinny jeans with artfully torn rips to reveal glimpses of tanned skin. Where did they find the time or the money to make themselves look so good? Compared to them she just felt monochrome. She never had the inclination to dress up. Even when she was photographing a politician or a celeb and was forced to make an effort, she wore boots under her dress. The whole fashion thing had just never made sense to her, though she did spend a lot on getting her short hair styled just right.

The bell trilled and she felt the familiar dread spread in her gut. Picking Will up always gave her this feeling. And the fact that she was feeling bad about picking up her own son on the only two days she was able to, made for a guilt that stuck to her insides all afternoon. It was clear he wasn't coping with school very well. He either lashed out physically when he saw her, or he was sullen and withdrawn. And more and more the quiet, melancholy slant of his personality seemed to be taking over. He seemed contented enough playing or drawing in his room but there was a negative energy about him that she felt overwhelmed by, weighed down by. She was worried about him and she knew she needed to talk to someone, perhaps the school, but she was working such long hours, and often on weekends, to simply have enough money to pay the bills that mental health seemed at the bottom of the priority list. And to be honest, she just didn't want to face it.

Sometimes she thought she was forgetting. Maybe Catelyn had been like this when she was younger. But when Pen really thought back, Cate had been, and still was, a pretty easy child. Sweet and fun, with the occasional difficult patch. Cate was the child that parents attribute to their own good parenting instead of just a lucky break. When you had a difficult second child you realised how deluded you'd been. That it was all just pot luck.

Pen spotted Emmie walking towards her. 'Hi,' she said and shifted over to let Emmie sit on the low brick wall in the shade. 'How was your day?'

Emmie touched her fingers to her temples gingerly. 'Serious hangover.'

'That's what the Melbourne Cup's for, isn't it?' Pen couldn't think of anything worse than dressing up and pretending to be interested in horses running around a track, but each to their own.

'Yes, but there was another reason. I was a little over-excited because I won the raffle at the concert yesterday and I never, and I mean never, win things.'

Pen laughed. 'Let me guess, a meat tray, a facial, a year's worth of stationery supplies?'

Emmie shook her head. 'Oh God, I need a facial. But no, it's actually pretty decent. It's a week in this huge holiday house on the coast. And it gets weirder. Findlay's mum and Thomas's mum – I'm not sure if you know them, they're Year 3 kids too – were with me at the time and now we're all going together. I'd never met them before yesterday.'

'Thomas Maxwell? His dad's that arrogant Maxwell guy on TV, isn't he?'

'Yeah, and I always thought his mum – Alexandra is her name – looked a bit stuck up but it turns out she's hilarious.'

'And who's Findlay's mum?'

'The stunning one who looks like a Russian model.'

'Oh yeah. We all know her. Bitch. I can't stop looking at that woman. I actually wanted to photograph her the other day. Just the way the light was falling behind her. It was, to be honest, a bit creepy and I caught myself.'

'I know. But she's so lovely. She cried about three times yesterday. Very sleep deprived. She's got two kids under five.'

Pen groaned in understanding. 'Oh, no, say no more. I wouldn't go back to having kids that young if you paid me.'

Emmie laughed nervously and Pen wondered if she'd said something wrong. She was always wondering this. Why she couldn't just talk to people like a normal person, without second-guessing everything she said, without feeling nervous and then replaying whole conversations in her head after the fact. Maybe that was why Will was so strange and sensitive. A friend who was a child psychologist had told her that he seemed like a normal eight-year-old boy, albeit a very sensitive and intelligent one. It was true, she never had to worry about grades or anything like that. It was more the social side of things that was his challenge.

Pen watched her son walk towards her. She felt her pulse quicken. He was the only one not buddied up with a friend, chatting easily. He walked with his head down, feet dragging. She knew this mood. It was the negative, passive–aggressive mood. Someone had probably said something to upset him. Sometimes food fixed it, other times it lingered all afternoon. He reached her and she took his bag, trying to lighten his load physically, if not mentally.

'Can Will come for a play date? Pleeease,' asked Seraphine, breathless as she ran towards them from the other side of the playground, red hair flying. 'Please, please, please, Mummy.'

She saw Will's whole mood shift, like the sun peeking from behind a bank of cloud.

Pen's heart squeezed with gratitude for this child. Seraphine and Will did seem to have a lovely bond and they hadn't quite got to the stage of feeling weird about their genders. She imagined having a beautiful, light-spirited child like Seraphine. She admonished herself silently. She was doing it again – comparing, being down on Will. She really did need to book in to see that psychologist for herself.

The kids bounced on the spot awaiting a response. Pen looked to Emmie hopefully. Seraphine genuinely seemed to have taken a shine to Will. If Emmie felt any negativity towards him, she hadn't shown it. She'd had him over to her house twice, which was one more time than he'd been to anyone else's house. Will would sometimes invite a friend to his house, but they were usually met with a barrage of excuses. It wasn't that Will was a bad kid, he was just different. He was awkward. He didn't connect.

'We can't today, sorry. Sera has swimming,' said Emmie. 'But hey, you know what? You guys should come away to this holiday house, too. Sera would love Will to come and you could bring Cate, too. We're still throwing around dates.'

Pen was momentarily stilled by the graciousness of the offer. Someone actually wanted Will to go away for several days with their child. She felt emotion ache in the back of her throat. 'That would be wonderful,' she said, holding her voice steady to quell the emotion.

The thought of going away with other mums – particularly the gorgeous one and the TV star husband one, was fairly terrifying. She didn't even know if she'd be able to get time off work. And God, how would she handle Will with other kids for a week? Probably perfect kids. The anxiety might push her over the edge. A week of battling with the threat that the other kids simply wouldn't like her child.

Emmie must have read her mixed emotions because she added: 'It'll be fun. Plus, I need someone down-to-earth to come along.'

'Are you sure we'll fit?'

'Plenty of room.'

Pen looked at Emmie's kind, thoughtful face. They weren't exactly close but she was the type of person that Pen felt she might even be able to confide in after a few drinks. She imagined saying the words out loud. The relief of getting the awful feelings out of her body. *I don't like my own son. See, I'm a monster. No, I don't just mean when he's being a handful, I mean ever. In eight years, I've never liked him. Deep down I wish*

I'd never had him. What mother feels that? Tell me, what mother feels that?

But Emmie was waving goodbye, Will tugging at the top of her jeans asking for a snack she didn't have, and her blood was rushing in her ears.

Jean
1948

The music was much louder inside the hotel. She could feel its languid beat inside her, intoxicating her. She followed Magnus into the foyer, the fabled marble staircase sweeping up to her left. She imagined ascending those stairs to see the richly decorated hotel rooms and the balcony that jutted over the hotel's entrance like a crown. He led her through a candlelit hall. The light burned from elaborate candelabra and the smell of wax mingled with other scents – perfume, whiskey, face powder, sweat. The walls were papered with blood red roses against a midnight blue and hung with pictures depicting nude women reclining on day beds, and various Australian bush scenes. She wanted to stop and admire them, run her fingers along the opulent wallpaper, but she didn't dare. Clara's slightly too-big shoes clicked on the ornate tiling under her feet, reminding her that she was an interloper. She smoothed her hair behind her ear, finding the beautiful clasp Clara had placed there. Before she could lose her nerve, they emerged into a big room filled with people. There was a magnificent chandelier at its heart, under which bodies moved lazily in the hazy air. All about the edges of the dance floor were small round tables filled with people smoking and sipping cocktails. Expensive jewels glittered on slim wrists. Vases full of wild roses overflowed and she longed to put her nose to the velvety petals. A band was set up in the corner, comprising of a piano, saxophone, violin, banjo and drums. She felt like she was in a Parisian salon, not a hotel in the middle of a vast Australian valley. A waiter appeared with a tray of champagne and she took a glass, heady suddenly with the smells and sounds around her. Magnus took the glass from her hand and put it back on the tray.

'First we must dance,' he said. She looked at him in profile as he guided her onto the floor. He was handsome, as though he should belong in films. She hadn't noticed that outside. A blush crept into her cheeks.

She laughed and let him guide her onto the floor. Chandelier crystals sparkled above her and diamonds on pale fingers caught the light. She had never danced this dance. The pulse of the music seemed to make her feet move independently to her mind, as was always the case. She copied the steps of the other dancers, her limbs finding their place easily. She had known she loved to dance as long as she'd known music. Now she taught ballet lessons to children in the valley, but there had been a time when dance was the very air she breathed.

Magnus guided her, his hand on her back. He was an excellent dancer. She tried to imagine Robert doing this and laughed to herself. She was so far from her normal life at this moment. He took complete control, and she took cues from his body, as though they were dancing some secret language that no one else understood. She was breathless when the music changed.

'You're good,' he said.

She felt her cheeks glow at his compliment. 'I must admit I do love to dance.'

'Come on, one more and then I'll let you have that champagne, Miss Rose.'

The music was slower, but their bodies felt equally in tune. He dipped her back and brought her up, face suddenly close to his.

His breath on her cheek, his body pressed to hers. She felt her body respond before her mind, a visceral reaction to his. Panic rose in her throat. God, what was she doing? She had no place here. Lied about her name. She should go, now. What was she going to tell him about herself if they talked over champagne? More lies?

But how she longed to sit at one of those elegant round tables. Just to pretend. Just for a few more moments. The song finished and he guided her to the edge of the dance floor. Jean felt self-conscious suddenly. Could people tell she was a miner's wife? Magnus waved over a waiter.

'This young lady has well and truly earned a glass of champagne.'

Jean fanned herself with her hands. 'Thank you.' She took a sip and the cool wine moved through her.

'So, what brings you out to the sticks, Miss Rose?'

Her mind reeled, spinning from the few sips of wine and the dancing. Oh, the dancing. How she'd missed it. 'I teach ballet lessons to the children,' she said. This, at least, was not a lie. 'There's a small school for the workers' children and I take their dance lessons.' She left out the small fact of her daughter being one of her students.

'Oh, well, that's a nice touch for them. I hear there's a lot of complaints about living standards, but the children are doing dance classes and school lessons. It can't be too bad.'

She said nothing. How to explain to a man like this, used to money and freedom, what they were living through in this valley? She needed to change the topic. 'So, what brings you out here, Mr Varesso?'

'Engineer by day. Chief engineer I should say. Entrepreneur by night. Let's just say I have a deep interest in shale oil. I come out here every few weeks from Sydney. Bugger of a journey but it must be done and occasionally I'll dig up a diamond in the rough.'

She pressed her cool hands to her burning cheeks and laughed.

'Where do they have the local ballet teacher housed then? Do say the hotel and not one of those ghastly houses.'

Jean grimaced.

'Oh dear. Let me see if I can remedy that. I have connections.'

Jean's heart was racing. The lies were getting away from her, spooling out. 'No, no, it's really not that bad. I'm very happy. It's close to the school. Please don't trouble yourself.' She should come clean. Tell this man she had a daughter, Liv, and a husband, Robert. A simple man. Not the kind of man to ever pine for this kind of decadent life. The guilt rose in her chest until she could hardly breathe.

'Well, I daresay you could give some lessons to some of the officials' wives. Perhaps that's something I could organise.'

'Oh no, I'm not sure I'd be good enough for that.' She knew it was false modesty, but would he even believe her if she told him the truth? That she was once the feted Serpentine Rose who danced on Sydney's finest stages. That it had all fallen away on the cold stage floor that fateful night. That the tastes and textures of her former life haunted her. The smooth satin against her skin, flowers in her hair and bare shoulders dusted with gold. The hot lights and long nights. The swell of the crowd. But it was the music and what it did to her body that lingered most. The music's seduction made it impossible to leave her past behind. Made it almost impossible to endure the daily hardship of this life as a miner's wife.

'And do you have any outstanding talents that you're nurturing in your class?'

She smiled. 'Well, yes, there is one little girl named Liv with a great deal of natural talent.'

The band began a popular swing song and the crowd let out a collective whoop, the dance floor filling with people.

'Well, we must dance this one,' Magnus said, leading her onto the floor.

The champagne made her more confident and she let her body really dance. She knew this one. And she could feel eyes on her. Magnus whistled through his fingers at her moves. She could feel the heat in her body rising, burning as the dance reached its crescendo, but she couldn't stop. It felt like letting go. It felt like coming home. It had been so long since she'd danced. Really danced. It was a part of herself that she thought was dead, but she realised it had merely been waiting to wake up.

They collapsed – breathless once again on the edge of the crowd as the music ebbed away into a slower song. He took her hand to pull her back onto the dance floor, but she could feel eyes on them now. Perhaps they were wondering who she was, this interloper who they'd not seen before trying to command the dance floor. Her face felt hot and her palms clammy. She couldn't breathe, as though all the air had been sucked out of the room. She broke away from him.

'Mr Varesso, I should be going now. It's late. Thank you for the dance.' She headed away from the mass of hot, moving bodies, down the candlelit hall that led to the foyer. She could feel the heat of him behind her. She was desperate now to feel the cool night air on her face. She swung the doors open. Her ears rang with the quiet and the scent of new rain thickened the air.

'Will I see you again?' he asked.

She was suddenly acutely aware of the stranger's gloves she wore, the unfamiliar shoes on her feet, and that there was no way to discard them. She shot him an apologetic look and disappeared into the night.

CHAPTER 6

Emmie

She typed *The champagne mothers*, and uploaded the selfie she had taken of herself, Nathalie and Alexandra at the Melbourne Cup party. They were laughing over glasses of champagne, the light soft behind them, lending their faces a sheen, a luminosity. She thought about uploading it to her Instagram account, but it was such a different photo from the everyday domestic ones that populated @Emmiewriter that on a whim she found herself creating a new account. The name came to her easily: @TheDaysofInnocence. She captioned it: *Mothers, love, friendship.*

The words flowed out of her. *I heard them before I saw them. They spoke in whispers, the secret language of women. Of mothers. The perfect shape of them transfixed me as they started across the hot asphalt.* Her hands hovered above the keyboard. She took a sip of tea and sat staring at the screen.

No, I can't, she thought and snapped the screen of the laptop shut. She should actually just go and bake that cake she'd promised Seraphine for afternoon tea. Emmie gathered the two empty teacups from her desk. She must stop drinking so much tea. She was certain Nathalie and Alexandra drank herbal blends, or something equally healthful, not pots and pots of English Breakfast with milk and sugar. She sighed as she ran her hand over the lovely smooth blond wood of her desk. She had a mood board for inspiration, a gorgeous French-style lamp, various expensive pens and note papers and a sleek laptop. It was a working-from-home study fit for Instagram, but the truth was, she had no work.

She went to the kitchen where she took the eggs and milk out of the fridge and began mashing three bananas with an aggression that made her arm hurt. There were probably loads of mums who would love to be baking a cake from scratch for their child to enjoy after school instead of working, she told herself, and paused to give her aching arm a break. *First-world problems*, she admonished herself. She took a deep breath and breathed it out slowly. *I am lucky, I am grateful.* She repeated the phrase in her head, willing positivity into her mind. Her shoulders slumped. She was even crap at gratitude. She just wished there was another aspect to her life. Something to take the focus off trying for another child and failing at it. Something just for her; something that allowed her to use her brain. She thought of her half-finished arts law degree. Maybe she could start that again. But she should be making money, not spending thousands on a degree that might not even lead to a job.

She was so lucky to have Dave. He would support her no matter what she decided. He was the one encouraging her to write while they tried for a baby. His faith in her writing talent was unwavering, which was beautiful, but she thought, misguided. She felt as though her real 'job' at the moment was getting pregnant, which her body was refusing to do. The image of her sweet husband's hopeful face as 'that' time of month rolled around nearly broke her. The way he raised his eyebrows, the eager twitch of his mouth, so ready to break into a smile. She had begun hiding her pain from him. Forcing a brightness onto her face and pretending it wasn't hollowing out her insides.

She sighed as she broke the eggs into the banana and added coconut oil. She took out her phone and took a picture for her blog. Homemade banana bread. She'd take another picture after it was baked, or maybe a selfie with Seraphine enjoying it later. Her life felt like a thin, brittle surface ready to crack. Everything she did felt fickle. Maybe if she actually had more than a handful of followers, it would make it all seem a bit more worthwhile. When had mummy blogging become a profession and the pressure to record the domestic monetised and scrutinised?

She thought about Alexandra and her chic gallery space, Nathalie and her effortless beauty and gorgeous baby, and Pen and her photojournalism. She knew that all of these things were superficial scratchings, the surface of complex lives underneath, that she was lucky to have even one child, and time to herself, but it didn't make the pain any less real. Of course, she knew there were other sides to these women. That was what made them so fascinating. Nathalie had a haunted air about her that Emmie sensed strongly but couldn't figure out. Pen struggled with her brilliant little boy, Will. And Alexandra was like a caricature of a successful working mother, with a famous husband to boot. But she was certain there was more to that story.

She stopped stirring the cake batter. She probably shouldn't use her new friends' pictures on Instagram without their approval. She laughed at herself. What did it matter? No one would read it anyhow. It would be lost in the sea of pretty pictures and pretty lives. She wouldn't use their names. Maybe she'd write fictional musings about motherhood. Short poems. Poetry was having a resurgence on Instagram, wasn't it?

Her failed attempt at a novel was proof that her creative writing wasn't really anything special, maybe she should try poems. The woman she'd hired to do a manuscript appraisal had told her that her voice was just not strong or engaging enough to make the story sing in a way it needed to. Of course, she'd charged her nearly $1500 for this piece of advice, along with lengthy changes to her manuscript to *find the music*, which Emmie never followed through with. She wasn't even sure why she was attempting to keep up the ruse that she was somehow a writer. Well, actually, she was. Her mother had been a successful literary novelist and Emmie had watched her from the vantage point of a young child who worshipped their parent. She had been tall and slim with pale hair that she'd worn just touching her shoulders. There was such a grace and elegance about her mother. She suspected it had skipped a generation and landed in her daughter's gorgeous looks and easy manner.

Emmie had done well in English at school and it was always assumed that she had inherited her mother's talent with words. Everyone had said so, but it was so many years ago now, and she had produced nothing of worth. People who knew about such things had even told her that she was no good. Why did she persist?

With this thought agitating in her head she unloaded the dishwasher, heaved the overflowing washing basket into the laundry and sorted the lights from the darks. She cleared the dining table of Sera's stickers and cuttings and coloured textas and the minefield of Lego from the rug. She was just finishing her cup of herbal tea when she smelled burning. Her heart fell as she opened the oven to a plume of smoke. The cake was blackened and the acrid taste of it was in her eyes and throat. She threw the pan in the sink and it hissed as it hit the cold water. She put her face in her hands. *Why are you crying?* she asked herself. *Why the hell are you crying?*

CHAPTER 7

Alexandra

'So, the girls and I are going away for a week.' Alexandra kept her voice light and upbeat. She could see Maxwell was in a good mood. He'd had an attractive fitness guru on the show this morning and his ego had obviously been well stroked.

It was rare for the two of them to be at home together before dark. They both worked 'til later the nights the nanny came, and the nights Alexandra left work at 5 pm and picked the boys up from after-school care, Maxwell was often at a work function of some kind.

He made a sound to indicate that he'd heard what she'd said but was not going to answer because what he was studying on his phone was more important. It was funny how all the tiny gestures meant something this far into a marriage. She waited. A small part in her contracted.

She sighed but she could tell he didn't pick up on her frustration. 'So, we've come up with a few dates and I just wanted to check in with you first. Or I can ask Kara.'

Maxwell's producer knew more about her husband than she did. Maxwell had always insisted that this was completely normal.

Silence. Expected.

'It's this magnificent beach house one of the mums at school owns. To be honest, I think it could do with an interiors overhaul, but the location is stunning.'

'We live on the beach,' he said, without looking up.

'Different beach. Bigger house. So, would early January work?' There was a false note of brightness to her voice. She hated how she sounded.

Alexandra straightened and breathed slowly in through her nose and out through her mouth just like yoga told her to. She managed to fit in yoga – her one luxurious hour to herself in the hectic week – on a Thursday morning, but that was only if the nanny came early to do the school run. She had tried everything to get the nanny to come early, but she was unreliable, skittish and prone to exaggeration about slight ills. Alexandra had been tempted many times to get rid of her, but the overwhelming anxiety she faced at the prospect of interviewing and finding a new nanny and then the possibility that she would leave abruptly, as some of these young women were inclined to do, deterred her.

He still hadn't responded. *Being ignored by your husband is normal. This is the reality of marriage. That's why everyone jokes about it*, she told herself. She studied the man bent over his phone as though he was devouring a meal and felt a twang in her chest. She began counting. She reached ten and looked out the kitchen window. The ocean was a slate blue, flat and opaque, like a drawing of an ocean. When had she stopped swimming in the sea? When had she stopped noticing it out her kitchen window?

Suddenly the desire to feel the sting of salt on her skin was overwhelming. Her counting was up to 30 now.

'You'll have to check in with Kara.'

There it was. A full half a minute to get a response that she already knew.

'But you're taking them with you, aren't you? The boys? What do you need me for?'

She sighed. 'I don't. I just thought you might like to know when your family was going to be away.'

He didn't respond.

'I'm going swimming.'

He looked up. 'What, at the holiday house?'

She didn't even try to disguise the resentment that she knew was on her face. 'No, now. In the ocean.'

He made a flicking movement with his hand, as though banishing an annoying insect. 'Just swim in the pool. That's what we bought it for. It's better for doing laps.'

'I don't want to do laps.'

'Well, take the boys with you, will you? I've got to work. Oh, and make sure Kara knows about the weekend.'

She felt a hot seam of anger open in her chest. She worked one day less than Maxwell, but it was as though she didn't even have a job. She earned much, much less, which somehow mattered a great deal in the power dynamic between them. She had fought and fought to get the nanny because somehow Maxwell believed it was solely her responsibility to raise their family. They had enough money for her to be a stay-at-home mum, but Alexandra knew Maxwell's stinginess would drive a wedge between them and that she'd have to beg for her own money. Besides, she wanted to work.

Sometimes her job felt like the only thing she had for herself. The boys, of course, felt like hers – all hers all too often. Maxwell seemed to regard his family in the same detached way he regarded his fans. Their marriage felt like it belonged to someone else. It was above and beyond her. It felt out of reach. An ideal rather than a real living thing, like an object behind glass in a museum. Something that other people admired but that behind the glass felt stultified, the air stale.

But, if she was honest, it had always been that way. There had been no big romance. No big emotional connection. They had met at a party and she'd been flattered by the attention of a young up-and-coming TV journalist. Twenty years ago, she'd had the kind of face and body that a man with Maxwell's looks and growing status was predisposed to pursue. And twenty years ago, she didn't even have a name for how she felt about women. Sexual orientation wasn't something to be pondered or explored, it was something to be concealed. And they'd both shared a dry humour, love of wine and that had been enough. He was a good catch. She'd benefited from the status of his growing fame, and she'd been an accessory for him. Now that the shine of those early lures had dulled, she wondered how they had ever been enough.

Alexandra began tapping out an email to her husband's producer on her phone, but she stopped. *This is shit*, she thought. *I need to swim.* She just wanted 20 minutes to herself, to sort out the strength of her feelings. Why was she reacting so strongly? Why was she on emotional tenterhooks and questioning her life choices? Life was always like this. He was always like this.

She left the room wordlessly. The boys were playing Lego in front of the TV. A flush of love ran through her, as strong as the resentment that had preceded it.

'Want to go for a swim with Mummy?' she asked, and the boys looked up. *At least they notice I'm here*, she thought, bending down to inhale the sweet, sweaty smell of them.

'Yeah!' they shouted in unison and it was a race to the bedrooms to get their swimmers.

'Meet me on the back step and bring your buckets.'

Jasper, who at six, had perfected the sort of whimper whine that needled into her skull like a tiny drill, started up. 'I don't waaaaant to go to the beach. I don't waaaaant to. I want to swim in the pool.'

Thomas joined in, breaking out his best puppy dog face. 'The beach is booooring. There are no pool noodles.'

Alexandra closed her eyes for a beat, counselling herself not to completely lose it.

I just want to fucking swim in the ocean for 20 minutes, to feel the wind on my face, she screamed inside. *I just want to be free. I just want to be loved. How have I ended up with everything except love?*

She felt an ocean of emotion, of longing swell inside her. It was so strong it felt like it was choking her. She swallowed it down and pressed her palms into her eye sockets. She wanted to run. Instead she said, 'Okay.'

'We're hungry,' Thomas whined. 'Can we get hot chips?'

'Where are we going to get hot chips?' Her voice had a hysterical tinge to it.

'Toby's mum gets them hot chips from the fish and chip shop for afternoon tea,' Jasper said.

Toby's mum is morbidly obese and passing on bad food habits to her children, Alexandra thought.

'How about some watermelon?'

They both made faces.

Why was everything such a mission with kids? Why couldn't they ever just agree to do what you wanted? It was like they were sent with the explicit purpose to test you in ways that only they knew would take you right to the brink. And if you went over, the guilt would consume you like a wave that bashed you against the rocks until you were a bloody mess. She didn't spend enough time with them. She wasn't there for every school concert and athletics carnival. Yes, motherhood. It was fun.

'I'm not swimming until we get chips,' said Thomas, crossing his arms across his skinny chest.

'Neither am I,' said Jasper, always quick to follow blindly in his older brother's footsteps.

She fought the urge to scream. Here was this behaviour again – entitled, demanding. Frankly, the pair of them acting like little shits. They were becoming mini-Maxwells. The set of their mouths frightened her. She wondered if she had somehow enabled this. She wanted to push back, to teach them that they couldn't just expect everything in life to be delivered to them on a platter, but she felt her strength waver. She didn't have the energy to fight. There were crisps in the pantry. Wasn't that a compromise? A good parenting outcome? She hated herself for doing it but goddammit, she just wanted a swim.

She followed the boys down to the pool, picking up the crisp crumbs as they walked. It really was a nice pool. She had taken months to decide on the tiles. What was she complaining about? The boys hooted as their long legs, tanned by the hot spring sun, kicked and flayed. She didn't feel like swimming anymore. She looked out over their perfectly manicured hedge towards the sea. The wind had picked up, carrying with it the sound of the waves rasping on the sand, the cries of gulls. She imagined the taste of the salt on her lips and the wet way of the sand between her toes.

An image of the woman from the shop came to her – the strawberry blonde hair, the expensive clothes and more expensive furniture purchases. She hadn't been able to place her initially. When Alexandra had first laid eyes on Macie, she had no idea who she was. She had changed so much since high school. If Alexandra was going to be entirely superficial, she was beautiful now. At school she'd had wild, curly hair and had been so awkward and shy. She had been an easy target. And Alexandra wasn't the only one. She didn't say the worst things. She was positive that Macie recognised her and yet she said nothing, she just kept coming in and buying the most expensive stock for the house she was renovating, as if to say, *Look where I am now.* Every time Macie came in it felt like Alexandra couldn't swallow, couldn't breathe, because the awful truth was that Alexandra had made Macie's life a living hell 27 years ago.

CHAPTER 8

Nathalie

The girls were playing on the trampoline, Richie was having a late nap and Nathalie was unpacking the dishwasher when she heard the key turn. Mike was home early. She wiped her hands on the tea towel and felt all the breath leave her lungs. Sometimes it felt as though she were clinging onto the side of a sinking ship. Sometimes it felt so easy – the thought of letting go. The thought of just letting herself float adrift. The squeak of his polished leather shoes on the entrance tiles made her skittish. She remembered when her husband coming home had heralded a feeling of relief and happiness. They were the days when they only had Findlay, when Nathalie was still working part-time and home in time to make dinner. Those days felt like another life.

Mike flung his keys onto the bench and wrestled the tie knot at his throat. Even now after all these years, after everything he'd done, she could still see at moments like these how objectively handsome he was.

'What's this?' he said, hands wide. 'No children. It's a miracle.'

He kissed her on the lips; his smell was of the clinical kind, of sweat made in air-conditioned offices. She felt herself subconsciously checking for the faint high note of perfume and chastised herself. What had the counsellor said? She had to stop looking for signs of infidelity. She had to forgive him and move forward if she was ever going to be happy again. She squashed the doubt down inside her, like the piece of Sim's play dough crusted onto the bench.

It was almost like the night at the hotel had never happened. She had composed herself the next morning, her hangover horrendous, and driven home at dawn. Mike begged for her forgiveness, promising he'd never see that woman again.

There was talk of how far they'd drifted from each other, the chasm expanding with each new child. She'd riled at that – as though his betrayal was a symptom of their joint failing. But now, with the perspective of the past eight months, she could see there was probably some truth in this. Now that night almost seemed like a scene she'd seen in a film once, not her real life.

After a few weeks of wrenching silence, of withering stares, of punishing remarks, she'd told him she didn't want to separate. She'd held him as he cried in a ball on the bed. Promised to change. Promised to be better. Promised they'd get counselling. What was she going to do? Become a single mother with three children? She'd forgotten how to even use her brain. She was surviving day to day as it was. The thought of trying to factor in working and providing for her children felt impossible. She was trapped. She knew it, he knew it. She didn't need for everyone else to know it. If she was going to stay with him, she may as well keep up appearances.

She wished she was a stronger woman and one who could tackle life as a single mother, for whom the moral transgression and the need for freedom was paramount, but the sad truth was she was simply too scared of being alone with three kids.

His hand lingered on her waist. 'What's our homework? Take any time we can to connect. Isn't that what Mrs Levy-Brown instructed?'

Mike had taken to acting like their counsellor was some kind of dominatrix. It was meant to be funny. An in-joke between them.

'Richie's about to wake.' Her voice sounded more clipped than she meant it to.

'Right. Well, no homework tonight then.' His voice lost its playfulness.

'I didn't mean—'

He turned away from her, the nape of his neck tanned. 'You're always exhausted after the kids are in bed.'

'The girls are right there on the trampoline.' A little huff escaped her mouth. He was probably thinking that his mistress would have had sex with him right there on the kitchen bench.

'As if they'd understand,' he said, loosening the watch she'd given him for his fortieth.

'I haven't slept more than a few hours in a row in nearly a year. Of course I'm tired at night.'

He raised his hands in exasperation. 'How did this turn into a fight?'

'We're not fighting,' she said, feeling tears of frustration building behind her eyes. 'We're talking.'

'Anyway, I've got the men's support group coming tonight.'

'What, here?'

'Yeah, I told you last week it was here.' He scratched behind his left ear. She wondered if that body language meant he was lying. No, being in therapy now, he apparently didn't lie because he was facing his 'deep truths'.

Nathalie scanned through the scattered pieces of her mind for this particular nub of information but found nothing. He may well have told her, and she didn't take it in. It seemed to happen often these days.

'The house is a total bomb,' she said, scanning the dirty dishes in the sink, the dishwasher needing to be unloaded, dining table covered with papers and craft, the toy-strewn lounge room floor. Every surface was covered.

'These aren't judgemental guys, Nat. They're not going to judge you on that.'

She waited a beat before replying. There were so many things wrong with his response. 'Yeah but they literally might not have anywhere to sit.'

'I'll help you clean up now.'

A sarcastic reply poised on the tip of her tongue, but she swallowed it down.

'Well, I hope they like screaming babies with their confessionals,' she said, picking up a pile of textas on the kitchen bench.

'I thought you could take Richie out in the car if he gets unsettled, see if he might sleep that way. You've been doing it a bit lately anyway.'

She felt her head shaking before she could stop it. 'So, we're getting chucked out of our own home?'

'No, I just–'

Nathalie scooped an armful of toys off the lounge room floor. 'Fine. But did you think that maybe not offering to have this meeting at your house might have been an option, seeing as we have a baby and two other children who don't sleep?'

He sighed and wiped a hand down his face. 'Everyone takes turns. That's the beauty of it. It's just a group of guys who have gone through shit and are trying to sort their shit out for their wives.'

She bit the inside of her lip. *For their wives. What about you just sort your own shit out?* She straightened and looked him in the eye. 'Sorry, but these are your friends and I feel like I'm being kicked out of my own house. I'm not whipping up dinner for them or something.'

Richie's cries came ricocheting down the hall and Nathalie jumped, as though a bolt of lightning had lit up her insides, so primed was her body to respond to her baby's distress. 'Shall Richie and I just leave you now?'

The way she said it, the certain timbre of her voice implied something bigger, more serious. She saw the hurt, bright and sudden flare in his eyes, and she knew she was being cruel. He was hopeless. He wouldn't be able to get the girls' dinner ready, to bath them and give them their puffers and various creams before his men's group arrived. And it was true, she resented him for it. His duty extended to reading them one short story. He then left her to scramble between settling them and Richie. Sometimes he helped clean up the kitchen.

'Sorry,' she mumbled and left the kitchen, wondering why, once again, she was the one apologising.

She heard him pick up the keys and follow her down the hall, his presence behind her like a shadow. For a moment she wondered if he would tell her to just get in the car and go. But then she realised. Of course. It was him who was going.

'We're going to need milk. And I'll pick up some cheese and biscuits or something, maybe something to have with coffee.'

She scooped Richie out of his cot and was calmed by the musky smell of him. 'What time are they coming?'

He looked at his phone. '7 pm.'

She felt her whole body float, as though she'd slipped off the side of the ship. 'In an hour and a half.'

So, she had to clean up the house to a presentable level, feed Richie, feed and bath the girls and put them in bed in an hour and a half. Part of her wanted to rally, refuse, but she was so used to it, so used to feeling alone with the emotional responsibility of the household while he appeared haphazardly to impose more work on her. A tiny voice inside of her said *it would be easier without you*, but he was swinging open the door and walking through it, leaving her alone, a great fear swelling in her belly and the sounds of the girls coming in from outside calling for food.

CHAPTER 9

Pen

The TV flashed with the trashy reality show Cate loved and Pen secretly did too, though she'd cultivated eye-rolling exasperation to make her daughter laugh. Cate propped her feet onto Pen's lap. Remnants of another frozen pizza dinner, with a hastily chopped salad to appease her mother guilt, lay on the coffee table. The small living room was cluttered with washing baskets of clean clothes that needed folding, toys that Will had been playing with and paperwork that Pen had yet to deal with. The guilt of the mess niggled at the back of Pen's mind, but she didn't have the energy to do anything about it. She had another 7 am shift at the paper and Will would need to be dropped off just as before-school care opened. A whole 'to do' list for tomorrow opened up in her head.

Cate wriggled her toes and Pen shot her daughter a sidelong glance. 'What do you want?'

'Paint my toes blue?'

Pen sighed. 'All right but you owe me about three pedicures. I'm counting.'

'Why can't I get mine done at the salon like all my friends? I mean, you're pretty good but it's just not the same. Not as shiny.'

'If you've got some spare money, knock yourself out,' she said.

'Sal's parents pay for a mani-pedi every two weeks. She gets nail art.'

Pen felt frustration buzz through her. Teenagers were obsessed with money and the status it gave them.

'You're going to have to go for the arty down-and-out vibe. Vintage shop clothes. Old books. Spend some time in Newtown. It's cool. It was when I was your age.'

Cate rolled her eyes. 'You just don't get it, Mum.'

Cate was 16 going on 23. Sometimes, Pen forgot that her daughter was still a child, save for moments like this.

'I might stay with Lucien for the rest of the week.'

'Can you stop calling your father by his first name please?'

'He doesn't care. He likes it.'

'Fine. But tidy your room before you go. I can't keep up with who's who on this show.'

'God, Mum, get with the program.'

Will came out of his room. 'Mum, can I use the iPad to Google something?'

'It's pretty late for screen time, mate. Bed in half an hour. What's so important?'

'On *BTN* they were talking about this man called Nostradamus and he could predict the future and I want to research it for a story I'm writing.'

'For school or for fun?'

'Fun.'

The familiar discomfort wormed in her gut and Pen shifted on the couch. 'Okay, that sort of stuff isn't really for kids, Will. I'm pretty sure that guy couldn't tell the future anyway. What am I saying? Of course, he couldn't.'

'Then why did they mention him on a kids' news show. At school?' Will's brow was crinkled in confusion.

'Weirdo,' said Cate. 'God, why do you have to be so strange? Just Google ... I don't know ... What are normal eight-year-olds into? *Transformers*? Soccer?'

Will's face darkened. He thrust his jaw out and his body stiffened.

Pen elbowed Cate and shot her a warning look. 'Don't be mean to your brother.' Her tone was heavy with the threat she hoped her daughter would heed.

'Half-brother.'

'Cate.' Pen's voice was a bark.

Will ripped the nail polish from Cate's fingers and threw it against the wall. They all watched in silence as the glass broke and blue varnish bled down the wall.

Pen grabbed Will by the arm, and he cried out as she dug her fingers into his flesh. 'Will! Why the hell would you do that?'

'She was being mean.'

Pen closed her eyes for a beat and released Will. 'She was.' She glared at Cate. 'She was being awful. Cate apologise to Will, please. That was *really* mean.'

Cate's face was stony, and her arms were crossed tight against her chest. 'You always take his side.'

Pen sighed and counselled herself to stay calm. 'I'm just trying to keep the peace. Cate, you're meant to be the mature one here.'

'I'm not his mother. If you were around more and I didn't have to always look after him maybe I wouldn't find him so annoying.'

'You're the annoying one,' said Will, his body rigid.

'You're *both* being annoying,' said Pen, her voice loud, full of exasperation.

'I wish you were never born,' hissed Cate. 'Our life was so much better before you came along.'

The words floated in the air, sharp and sickening like the smell of nail varnish.

I wish you were never born. The words cut close to Pen. She recognised the shard of truth in them that had been edging up against her own heart. She had thought them. She had. Cate had just articulated the awful truth of what she had thought inside her head. The guilt came next, crashing through her, making her reach for him.

'Will,' she cried as he flew from the room silently.

'Cate. Clean that up right now. How dare you say that to your brother.'

'Why do I have to clean it up? He's the one who did it.'

'Do it!' She screeched the words and saw the impact on Cate's face and again, the guilt. She headed down the hall towards Will's room.

'It's true,' Cate cried behind her. 'We were so much happier when it was just you and me. You were so much happier.'

Pen felt her whole world narrowing with the pain of those words. As she knocked on Will's door, imploring him to let her in, she thought back to that decision. She had been so close to having an abortion. So close. She was a single mum-of-one already. Struggling to make ends meet. Will's father was no one. A butcher with a sexy accent and a sense of humour who she'd had one night with after a friend's party. But she'd made her choice. She'd chosen to keep her baby.

She had wondered at times if there was something else at play. Did he have ADHD or autism or anxiety that was just masked by his intelligence? She'd asked one of his teachers if he had oppositional defiance disorder and she'd laughed. He was intelligent and diligent, the teacher said. He was a sweet boy, Emmie said. And so, she couldn't help thinking that what Will had was a mother who didn't love him. As she walked away from the door he would not open, she realised she was crying.

Jean
1948

The day was hot, like all the other days here, the heat twisting itself into her limbs, bedsheets discarded in the night. Liv's body spooned into hers and Jean wiped the damp hair from her daughter's face. She was home. Last night seemed like a wild dream. Another life. The dancing. That man. She had snuck into the house before dawn began to glow behind the valley walls, the birdsong rising softly in the air. Robert left at first light for the mines. He slept like the dead. Twelve hours of physical work did that to a man, she knew. He would never know she had gone. Had he found her side of the bed empty he would have assumed she was curled up with their daughter in the other bedroom. Liv had stirred as Jean had tiptoed down the hall, and there was a moment when her daughter might have seen her red lipstick, her satin gloves. But Liv was sleep-addled as she shifted in her bed. Jean stripped off in Liv's room and pushed her clothes under the bed, got between the sheets and wrapped her arms around her daughter. It took a long time to get to sleep.

When Liv woke, Jean spent the morning making her meagre school lunch and drinking all of their coffee ration. She watched Liv trace out dance steps with her toes on their dusty kitchen floor. She took her daughter's hands and twirled her until she giggled, and they did the jitterbug to the whistle of the boiling kettle. They walked to the school gate and she hugged her daughter at the door of the classroom, saying hello to her teacher, Mrs Appleby.

The day passed like all the others. Jean prepped the evening meal from what little she had. She wished they had the money to go to the Silver Bell cafe to treat Liv, but she managed to use the last scraps of meat to fashion a steak and kidney pie. She washed Robert's filthy work clothes until the water was black and smelling of shale oil. But in her belly was a curl of excitement the like of which she had not felt for a very long time. There was guilt, too, and the two feelings slipped around inside her like the soap on her fingers.

At the school gate she saw Pam, the mother of Liv's best friend, Bertie.

'Jean, have you heard? There's a woman gone missing. In the valley. Clara Black is her name. She was last seen at the ball at the hotel last night. Did you hear it? You couldn't have not. The music was terribly loud, and it went all night. Can you imagine? Her husband's my husband's boss. Apparently, the poor man is beside himself.'

Jean's mouth went dry and she felt sweat prick her brow. The nerves already inside her belly tightened and she pressed her hands to her hot cheeks. 'Oh no, that's terrible,' she said.

'Of course, everyone's saying something like this was inevitable. All the poverty, the terrible working conditions, the disparity between them and us. Imagine, even I was jealous hearing that party going all night. And here we are with barely enough to feed our children and having to buy water from the water cart. There's talk of one of the miners losing their mind and deciding to take revenge.' Pam lowered her voice. 'Sometimes, something doesn't feel right here. All those rumours of the massacres of the Blacks and the valley ghosts.'

Jean's skin crawled and she shivered despite the hot sun above them. 'Maybe they'll find her. She hasn't been gone for long. You know how these missing person things turn out. Most of the time they're found, aren't they?'

'They're bringing in police from Sydney to search the bushland but, gosh, there's a lot of bush out here. It's like something out of a crime novel. Imagine.'

Jean's mind reeled as their conversation turned to domestic things and the girls. She searched frantically for her final words to Clara Black. She'd asked her if she was sure she should go into the night alone. What had Clara said? That she'd wanted to. That she felt like walking barefoot, being free. Getting away from the party. Jean remembered how dark the night was. How dreamy Clara had seemed. What if she had gone with Clara? Been more insistent. Could she have saved her? Or would she too be missing? A name on the lips of the valley's gossip? She felt a wave of nausea roll through her.

Clara Black wasn't tough like Jean knew she herself was. She hadn't grown up in poverty, in hardship. She hadn't learned the ways to keep herself safe as a matter of course. This was a woman to whom harm could come. If only she'd gone with

Clara on her silly walk. She would never have met Magnus. Would that have been better? Yes, of course it would. She wouldn't be responsible for a poor woman going missing and she wouldn't be having all these silly feelings for a man she'd only met once.

She was relieved when she saw the girls skipping towards them, hand in hand. Not to have to speculate anymore, gossip anymore about Clara Black. She made her excuses to Pam about being in a rush to get to teaching. She had classes starting shortly but she returned to the house and while Liv was drinking her milk and eating a biscuit on the back step, she got down on her hands and knees and pulled the clothes she'd discarded last night from under Liv's bed. The red gloves, the red hairclip. The shoes. Would they find Jean's dusty old shoes stuffed under the seat out the front of the hotel? She touched her lips. She had been wearing Clara's lipstick. She remembered the beautiful silver cigarette case. Where was that now? Had she been the last person to ever see Clara Black? She squeezed her eyes shut. The poor woman's husband.

She gathered the gloves and shoes and stuffed them into an old pillowcase. Were they some kind of evidence? Of what? She hadn't done anything wrong, had she? What good would it do to tell the police that she'd seen this woman? She would look entirely guilty to have put on this woman's shoes and make-up and gone into a dance where she hadn't belonged. And how would she explain why she was there in the first place? That the music had drawn her? That it had called to her over the valley and made her sneak out of her own house? That the music had bewitched her body and taken her back to a time when she had everything before her? When dancing had been her life?

Her very soul. That a man with an impossible name had seen what she used to be? That she had lied about her name? No. It all looked completely suspicious. They would think she was somehow involved when all she'd been was a spectator. She went to her wardrobe and used a chair to get to the highest shelf, where she stuffed the pillowcase in the back. She would need to forget about Clara Black, forget about Serpentine Rose. It was her name, but from another life. That life wasn't hers anymore. That person no longer existed.

CHAPTER 10

Nathalie

December

The glass of wine sat sweating into the still, warm air. Nathalie ran her fingertip around the rim, just to feel the moisture, just to appreciate the quality of the crystal. She took a slow sip and felt the liquid dissolve into her body like a balm. She felt everything relax, lulled by the soft rush of the waves meeting sand. The evening was turning purple at its edges as the sun slid below the clouds at the horizon. She had chosen seats that overlooked the ocean. She swept her hair back, hoping to feel a sea breeze on her neck. It licked at her nape and she closed her eyes.

The ever-social Alexandra had insisted that they all catch up here for a pre-Christmas drink before their week away together in January, but now she wondered if the trip was actually going to happen. Amanda O'Neil had texted to say that recent heavy rains up the coast had caused a significant leak in the roof and now the house had water damage. She wasn't sure it would still be available for their dates. Nathalie had meant to pass this onto the others when the text came through, but she'd been mid vomiting bug with the girls, and she'd completely forgotten. And now, here they were ostensibly meeting ahead of a holiday that might not be happening. She felt pathetic to have completely blanked on this, but it was hard to project a few hours, let alone a few weeks into the future. It felt like she was on a sand dune that kept shifting, and it was all she could do to stop herself being scattered by the wind. She took out her phone and texted Amanda, asking for an update. The response was almost immediate.

Sorry hon, it's not looking good. I was just going to talk to the builder before confirming with you, but I think it's going to be safer to postpone until Feb.

No. I needed this holiday, she thought. *The others are going to be so disappointed.*

She took a large sip of her wine. Dammit. She wasn't going to let this spoil such a rare mid-week escape. She had lied outright to Mike, to make sure she got a half hour to herself. Didn't self-help books for mothers always talk about taking time for yourself? Well, these 30 minutes were hers and she wasn't going to feel bad. She sensed the eyes of others slide over her body and she luxuriated in the feeling. She wore a cream sleeveless silk shift, and bare legs. She finished the glass and poured herself a second. Sometimes, after a few glasses, she imagined that she too could have an affair.

She wondered when Mike had made the decision. Had it been as soon as he'd met the woman? Had her beauty been so astounding that he'd felt his whole body react? She'd seen a picture. She'd made him show her. She was attractive, but not a great beauty as far as Nathalie was concerned. Their counsellor said that it was part of her need to know and process the affair;

that he needed to answer all her questions. How often did they have sex? Every time they met. Had he given her oral sex? Yes. Had they used a condom? Not always. Each word had felt like a sharp slit into her skin. Wounds that she didn't know would ever heal. Yet he'd answered her questions with a deep, earnest look in his eyes, as though he was the most honest person alive. But there was one thing she hadn't been able to ask him. *When was the exact moment you decided you would jeopardise our children, our family for another woman?* She couldn't bring herself to ask, because maybe some part of her knew that it would push him over the edge, and she was scared of what would happen.

She took another luxurious sip of wine and closed her eyes. No, she wasn't going to spend her precious moments to herself going over this again. She searched her mind for something positive to think about. Findlay had received a merit award in assembly, Sim was happy at preschool. *Something positive about myself*, she thought. But all she could come up with was this moment. Alone. Softening from the warmth of the wine inside her.

'Hey, girl.' Alexandra gave her shoulder a quick squeeze from behind. 'Yay! No bedtime routine! Did you get out of bath as well?'

Nathalie gave her the thumbs up, even though she had bathed and fed the kids early so Mike didn't have to do it. She felt suddenly teary and wiped the moisture from under her eyes, hoping Alexandra hadn't seen.

'Ah, sweet freedom.' Alexandra flung one of the designer leather bags she was so fond of onto a stool and made a gesture towards the bar.

'I'm already on my second glass,' Nathalie indicated to the bottle. She felt her face colour, partly from the wine, partly from her confession about the wine. Alexandra waved her hand as if to say, 'that's nothing', but Nathalie suddenly felt self-conscious.

'Hey, I've got bad news. Amanda's house has water damage. We can't go away in January. It won't be available 'til February.'

Alexandra's face fell. 'What the hell? What's the good of February? The kids will be back at school.'

Nathalie winced, feeling somehow like it was her fault. 'I know. Shame. I've been dying for a break. And with Christmas on the horizon and all the shopping and cooking … it was going to be the calm after the storm.'

'Shit. Exactly. The next two weeks are going to be insane. I haven't even started my present shopping.' Alexandra rubbed her temples. 'The kids will be sad, too. And now here we are getting together with Emmie and Pen, who frankly …'

'What? We usually wouldn't be having drinks and going away with?'

'Well, yes. No. I don't know. We hardly know them. But I guess it is technically Emmie's prize. It just feels like yours, 'cause you know Amanda.'

'It's totally her prize. Emmie seems nice. I like her,' Nathalie said.

'You like everyone. Bugger it. Oh well, we're out. We're never out mid-week. It's nearly Christmas. We are *doing* this, holiday or no holiday. Rosé good for the second bottle?' Alexandra stormed off through the crowd to the bar.

Nathalie studied her half-empty second wine glass. Alexandra treated this as a blowout, a one-off but the truth was, it was a constant. Nathalie tried to locate the last night she hadn't had a drink. She was surprised by the relief she felt when she realised it was a few weeks ago when she had been sick with a cold.

She told herself that it was normal to have a few glasses at night. Richie took a bottle of formula overnight, and after that last afternoon feed, it was her treat. Her one thing for herself. So, they had big wine glasses. They were Waterford crystal and part of the joy was the beautiful glasses, the ceremony. That first sip. Sometimes it was the only thing getting her through the day.

Alexandra returned with the wine and a buzzer for sweet potato fries, salt and pepper squid, and prawn pizzas.

'How many glasses do you have a night? Of wine?' Nathalie asked with a breezy, casual note in her voice.

Alexandra snorted. 'Depends how shit my day has been.'

'How about a seven out of ten. Seven and a half. That'd be most of your days, right?'

Alexandra gave her a reproachful look. 'Are you kidding?'

'You've got the studio, famous husband, your boys …' Nathalie's voice trailed off as she watched Alexandra's face contort in disbelief.

Alexandra twisted the stem of her glass. 'Truly. Does anyone have a seven-out-of-ten life? I mean, in real life. Not on social media.'

'Well, clearly I do,' Nathalie laughed darkly. *My life is a joke*, she thought, but it felt good to laugh.

'Well, clearly. That's why we're all not-so-secretly jealous of you.' Alexandra put her hand on Nathalie's arm. 'How are things with you anyway? I feel like we haven't talked in ages.'

Nathalie took another sip of wine. Alex knew nothing of the affair. She hadn't told a soul and she intended to keep it that way. Part of her wished she had the courage to tell her closest friend. Why was it so hard? *My husband had an affair. It's over now. He said it didn't mean anything, not really. I haven't kicked him out. He's in therapy. We both are. He's sworn he'll never do it again. I'm shameful and weak.* She poured more wine into her glass. 'Oh, same old,' she said. 'Surviving. Just. Thank God I'm not pregnant again.'

'What have we missed?' Emmie and Pen arrived, giving shy little waves. New friends. They weren't quite at the kissing on arrival stage yet.

'Our holiday's off. Boo,' Alexandra said, frowning dramatically before brightening suddenly. 'So, we're drinking *all* the wine. Come and commiserate with us.'

'No! What? How? It's mine, I won it. I never win anything,' said Emmie, effecting faux horror.

'Yeah, well your luck has run out, lady. Nat has been texting Amanda and the place has water damage and won't be available 'til February, which is pointless because school's back.'

Emmie made a face. 'Damn. That really sucks. Sorry.'

'It's not your fault,' Nathalie said.

'What a shame,' said Pen. 'My holidays just got approved, too.'

'Look, it's not ideal, but we're being grown-ups and rolling with the punches because there is fried food and carbs on the way ... and wine,' Nathalie said, raising her glass.

'If you say so,' said Emmie, looking uncertain.

'I do. Sit, sit. Drink.'

'This place is nice,' said Pen.

Night had snuck up on them and candles lit the tables, a string of bare bulbs illuminating the deck. Things spun pleasantly. Nathalie knew she shouldn't have any more wine but she poured the others' glasses before topping up her own.

She'd seen Pen around the school. She had the cool mum thing going on. Short dark hair, wet, as though she'd just stepped out of the shower, a piercing in her nose, bright lipstick. This was a woman who said it like it was. This was the kind of woman who would kick a cheating husband to the kerb.

'Nat's nearly three glasses in so you've got some catching up to do.' Alexandra held up her near-empty glass.

Emmie laughed awkwardly and mimed a drinking gesture. She was more dressed up than usual, in a floral dress that showed off her curves. Nathalie was always envious of that body shape. Women with boobs and a butt looked so amazing and yet her own skinny, tall waif-like body was considered somehow aspirational.

'You ladies look gorgeous,' she said.

Emmie's cheeks blushed to a shade of high crimson.

'Hi, I'm Pen.' Pen extended a hand as she sat down. 'I don't think we've met properly.'

'You did Sophia Smith's wedding, didn't you?' Alexandra nudged Nathalie. 'Pen's an amazing photographer from what I've heard.'

Pen worried a small hoop earring in her lobe. 'That's great to hear she liked the photos. She was an ace bride. Very laid-back. My favourite type. I don't do heaps of weddings. I'm really a news photographer but, sometimes, I'll do them if I know the couple aren't going to be a nightmare.'

'You mean not all brides are laid-back?' Alexandra raised an eyebrow sarcastically and they all laughed.

'Oh my God, the stories I have to tell, you wouldn't believe,' said Pen.

Alexandra moved towards her conspiratorially. 'Oh, do tell.'

'I think I'm going to need a bucket of wine first,' said Pen.

'On it,' said Emmie, leaving for the bar.

CHAPTER 11

Emmie

Emmie made her way back to the table with a bottle and four fresh glasses. She'd ordered the most expensive bottle of prosecco on the list, which was something she'd never normally do. But she felt bad, as though it was her fault; her bad luck had rubbed off on their holiday. Who won a holiday and then lost it? *Pathetic.* It had all seemed a bit too good to be true. Who knew if it would even end up happening now? They were all so different and now there was no reason for them to go away and Alexandra didn't seem that keen to reschedule. A thick wave of disappointment moved through her. But Nathalie was right, they were out, and she was going to try to enjoy herself. The bar buzzed with the allure and anticipation of the long stretch of summer holidays and Christmas. Everywhere the glint of sun-licked skin, bejewelled limbs and painted nails. It was as though the night-time had unleashed this gorgeous tribe that Emmie had almost forgotten existed – young people.

Of course, Nathalie and Alexandra fitted with this crowd. Was it their clothes, their nonchalance? The fact they didn't look like 'mums'? And why was it an insult to actually look like a mum anyhow? 'Mumsy' was a derogatory term and yet she knew that she embodied what it was to look mumsy: a little soft, a little boring-looking. She wasn't sure why this bothered her. Maybe it was being in the proximity of yummier mummies. She thought of a newspaper article she had read about how the people you socialised with informed the way you thought about yourself. If you hung out with richer, more beautiful people your self-esteem would suffer. But on the plus side, you would be judged as better-looking yourself if your friends were good-looking.

As she excused her way through the crowd she observed her new friends – were they friends now that the reason for them getting together was gone? Alexandra and Nathalie were laughing at something Pen was saying and Emmie felt a spike of ... what? Was she jealous? *How infantile*, she thought. *Friendship isn't a competition.*

She placed the bottle carefully in the middle of the table, self-conscious of her low-cut dress as she bent over. Dave had made a low whistle when she'd walked into the lounge room wearing it and she'd felt a surge of confidence at his appreciation. Why was it that all that disappeared the moment she went out into the real world?

'And then she – I kid you not – threw the bouquet at the groom's face.'

'Noooo,' Alexandra and Nathalie cooed together.

Emmie proceeded to pour the prosecco, trying to pick up snatches of this dramatic wedding story. Now she really felt like the mum, slightly on the outer, doing the practical stuff while everyone else was having fun. *Oh God*, she thought to herself, *pull yourself together.* She was so prone to overthinking social situations, and victim mentality. She really didn't like herself at times like these. She handed around the glasses and got out her phone to take some shots. It was a beautiful night. Light still hovered just where the horizon met the sky, as though the seams of the earth were on display.

'Cheers. Smile everyone,' she said. 'Let me take a selfie. For the Mum's Gone Wild Holiday Club that isn't happening anymore,' she said. 'Ugh. Sounds like a lame movie I'd like.'

They all laughed, leaning in together as Emmie took a quick snap.

She snuck a look at the picture. It was impossible to get past how Nathalie looked. She was in a giggly mood, her cheeks flushed and her eyes shining. Emmie had already noticed the attention she commanded in the bar. People's eyes lingered over her in a way that she didn't even seem to register. *What would it be like to hold that much power?* thought Emmie. It was so easy to look at someone beautiful and believe that they had no problems. Or that if they did have problems, they would somehow be softened by everyone's constant adoration.

Nathalie was describing a funny moment at her own wedding now and Emmie detected a slight slur to her words. She was obviously making the most of time away from her family.

'We had like, 300 people, Mike comes from a big family. Italian heritage. His great-uncle was cracking on to me the whole time. It was hilarious.'

Emmie would have secretly loved to have had a big wedding. Instead she had pretended to be the kind of person who wanted something small and intimate. That's what Dave had wanted and the shy part of her was relieved, but there was somewhere in her that longed for a bigger life, a brighter life. She imagined Nathalie before having kids, in a wedding dress. She wondered if her husband was insanely good-looking too.

'Well, at least you didn't have the paparazzi at your wedding. Maxwell insisted on selling ours to the trash mags. I was mortified,' said Alexandra. 'And I'm not just saying that for false modesty. It ruined our wedding day. Everywhere I looked there was either a camera or a white umbrella in my face.'

'Oh, to stop the other media from getting the pics?' asked Pen. 'Yeah, I've done some high-profile weddings and it takes away from the intimacy. You can almost see how it's setting the marriage up to be a certain way.' Pen nudged Alexandra's arm. 'Oh, I don't mean yours, sorry.'

Alexandra arched an eyebrow and waved away Pen's apology. 'Oh, don't apologise. You should write a tell-all book.'

'So, can you tell which marriages are going to fail?' asked Nathalie, her body swaying very subtly, her eyes fixed on some distant place.

She is completely drunk, thought Emmie. She wondered if the others had noticed. Nathalie had begun on the glass of prosecco.

Pen cocked her head thoughtfully and pressed her lips together. She had the kind of lips made for bright red lipstick. As far as Emmie could see that was the only make-up she wore, and she'd never seen her without the lipstick.

'Yeah, I guess so.' Pen chewed on a dark painted nail. 'Sometimes there's just no emotional connection to capture in the photographs. It's pretty clear when you're capturing something real. And the sarcastic comments. If one of them is putting the other down in a sarcastic way the whole day I know it's doomed.'

'Oh God, I'm pretty sure that was me and Maxwell,' Alexandra said, rolling her eyes. 'Or maybe it's only come on in later years now we're sick of each other. I can't remember.'

'Oh, come on, he adores you. He's always talking about you on air,' said Nathalie.

'But, you know, I've been wrong. Relationships are weird beasts,' Pen said.

'Or wild beasts, in the case of my husband,' Emmie said. Everyone looked at her. She swallowed and felt a trickle of perspiration run down her back. *Why did I say that?* It was really too early in their friendship.

She made an awkward hand gesture and wobbled her head in a way that she assumed made her look like a crazy person. The irony of the fact that she couldn't fall pregnant was not lost on her.

'Don't know why I said that.' Emmie hid behind her glass.

Alexandra's eyes narrowed. 'Your husband a bit of a wild thing, is he? Go you.'

Nathalie shot Emmie a smile, as though she intuited her awkwardness. 'How's your novel coming along?'

'Good, good,' Emmie said touching the nape of her neck and averting her eyes. *It's not a novel, it's an Instagram account and your picture is on it. And that one photo has got me more likes and follows than anything I've ever posted before.*

'What's it about again?' Nathalie asked.

Emmie froze, not knowing what to say. Her mouth twitched but could not find the words.

'Let's hope the wild husband,' said Alexandra with a sly smile.

At that moment the waiter brought out two pizzas and a large bowl of sweet potato chips and another of salt and pepper squid. Everyone murmured appreciatively at the carb-fest and Emmie breathed a sigh of relief that the focus was no longer on her.

CHAPTER 12

Alexandra

Alexandra snuck a look at Emmie, sipping politely on her prosecco and cutting up a piece of pizza with her knife and fork. She wouldn't have picked her as someone who was still having wild sex and had a functioning relationship this far into marriage and kids. She was awkward and self-conscious, prone to babbling to fill up silence. And yet Alexandra realised with a shock that she was jealous of Emmie. How on earth did you keep that kind of connection with another person going for so long without the resentment eating you up? Sex for her and Maxwell felt like another thing to be ticked off on the 'to do' list. And if it was suffused with anything more than that, it was simply a need to be met. Alexandra felt uneasiness shift inside her once again. *You could have had more. If only you'd listened to what you really need. What you really desire.*

'So, how's work? Is that woman who gave me her scarf still coming in to buy half the shop?' asked Nathalie.

Alexandra waved a hand, trying to look nonplussed. 'Oh, not as much. Must have reached her budget limit.'

Macie was still coming in every second day. She wasn't sure why she'd lied about that. She had come into the shop today and Alexandra had felt the hairs on her arms rise, as usual.

'What can I help you with? Thought any more about the lamps for the lounge?' Alexandra was always the first to speak. Macie had a self-possession that unnerved her and made her over-talk. 'Isn't it a divine day?'

Macie ran her fingers along the grain of a custom-made timber dining table. 'Yes, gorgeous sunshine.' Today she was wearing a long pale blue dress that showed off her milky skin. She shot Alexandra a smile. Those braces had certainly been worth it. She had the straightest teeth. 'Oh, I'm not here to talk shop for once. I wanted to ask a favour.'

Alexandra felt her heartbeat accelerate a little. This sounded personal. Their conversations always revolved around fabric swatches and the measurements of sofas. This Alexandra could do, but apart from knowing each other's names, there had been no talk of anything else that might have placed them once at the same school. Anything that skirted close to the unacknowledged truth between them.

Alexandra tapped her nails nervously on the counter in front of her.

'I'm putting together a creative talk at the local art gallery where my friend works. She's lent us this most amazing space. And we just lost our designer. It's an all-women thing and I just thought of you.'

Alexandra's hand went to her chest. 'Me?' It was the feeling, so ingrained from childhood. Being picked. Singled out of a line of others.

'Well, you've basically decorated my entire home and everyone who's seen it so far has been so blown away. I know you may not technically be a designer, but you've definitely got the natural eye to be a designer.'

Alexandra felt her chin wobble a little and she bit the inside of her lip to stop it. She was so used to feeling like a complete fraud. She had only got the job because Elizabeth, the owner, was friends with Maxwell's boss's wife. Everything she did felt somehow mediated by her husband. And now here was this woman who she'd spent a good deal of her adolescence tormenting making her feel acknowledged and worthy.

'And you're such a big personality. It'd be a cinch for you to get up and talk.'

Alexandra blinked several times and worried a ring on her finger. 'Am I? Would it?'

'You'd just have to talk a bit about your creative process and it's a women in business talk, so a bit about that.'

She felt her face flush. She never went red, but her cheeks felt like they were on fire. She didn't truly see herself as a creative person. It always felt like she was faking it.

'Ah ...' She was lost for words.

'It is quite soon though. Next week. Monday night. We've got an author and a winemaker. She's providing the wine.'

Alexandra was so close to nodding, accepting this unexpected flattery, but something inside her shifted, uncertainty rising to the surface.

'Oh, I'd love to, but I think that might be too close. Even with Maxwell giving me public speaking tips I'm not sure I could pull it off.' She realised she'd never mentioned her husband to Macie. She watched her face to see the usual spark of recognition but found nothing.

Macie smiled. 'I understand. But come along. It'll be a great night. Good wine. I'll shoot the details to the shop's email address.'

Alexandra nodded. 'Okay, great.'

Alexandra watched Macie turn and walk away. 'Thanks,' she said. She knew the other woman couldn't hear her. But she couldn't speak any louder. She felt the familiar stab of shame in her gut. An image flashed into her mind. Macie walking away from them all in the playground, her back and shoulders straight, even with the sticky mango skin and strawberry hulls caught in her curly hair. The chant *Macie likes girls* echoing, the cruel smiles curled on their lips. Macie never turned around. She just kept walking, as though their sniggers hadn't sliced through her skin like sharpened knives. But Alexandra saw the very slight tremor along Macie's shoulders. She should have done something. She should have stopped it. But she couldn't. She hadn't been strong enough. She hadn't been able to face her own feelings. And now Macie was here, beautiful and gracious, and it was all Alexandra could do to stop the shame and regret from suffocating her.

CHAPTER 13

Pen

The four of them had outlasted the shiny young people, the candles on their table long extinguished, the wine bottles empty. The bustling boardwalk outside the bar had quietened and the moon had risen, a shiny puncture in the blanket of black. The only sounds were the gentle wash of the waves against the pylons and the soft clink of cutlery being cleared. The ocean had breathed a salty mist over the night and she felt enveloped in its silky cocoon. Pen knew she should probably say her goodbyes and go home. She had a wedding job tomorrow and she needed to be out of the house early. But the truth was, she was enjoying herself for the first time in ages. Nathalie had her head on Alexandra's shoulder and Emmie was still chastely cradling a glass of red wine.

She had seen Nathalie and Alexandra in the playground and always assumed they were somehow stuck up because of the way they dressed, or looked. But that couldn't have been further from the truth. Nathalie was drunk and giggly, which made Pen want to look after her and Alexandra had a dry wit that made her cheeks hurt from laughing.

Pen had seen Alexandra's husband, Maxwell, on morning television. It wasn't the kind of TV she watched, even though she was partial to crappy reality TV shows. He was handsome, in that bronzed, stiff Ken-doll, plastic-hair way. Alexandra was also super fit and toned, her nails perfect, her hair blow-dried to the kind of smooth straightness that defied wind. But there was something about her illusion of perfection that shimmered with uncertainty. And it was this that Pen found interesting. She found them all interesting. They were so different from her, but they all had vulnerabilities and wore their hearts on their sleeves. These were women she might just be able to be friends with.

They'd spent the past hour whispering stories of what little shits their children could be in the way only drunk mothers could. For Pen this was a revelation.

'My boys once smeared sunscreen on my Turkish rug,' Alexandra said. 'It's just as well the nanny found it, or I would have throttled them.'

'Got a better one. Permanent marker on the leather lounge,' Nathalie said, her words slurring and her eyes heavily lidded.

'Nappy removed in the cot. Poo smeared everywhere,' Pen said. They all made grimaces of understanding. She thought about the time that she'd found Will as a toddler lying on top of a friend, the other child struggling to breathe. That wasn't the kind of story that you could share, even after several wines. Had that been the day everything had shifted? When it had become hard to feel love for him? No, it had been a one-off. He'd never done anything like that again. It was likely he had no idea the other boy couldn't breathe.

She felt the familiar stab of guilt. All these women found their children frustrating at times. But from the way they spoke it went away and was replaced with love and a hopeless, endless affection that it seemed they couldn't turn off, even if they wanted to. She envied this. She wanted desperately to feel what they felt.

'So, I think we'd better get this one home,' said Alexandra, smoothing Nathalie's hair, who was dozing against her shoulder.

'I'll drop her home. I'm getting an Uber,' said Pen.

'No, no, you're all coming with me.' Emmie waved away their protests. 'I drove.'

'Are you sure?' asked Pen, knowing Emmie would have to go out of her way to get everyone home.

Emmie pushed her glass away from her. 'No problems. I've only had a glass and a half.'

'You're so good. Thank you and, hey, thanks for inviting me. I feel like I really needed this. Work has been non-stop and I didn't realise that I hadn't actually done anything nice for I don't know how long,' said Pen.

'I have no idea how you do it. You're a single mum working full-time and doing extra hours on the weekend,' Alexandra said.

Pen shook her head and took a deep breath to calm the emotion building in her throat. 'I don't have a choice, unfortunately. There needs to be a roof over our heads and food on the table.' She hesitated. Maybe it was the wine or just the warmth of the solidarity they'd all shared. 'But I do feel bad for my kids. They don't get the best of me. They get the stretched, exhausted mum who's just cobbling everything together as she goes and hoping it won't fall apart. But I feel like they know it kind of has fallen apart, it never was together, and that I'm making all this up as I go along.' She felt tears prick her eyes and she brushed them away.

'We all feel like that,' said Emmie, her mouth pressed down in empathy.

Not all the time though, thought Pen.

'That's why we all need a holiday,' said Emmie. 'Pitching in to look after the kids, sharing the cooking. Not having to spell things out to men. We can even take turns having nanna naps.' Her mouth drew into a thin line. 'Oh yeah, it's not happening.'

Pen squeezed Emmie's arm. 'We'll make it happen somehow. This has been so nice.'

Nathalie was standing suddenly, and Pen realised she was going to fall. She braced the other woman's shoulders and steadied her. She was really in a bad way. She felt a rush of affection for Nathalie, who was very possibly also not coping.

'We can tell you're an expert at this,' Alexandra said. 'Lots of drunk brides?'

Pen laughed. 'Oh my God, yes. You should see some of the photos I get that never see the light of day.'

'Slide night. You can bring them to our holiday if we ever get it, and we'll all feel better about ourselves.'

I wish, I really wish, it was that easy, thought Pen.

CHAPTER 14

Nathalie

'Are you sure you're going to be okay with her?' Nathalie heard Alexandra's words, but everything was spinning, and she was so tired. She could just lie down right here. She felt her body falling but a strong arm was around her waist. Wait, where was she? Oh, a car park. How had they got here? Somehow her head was still in the warm cocoon of the candlelight. The rush of the sea was still in her ears. It was hard to concentrate on any one thing. Hard to keep her eyes open.

She felt Alexandra pat her head. 'Goodnight, Sleeping Beauty. You're going to have one hell of a hangover tomorrow.'

She realised she was in a car. Emmie's car.

'You okay?' she managed to ask Emmie, who was in the driver's seat, her hand on the ignition.

'All good,' said Emmie brightly.

Nathalie forced her eyes to open wider. Her lids felt too heavy.

'Where are the others?'

'Oh, I've already dropped them off.'

She must have fallen asleep. How embarrassing. She did feel a little bit less drunk, but tired. So tired.

'You're like an angel,' said Nathalie. 'So kind. So thoughtful. Driving me home. I can't believe you're not drunk and you're sharing the holiday with us.' She was babbling. She forced herself to stop talking and let her head rest against the cool glass of the window.

Emmie started the engine. 'I really hope it ends up happening. We all deserve it. You deserve it. What, with three kids, I don't know how you do it.'

Nathalie laughed but the sound was thin. 'Yeah. This is me doing it.'

She glanced sideways and met Emmie's eyes and she saw pity, plain and naked. She put her hands to her hot cheeks and tried to breathe. She felt nauseous and ashamed. She could feel herself unravelling, a spool of emotions that she couldn't pull back.

'I don't know why I got so drunk. I'm so sorry.' She let her hair fall forward so Emmie couldn't see her face.

'Oh, no. You just need a bit of a release sometimes. We all get it. Motherhood is hard.'

'I'm pathetic. I can't even keep my shit together enough to have a nice meal with friends without embarrassing myself.' She could feel her face was wet and she wiped under her eyes and sniffed.

'Please don't say that. You know we all worship you. Everyone does. You're so pretty. We all want to be you.'

A puff of air came out of Nathalie's mouth, like being winded by an invisible force from behind. Is that really what Emmie thought? That being pretty was somehow the answer to life's problems? She wasn't arrogant enough not to be grateful for being attractive, but it didn't stop the pain. It didn't make your husband love you enough not to cheat on you.

She looked out the window. It had begun to rain. She wanted to dissolve into the drops on the glass. She had no idea what time it was. Mike would be annoyed if it was late. The car stopped and she realised they were outside her house. She didn't even remember giving Emmie her address. She did love her house. It was all her. Federation style with a sandstone base and an easy charm that the mess of three children didn't entirely diminish. Sometimes, when all the children were asleep and she'd tidied the whole house sufficiently, she felt at peace, happy even. Being in calm, beautiful surrounds was such a luxury when you had kids. She could almost remember the person she used to be.

She knew she should get out of the car, but it was so warm and clean. She hadn't had a clean car for as long as she could remember. And sitting here looking in from the outside she could almost see her life as Emmie saw it. Her lovely home with the stained-glass windows that dispersed rainbows of light into the lounge room on sun-drenched afternoons. How handsome her husband was. Three adorable children. Why couldn't she stay here forever, looking at her life from the outside in, like a snow globe shining in the rain? The wet night glimmered as though someone had shaken the dome. Everything looked clean, new. As though she could start again. Wipe away everything that had happened to dull her life. But she knew it was an illusion.

'Do you ever think about just getting in your car and driving and driving and not coming back?' she asked into the dark glow of the cabin.

'God yes. All the time. I remember when Seraphine was born, right after I'd come home from hospital, I was so tired I just wanted to run away so I could sleep for a million years.'

'I don't think that feeling has ever gone away for me.'

'Well, you have three kids.'

Nathalie took a deep breath. She still didn't want to go inside. It was teeming now, the rain a loud thrum against the car roof. She wondered if Emmie was just saying that about leaving. Probably. *No one is as bad a mother as me.*

'Sometimes I wish I'd only had one, you know. My first is my favourite. You're not supposed to say that, are you?' God, she should shut up. Emmie didn't want to hear what an awful person she was.

'I'd love to have three kids,' said Emmie, her eyes staring straight ahead. 'I always wanted three. It was my number, you know?'

'Yeah, it was my number too, until I had them.' Nathalie laughed but the look on Emmie's face told her she'd misread something.

'Oh, sorry. Sorry Emmie, I didn't realise.' She reached out to touch her shoulder.

Emmie shook her head fast and a sad smile played on her lips. 'We've been trying for years.' She laughed lightly. 'So many babies that never made it.'

'Oh no. I'm so sorry. Sometimes I'm so insensitive.' She shifted in the car seat, trying to snap her body out of its stupor.

'It's okay. I'm used to mothers complaining about their children. Being told how smart I am only having one.'

'That must be hard. Or people asking you why only one.'

'Seraphine's preschool teacher once lectured me about how having only one child was doing Seraphine a disservice. I couldn't believe it. I let her have her rant and then said, "I've had six miscarriages."'

'Oh Emmie, no.' Nathalie felt a wash of sorrow mixed with gratitude and guilt. She suddenly felt very sober. 'I had no idea. How awful for you.'

Emmie shook her head and tucked her hair behind her ears. 'Sorry, I don't know why I'm telling you all of this.'

'No, no, it's okay. You're safe with me. Sometimes just saying it out loud takes the sting out of the pain, you know?'

'I've actually started using contraception again. My husband has no idea. He would never in a million years want to give up. But I just can't do it anymore. I can't have the hope and then the pain.'

Nathalie rubbed Emmie's shoulder. Emmie was crying but her tears were silent, overtaken by the voluminous downpour outside. 'I'm a terrible person. I don't even know why I'm telling you this.'

'Probably because I said I wanted to just drive away from my life.'

Emmie laughed. 'Yeah, maybe.' She searched in her handbag and found tissues. 'But I don't understand how you can have a shit life.'

Nathalie snorted loudly and shook her head slowly. If ever she was going to tell anyone about Mike, about the shambles she was living beneath the shiny veneer of their lives, this was it. Her inhibitions were loosened and in the cocoon against the downpour she felt safe. She opened her mouth to speak but it wouldn't come. She closed her mouth. No. She couldn't. It was too scary. Too close. Her heartbeat too fast.

'Want to go to McDonald's drive-through? I need a burger,' she said.

Emmie gave a teary laugh. 'I'm more a chocolate thickshake kind of girl.'

'Yeah, I could do one of those, too. I have to sober up.' Emmie's estimation of her was probably low now. Imagine, falling asleep in front of all the school mums. She felt a wave of self-loathing.

Emmie started the car and pulled out from the kerb. The rain had eased.

'You don't have to pretend having three kids is perfect. I know it's not. I don't know why I'm so hung up on having another. I actually want to do something with my life.' She shot Nathalie a glance. 'Not that being a mum is not doing something, but if I'm not raising another child, I feel compelled to be achieving something else at least. But I'm not.'

'You're driving a drunk woman to get McDonald's. That's a pretty important public service.'

Emmie laughed. 'Maybe I could be an Uber driver for drunk mothers.'

Nathalie shrugged. 'Note that I'm not laughing. It would be a legitimate business concern.'

Emmie went through the drive-through and ordered two burgers and two chocolate thickshakes from a server who sounded like he had just hit puberty. She stopped the car in the car park and turned to Nathalie.

'You know what? I can't damn well wait until February or whenever it's going to be for this week away. We're all desperate for some time away from our lives.'

Nathalie took a large bite of her burger and spoke through her mouthful. 'We're clearly women in crises. Look at us. Well, look at me: drunk and eating burgers on a school night.'

'Let's get a selfie and text it to the others,' said Emmie.

'I'm hopeless at selfies.'

'Don't even. You're going to look good even with mascara running down your face.'

'Is there?'

'Yes, but it looks ironic.'

'Oh, okay, is that good?'

'Very.'

Emmie took the selfie, making sure to get all the takeaway food in it, and captioned it: *Clearly we are having a mid-life crisis. And on a school night! Can we just find an Airbnb already and keep our January dates?*

Pen wrote back immediately. *Please. It's going to be impossible to change my holiday dates with work. Oh, and I want burgers!*

Alexandra responded: *Yasss, we need this, ladies. Had such a good time tonight. Emmie, are you on it? Glad to see you're keeping Nat alive.*

Humiliation ran through Nathalie but it was overlaid by something warmer. The tiniest inkling of hope.

CHAPTER 15

Alexandra

Alexandra sat in the back row of the gallery and took great gulps of her wine. The space was white, with shiny, parquetry floors and the air was cool and dry, a reprieve from the sticky heat outside. There were about 50 people arranged neatly on plastic seats nursing wine glasses and serious expressions. The walls were filled with vast canvases overlaid with earthy hues, paint that bubbled and cracked and sang with the textures of the Australian bush.

The woman who Macie had found to do the designer talk instead of Alexandra was infinitely more eminent than she could ever hope to be. The hard, plastic seat bit into her thighs and a deep vein of regret, and relief, flowed as she listened. This woman had travelled to all corners of the world, done charity work with poverty-stricken children and as if that wasn't enough, had dedicated herself to sustainable design. She owned and ran a five-star eco resort in the bush. Alexandra could feel herself shrinking, mortified at the thought she had even contemplated getting up and talking about her own meagre design interests. She was still bemused that Macie had even offered her the speaking role.

Macie sat in the front row looking serene as usual. She had insisted on her coming along tonight. And after a long day at work, it was a rare treat to come straight out to have a drink, and brie on crackers for dinner. Sipping wine in art galleries listening to eminent artists speak was the kind of thing she had always imagined herself doing as an adult. But she still felt like an impostor next to someone like Macie.

Some people appeared lit from within, their trajectory through life more otherworldly than others. Nathalie had it; Macie, too. What was that? Was it real? People said that Maxwell had 'star quality'. Alexandra thought that probably meant he just had good grooming. He spent enough time in the bathroom. But there was something about Macie that she couldn't put her finger on. She was beautiful, but it was something other than that.

The audience was clapping, and the designer was doing some kind of namaste bow as though she was in a yoga class. She could probably put her legs behind her head as well. Alexandra chastised herself. She was such a bitch. She wished Nathalie was here, she would have laughed at that. Alexandra was worried about her friend. She was completely wasted the other night. She shuddered at the thought of a third child. It had obviously tipped Nathalie over the edge.

She shifted on her seat and looked to see how much more wine was left on the cheese table behind her. She felt her glass being lifted from her hands. Macie poured sparkling wine into it and flashed her a smile. 'Thanks for coming.'

Her face flushed. 'Thanks for inviting me. Oh my God, Tina is so accomplished. I can't even believe you wanted me to speak.'

Macie handed back her glass. She wore fine gold jewellery on her fingers. 'Well, there's a bit of a story there.'

'Really?'

'Want to bring your wine outside? I need some air.'

The gallery was by the sea and the evening was salt-laced and still warm. The soft, rhythmic wash of the waves greeted them. Macie took off her sandals and unravelled her hair from the French roll at the nape of her neck. The only light came from the reflection of the restaurants over the water.

'Want to dip our toes in?' Macie asked. She unwound the sparkly scarf at her throat and the skin on her chest looked pink.

'Did you get some sun today?' Alexandra asked, then immediately felt self-conscious for staring at another woman's boobs.

Macie touched the tops of her breasts lightly. 'Oh God. I just went for a short walk at lunch, but the sun is so strong now.'

She took a hand-rolled cigarette out of her pocket and cupped her hand to light it. 'Sorry, do you mind?'

The pungent smell of marijuana filled the air.

Alexandra felt a little jump of something she couldn't name in her stomach. She had no idea Macie smoked weed. It seemed so young and cool. She would have pegged Macie more as being part of the cocaine crowd. She took off her heels, wondering why she wasn't wearing soft leather sandals like Macie and sank her feet into the cool sand.

Macie walked ahead, wavy hair catching the breeze. Alexandra had the urge to reach out and feel its consistency between her fingers, feel its smoothness, so different from the wiry texture it had been at school. Her heartbeat accelerated. They reached the part of the beach where the sand was wet, and the salt foam fizzed between her toes. She shivered.

Macie was holding the joint out to her. Alexandra hesitated. She hadn't smoked since she was in her early 20s. But the heady curls coming out of Macie's lips, combined with the salt in the air and the wine made her reach out and take the offering. Her lungs burned and she let out an awkward cough and then a grunt of embarrassment.

'I didn't know you were a smoker.'

Macie took back the joint, her eyes narrowing against the smoke. 'Terrible habit but I've taken to smoking when I paint. Some of the paintings in this exhibition had a little help from the old weed.'

Alexandra took a moment to absorb this, to register appropriate shock on her face, as though she hadn't Google-stalked Macie to find she was now an artist. What she was shocked about was that the paintings on the walls of the gallery were Macie's. 'The paintings in the gallery are all yours? They're incredible.'

Macie passed back the joint. 'They're all just a big messy experiment. I just have them laid out in my studio and come and splash some paint about when the mood takes me. I have no idea why people are willing to part with their money for them but who am I to judge?'

'They're so passionate. So raw.' She wanted to say 'Macie' but Alexandra realised she'd never actually spoken her name. It felt somehow, too intimate.

'You think so? My agent wanted me to have a proper

opening, but I wanted to hear other artists talk about their own work rather than just me talking about myself.'

'But you didn't talk about yourself at all,' Alexandra said.

Macie shrugged and gazed out to sea.

'Well, congratulations.' Alexandra held her wine glass up in a toast. 'I'm in awe of your artistic ability and your humility.'

Macie scoffed. 'Humility is the antithesis of art. If I were truly humble I would never subject other people to the crazy whims of my emotions.'

Those are big emotions, thought Alexandra. *Big emotions.* Macie's gaze was still trained seaward. It was too dark to read her expression. 'So, you said there was a story with Tina, the sustainable designer who helps orphaned children? I wonder if she introduces herself that way. She absolutely should. I would. Oh my God, that woman is a saint.'

'Try being romantically involved with a saint. Not as easy as it would seem.'

Alexandra felt guilt churn in her abdomen. Her own taunting voice came back to her. *Lemon cake, lemon pie, Macie likes girls and we know why.* God, how had they all been so cruel? The words ran through her mind now like a demented carnival song.

'Anyway, what about you?' Macie turned towards her, a thin mist of smoke escaping her lips.

Alexandra pushed the churn of her feelings down and looked at Macie. 'Maxwell is—'

'I don't want to know about your husband. We all know about him.' She flicked ash away, but her eyes didn't leave Alexandra's.

It was, she realised, what she had become accustomed to. She was lost for words.

'Do you get sick of everyone always talking about him?'

Alexandra felt the hairs on her arms lift. She didn't know what to say, or where to start.

Macie touched her arm lightly and passed the joint. 'Sorry, I'm so nosy about other people's business. I mean, he seems like a very charming man.'

Alexandra laughed nervously. This woman's confidence was absolute. It made her so edgy and yet she was drawn to her. She took a drag and passed the joint back. The drug began to ease into her. She felt herself relax a little. 'Charming is one thing my husband has down pat.'

She wanted to share everything with this woman, who she intuited actually wanted to hear it, but she couldn't traverse the chasm of what had happened all those years ago. Why couldn't she just breach it? Say it out loud? Macie didn't seem like the kind of woman to hold grudges. She was a free spirit, a bohemian. Probably if she had been a millennial, she would have been the coolest girl in school, not the one who was teased constantly.

Alexandra's phone buzzed in her bag. It would likely be the nanny. She fished it out, the world spinning a little from the collision of the drug, the wine and the memories.

Emmie thought she'd found a great place for us, but our January dates are gone now! Noooo. It doesn't look like we're going to find somewhere at this short notice. Maybe it just wasn't meant to be. Sob. Nat x

'Damn.' Alexandra sighed deeply and closed her eyes. They felt dry from the salt and the smoke. She felt suddenly parched, dizzy.

'What is it?'

'Some friends and I – school mums – the ones you met at the studio for Melbourne Cup drinks ... we won this random holiday in a school raffle, this great house up the coast. We finally all found a time that worked, took time off work. And the house fell through. It's impossible to find another at such short notice and during school holidays. And of course, we're all madly running around trying to organise everything for Christmas.'

'How many of you are there?' Macie dug her toes into the sand.

'Um, about ten, I think. Four adults, all mums, six or seven kids, depending on who comes. Maybe a baby.'

Macie squatted and stubbed the tiny nub of joint in the wet sand. The night was becoming darker, rain clouds looming at the horizon. Alexandra felt moisture mist her skin.

'I've got a place you can stay.'

'Really?' She hadn't realised just how desperate she was for this getaway until they'd had that great night at the bar. The thought of having a week alone at home with the boys instead of with Nathalie and the others depressed her.

'It's a hotel actually. Art Deco style. Built in 1939. Around 18 rooms. It's been in my family for years. It's a bit remote but that's part of the appeal. Patchy phone reception. Pool that's pure 1970s Hollywood. River to swim in. It's actually a pretty amazing part of the world.'

'It sounds extraordinary, but we couldn't.'

'No, seriously. You're welcome to it. It's got beautiful gardens for the kids to play in. It's just over the Blue Mountains. About three hours away. You'll love it.'

'Really? And you'd have room in early January?'

'There's plenty of room and its remoteness puts the crowds off, even during peak seasons. I've been meaning to get back there myself. I split my time between Sydney and there.'

'We wouldn't want to put you out. It's pretty short notice.'

'No trouble. I'd love for it to be full of people again. We get a lot of fortieth birthdays and some weddings but it's been a while since we've hosted a group.'

'Sounds magical.'

'It forces you to have a break from your real lives.'

'God. I think we all need that. We'll pay you of course.'

Macie waved her hand. 'Honestly, happy to help out. I'll give you mate's rates. It's nothing flash.'

'That's so generous, thank you. But are you sure it's not too much trouble?'

'No, I insist. Serendipity works in mysterious ways.'

Alexandra began typing back to Nathalie, relief and elation mixing with something else. Something she couldn't quite put her finger on.

Jean

1948

Men fanned out across the green paddocks for as far as the eye could see. The search for Clara Black had resumed at daybreak. Jean awoke to the men calling out Clara's name as they scanned the mines, the dusty roads, the surrounding farmland and the thick scrub. Police motorbikes left trails of engine oil in the air and Jean's stomach twisted into knots from morning to night, praying Clara would be found. Hoping no one would find her dusty shoes abandoned under the chair in the hotel garden.

A crowd of women gathered outside the hotel gate as though there was some spectacle to be seen, instead of quite the opposite – a woman gone. And Jean found she could not stay away either. After she dropped Liv at school she hovered on the edge of the crowd, standing back, under the shade of a gum tree. She didn't want to have to get into another conversation about Clara Black. She observed some of the other women, their heads bent together, their whispers carrying on the hot wind. There was a buzz; that strange, misplaced excitement that even tragedy could conjure up in humans. It felt wrong, yet addictive. It was so rare for these quiet parts.

An army tent had been set up just within the hotel grounds and that's where she spotted him. He must have been volunteering for the search. She almost didn't recognise him dressed as he was in casual clothing. His hair wasn't slicked back as it had been at the party, and he wore army boots and loose cotton shirting. She fought the urge to wave to him, instead becoming self-conscious. She was dressed differently too, in her faded cotton day dress and an old sun hat. He headed out towards the mines with a group of men and disappointment swelled inside her. It had just been one magical, dangerous night. She needed to forget she'd ever met Magnus.

* * *

The afternoon shadows were lengthening along the dusty road as she farewelled the children and their mothers at the door of the hall. The air was still warm and smelled of eucalyptus and the early beginnings of supper being made in the township. She had been distracted the whole class. Usually she loved her lessons with the older girls as they were so much more focused than the little ones Liv's age, but she couldn't stop thinking about Clara. She knew the search party would be reeling in as night approached. Another night that Clara would be out there all alone. Guilt crushed against her chest.

A small crowd was gathering on the front steps of the church adjoining the hall.

'What's going on?' she asked one of the departing mothers.

'I think it's a meeting for an update on the search for Clara Black.'

'Oh,' said Jean, wishing she wasn't in her ballet costume, so she could go and listen.

'I don't think the news is good. They're probably calling it off soon.'

'Oh dear,' said Jean, the doom that had been building like a storm these past days thundering inside her.

She waved as the last of the mothers and children filed out of the hall and dispersed into the street. From her vantage point at the hall's entrance she could see that the crowd was growing. It was mainly men but some of the women lingered with their children. Someone important-looking was standing on the top step in front of the church. He held a bible in his hands. No, it didn't look good at all. Regret and guilt mingled together, and she felt tears build behind her eyes.

She saw him crossing the lawn in front of the hall, those same loose confident strides that she'd spotted this morning. She gasped and pressed her hand to her mouth. Their eyes met and she disappeared into the hall. No. He couldn't see her like this. In her flimsy black leotard and second-hand ballet slippers with the satin fraying around the edges. Thank God Liv wasn't here.

'Hello there.' His voice was the same. Melodious. Confident. 'I wondered if this might be the ballet hall when I saw all the little ballerinas filing out with their mothers.'

'Oh, hello,' she said, her hand fluttering to her throat, her heart hammering. She was trapped, exposed, almost naked in her nude stockings, her figure-hugging leotard. And yet part of her was giddy, as though she'd just executed a triple pirouette. 'Are you here for the meeting at the church?'

'Yes, sadly they've not had any luck finding the missing woman. I've been out there and there's so much land to cover. You could search for days. This valley is a strange place. There's something rather mutinous about it. Something ancient. Women shouldn't be walking around alone at night with all those restless spirits. Not to mention the miners, with dark things on their minds.'

Jean bit her tongue. The only thing the miners had on their minds was sleep, a feed and a bath. So, he'd heard of the massacres, heard the ghost rumours. An Aboriginal tribe was slaughtered here at first settlement. They did not want to give up this place, their place. But the white men stole it from them anyway with their rifles and their horses and their awful self-righteousness. Some said those unsettled spirits still lingered here. Perhaps the stories of what had taken place had been passed on by the ancestors, to become a kind of whispered lore. Jean found herself drawing her arms around herself.

'Oh, that's very sad they've not found anything,' she said. 'I saw you at the volunteers' tent this morning.'

'You should have come and said hello.'

'Oh no, I–'

He took a step into the hall and she took a step back. Like a dance. 'Well, isn't this charming. You look like the perfect ballet mistress,' he said, his eyes crinkling in a way that she wished she found less attractive. 'I bet all the little girls adore you.'

She saw up close and in the daylight that he was a bit older than she had thought in her over-excited state at the party. Possibly late 30s or early 40s. He ran a hand through his dark hair. She hadn't remembered his hair being so black, nor his skin so tan. He had the look of a Mediterranean heritage. Everything about this man was dark, except his pale blue eyes.

'Yes, the children are very sweet.'

'I bet they bring their pretty ballet teacher gifts. Things they've picked up and slipped into their pockets.'

He reached into his own pocket and brought out a beautiful smooth jade-coloured stone. He placed it in her palm. His hands were rough and warm and the touch took her back to the way they had danced.

'Oh, this is beautiful. Where did you find it?'

'By the riverbed on the search. I thought of another rare jewel I'd just stumbled across.'

Her face coloured, the rush of blood making her even more dizzy. She laughed, unable to find the words to reply to such unwarranted flattery.

A loud horn sounded outside the hall and Jean jumped. Shadows were gathering in the corners of the hall. Pam would be expecting her to pick up Liv, and Robert would be home soon.

'Thank you, Mr Varesso, that's so very kind of you,' she said, shyly meeting his eye. The rush she felt when he held her gaze made her breathless.

'Please, call me Magnus.' His eyes were intensely blue. She could feel them burning her skin, like the summer sky.

She nodded. 'Magnus.' His name felt strange and foreign on her tongue. 'I should really go now, it's getting late.' She collected up her bag.

'You won't join me for a drink at the hotel bar?'

Her heart lifted into her throat, but her head dropped. How to explain to a man like Magnus that women like her didn't go into the hotel bar. That the night they'd met had been an anomaly and one that couldn't happen again. She opened her mouth to speak but no words came.

He must have read her expression because he bowed his head in some kind of apology. 'Oh, I see I've been too hasty. I can be a little like that when I see something I like. I do apologise. And you're in your dance costume, no less. Where are my manners?'

He took a step backwards towards the door and bowed as though he were a butler at her service. 'Well, I'll take my leave. I know where to find you, Miss Rose.'

Jean watched him disappear out the door as though he'd been a mirage, a spectre. She realised she was clutching her bag to her chest, her heart beating as though she'd just finished dancing a concert.

PART II

Mummy always says, 'If you get lost you know my mobile number by heart, so you should tell a stranger and they will call me.' She said that only some strangers are safe. We need to look out for other mums with kids. That they're the ones to go up to if you're lost. Not men. Not security guards because they look like they can be trusted but they can't always be trusted. It's the mums who can always be trusted. She also said bananas are the best thing to have if you get lost and hungry. They're the perfect package without packaging. That's why I can't understand how it's Mummy who is lost. I can see all these people who are looking for her, policemen and other strange men in uniforms, but I can't see her, not anywhere. I hope she has a banana with her but whose mobile phone will she call? I don't have one to answer. It was me who was meant to get lost and someone would find me because I know how to get a stranger to ring Mummy off by heart.

CHAPTER 16

Nathalie

January

She unwound the window and let the air rush in, caressing her face with its hot, dry breath. Nathalie inhaled deeply. Grass, eucalyptus, sunshine, dust. It felt like they were so far from everything. The last signs of civilisation had been 40 minutes ago – a set of run-down shops with a bakery and a dilapidated Chinese restaurant on the highway, just before the turn-off. It had been such a small sign she'd nearly missed it. And now they were driving through a vast, empty valley with only green grass and bush on either side of the car. She felt a rush of emotion. Uncertainty at being somewhere so remote. Elation for the same reason.

Farmland stretched before her, delineated by long, low fences and the occasional rusty car that was slowly being swallowed by the land. This country felt so foreign sometimes. So ancient and unknowable and vast. She had only lived on the coast, in the city. Every time she went into the bush, she realised how much of a stranger she was. The unsealed road was the only man-made thing as far as the eye could see. A few cows dotted the pastures. The car rounded a corner and the valley's cliffs rose into a cerulean sky, like rough hands cupped in worship.

She glanced in the rear-view mirror. The low roar of the engine had lulled the girls to sleep. The car rounded another bend and the countryside opened up like the pages of a children's picture book. Hillsides covered in wildflowers and carpeted in green grass. Greener than she'd seen it in months, as though this place drank from a deep secret well. And then the foliage encroached. White-trunked gums gleamed as they formed a tunnel, steepled, like fingers. The sun flickered through the branches, light and shadow making a play for dominance. She was reminded of the stories of enchanted forests from her childhood. She shivered despite the warm air.

She drove on and on. The mild sense of panic mixed with a heady sensation of freedom. Did she have enough petrol? Should she have brought more snacks for the girls? This place was a lot more remote than Alexandra had made out. She'd envisioned a ten-minute drive into a small valley, not this place of majestic cliffs and wide, empty grasslands.

Now the cliffs were on either side of the car, sheer walls of rock honeycombed by the sun. The road petered out to a dirt track. It was the only way to go as the valley narrowed in the distance to an end point. No signage. No reception. She drove carefully, pebbles and rocks pinging against the body of the car. She eased the car over a narrow wooden bridge, a gently flowing stream glistening and edged with greenery below. She passed the façade of a shop but realised it was derelict; an old pharmacy with signage that looked frozen in time. Further up the dirt road to her right, she could see the shells of other buildings. The remains of a tiny township. But they too seemed empty, abandoned, their tin roofs rusted, and bricks crumbling, eaten away by time. This really was a ghost town. She was tempted to drive up to take a look, but just ahead she could make out the hotel behind a stone wall and metal gates.

She slowed as she reached an ornate gate flanked by two palm trees, tropical interlopers in the native bush. The sign had a dilapidated elegance: The Valley Hotel. She got out of the car and opened the gate. Beyond it the hotel crouched self-consciously in the shadow of the cliffs, an anomaly of elegance in the middle of the bush. It was a structure from another time, another place. And yet here it was, like a lady all dressed up with nowhere to go.

It wasn't exactly going to be the luxurious coastal holiday they'd all been anticipating, but everyone had been so thrilled to be able to keep the plans. And maybe they'd be able to go to the beach house next school holidays, if this one went smoothly. It was always a little nerve-racking going away with other families, but she was so desperate for some time away from her life. Her mother-in-law had insisted on having Richie for half the week, and Mike had stepped up to the plate and said he'd take two days off work to mind him. She had been surprised that he would offer such a thing. She had felt herself softening towards her husband. It was the biggest indication yet that he was actually trying. She knew it would pain her to be away from her baby, she was still getting used to not feeding him from her own body, but she couldn't deny there was also a sharp sweetness to that pain. Like a tight muscle being forced to relax. She knew with just the girls she'd be able to let go, because women forged a kind of organic community, a net that held everything together, helping each other without the need to spell it out.

Nathalie pulled into the gravel car park under the shade of the poplar trees that lined the drive. The girls were still asleep. She stretched and took a sip of water from her bottle. She opened the window and heat pressed down on her and sleep felt close suddenly. She wanted to curl up and doze for a moment like her sweet girls. There was no sound except the soft twittering of birds. It felt peaceful. She looked at her phone. No reception. Again, that feeling; mild panic, mixed with relief. She opened all the car windows and her door to let the air circulate. She grabbed a warm apple from the food bag beside her and got out.

The flesh was sweet, and she walked across the gravel to the garden that flanked the hotel's entrance. Crepe myrtle trees flaunted pale pink and white blooms, urns overflowed with lavender and wild rose vines crept and weaved knotty tendrils up walls and over statues. There was a bank of fledgling citrus trees – the smell of tart fruit was intoxicating. Nathalie crushed a sprig of rosemary between her fingers and held it to her nose. Statues of women in languorous repose surrounded a fountain at the garden's heart. Winged angels, children holding water jugs and bird baths were hidden throughout the foliage. She might have been in the English countryside except for the raw sandstone cliffs above and the calls of currawongs.

At the side of the hotel Nathalie spotted a large trampoline, the old style with no safety nets and behind that a horse munching grass in an adjoining paddock. The kids were actually going to love it here. There was no sound coming from the car, so she headed over to the horse. The smell of manure and freshly turned earth enveloped her and she felt her shoulders drop as she ran her hand along the animal's flank. She took her sandals off to feel the soft grass between her toes and fed him the rest of the apple.

She heard the high note of her younger daughter's voice calling out. There was an edge of panic to it. Nathalie ran back to the car. Sim's eyes were puffy with sleep and heat. Findlay was just rousing.

'We're here,' she said, smoothing their sweaty hair off their foreheads. 'It's a magical garden in a secret valley.' The girls got out of the car and walked on unsteady legs into the garden. The sight of their little fingers trailing in the cool water of the fountain, their sleep-flushed cheeks among the flowers, calmed her. They played hide-and-seek behind the statues, picked wildflowers from the grass. The only sound was birdsong and the soft rush of the breeze in the willow trees. She adorned their hair with daisies and kissed their hot cheeks until they laughed. She looked towards the hotel, with its majestic white stone pillars, bright against the dark escarpment behind and wondered what was inside.

CHAPTER 17

Emmie

Nathalie and her children already looked at home in this valley. They all wore light summer dresses, and flowers in their hair, as though they were the living embodiment of the nymph statues that appeared to dance in the garden. Nathalie was reading a picture book to the girls under the shade of a crepe myrtle. She waved and Emmie waved back and cut the engine. She cracked the car door and felt the thick heat seep in. It smelled like sweet roses, eucalyptus and freshly turned soil.

They'd just passed the old township and Emmie hadn't been able to resist driving up past the abandoned pharmacy, the crumbling post office and the rusting remains of a few other shopfronts. Further up she could see the bones of old miners' cottages, bricks bleached with age under the bright sun. The bush had encroached – tree roots cracking through crumbling walls as though they were chalk, birds nested in chimney stacks. It smelled like dust and crushed ants.

'Who used to live here?' Seraphine had asked, her face pressed against the car window.

'People like you and me. This was a busy town in the olden days.'

'Where did they all go?'

How to explain to her daughter that these were the forgotten remnants of lives that had once been lived and taken for granted in the same innocent way hers was. And now all that remained of their stories, the important rhythm of their days, was dirt and dust and words in books. *It will happen to us all*, thought Emmie. *We too will pass into the land of lost stories.*

'Mum? Are you okay?' Seraphine asked, her little face scrunched with concern. Emmie had brightened and given her daughter a boiled lolly and now they were here, in front of this magnificent hotel, the only thing to remain alive, to have been preserved. Emmie couldn't wait to go inside.

'Can I go play with the others, Mumma?' Seraphine's little face was hot and flushed as she hopped out of the car.

Emmie nodded, handing her a hat. 'It looks like this garden has so many nooks and crannies for you to explore.'

'Look, there's a trampoline.'

Emmie stood and stretched, watching Sera fly off to greet the other girls. She didn't know where this child came from. So socially at ease.

She greeted Nathalie with a kiss and the other woman gripped her arms. 'Can you believe this place? Where even are we?' Nathalie asked.

'I know, I had no idea it was so far. I kept thinking a town would appear just around the bend and then there was another bend and another.'

'Did you see the abandoned township just up the road?' Nathalie asked.

'Oh, I know. It's like it's been frozen in time. The pharmacy still has old medicine bottles and syringes in the window. I did a bit of research and this valley has such a rich history.'

'There you go, always the writer, researching. All I knew was that it was a three-hour drive and in a valley. I did know about the ruins though.'

They both squinted into the distance, towards the place where the valley became a dead end. Skeletons of old industrial buildings shimmered in the heat, shy dinosaurs peeking through the bush. Crumbling brick towers and rusted steel scaffolding nestled into the side of the cliff wall at the far end of the valley.

'I hope we can have a good look around the mines. The kids will love it. And this hotel's incredible, isn't it?' said Emmie, walking through the garden towards the entrance. 'Smack bang in the middle of nowhere. I can't wait to look around. It's been restored to a proper working hotel. But somehow it doesn't look like it gets that many visitors.'

'Well, there's nothing out here.'

'I think that's the point though. It's so rare to find somewhere untouched now. No internet. The hotel was left abandoned for years after the mines were closed in 1952. A real ghost town but this family, it must have been Macie's, came and resurrected it from the dust. It was a complete hovel for years, filled with bats, spiders, squatters. Before that it was reportedly a monastery and then a horse ranch.'

Nathalie's eyes were wide. 'You're not serious.'

'I'm totally serious. This whole valley used to be a thriving shale oil town. It supplied petrol and gas during the war. Thousands of people lived here, if you can believe it. Hence the abandoned shopfronts when we drove in. There was also a post office, a cafe, churches, a school. The hotel was considered the jewel of the valley but then it lay in ruins for years.'

'Oh God.'

'Oh, come on, it'll be an adventure. Look how happy the girls are.'

'You might get a book idea out of it.'

The tendril of guilt that had already budded wove itself tighter in Emmie. Not a book. She wasn't writing a book now. Emmie thought of the last selfie she'd taken of her and Nathalie. At McDonald's, Nathalie with her eyes shining, mouth full of burger. Emmie's caption had read: *Wagging the bedtime routine at Maccas on a school night.* Everyone had commented on Nathalie with her gorgeous face lit with child-like delight.

Somewhere along the line someone had assumed that it was Nathalie's account. Maybe because when Nathalie was in a picture, she took up all the space, like a low moon on a dark night. Some people's music or writing stirred people; Nathalie's looks did that. Emmie hadn't confirmed whose account it was, but she hadn't denied it, either. She'd had more hits with a few posts in this new account than she'd had in total with her own @Emmiewriter account.

Maybe it was because these new posts were of people actually having fun. There was *life* in these pictures with her new mum friends. It was the first time she felt included in something special. She didn't care that they were in the middle of nowhere; in fact, the remoteness would only serve to make it more of an adventure, to bond their fledgling friendships.

'Sorry, I don't know why I'm being a bit negative. It's actually beautiful out here. And the girls haven't harassed us for at least five minutes. Maybe it's being away from Richie for the first time.'

'Who's got him?'

'My mother-in-law for three days and Mike will have him for the last few nights. He's on a bottle now. And they might come up for the weekend before we go.'

'That's a big thing leaving him for a week.'

'Do you think I'm a bad mother?'

Emmie touched Nathalie's shoulder. 'Of course not. You need a break. We all do, having survived the insanity of Christmas.'

'Oh my goodness. How was yours? Mine was complete madness. So much shopping, so much cooking. So many relatives. This feels like the first time I've stopped in weeks.'

'Ugh, I hear you. The whole month of December feels like a blur.'

'What we need right now is holiday wine,' said Nathalie, brightening. 'Let's go over there, to that lovely table under the tree. Maybe I should get a bottle of white out of the esky. Day drinking is mandatory on summer holidays.'

'Exactly. Glasses?'

Nathalie paused. 'Are we game to go inside and ask for some?'

'I will. I'm dying to get a look inside. You stay out here with the girls.'

'Okay, I'll get snacks from the car.'

Emmie could feel Nathalie watching her as she walked towards the hotel. She turned and gave the thumbs up. The French doors were heavy timber, but they opened easily when she pulled. It took a few seconds for her eyes to adjust to the dim light in the foyer. It felt ten degrees cooler inside and she was grateful for the reprieve.

'Hello,' she called, peering at the elegant marble staircase that swept to the upper level. It smelled like furniture polish and perfume. There was a door into a dark lounge room off to the left, which she peeked into. There was an open fireplace and bookcases overflowing with books, a beautiful drinks trolley and a vintage lounge setting. Wood fire and tobacco lingered in the air. She could just imagine them sitting in front of the fire after dinner. To her right stretched a long, darkened hall and up ahead were glass doors, behind which she glimpsed dining tables. Paintings decorated the walls of the foyer. Sleeping Beauty with heavy lids on a bed of roses, and Ophelia's pale gaze from her watery grave. Two lavishly framed canvases depicted Tennyson's haunting Lady of Shalott, floating in her boat, and trapped in her tower. There was a definite theme. Statues of women in flowing gowns reclined on the surface of antique tables. The only light came from a vintage lamp at a counter under a sign reading Reception. There was a bell and she dinged it lightly.

'Hello, you're here.' She heard the voice and turned. It was Macie. She was dressed to match the vintage style of the hotel, in a delicate embroidered silk gown and dark lipstick. She moved forward and kissed Emmie's cheek. She smelled like the powdery perfume that permeated the foyer. 'So good to see you again. I'm so glad you could all come. I thought I heard children's laughter in the garden. It's so lovely to have children here.'

'Macie, isn't it? We met at Alexandra's gallery. Or shop. Though it's more like an art gallery.'

'I remember.'

'Thanks for having us at such short notice. We were devastated when our holiday house fell through. This place is magnificent. I've just been having a peek around. The lounge room is gorgeous. And all these paintings and statues. Did you decorate it?'

'My family did. It's been a labour of love to restore. I spent my early childhood here while my parents brought it back to life.'

'I read all about that online. How incredible. Such history.'

Macie took her arm in a sweet, old-fashioned kind of way that Emmie thought utterly charming. 'Come, come, I've got afternoon tea prepared and we'll take it out the front in the shade of the willow trees and then the kids can have a swim.'

'That's so thoughtful of you to make afternoon tea,' said Emmie, as they walked through a handsome dining room with impossibly high ceilings, stately red walls and gilded mirrors.

'Wow. I feel like I'm in Buckingham Palace.'

Macie laughed. 'Perhaps if the Palace had been neglected for a few decades.'

Emmie followed her through swing doors into an industrial kitchen. 'It looks like this place could feed an army.'

'It fed the whole hotel at one point. There are 18 guest rooms and the dining room seated 75. In 1957, it was bought by the Marist Fathers and turned into a monastery. All the books are in the lounge if you're interested in the history.'

'Oh, how fascinating, yes, I can't wait to have a look. This spread looks wonderful, Macie. We weren't expecting anything so fancy. Afternoon tea at ours is cut-up apple and crackers.'

Macie smiled and shrugged. 'It's really very simple. I enjoy it.'

'Oh, and I just need wine glasses. We're celebrating being on holidays.'

They took the afternoon tea on trays to the tables under the soft leaves of the willow trees. Nathalie's eyes were closed, her feet up and her hair bundled into a top knot.

She and Macie exchanged pleasantries and then Nathalie got up and went to find the girls in the garden.

'Oh, Pen and Will are here,' said Emmie, waving them over to the shade. She hugged Pen and patted Will's head. Sera was beside him, explaining the currency she and the other girls had established. She put pebbles, flower buds and leaves into Will's palm, explaining what each one purchased. *Extra hiding time for hide-and-seek, the last piece of cake, and immunity from being 'it' in tip.*

'Oh, it's so cool under the trees,' Nathalie said. 'Kids, come and rest out of the sun for a bit and eat something.' She poured white wine from a sweating bottle into glasses and passed them around.

The crisp, cool wine went down a little too easily and Emmie felt its effect almost immediately. Everything felt slightly surreal, like a dream you didn't want to wake from. The table was filled with delights. There were vintage teapots and matching floral cups with saucers, sugar cubes with tiny spoons and a pitcher of cloudy lemonade. Homemade scones with strawberry jam and cream, and a glazed orange cake sat next to jars of fresh flowers and linen napkins. There were thick slices of watermelon and bunches of grapes, which the children descended on like the small darting birds in the garden.

'How idyllic is this?' Emmie said, sneaking a quick photo of the spread with her phone. 'You'd better wash your hands,' she told the children. 'You've already collected quite the treasure trove, Seraphine.'

'There's a tap and drinking fountain just over there,' said Macie, pointing to the far side of the hotel, across the garden.

'Go on, we'll save some cake, but only if you're quick,' said Emmie, watching them disappear, hooting in delight as they raced each other.

She was just pouring the fragrant Earl Grey tea when Will and Sera came running back.

'Mum, there's a lady there. We can't wash our hands,' said Will, his eyes wide.

Pen turned from where she was chatting to Nathalie. She was silent for a beat and then she spoke quietly, taking Will's arm and leading him away. 'Will, please don't annoy the other guests, we've only just got here.'

Macie put the teapot down. 'We don't have any other guests.'

Silence thickened the hot air, making the nape of Emmie's neck tingle.

'I'll come with you guys. You can show me.' She flashed Pen a reassuring look. She could tell she was on edge. Maybe she was worried about whether Will would fit in with the other kids. She knew Seraphine would be fine. She'd have to speak to her about making sure he was included at all times.

Will looked relieved as she followed them across the garden to the far side of the hotel. You could see the aging bones of the structure here, cracks in the brickwork and spider webs in corners, a bird's nest poking out from the eaves. There was an old-fashioned water fountain with a tap next to stairs leading to a back entrance, presumably the kitchen or perhaps staff quarters.

'She was right there, in the doorway.' Will pointed to the top of the steps.

Emmie felt a chill run over her, and she stepped out of the shade, back into the sunshine. 'Oh, maybe you just saw a movement. Our eyes can play tricks like that sometimes.'

'I didn't see anything, Mummy,' said Seraphine, shaking her wet hands before drying them on her top.

Sim and Findlay were busy flicking water at each other and squealing.

Emmie bent down so she was at their level. 'Or maybe Macie has a secret guest – maybe it was a garden sprite, like the statues everywhere.'

'No, it was definitely a woman,' said Will, his eyes serious. Emmie pushed her discomfort down and nodded brightly.

'She seemed upset.' His eyes trained on the empty space at the top of the steps.

Emmie shivered and rested her hand on his shoulder. 'Sometimes we imagine things. Seraphine's very imaginative too, aren't you darling. Always writing stories.'

'I write stories,' said Will, his eyes lighting up.

Emmie took advantage of the distraction. 'Oh, you'll have to tell us about them. Okay, let's go back and eat cake before the mums eat it all.'

The kids took off and Emmie looked back to the top of the steps. She wished she hadn't read all about the valley's ghosts.

Jean
1948

He brought her small gifts, leaving them on the steps of the hall wrapped in shiny paper, like a satin bowerbird preparing a nest. A bag of scorched almonds and a Cherry Ripe, chocolates in delicate gold tissue tasting of coffee. And then a pair of silk stockings, a tiny bottle of perfume that smelled like roses in full bloom. Liv had asked what was in the packages and Jean had been flustered, sick at the thought of lying to her daughter. *Special balm for my sore feet*, she had said, pointing to her calloused toes. *A balm for my heart*, she had thought. She was, at once, flushed with the attention and the beautiful presents, looking forward to the end of class to see what small treasure would be waiting, and filled with guilt and trepidation.

Once he waited for her. As she was locking up the hall he came out of the church next door. Liv and Bertie were playing in the tree outside, like pink plumaged birds. Her heart had raced and, in hushed tones, she'd dismissed him, insisted he stop bringing her precious things, but he had only winked and told her she deserved them and that he would only stop if she agreed to spend time with him. She'd needed him to leave, so she'd agreed upon a day she knew Liv would be with Pam.

And so now he was here, the afternoon sun streaming through the high windows, their shadows stretching along the hall's timber floorboards, elongating their bodies like spirit creatures.

He put his hat on a chair and took a bottle of red wine and two small glasses from a bag.

She gasped. 'You brought wine?'

'You sound surprised. Here's one more. Surprise, that is. It's the last one, I promise.'

He reached into his pocket, taking out a small box. 'Open it.'

Jean's heart was beating fast. 'Oh no, I couldn't possibly take another thing.'

He shrugged innocently and she laughed despite herself. 'It's naughty of you. You said you'd stop.' She had already taken too many things that weren't hers. She tried to press the box back into his hand.

'Please. Let a man give a woman a small gift.'

'You have already given me too much.'

She shook her head but opened the box nevertheless, nerves like butterflies, at once seductive and skittish. Her hand went to her throat. She had never seen such a beautiful piece of jewellery. A tiny diamond embedded in the face of a gold locket on a fine chain. It was like something out of a fashion magazine. 'Oh, my goodness, it's stunning. But it's not a small gift, Magnus. I cannot accept this. Please.'

'I would be offended if you didn't take it. Please, try it on.'

She hesitated. She didn't want to offend him but at the same time she knew she couldn't take this, couldn't be beholden to him. The other presents were small, sweet gifts but this was something altogether different.

He walked away from her towards the record player, began flicking through her measly collection of six records. He chose one, took it out of the sleeve, placed it on the player and put the needle down.

The swell of Vivaldi's *Four Seasons* filled the small hall. She felt it well in her chest, behind her eyes and she thought she might cry. She stood there, immobilised. He stayed with his back to her, bent over the record player. What was he doing here? Giving her this? She wanted to drop the necklace and run from the hall. She wanted to feel the precious metal against her skin, she wanted to dance. And so, she just stood there, paralysed by conflicting emotions.

The music peaked and then softened. He walked towards her and took the box from her hand. For a moment she thought that he had understood and that he was making the decision for her, taking back the extravagant gift. But then she felt his hand brush away her hair from the nape of her neck. It sent a quiver through her whole body. He gently fastened the necklace. She could feel his breath on her hair. Her hand found the stone. She knew it was real. This was not a man to give something fake and yet fake was all she was.

'Could I have this dance, Miss Rose?' He held out his arm.

'I don't really have anything aside from ballet music to dance to.'

He smiled. 'Something tells me we don't even need music.'

She felt her cheeks flush. Her body grew too warm. She crossed her arms across her chest. 'Magnus, I'm afraid you think me something that I'm not. I'm not glamorous, nor deserving of all these charming gifts. I'm just a dance teacher in a makeshift hall in the middle of the bush.'

He took a step towards her and pulled her into him. He smelled so clean, like the morning air, like eucalyptus and rain. He twisted her out from his body and she spun on reflex. He pulled her back in, resting her cheek against his chest, and then he dipped her and her back arched to the curve of his arm.

'I know who you are. A beautiful woman with a sweet nature living in the middle of a valley, when really she belongs somewhere far more sophisticated.'

Sweat beaded at her brow and the hall felt hot and the air close.

She laughed, despite herself, and desire curled inside her, like cold toes in front of a warm flame. She was still in his arms and they were moving, a slow waltz.

'The fact a woman like you ended up in a place like this makes you even more intriguing.'

She was silent. She should tell him right now about Liv and Robert, but her mind was somewhere else, backstage, waiting in the wings, the music swelling around her, her body poised.

'Will you come on a trip to Sydney with me?'

'Sydney?'

'I need to return in a day or two and I can't bear the thought of not seeing you again.'

She felt herself blush a deep shade of crimson. 'Oh, I don't know Magnus ...' But her mind was spinning like *fouetté* turns in a complicated dance. How she had longed to see her hometown during the long, hot months and years here. The beautiful cafes and the dance halls, the department stores, the sea. Oh, to see the ocean again.

'Just for a weekend. I'll organise us rooms in a hotel, we'll go to dinner, go dancing, of course.'

Memories of this life glimmered as they came into her mind. They were full of light, but it was like staring into the sun. Dangerous to linger there too long. It wasn't her life anymore. It was simply the trick of light youth played. She was nearly 30 now. She was a wife and mother. And yet something had made her sneak out of her house in the middle of the night to go to that party. And now, this man in front of her was offering her a glimpse, just a glimpse of what used to be.

'My father's in Sydney. He's in a share home and quite poorly. I haven't been able to see him in such a long time,' she said tentatively, the guilt and shame crawling through her as she spoke.

'Well, it's decided then. You must come, and pay him a visit.'

'I'd only be able to go for a night or two. I'd be letting too many people down.'

'What, your little ballet dancers?'

No, my daughter, she thought. *But I could visit Father. I've been promising to forever, but there's never enough money.* She had asked around and you needed to take a bus from the valley to Katoomba and then a train to Central Station. And accommodation in Sydney was extremely dear.

'We could leave at the weekend,' he said, letting go of her and picking up the bottle of wine. He poured a glass and handed it to her. 'This is just a taste,' he said.

She took a sip. It was so sweet, so rich that she closed her eyes in pleasure.

'All right,' she said, her eyes still closed, her heart humming.

The needle of the record player must have slipped because the Vivaldi suddenly swelled, filling the hall and her body with hope and fear.

CHAPTER 18

Pen

Dust motes floated in the soft early evening light streaming in through the window. The cliffs shone as the last of the sunlight warmed them. She had pulled the sheer curtains aside from both windows so the landscape could come in. The garden hummed below with dusk birds and insects and the view was out across the green paddocks, flanked by the rising escarpment. A horse whinnied in the distance and Will leafed through the pages of a book, making soft clicking sounds with his tongue. The room smelled like lavender and tea leaves. Pen wondered if the others' rooms were as charmingly dilapidated. They were on the second floor and the room held a trove of vintage wonders. An ornate wardrobe, double and single beds covered in faded floral bedspreads, and a small sink in the corner of the room with a pretty mirror above it. There were fresh flowers from the garden in glass jars on the bedside table and on the vanity. Nothing in the room suggested they were in modern times, save the invasion of their open bags, Will's already spilling with clothes.

She'd been mortified by Will's comment about the lady. She'd seen everyone's faces – he'd spooked them. All she wanted was for him to act like the other kids. Blend in. Relax. But how could she ask that of her son when she struggled to do the same? Thankfully they'd enjoyed the lovely food under the willow tree and the rest of the afternoon had passed uneventfully. He was happy now, absorbed in a book. She'd tried to suggest he go and find the other kids to play with, but he'd wanted to stay in here.

Macie had announced rather formally that dinner would be served in the dining room at 7 pm. Will had already devoured a packet of crackers and two bananas on the bed. No one had dared inform Macie that 7 pm was probably a bit too late for young children, who'd been travelling and then running around, to eat dinner. Everyone was likely just as glad as her at the prospect of not cooking.

The dining room was like a grand old lady wearing her Sunday best. A dimly lit chandelier hung from the high, ornate ceiling, which was cracked and stained with age. Four large round dining tables, all of them lit with long candles and covered with lace, filled the space. The red walls and beautifully framed paintings made the room feel warm and cosy despite its size. The effect was one of old-world grandeur. A sense of occasion. It was quite lovely. Pen cringed as she thought about all the dinners her family ate in front of the TV. Will joined the kids doodling with coloured pencils at a table next to the adults. Pen felt a wash of relief as Seraphine made room for him next to her and handed him a sheet of paper. The adults' table was set immaculately, with shining silver cutlery, vintage glassware, linen serviettes and several bottles of red wine. Pen was taking a seat when a man appeared carrying a basket of bread. He had a striking face. Dark, deep-set eyes and the kind of incredible, angular cheekbones she would have liked to photograph in black and white.

'Pen, this is our manager here, Caleb. He's the resident chef. He was responsible for the cakes and whatnot this afternoon. And this is his famous sourdough,' Macie said.

Pen noticed Macie had changed for dinner into a silky navy blue dress that swept to the ground. Even Caleb wore a crisp white shirt opened at the collar. Pen felt a fizz of embarrassment. Everyone was far more dressed up than her and Will. Nathalie and her girls still had flowers from the garden in their hair, but they had all changed into fresh dresses. Dinner was obviously going to be a rather formal occasion.

Caleb offered the basket to her and Pen took a piece of the warm bread. He looked too young to be a hotel manager all the way out here in the middle of nowhere, despite his ironed shirt.

Macie was beside her with a bottle of red wine, pouring her a glass.

'Thank you, this is all quite lovely,' she said, taking a sip of the wine. It was as rich and delicious as the smells coming from the kitchen. She tried to think of the last time she'd made her kids a proper home-cooked meal that wasn't sausages.

'This is a pinot from a local vineyard. Do you like it?'

Pen nodded. 'And thanks for setting the kids up with pencils and paper. Brilliant idea.'

Macie looked over towards the children. 'Your son is quite perceptive, you know. I don't think you should be so quick to dismiss him. Will, is it? We do have a resident ghost here, you know. The valley's known for it, for being a bit of a ghost town. You can see that for yourself. Half the people who stay here are bird watchers, the other half are those interested in history,' Macie said.

Pen felt a rub of annoyance and her face grew warm. 'I'm not dismissing him. He can just be silly sometimes.'

'Children are much more intuitive than we give them credit for.'

'Yes, I do realise that. But they also have big imaginations, especially my son.'

'Oh wonderful. That's what we need more of. Kids today spend far too many hours on screens. That's why somewhere like this is so good for them. Fresh air, home-cooked food and no internet connection.'

Pen nodded and took another sip of her wine. It was going down a little too well, and she realised how anxious she was feeling. She couldn't tamp down the annoyance Macie's comments were sparking in her. 'And you have kids then, Macie?'

'Yes. A boy.'

'And he is where?'

Macie's face closed down, like a door swung shut. 'With his father.'

Pen felt her anger dissolve. She'd been rude. There was obviously a broken marriage – Pen knew about the nightmare of living that. The poor woman was just making polite conversation, taking an interest. Why did she have to overreact so badly? 'Sorry, I'm sorry to hear that.' Her voice softened. 'That can be hard.' She paused, unsure if she should inquire further. 'Do you get to see him?'

Macie shook her head, her eyes downcast. 'Not as often as I'd like.'

Pen nibbled at her bread. 'I have shared custody of my daughter with my ex-husband. She's staying with him this week. I know it can all be ... difficult.'

Macie looked up. 'Does Will get to see his father much?'

Pen didn't want to talk about this, but Macie's vulnerability had softened her. 'No, he's not in the picture. And Will's just getting to that age where boys probably need their dads more than their mums.'

'Oh, they always need their mums, especially at Will's age.'

'Do you think so?' Pen thought about all the times Will had probably needed her and she hadn't been able to give him anything, not emotionally. Her heart ached.

Macie nodded. 'There's so much written about fathers and sons, but we're the ones who teach them compassion and how to treat women.'

Pen took a large sip of wine. This conversation was depressing the hell out of her. God, imagine the damage she'd already done to Will. The times she'd shut him down when he was talking at a million miles an hour and she couldn't handle his intensity. The way she yelled at him if he was having a meltdown and couldn't manage his emotions, the way his moroseness made her shut down.

'Chin chin.' Alexandra took a seat next to her and clinked glasses. 'Have you tried this wine? It's delish. Where did you find this, Macie?'

Pen was relieved for the distraction. She sipped her wine. 'It is rather good.'

'Caleb sources all the food and wine for our guests. He's quite the epicure,' Macie said.

'How often do you get guests? It's a bit of a drive from anywhere,' said Pen.

'As I said, there are a lot of history buffs, bird watchers. We get motorbike riders taking weekends. Sometimes people will book weddings or occasion birthdays and hire out the whole hotel for their guests. We had a *Great Gatsby*–inspired fiftieth not that long ago. It was fabulous.'

'And how often are you here, Macie, given … I take it your son is in Sydney?' Pen asked.

Macie paused, poured more wine.

'Macie's gallery is in Sydney,' Alexandra said. 'She's a brilliant artist. Have you heard the name Macie Laurencin? She's represented by Nick Wilson. Bigwig in the art world. I knew you'd get on, both being creative types. Pen's a photographer,' said Alexandra.

'Oh, you'll love it here. Such incredible light,' said Macie.

'What type of art?'

'Landscapes. I do the big ones here and sell them in Sydney.'

'I'd love to see them. What a perfectly balanced life,' said Pen. 'Sometimes I'd kill for somewhere like this to escape all the noise.'

Alexandra flashed her eyes in agreement. 'You should set up a day spa here Macie, and advertise it as having zero internet access. You'll be overrun with mums.'

'I actually had the CEO of a huge corporation spend a week here with his family. At first, he didn't cope well without internet access. But then he actually wept when he left. He didn't want to go back to his life.'

'Wow. I must admit I felt bereft when I lost mobile reception. I still keep reaching for my phone,' said Pen.

'So, what's the deal with this gorgeous manager of yours? Why is he here serving a bunch of middle-aged women dinner in the middle of nowhere with no phone reception instead of partying with friends?' asked Alexandra, a smile on her lips.

'Oh, I wouldn't say we're all middle-aged yet,' Pen said, elbowing her.

'He likes the quiet life. He's an artistic sort. A loner. And he's not bad in the kitchen, either.'

Alexandra raised her eyebrows. 'Intriguing.'

Caleb arrived at the table carrying a deep dish of lasagne. 'I thought the kids would like this type of food,' he offered, placing it in the middle of the kids' table.

'Perfect,' said Alexandra, serving a green salad onto her boys' plates. 'Thank you, Caleb, we've just been hearing how amazing you are.'

'You should taste his coq au vin,' said Macie, indicating to a fragrant dish of marinated chicken and vegetables.

Colour crept into Caleb's face and Pen immediately warmed to him. He was shy. She served the lasagne and salad onto a plate for Will. It all smelled delicious and Pen realised the fresh air had made her hungry.

Will was drawing on a sheet of paper using the pencils from a jar in the middle of the table. She glanced at the paper. Will had always been a good drawer. He almost had the proportions right. The face of a woman stared from the paper, hair long, high cheekbones.

Pen bit her lip as a spike of dread drove through her. She spoke quietly, without letting her voice betray her. 'What are you drawing, mate?'

'Nothing,' said Will, his voice emotionless, his hand moving deftly. Pen squeezed his shoulder, pushing back against the cold creep in her chest. She looked at the drawings the other kids were making. Rainbows and flowers, trees and dinosaurs, a planet on fire. Why did Will always have to be the weird one? She berated herself. She wasn't being fair. It was actually a great sketch. Maybe he'd drawn Nathalie. There was something about the eyes and the slope of the mouth.

'She's beautiful,' said Macie, coming up behind them with a tray of water. She placed a glass in front of Will. 'Is that the woman you saw earlier, near the drinking fountain?'

Pen's pulse quickened. How dare Macie put ideas into Will's head.

Will nodded without looking up and Pen bit her lip harder. 'And what's that?' she asked, pointing at something in the corner of the page, trying to be supportive, despite the loud churn of her feelings.

'What?'

'That thing in the background.'

'I don't know,' Will said.

'You know, it looks a little bit like this thing over here,' Macie said, pointing to an urn in the corner of the room. 'Is that it?'

Will shrugged. 'Yeah.'

'Is that where she's standing now? In front of the urn?' Macie asked.

Anger surged through Pen and she yanked the paper out from under Will. 'Enough drawing. It's dinnertime.' She put the plate of lasagne down in front of him with a thud. 'And eat your salad, too.'

'Hey,' he said, grabbing the paper. She realised everyone was staring at them now. She fought to calm herself.

'That's an amazing picture,' said Alexandra, looking over his shoulder. 'Will, you've got a lot of talent. Who is it?'

'It's our resident ghost, of course,' said Macie, winking at Will, who smiled.

'That's giving me the heebie-jeebies,' said Nathalie, who was serving food onto her daughters' plates. She and Pen exchanged a look. 'We don't want to freak the kids out.'

'Freak us out about what?' asked Findlay, her eyes huge.

Pen felt an irrational urge to slap Macie. 'Will just has a very vivid imagination. And Macie is encouraging him.'

'He really is a very good drawer,' Macie said.

'Yes, I'm aware of that,' Pen snapped as she turned away from her son, her heart as crumpled as the piece of paper in Will's hand.

CHAPTER 19

Alexandra

The heat of the fire combined with the wine to make Alexandra's eyes close. The room had the delicious smell of burning wood, and the rose-scented candles Macie had lit on the coffee table. The only sound was the crackle and burn of the wood popping in the grate. They'd finished dinner with a creamy tiramisu and after they'd put the kids to bed, they'd opened another bottle of wine. She was probably a little drunk. The room danced with the light of the flames in the fireplace. It was cold here at night despite the heat of the day. She felt its icy fingers lick under the doors, and through the dark passageways of the old house. The windows were hung with heavy drapes and the furniture was vintage, an old green velvet lounge with matching armchairs. Pen and Emmie were still upstairs with their kids. Alexandra's boys had passed out as soon as their little heads had hit the pillow, bless them, but it wasn't surprising that the other kids were finding it hard to sleep.

Alexandra had to admit, Will's drawing of the lady by the urn had made the hairs on the back of her neck stand up. When she was walking down the dimly lit corridor to their room, she had felt a tremor of fear snatch at her unexpectedly. She'd turned to see nothing but shadows. Her boys didn't seem fazed, though she wasn't so sure about Jasper. He was likely putting on a brave face to match his older brother's bravado. Maxwell loved scary movies and her boys had probably seen way too much for their age, but it seemed to have desensitised them rather than making them more scared. She wasn't sure which was worse. Maxwell was always trying to toughen up the boys, especially Jasper. He was more the mummy's boy of the two and Alexandra loved that he still came to her for comfort and cuddles. But Maxwell singled him out with stern words when he showed his softness. Just recently at summer soccer, Jasper had come to her on the sideline, silently devastated after he let a goal in. Maxwell had taken him out of her arms by the elbow, and dragged him back to the goal post. She wanted to snatch him back, tell Maxwell to stop beating the sensitivity out of his son, but she never had the words, especially with all those eyes trained on them.

Her thoughts returned to Will. There was something a little odd about him. He was just slightly different from her boys. It was almost impossible to pin down exactly what it was. Maybe it was his intelligence. She'd heard on the school grapevine that he was very smart – he'd won several academic awards already. He was clearly a gifted artist, too. She wondered what that would be like, to have an academic child. Her boys were both very average at school, slightly better on the sporting field. She foresaw tutors in high school, and it was only her constant refrain of 'let them be kids' that stopped Maxwell from engaging tutors already. Mediocrity was not something he was fond of.

Nathalie poured more wine into Alexandra's glass and melted into the lounge next to her, cradling her own glass. She was languid with wine and food, too. Alexandra wondered if she should say something about the drinking. She'd found herself sharing glances with Emmie, especially after how wasted Nathalie had been on their night out. On the surface, Nathalie's life was perfect, but Alexandra knew deep down that something must be going on. It had been a while since they'd had a real heart-to-heart. Maybe she was missing her old life and she needed to go back to work and remember who she used to be. There was no way Alexandra could stay sane being a stay-at-home mum. She patted her friend on the knee. 'Comfy there?'

'Hmmm, what?'

'You okay? The girls asleep?'

'Yes, their eyes were hanging out of their heads. I could really do with a cigarette right now.' Nathalie propped her feet on the coffee table. 'I've broken my ban and now I sneak them on the back porch when the kids are asleep, and Mike is late. How bad am I?'

'Well, a girl's got to do what a girl's got to do.'

Nathalie made a snorting sound.

They both watched Caleb enter the room, crouch in front of the fire and stack fresh wood in the grate. His body was strong and lean, and with his angular jaw and wavy hair pulled into a low ponytail, Alexandra felt like she was watching a commercial for Levi's jeans. She was about to whisper as much to Nathalie when she spoke.

'*Merci monsieur*,' Nathalie said, her lids heavy.

'*De rien*,' Caleb replied, glancing at her while stoking the flames.

'Oh, you speak French?' Nathalie pulled herself up straighter.

'*Un peu*.'

The pair of them rattled off a conversation in French. Alexandra was sure going back to the French department at the university would help Nathalie's mental health. She would raise it with her at some point. Caleb got up from the fire and poured himself a glass of whiskey from the gorgeous Art Deco bar trolley in the corner of the room. He leaned against the mantlepiece above the fire as he sipped his drink. Caleb had barely spoken a word during dinner, so it was nice to see him animated, even if she had no idea what they were talking about.

'What are you two chatting about in that sexy accent?' Alexandra asked.

'Oh, sorry. I always get carried away in French when I'm tipsy. Caleb's just telling me he's taught himself French and I've got to say, he's good. His accent is excellent. He's never been to France and I'm telling him he should go.'

'Never been overseas,' Caleb said, crouching again to stoke the fire.

'Really? Shouldn't someone your age be partying in Bali or Ibiza?' Alexandra asked.

Caleb shrugged and looked into the flames. 'Not really my thing.'

'What is your thing, Caleb, aside from cooking excellent French and Italian food?' Alexandra asked.

'I like the simple life,' he said, his eyes flickering towards Nathalie. 'Give me a campfire under the stars, a nice bottle of wine and a good book over a party any day. The bush around here is pretty special. There are some great hikes and there's the river to swim in. I've got a dirt bike and a horse to ride. I keep myself busy.'

'That sounds just perfect to me,' said Nathalie, her eyes shining as she smiled at Caleb. She had finished her wine and was now lying on the lounge, her bare feet resting on Alexandra's knees.

'It could be worse.' Caleb returned Nathalie's smile.

Oh God, thought Alexandra. *Look at these two.*

'How do you survive without internet though?' she asked.

'I've got plenty of books, a vintage record player, a clunky old typewriter. I happen to like old school.'

'Very hipster. I feel like we're in a time warp being in this valley,' Alexandra said. 'How did you even end up here?'

'Caleb is a bit like this house – charmingly old-fashioned,' Macie said, entering the room with a tray of coffee. Pen and Emmie came in behind her, settling into two armchairs.

'Kids go down okay?' Alexandra asked.

Emmie gave the thumbs up and went over to inspect the drinks trolley.

'He's quite a history buff too, and he runs tours of the old mines.'

'I'll take you all for a tour tomorrow,' said Caleb. 'The site's been abandoned since the early 1950s. The government just pulled the plug on a township of more than 2000 people. It went from a thriving shale oil mining town to a ghost town almost overnight.'

'And what do you make of all this talk of ghosts?' Alexandra asked.

Caleb rubbed his jaw and looked into the fire. A sad smile played on his lips. 'There's all this mythology around the ghost of Clara Black, a woman who went missing in the valley in 1948, but there are other ghosts in these parts. The custodians of the land surrounding the valley were the Aboriginal Wiradjuri people. Some of the rocks here are still decorated with their paintings and ancient sites have been found, filled with Aboriginal stories about how they lived. Bone needles for stitching skins, axes, hammers, history hundreds of years old. There were massacres of First Nations people when the white men came. You might have heard of the Bathurst Wars in 1824. Martial law was declared and another brutal period in Australian history ensued. The use of firearms against the Wiradjuri peoples was sanctioned throughout the region. Soldiers were told to round up all the Aboriginal people and move them into the valley for stealing food. Their traditional hunting grounds had been destroyed. They were massacred here. But some say a woman and her baby managed to escape the killings and her descendants are still alive today.'

Alexandra inched closer to the fire. 'I just got shivers.'

'So much of this has been forgotten. Few want to talk about it. Many Aboriginal people were slaughtered. There was also a massacre nearby, the Potato Field incident, which sparked revenge attacks by the Wiradjuri nation. The majority of victims were believed to be women and children. Personally, I believe the feeling in this region comes from these restless spirits. Of course, all these stories are now lost to history, confined to books, unspoken, to make white men feel better, but the feeling still lingers, as though the land holds onto the memory.'

'Oh my goodness, I know exactly what you're talking about,' said Nathalie.

'Me too,' said Pen, hugging a cushion to her chest.

'To quote Indigenous writer Raelee Lancaster, "... all land on this land, since the landing of the white man, has been haunted." Is it so strange to think that places have a memory, too?' Caleb asked. 'It's in the soil and the trees and these ancient cliffs.'

'*Une vieille âme dans un corps de jeune,*' Nathalie said.

'Translation please,' Alexandra said, nudging her.

'An old soul in a young body.'

'*Peut-être,*' Caleb said, looking self-conscious, dusting his hands of ash from the fire.

'Well, you two seem to be getting along rather well. I didn't know you spoke French, Nathalie,' Macie said, opening a silver cigarette case and offering one to her.

Nathalie paused, seeming to study the cigarettes.

'Oh, go on. You were just saying you felt like a cigarette,' Alexandra said. 'Macie, you're a mind reader. Your hospitality is just beyond. Personal chefs, and now coffee, cigarettes and what are these? Chocolate truffles by the fire.'

'Caleb made them. He's quite the chocolatier.'

'Of course he is,' said Alexandra.

'They're exquisite.' Nathalie waved the cigarette away. 'No thank you. I really shouldn't.'

'It's what I grew up seeing my mother do,' Macie said, handing around the coffee. 'She was *the* perfect hostess. And this place was her big love. When my father left us, she poured everything into restoring it. And, all that time ago, a woman renovating somewhere like this was a big deal. It wasn't done. It was a man's job. But she knew she needed to make it somewhere to host people so she could make a living to provide for me. She did all the cooking and the cleaning. The only help she had was from our gardener and groundskeeper. She's passed away now, but I have this home as her legacy.'

'Your mum sounds incredible,' Alexandra said. 'I never met her, did I? But I guess boarding schools are like that – shipped off by the parents.'

'You went to school with Macie?' Nathalie asked.

Alexandra's stomach tightened and her face grew hot. The room spun. What was she doing? She hadn't told anyone about her school connection with Macie. She hadn't even voiced it out loud with Macie herself. She was clearly drunk. All that talk of ghosts and spirits had unhinged her. The fire was too hot, roaring in the grate. Nausea washed over her.

'Goodness, I thought I recognised you from somewhere,' said Macie, her eyes narrowing and a smile playing on her lips. 'How have we never worked this out?'

Alexandra waved a hand, tried to be casual, but her mouth was dry. She gave a little laugh. 'I think I suspected early on but then ... it just got past the point of being able to say something—'

'Oh, like when you don't know a school mum's name but it's literally been years so you can never ask,' Emmie said.

'Exactly,' Alexandra said, pressing her hand to her chest.

'So, were you friends at school?' asked Nathalie.

A lump formed in Alexandra's throat. 'Oh, ah, well, we ...'

'I'd say we were acquaintances. We were in the same year,' Macie said, lighting her cigarette and inhaling.

Alexandra's sick feeling intensified with the sweet smell of tobacco. 'I mean, it was a big school, wasn't it?'

'Enormous. Very easy to get lost in.'

Alexandra's heart was beating fast. She stood. She needed to escape this too-close room. 'Where did you go to school Caleb?' she asked, desperate for a diversion. She walked over to the bar trolley filled with spirits in beautiful cut-glass decanters. 'Here, let me pour some whiskey, is that what this is? Does anyone want any?' She poured the amber liquid into several glasses, which she handed around.

'Thanks,' said Caleb, as she topped up his glass, settling into a chair next to the fire. 'I wasn't really much of an academic,' he said. 'I'm largely self-taught. Home-schooled.'

'I think we could call Caleb gifted,' Macie said. 'History buff as we just heard, prolific reader, writer, musician, cook, handyman – can fix anything that breaks.'

'Well, if your mastery of French is anything to go by, I'd have to agree,' Nathalie said. 'So, back to this high school connection. How intriguing. Which school did you go to again Alexandra?'

'Prushville Girls, in Sydney,' Macie said. 'I was a boarder. Alexandra was a day girl, if I remember correctly?'

Their eyes met and Alexandra felt a frisson run from the hairs on the nape of her neck to her toes.

'Are all of those awful stories true about boarding schools? Cruel initiation rituals and strict teachers and rebellious girls?' Nathalie asked.

Alexandra felt paralysed, her limbs heavy. She forced the hot spirits down her throat in one gulp. 'Oh, of course. School was a drag.' She waved a hand. 'You know, I think I'll nab one of those cigarettes and go outside. It's getting a bit stuffy in here with the fire.' She took a cigarette, let Macie light it and prayed she wouldn't follow her as she walked out of the lounge. She pushed the French doors open to the night, gasping with relief at the smell of eucalyptus on the cool breeze.

She listened for the echo of steps on the marble entrance hall and felt her shoulders drop with relief when she heard nothing. She let out a shaky breath. Why was she getting so tense about this? It was a lifetime ago. If Macie hadn't raised their connection maybe she didn't care about what had gone on at that school anymore. It was probably better it was out in the open now. People moved on.

Macie was a successful artist who owned a Sydney mansion and practically a whole valley. She'd been the perfect host. She wasn't acting like a woman who was holding a grudge from something that happened when they were kids. Alexandra moved further into the cool night. The dark cliffs loomed above her, a reminder of just how far they were from everything. There was no sound save the movement of leaves in the breeze and the occasional hoot of an owl. But she sensed the thrum of life under the inky blanket. She looked up. The sky was clear and star-strewn. There was a brightness to the night sky that you didn't get in the city. It was like looking to the edge of the universe. *Perspective.* How tiny her worries. How small her world. She took a deep breath. They really were in the middle of nowhere. There was a sound of scurrying from a bush nearby and Alexandra hurried back to the hotel porch. Her head was swimming. She sat down and extinguished her cigarette. Here she was judging Nathalie for her proclivity for wine, while she was totally drunk herself. Maybe it was just being here that was making her anxious. So many ghosts. So much history buried and a whole town abandoned and sunk into the earth.

CHAPTER 20

Nathalie

She felt a hand, cool on her forehead. So good. So cool. She tried to open her eyes, but her lids were impossibly heavy. The flickering light of the flames played behind them. She must still be in the lounge room. It was like a cocoon. Was Caleb still here? How long had she been asleep? *Open your eyes*, she willed herself. But it was as though her body was a weight, sinking, unable to rise to the surface. There was a ripple, an arm behind her. She felt herself rising now. Her neck fell back and her eyes snapped open. She blinked until she could focus. Macie. Rose and sandalwood-scented hair fell over Nathalie's face as she helped her to her feet. She heard herself grunt with effort as though she was outside her own body.

'Where is everyone?'

'Everyone had a bit too much to drink, but they're all in bed now. We thought we'd let you sleep for a little bit longer. I was going to let you stay on the lounge, but those beautiful little girls of yours will be worried if they wake up and

Mummy's not there.' Macie's voice was soothing, and it drew Nathalie back to a memory of her own mother putting her to bed, sleep-addled and safe. The comfort, the warm smell of her neck. A sickening wave of emotion pulled through her and she heard herself moan.

'Are you okay? Are you going to be sick?' Macie asked, smoothing her hair. They were moving, out of the lounge and into the foyer, Nathalie's arm around Macie's shoulders for support.

'I'm so sorry.' Nathalie's voice was a whisper. Her words were too slow, like moving underwater. Like drowning. Her hand went to her face. It was wet with tears. 'I'm so drunk. I'm so embarrassed. I'm such a terrible mother.'

'No, no you're not. You just needed to let off some steam. Everyone did. It's always what happens on the first night.' They were at the stairs. Nathalie didn't know how she was going to climb them. She sank onto the cool marble step. Macie sat down next to her and pulled her damp hair off her face. 'Come on, we just need to get up the stairs. Get you into bed.'

'I am. Terrible. You don't understand. I almost left them forever. My own children. I almost never came back. I wanted to go to Paris. To escape them all. I left them for a whole night, and I had a newborn baby. I left him. I got drunk at the hotel. He'd just hurt me so much, I didn't know what else to do.' She was babbling but she couldn't stop the words bubbling out of her mouth. The room spun tighter.

Macie rubbed her back. 'Who hurt you? It's okay. It's okay. Breathe.'

'Mike. My husband. He cheated on me. Everyone thinks I have the perfect marriage.' Laughter. Loud. Manic. Echoing off the cold stone stairs, through the dark foyer. She stifled it with a palm over her mouth. She was cold now and she convulsed, sickened at her own state. Unable to get up. Unable to get away from herself. 'It's all a lie,' she whispered. 'But I can't tell anyone.'

'Why not?'

'Because I want it to be perfect.'

'Of course you do,' Macie said, their eyes meeting. Nathalie thought she saw tears shining in her eyes, but then she felt Macie pulling her up and they climbed the rest of the stairs in silence. Macie opened the door to the room and moonlight streamed through the naked windows. Her little girls were clinging together on the bed, intertwined, hair like pale mermaid tendrils. Nathalie's heart hurt with love for them. As Macie pulled back the covers on her bed and she sank into it, Nathalie grabbed her arm. 'Please don't tell anyone. I can't. I can't do it. I can't leave him. I'm too weak.'

She saw Macie smile, felt her hand on her face, before sleep closed over her like a glove.

Jean
1948

She squeezed Liv's little hands and pulled her into a big hug. Her daughter's skin smelled of honey and the soap she'd washed in last night. The scent of it made Jean's heart ache. *What are you doing? You can't leave her*, she thought. But it was fleeting, replaced by an urgency, an excitement that curled in Jean's belly. *It's just for the weekend. I'll be back so soon. I just need this one thing for myself. And I need to see Father.* But still the guilt was there rippling just beneath the surface of her skin. She pulled herself together and brushed away the moisture in her eyes.

'I'm going to miss you so much, my darling. Now you be a good girl for Pam, won't you? Eat all your supper and remember all your manners.'

'I will, Mamma.' Liv kissed her, waved and ran into the house with Bertie. She was grateful that her daughter seemed to have more of her father's stable, easygoing temperament. She was such a good girl. Jean had to admit the only part of herself she could see in Liv was her love of ballet. She was relieved to not have a passionate, stubborn child, as she herself had been. Or perhaps it was this place, the valley, that had formed Liv. Grounded her. The days spent running with the other children, the hot sun on their faces, the cool river water on their backs. Always moving. Always outside.

'I can't thank you enough for having her,' she said to Pam. 'This trip to see my father is something that's been playing on my mind for such a long time. He's really not in a good way. He gets very confused. His memory is quite bad, it's upsetting.'

'Oh, that's very sad. Yes, it's best for Liv not to see him like that.'

'It's quite heartbreaking, but I do need to check in on him, see he's being cared for properly. Thank you for having her. And you're sure you won't be too tired to have another child while you're expecting?'

'Well, I'd better be getting used to having another,' Pam said, smiling and rubbing her growing belly. 'Now, I hope your father is okay.'

Jean felt guilt burn in her stomach, but she squeezed Pam's arm warmly. 'Thank you so much, I hope so too.'

'Well, make sure you take a little time for yourself in Sydney, too. It seems like another world, doesn't it?'

Jean felt terrible for making her father the reason for leaving Liv when there was so much else she hadn't disclosed. But she reasoned with herself that she never would have had the money to visit her dad without Magnus. She'd told Robert that her father had come into a little money and sent her some to make the trip. Money for a bus to the train at Katoomba, and a train to Central Station, where she'd then catch a bus to Sydney's north and stay with him in the boarding house. More lies. She felt sick with nerves at what she was doing. She didn't even know herself this past while. Wearing the clothes of a missing woman, leaving for Sydney with a man she barely knew. Who was she? And why was she acting in this way? She felt deeply ashamed, but she couldn't seem to stop herself. She took a deep breath to still her racing mind.

She checked her wristwatch. It was an hour until Magnus was due to pick her up in front of the dance hall. She walked back to her house quickly, went inside and checked her reflection in the glass. She was wearing a deep red felt hat that had once been pretty but now had moth-eaten holes that she'd tried to patch over, and the best day dress she owned, also patched in places. Her hair was in the rolled curl style she'd read Sydney women were wearing. It would have to do.

Her breath was quick as she walked to the dance hall with her small case, her hat pulled low over her face. The late morning sun was hot and the sheer cliff faces shimmered with heat. It had been so long since she'd left this place – she had almost forgotten there was a world beyond its walls. Of course, she wasn't the only one confined to this place. Petrol rationing made it difficult for families to leave the valley. She waited beneath the shade of the eucalypt in front of the hall, angling herself away from the street. It was quiet but the miners would be on the road soon for tea break. She hoped Magnus wouldn't be late.

The car pulled up. Even coated in valley dust its surfaces gleamed. She walked quickly towards it, acutely aware of whether anyone was watching them. She didn't wait for him to come and open her door but quickly got in, her small suitcase on her lap.

'Someone's in a rush to get out of here,' Magnus said, an amused smile playing on his lips. His shirt sleeves were rolled up to reveal tanned arms. They were not worker's arms, worker's hands. They were the type of arms that rested casually on leather steering wheels.

'I may be a little excited,' she said, feeling that hot guilt rise from her gut again.

Magnus shook his head. 'Here, let me at least get that case off your knees.' He took his time finding a place for her bag in the boot, Jean willing him to hurry, to get them out of here, lest they be seen.

The car had a radio and Jean felt herself relaxing with the music, the warm wind in her hair. As they left the settlement behind, the valley and its cliffs rose around them, magnificent and imposing before receding like a hazy dream. And then they were travelling up, through dense bushland.

'We're climbing out of the valley,' said Magnus.

It was hot and his words were lost in the air rushing through the open windows. It was easier not to chat. She felt relieved by this and the languid sunshine on her arms.

They drove over the Blue Mountains, Jean admiring the small towns they passed with their shopfronts and charming restaurants. Magnus asked if she wished to stop for lunch at the famous Paragon restaurant in Katoomba, but she just wanted to be in Sydney. She couldn't risk being seen in the Mountains, where on a rare and special occasion families from the valley visited a restaurant.

The traffic became more congested as they reached the outskirts of Sydney and the car slowed. The smell of petrol fumes and something else, perhaps the salty breeze from the ocean now nearby caused her whole body to tingle in anticipation. It had been so long since she'd seen the sea.

'I had intended we stay at The Australia Hotel on Castlereagh Street, but a friend of mine, Mr Parker, has offered to host us at his home in Kirribilli for the weekend. It's right on the harbour. A magnificent sandstone building.'

Jean felt nerves as well as excitement buzz along her shoulders. The harbour. The ocean. She couldn't wait to cast her eyes over a large body of water. She'd grown up by the sea and hadn't realised how entrenched it was in her psyche until she was forced to be so far from it. But who was this Mr Parker? She'd pictured herself having her own room in the hotel and even enjoying some time alone, without the burden of constant chores. Perhaps reading a novel. She realised she'd misread the situation.

But before she could panic, they were entering the city, the buildings rising around her, the people dressed in fine clothing; the extravagance of the women's dresses, the tailoring of the men's suits. She drank it all in, speechless. Magnus stopped the car outside a handsome building on Martin Place.

'But before we head over the Harbour Bridge, refreshments my lady.'

'Oh, I've heard of this place. The Black and White Milk Bar. It's in all the women's magazines.'

They entered the cool milk bar with its ornate tiling and shining silver milkshake makers and anticipation skittered over her skin once more. The servers were dressed in starched white pinafores with scalloped black collars and pretty little white caps. Art Deco lights were strung from the ceiling and behind the bar were elegant mirrors and elaborate half-moon plaster work.

'Oh, it's so glamorous. I feel like I'm in a Hollywood movie.'

'It's something, isn't it? Sydney's original milk bar.'

They took a seat at a glossy booth painted in the bar's namesake, black and white.

'What do you fancy? Order anything you like.'

Jean tried to hide her shock at Magnus's excess. At home there was no extra money. Not enough money. Every morsel of food needed to be stretched as far as it could go and most of the time she went hungry, preferring Liv to eat her share to fuel her growing body and Robert needed a large serving for his long days in the mines.

'A milkshake? Ice cream sundae? Some homemade chocolates? Or shall we just order all of it?' asked Magnus, his eyes glinting, teasing.

Jean laughed and watched in amazement as he ordered with the elegant server. The woman had the most beautiful green eyes, which were offset by her taupe eyeshadow and dark hair that curled into a bob cut at her neck. Suddenly Jean wanted the same haircut. The same make-up. To be working somewhere glamorous like this. She knew her old clothes singled her out here, but she pushed down the feeling of inadequacy. She refused to not feel happy. This was a single weekend of freedom in her life, nothing more. She needed to not let herself get caught up in things. That's what had led her to where she was now. Her passion. Her impetuousness. Her mother had always said she did things without thinking about the consequences. She never dreamed the consequences would be giving up her dancing to live in a faraway valley, struggling to feed her family with a man she was devoted to but felt no connection to. Struggling with the pull of the past.

'After this we'll swing by the department store around the corner. I think that now we're in Sydney we need you dressed with a little more panache.'

Jean's heart raced. 'Oh, Magnus, I can't afford all this. You've been so kind but we said no more gifts—'

Magnus waved her protests away with a flick of his wrist. 'I lied.'

She shot him a reproachful look and he laughed. She couldn't help but laugh as well. A zing of happiness shot through her.

But then two enormous frothy glasses topped off with whipped cream and maraschino cherries were placed in front of them.

'I hope you like rum with your banana milk,' Magnus said. 'This is called the bootlegger punch, with a dash of rum essence.' They watched the women pouring the shakes at the counter, stretching out the milk between silver cups as though it were an elaborate cocktail.

The milkshake was cool and creamy, and she savoured its deliciousness through a chilled straw. They brought out hamburgers with thick slabs of juicy meat the like of which she'd never tasted. The juices ran down to her elbows. And then there was coffee and rich chocolates in ornate wrappings.

Magnus smoked cigarettes and mostly talked about business deals he was doing in Sydney. He was considering purchasing his own milk bar as it was the 'Hollywood' trend. Jean was grateful that he was happy to talk so much about himself. She was a good listener and preferred it to talking about herself. And she didn't know what she'd say if he wanted to know more about her. Her lies about simply being a ballet teacher in the bush felt flimsy, paper-thin and likely to tear at the first hint of deeper probing.

She wanted to say out loud what was playing on her mind. *Magnus, I'm so grateful but I'm hoping you're not expecting more from me than I can give you.*

With bellies full and a little buzzed on caffeine, they walked around the corner to McDowells department store. It was more beautiful than she'd remembered. The window displays held the latest fashions, beautiful full skirts and elegant slanted hats. A tremor of excitement ran through her as her fingers found the silky, gossamer fabric of a dress in the ladies' department. It was a pale pink with fine white roses sewn into it, but Magnus tapped her on the shoulder. He led her to a mannequin in the centre of the store dressed in a floor-length gown in the most stunning sapphire silk.

A memory flitted across her mind, shadowy, unformed.

Magnus indicated to a girl on the shop floor. When Jean tried to protest, he flicked his wrist again and mouthed the words, 'Last gift, I promise'.

'We'll take the pink one and this blue dress. In mademoiselle's sizing,' he said. 'Oh, and matching hats and gloves for both.'

As she stared at herself in the glass, the striking gown draped perfectly over her body, an image came to her, vague, buried, but she let it form, sink into her, like ink on rich parchment. She'd worn a dress similar to this once. She'd worn feathers in her hair. It had been the after-show party for the opening night of her first big performance. She had paid for it from her own earnings. From her split toes, from her aching muscles, from her tired mind. From her dancer's spirit. She remembered the pride, the sense of otherworldliness as she stepped into the ballroom to greet their applause, wearing something she had worked so hard for, dreamt so long for. She had felt like a queen. She could still remember the scent of the roses they'd thrown. And now here she was having a dress like this bought for her. Caught in a web of lies. She took the dress off.

Jean knew that he'd want her to wear the pink one now and the sapphire dress for some kind of evening engagement. She pulled on the pastel frock and balled up her dusty one. She had forgotten how it felt to have new fabric against her skin. The greasy soap she washed their clothes in never seemed to clean them of valley dirt.

'Fresh,' said Magnus, as she emerged with the new dress on.

'Thank you,' she said, allowing herself a small smile. 'I don't even know how to begin to thank you, my gratitude … it's overwhelming.'

'You can start by joining me for drinks this evening wearing that blue dress,' he said. 'Mr Parker is expecting us shortly in Kirribilli.'

'Magnus, I do need to visit my father this weekend. He's very ill. In Mosman. It's not too far.'

He patted her arm as he paid for the clothing. 'We'll have plenty of time tomorrow to pay him a visit, don't you mind.'

They crossed the Harbour Bridge and the smell of the salt intoxicated her. She closed her eyes to focus on it. The screech of gulls reached her, the slosh of waves against rocks. She watched the white caps of the water tossing the vessels below as though they were children's toys. Magnus pointed to the grand homes that lined the foreshore.

'See the sandstone one there? That's where we're staying. Right on the water.'

'Oh my,' she said, excitement and trepidation wrestling inside her chest. She wondered what Liv was doing now.

If Robert was kicking off his black, oily boots on the porch, finding the meagre loaf of bread in the pantry, throwing his soiled clothing in the laundry tub. Her heart contracted with guilt at the same time Magnus took her hand and squeezed it. She hesitated a second before she squeezed back.

CHAPTER 21

Emmie

The children squealed as they splashed in the shallow stream. The morning sun cast a dappled tapestry through the gum trees and smooth white pebbles clunked as they were skimmed over the water and piled into towers. The air was as fresh and clear as the water under the little wooden bridge. It smelled like cut grass, wet soil and river moss. There had been dew through the garden this morning, and mist hovering at the valley walls, as though the earth had been breathing all night.

Emmie had taken so many gorgeous photos this morning, she wasn't sure which ones to upload.

'Don't throw stones that are too big, please,' she shouted. 'And Seraphine, please keep an eye on the younger ones.'

'Okay, Mummy.'

She hadn't expected to get any reception at all, but right in the middle of the bridge, not an inch either side, there it was: a full four bars on her phone. She'd left everyone else finishing their morning coffees in the sunshine at the table on the patio overlooking the garden and offered to take the kids for a walk. It was only a short stroll out the hotel gates, past the old pharmacy, which the children were fascinated by, and to the bridge over the stream. Yes, she had slightly ulterior motives, but at least the kids were having fun and the girls were getting their sacred coffee-lingering time.

There had been a lot of talk of a sleepless night and the kids getting spooked. Sim had even started crying over breakfast and wanted to go home. But Seraphine seemed enchanted by the gardens and all the old furniture, and Emmie felt the same. She'd never been anywhere quite like this. There were so many stories here, she could almost feel them echoing off the majestic sandstone escarpment. Where the others felt fear or trepidation, she felt awed, inspired.

She opened Instagram and chose some of the photos she'd taken of the kids playing in the garden just as evening fell: one of them all over by the horse with the cliff face honeycombed in the background, and a photo of the beautiful afternoon tea Macie had served under the willow. She hesitated over the final image. Nathalie's profile, framed against bare branches that were softened by the sinking sun. Her fingers moved quickly over her phone keys.

Time in nature creates space around and within us. These wild places refresh our spirit, free our minds to wander and wonder. And we wonder why we don't seek out her beauty more — the touch of her sunlit fingers, the warmth of her breath in our hair, her high skies. And we know we are reconnecting to something bigger, something we forget about in the ordinary days of our small lives. #DaysofInnocence.

She was gaining more followers each day.

So idyllic, someone wrote as soon as she posted the images. *Love the sense of whimsy and beauty in your posts.*

OMG, you and your friends and the kids are so gorgeous.

Excitement zipped through her. Maybe she'd finally found her thing. She thought of all those manuscripts she'd spent years writing. The blog posts she'd spent hours perfecting.

'Hey.' Nathalie crossed the bridge towards her, a coffee mug in her hand. Her summer dress was the same muted greens as the tree leaves overhanging the bridge and her hair was plaited, falling loose at her back, but her eyes looked tired.

Emmie put her phone in her back pocket. An inkling of guilt wormed in her gut. Part of her felt like she should mention the Instagram account to Nathalie and the others, but she felt stupid. She had a few hundred followers. That was a drop in the ocean. Half the pictures were of the countryside or food, and there was kind of a fictional aspect to it. It also felt weirdly self-important to announce that she had set up an Instagram account.

'Sim's happy now, thank God,' Nathalie said. 'Thanks for the distraction.'

They waved to the kids playing below them. The three boys were piling the pebbles, one on top of the other, seemingly making a stone city, while the girls had taken off their shoes and were squishing their toes in the sandy bank.

'Mummy, Sim keeps stealing the boys' pebbles.' Findlay was looking up at them, her hands on her hips, her little body rigid with indignation.

'It looks like you're all sharing pretty nicely to me,' Nathalie said shading her eyes against the morning glare.

'Well, she's not sharing.' She stomped her foot.

'I am so,' cried Sim, her little mouth set in a pout. Sim pushed Findlay, who landed on her bottom with a wail.

'Oh God,' Nathalie said under her breath. 'Hangovers and fighting kids do not mix.' She made her way down to them and crouched. 'Sim, you can't push your sister. And Findlay, you shouldn't be dobbing on Sim. Everyone was playing nicely.'

'I wasn't dobbing.'

'Dobbers wear nappies,' said Sim, poking out her tongue.

'Sim.' Nathalie shot her daughter a death stare and the child began to cry. Nathalie looked up at Emmie and shook her head helplessly.

'Seraphine, why don't you see if you can find tadpoles, or a frog,' said Emmie.

'A tadpole. I see one,' cried Seraphine, pointing into the water. In an instant the tension was gone, as though it was a momentary ripple on the surface of the water, and all the children were peering into the shallows.

'Ugh, thank you,' said Nathalie, returning to the bridge. 'That dynamic is happening way too often. Findlay trying to get my attention by telling on her sister. And Sim is just a mess. So many tears and it's not even 9 am.'

'She was really upset at breakfast, huh?'

'Yeah, she can't really verbalise how she's feeling, but I think she's picking up on the vibe out here. Speaking of which, Caleb wants to take us all on a tour of the ruins this morning before the day gets too hot.'

'Oh good, I've been dying to see them up close. He seems to know what he's talking about. And he seems quite taken with you.' She nudged Nathalie.

Nathalie shook her head, embarrassed. 'Oh, God, no. He's half my age.'

'When did that ever stop anyone from crushing?'

'I think you're the only one who's keen on seeing these old mines. Pen is probably dreading it in case Will starts drawing another ghost.'

'She's coming over,' said Emmie, spotting Pen walking up the unsealed road towards them. 'She was so apologetic last night for Will spooking everyone. And then with Sim freaking out this morning.'

'It's not Will's fault. He's just drawing what all of us are feeling.'

'To be honest, I was a little rattled when he first said he saw the lady on the back steps. I definitely got tingles down my spine,' Emmie said.

'Gosh, isn't it pretty here? What an idyllic little stream,' Pen said. 'Should have brought my camera from the room.'

'I know, it's paradise for the kids. Just give them some sticks and stones and a bit of water and that's them sorted for a few hours,' said Nathalie. 'Unless someone steals the stones.' She exchanged a sarcastic smile and Emmie couldn't help but feel warmed by their shared understanding.

One of the girls squealed below them. 'He's splashing me. Stop it.'

'Okay, no splashing each other,' called Emmie.

'It's Jasper. He keeps doing it,' said Findlay.

'See, the dobbing again. Come on, you can deal with some water,' said Nathalie. 'Splash him back.'

'Here we go,' said Emmie, and they all laughed.

'Look, I just wanted to apologise again for Will scaring Sim so much. I had no idea she understood what was going on last night with the drawing of the woman,' said Pen.

Nathalie waved a hand. 'It's fine. It's not Will's fault. This is a really old place in the middle of the bush. The doors to our rooms don't lock, which is apparently an issue with my girls. Findlay spent half the night telling me that anyone could come into our room. The kids aren't the only ones who think it's a bit … atmospheric. Sim just misses home, but look at her now.'

The little girl was giggling at something her sister was whispering in her ear.

'Are you sure?' asked Pen.

Emmie put her arm on Pen's shoulder. 'Of course. Try to relax and don't worry about Will. He's a sweetheart. And we're all here to keep an eye on all of them. Four mums. What could go wrong?'

They all laughed.

'So, apparently we're off to see the ruins of the mines shortly, which attract ghost hunters from all over the country,' said Pen a tad too brightly.

'Oh, come on, it's an adventure. The kids will love it,' said Emmie. 'And it's daytime. I'm pretty sure ghosts only come out at night.'

CHAPTER 22

Pen

The ruins were like uneven teeth, jutting sharply from the lush mouth of the valley. Pen couldn't deny there was a stark beauty to their decay. Pillars of brick and steel, long-forgotten markers of a dead industry were dissolving slowly back into the landscape. Long grass crept between cracks, and tree roots choked the concrete, like wilful serpents. A flock of cockatoos took off from a gum tree, their screeches echoing through the hot blue sky. As their cries died, Pen felt the silence of the past settle around her like fine dust. There was a feeling here, like walking into an old, empty church. A reverence for something unseen.

The walk wasn't as far as Pen had expected. The mines had looked distant, shrouded in morning mist out her window, but it was only a short stroll up a dusty road from the hotel. The air was dry now, as though the wisps of mist had been a dream. It was getting hotter as the sun moved towards its zenith in the sky.

She held her camera steady and snapped the graceful arch of a long abandoned building. A tin drum overrun with wildflowers.

An army of beetles, their shiny backs catching the light like glints of metal. The contrast between the man-made structures and nature was something special. Nature was winning.

She urged the stuff with Will to the back of her mind. She'd had a talk with him last night and he'd been adamant that he was just drawing what he saw. He said it didn't look like a ghost – it wasn't see-through – it looked like an actual lady. And then when he must have seen Pen's look of horror, he revised and said he didn't know, and it was just from his imagination. He shut down then and wouldn't talk about it further, and she felt like the worst mother for not believing him.

She thought back to all those imaginary friends Will had had over the years. She'd just put them down to the loneliness of being essentially an only child, with his sister so much older than him. Now she wondered if he'd been seeing things for years and she hadn't even noticed. Guilt lanced through her, hot and fresh, as though it was a new emotion, not one as familiar as her own face.

Caleb unlocked a rusted barbed wire gate and told the kids to keep away from the long grass because there could be snakes. That was like asking tiger cubs to keep out of the jungle.

'Did you hear that, kids?' asked Emmie, her voice clear and authoritative. 'And keep your hats on or you'll get sunburnt. Quick, let me get a photo.' She somehow managed to assemble them into a line and take a photo on her phone.

Thank God for Emmie. She must have been a schoolteacher or a saint in a former life. She had so much patience.

'So, it's hard to imagine now but this used to be a thriving shale oil works,' said Caleb standing at the entrance with them all gathered around. He was wearing a battered straw hat, and what appeared to be his uniform of jeans, a white shirt and leather boots. 'The shale oil was turned into petrol and gasoline for use during World War II. It provided roughly 2.5 million gallons of oil at its height. And the mine's workers and their families lived here between 1938 and 1952. There was lots of poverty and it was known as Bag Town early on, because the miners had to build their accommodation out of hessian sacks. Later a township was established. It included a post office, butcher, baker, bank, school, a Catholic church, and even at its height, a picture theatre and greyhound racing track. There were suburbs called things like Happy Valley, River Bends, Frog Hollow and Tweedies.

'You would have seen some of the remains of the shops after you crossed the bridge, just before the hotel gates. Some of the shopfronts are frozen in time. The government pulled oil production in 1952 but it wasn't until 1954 that the township was finally abandoned, many families losing everything they owned. There were roughly 2500 people living in the valley at its height.'

'Where are they all now?' asked Seraphine.

'Dead, dummy,' said Thomas.

'Except the lady that Will saw,' said Findlay. 'She's still here.'

'Hey, what did we talk about, no more about that stuff,' said Nathalie.

Pen cringed, feeling the sun bore into her bare shoulders, the glare sting her eyes.

'Well, we are doing a ghost tour,' said Will.

'Touché,' said Nathalie, nodding. 'Yeah, true Will.'

'Will,' said Pen, with more warning in her voice than she'd intended. Everyone turned to her. *God.* 'Quiet please, honey. Caleb is trying to talk.'

Will shot her an angry look and stormed off the rough path that seemed to meander through the centre of the ruins. *Ugh. It would serve him right if he got bitten by a snake*, Pen thought, then hated herself. God, if people could hear the things she said in her mind about her kid. Was it just her? Did other parents have these thoughts?

'Over there you'll see some of the remainders of old kilns that made bricks for the valley. And these are old petrol pipelines running through the bush, and this here was a cooling tower,' Caleb said. 'Oh, yeah, maybe the boys shouldn't go in there.'

'Boys, out!' shouted Alexandra, pulling Thomas and Jasper from a concrete tunnel wide enough to fit a small car. Will was up ahead, walking beside Macie. He bent and picked up a piece of rubble and handed it to her. She tried and failed to fit it in her pocket and they laughed. Pen felt a sharp stab in her chest. Was she really feeling jealous of her son's relationship with a stranger? When was the last time she and Will had shared a laugh about something? She lifted her camera and took a photo of them. She wasn't sure why.

'You should get some nice shots out here,' said Alexandra. 'Now keep out of trouble and don't go in the long grass.' Alexandra ruffled her boys' hair and rolled her eyes at Pen.

'Who knew all this was out here? And all that history. And just to think we could have been by the pool at the boring beach,' Pen said.

Alexandra rolled her eyes. 'I heard that sarcasm. Oh, I know. I must admit, when Macie offered us to stay at her place, I didn't expect it to be this.' She made a sweeping gesture.

The group had dispersed, and she looked back to find Caleb and Nathalie craning their necks to study some sandstone pillars that looked particularly Romanesque.

'We've got to watch those two, I reckon,' said Alexandra, following her line of sight. 'What with the amount Nathalie drinks and the way I've seen him looking at her.'

Pen scrunched up her face. 'She could have anyone. You really think she'd cheat on her husband with some reclusive guy in his 20s? Who does tours of old mines?'

Alexandra shrugged. 'You've got to admit, he's pretty sexy for a recluse. And don't you feel it? There's something about this place. This whole valley. After what Caleb described. I'm not spiritual, but I don't know … I can't really articulate it. I feel like anything could happen. I'm not sure if that's good or bad, given I live such a boring life.'

Macie and Will were beside them suddenly. 'Mum, Macie's going to show me how to make earth pigment out of some of the rocks we've collected. You crush it and mix it with …'

'Egg white and water,' Macie said. 'Will's very interested in the Aboriginal history, too. Caleb can show us some of the cave paintings in the valley. You've got a budding little historian and artist here, Pen.'

Will's face glowed as he pocketed the rocks and ran off to join Jasper and Thomas who were kicking a rusty can between them.

The hairs on Pen's arms rose despite the sun burning her skin. 'Oh, I feel it all right,' she whispered to Alexandra, as Will hesitated in front of the other boys, then ran back to Macie.

CHAPTER 23

Nathalie

The gorge echoed with kookaburra song and the low croak of frogs. The afternoon air was cooler here, tempered by the cold water moving over smooth black rocks. The narrow green snake of the river sunned itself under a violent blue sky. Wildflowers bloomed unbidden among the river stones. Dragonflies hovered low, and rock pools gurgled with soft rapids. The banks were lined with spindly gums on one side and willows on the other, their leaves licking the water.

The children played in the shallows, yelping with delight as they hopped from rock to rock. The mothers stood ankle-deep, watching. Macie had packed a picnic of cheeses, fruits and French champagne, and it was laid out on a white cloth in the shade of a willow tree. Nathalie had to admit, Macie had a charming flair for entertaining.

She eased into the water, feeling the dusty heat of the day slough off her skin. She dipped her head under. The water was so cold it took her breath away and an exhilarating jolt shot through her. Her toes found the smooth pebbles on the river floor and she dived down and chose one to hold in her palm. From the lip of the water the afternoon looked hazy, the champagne in her body rendering it all the more like a dream. They had only been here one night, and it was like they were in a new land. One where the hum and sparkle of nature was impossible to ignore. City life seemed so distant, so dull and monochrome in comparison. She was trying not to think about Richie too much, though her body memory of him was as loud and sharp as the cicada drone in the trees above.

Macie was knee-deep, heading towards her through the water. Nathalie felt shame shimmy along her shoulders. Fragments of their conversation last night returned, as though she was looking at her own reflection in a cracked mirror. The memory was as hazy as the heat hovering over the water, but she knew she'd told Macie about Mike's affair, about the night at the hotel. Abandoning her children. *Oh God.* She must have been so drunk. Should she acknowledge it while they were alone, or keep silent, hoping Macie would, too?

Macie was coming in deeper.

'Every time I'm back here I wonder why I stay in Sydney.' Macie sank to her neck and sighed wistfully.

Nathalie forced a smile onto her face. Perhaps it was going to be okay. Perhaps they'd skim the surface of things, like the insects over the water. 'You're very lucky to have the best of both worlds.'

'So, tell me, are you married Nathalie?' Macie asked, her face trained towards the sky.

Nathalie paused for a moment longer than what was natural. 'I, ah, yes,' she said, trying to make her face, her voice, impassive. Was Macie really going to play it like this? It was one thing to pretend last night had never happened, it was another to ask directly something she clearly knew. Part of her wanted to say, 'Why are you acting like you didn't put me to bed and listen to me spill the guts of my life?' But a larger part of her wanted to forget she ever had. Maybe Macie was just giving her this out. Maybe it was graciousness.

'Is your husband at home with your baby? Your little boy must be getting so big by now.'

'Yes, he's going to be one soon. I'm missing him a lot, actually.'

'Oh, they're beautiful at that age. It must have been hard to leave him. That's nice your husband is looking after your son.'

Nathalie scooped a tiny white butterfly from the surface of the water. Its limp, translucent wings made her feel unaccountably sad. She nodded, feeling her unease intensify. She wasn't going to tell Macie that Mike's mother, who was actually amazing and one of the good things about her marriage, had insisted on spending time with her grandson and giving Nathalie a break. She wanted out of this conversation. Her teeth chattered. 'I'm getting cold. I might head over and warm up in the sun.'

'I hope you're wearing sunscreen. You have the most incredible complexion. We all wonder at people like you with your easy beauty.'

Nathalie laughed awkwardly. 'Oh, thanks. No, I put it on the girls. I always forget myself.'

'There's a bottle on my towel if you'd like to use it,' Macie said, stretching languidly.

Nathalie felt Macie's eyes on her as she stood to move towards the sun and the other women.

'I bet he's super handsome.'

'Who?'

'Your husband.'

Nathalie laughed to hide the unease chilling her skin like cold water droplets.

'Sorry, it's just you're so gorgeous, I can only imagine you paired with another alpha human.'

Nathalie shook her head, totally lost for words. *Who talked like this?*

'You probably don't see it but everywhere you go, you're given respect and deference because of your beauty. You're the top dog here in this group of women.'

The hairs on Nathalie's wet, bare arms rose. 'I don't really think it works like that.'

'I've studied psychology. Sometimes we over-complicate what is really just biological fact. You're a nice person, so you don't take advantage of your power, but you could.'

'I don't think it works like that between female friends. Well, not at this age.'

'What, power play? Of course it does. It underpins everything.'

'I just think that's a really cynical way of seeing things.' Nathalie couldn't help the hard edge that had crept into her voice.

Macie shrugged her shoulders. 'That just shows that you've never been at the bottom of the power struggle between women.'

'What the hell would you know?' The words snapped out of her before she could stop them. Nathalie felt her face redden and her hands clenched into fists below the water.

Their eyes met and Nathalie was sure she saw a dark amusement playing in Macie's. Bloody hell, she was so sick of people making assumptions about her because of how she looked – like her life was somehow easy, or better. Surely Macie knew this more than anyone after she'd confided to her about Mike's affair. She just wanted to get away and join the others.

'I'm getting cold,' she said, her tone flat. She swam around Macie, the stones slippery under her feet. She found her daughters and gave their sun-warmed little bodies a cuddle, pushed their wet hair behind their ears. They ignored her, engrossed in an elaborate game that involved sand and sticks.

She looked back over her shoulder. Macie was floating on the surface of the water. She felt a surge of annoyance, as quick and strong as an underwater current. She shook the feeling from her body as she warmed herself with the towel. She sat with her back against a rock, feeling the heat absorb through her skin. She closed her eyes against the sun. She thought about the sunscreen Macie had mentioned. She didn't put it on.

She watched with half-closed eyes as Macie came out and squeezed the water from her hair. She picked her way across the rocks to the others. They all seemed to like her. They laughed at something she said. Maybe she was just overly sensitive, hormonal being away from Richie. She got up and poured herself another glass of champagne, then went back to the warmth of her rock.

CHAPTER 24

Alexandra

Dark clouds loomed at the lip of the escarpment and thunder grumbled through the valley. It had felt like 40 degrees by the river. Now it smelled like rain and cooling soil. The birds in the garden had grown silent, as though already hiding from the scent of the coming storm. The air felt taut, as though it could coil and snap at any moment. From the hotel's front porch Alexandra watched the children play on the trampoline, their swimmers dried and hair flat against their backs. Nostalgia washed over her, sweet and tinged slightly with sadness. The trampoline was one of those big old spring ones that every kid in the '80s grew up with. The kids were all spellbound by the fact that there was no safety net.

'What if we jump and fall off the sides?' Findlay had asked.

'Ah, well, you fall off the sides,' Alexandra had replied. 'You sprain your ankle or get a big bruise and you quickly learn how not to fall off.'

Jasper, the younger and more cautious of her two, blanched. 'But we don't know how. We like to bounce against the net on the sides.'

'Well, honey, you can't do that here, can you?'

The kids had looked back at her with wide eyes. She rolled hers.

'You'll be fine. You just have to be a bit more careful than usual. No more than two people on the trampoline at a time, okay?'

Thomas, being physically the biggest of all the children, was the first to try out this strange new and dangerous breed of jumping device. Of course, of all the kids, Jasper had been the one to jump too close to the edge. His high cry had snapped her neck up from the magazine she'd been flicking through.

'My leg,' he cried, his little face scrunched in agony. Alexandra had picked him up and checked the leg that had slipped into the gap between the springs. She gave it a quick rub. He winced and pulled it away.

'It's fine. You just got a shock. This used to happen to us all the time.'

Jasper wailed.

'Come on, you're overreacting, mate. Dust yourself off and get back on the horse.'

'It hurts.' He flung his arms around her neck.

She extricated herself and held him firmly by the shoulders. 'Come on. You're a big boy now. Stop crying.'

His wails reached a new intensity. 'Your leg is fine, Jasper,' she snapped.

He went quiet suddenly. She looked into his eyes, watery with tears and hurt, and felt a rub of doubt. Guilt. God, was she doing what Maxwell did to him? Squashing his emotions down? Telling him to harden up? Her throat ached with repressed emotion and she softened, pulling him into a hug and rubbing his back until he calmed down. *You're a bully*. The thought came at her unbidden and she bit back the tears that threatened.

God, what the hell was wrong with her? Snapping at her kids. Crying. At least she wasn't the only one acting off-kilter. Nathalie seemed distracted and distant, Pen seemed on edge, while only Emmie and Macie seemed to be on an even keel. Perhaps it hadn't been a good idea to come away with acquaintances on a whim, on the draw of a ticket. Or maybe if they'd been in the luxury home at the ocean, things would have been simpler. Still, she thought about what she'd be doing right now at home. Probably half-heartedly making dinner while aimlessly scrolling social media, for what, she didn't know, and trying to get Maxwell to tell her if he'd be home to eat. It felt good to be away from her life. Even if this place seemed to be bringing up all sorts of feelings.

She took a last sip of her cold tea. She needed a wine. Emmie and Pen had gone for a walk over the bridge, and Nathalie was taking a nap. She wasn't sure where Macie was.

Now Seraphine was acting as the trampoline gatekeeper, making sure no one broke the two-at-a-time rule. She was a mini Emmie. The kids would be fine for a moment.

'Seraphine, you're doing a great job making sure it's two at a time. I'll be back in a minute,' she called. Seraphine waved. Emmie had really lucked out there. She was a great kid.

Alexandra padded through the dark entrance hall, the tiles cool on her bare feet. This place was pretty amazing. She stopped to admire a beautiful lamp, the base shaped into the body of a writhing mermaid. There was a bookcase filled with old tomes, the gold lettering on the spines shining in the dim lamplight. A framed photograph taken outside the hotel long ago. Faces from the past stared down at her from their sepia tomb. Being in the empty hall alone made her think of when she was a child, in her dark bedroom at night. She fought the urge to look behind her, to stare into the dark corners. She pushed the glass swinging door into the dining room and headed into the industrial kitchen in search of the fridge. Caleb and Nathalie were at one of the long metal benches. He was chopping vegetables and she was sitting on the bench cradling a glass of wine.

'Oh, hi,' Alexandra said.

Nathalie startled. 'Hi.'

'I see you've beaten me to the wine.' *No surprises there.*

Nathalie held up a bottle of rosé. 'Here, I'll get you a glass.' She went to a cupboard and took one out. 'I just came down here to try to find some Panadol, and Caleb ended up finding me wine as well. Apparently, the combination works.'

I'm sure he did, thought Alexandra, taking the glass of wine from Nathalie and clinking cheers. Her friend could be so naïve sometimes.

'Caleb was saying there's a big storm forecast.'

'I was just watching the clouds come across,' Alexandra said.

'We get some pretty spectacular storms after really hot weather. The thunder echoes off the valley walls. It's pretty intense,' said Caleb, looking up from his vegetable chopping.

'Oh, and we know how much the kids love storms,' Alexandra said. 'Last night it was ghosts, tonight it's going to be thunder and they're already freaked out about a trampoline without a safety net. I'm going to need this to get through tonight.' She topped up her glass. 'I guess it's probably good for them to be exposed to all this drama. They're so used to having everything so vanilla in their suburban lives. So, are you a city boy or did you grow up in the country, Caleb?'

Caleb stopped chopping the carrots for a moment and then continued. 'I, ah, yeah, I've never lived in a big city.'

'You grow up near here?'

'Yeah.' He slid the carrots into a pot.

Alexandra stopped herself from prying further. It was like pulling teeth trying to make conversation with this guy. He really needed to get out more. She changed tack. 'What are you cooking?'

'It's a lamb and vegetable stew. I'm keeping the food pretty simple for the kids.'

'But he's made the stock from scratch and there's also homemade choc-mint ice cream for the kids' dessert, and roast duck and a pear and almond flan for us,' Nathalie said.

'Wow. I had no idea we were going to have a gourmet chef on site.'

'Well, there has to be some kind of incentive to come all the way out here,' said Caleb. 'We kind of market it like a bit of a foodie tour. There are some wineries just outside the valley and a dairy farmer and cheesemaker where we source a lot of our cheese and milk. People like to visit those things.'

'Are you a self-taught cook Caleb, or did you study it?'

'He's self-taught,' said Nathalie, who was obviously better at getting information out of Caleb.

Caleb shrugged. 'Well, Macie's a pretty good cook. She taught me all the basics and I improvised and found good recipes. Kind of took me under her wing,' he said.

Alexandra was about to ask how long he'd been working here when she heard the high sound of the kids' voices float through the house. She pushed open the door to the dining room and found them all standing there, their little faces flushed.

'We can't find Sim, we were playing hide-and-seek and ...' Seraphine burst into tears. Alexandra crouched down and hugged her.

'It's okay. Slow down. Tell me what happened. Thomas, Jasper?'

Thomas looked sulky. 'We were playing hide-and-seek, and we thought she was under the trampoline or in our cubbyhouse place in the bushes, but we can't find her.'

'And it's raining, Mummy. She'll be all wet,' said Jasper, his little face stricken. She hugged him too.

'Sim's missing,' said Will, as Nathalie came into the dining room behind her.

Findlay ran to her mother and buried her face in her dress. 'What happened, sweetheart?' Nathalie crouched beside her daughter.

'We were just playing hide-and-seek,' said Findlay, her voice muffled in Nathalie's neck. 'What if the ghost got her, Mummy?'

The mothers exchanged a look. 'It's okay, I'm sure she's not far. Let's go and look for her,' Nathalie suggested. 'She's probably somewhere really obvious and she's so stubborn that she doesn't even care that it's raining. She just wants to win.'

'Yeah, that does sound like her,' said Findlay, brightening.

They all went through the foyer and out onto the hotel porch to find fat droplets of rain falling and heavy, dark clouds above. Alexandra felt a twinge of anxiety as the rain intensified and a crack of distant lightning lanced the warm air.

'I'll get Caleb to come out here with the kids while we look,' said Alexandra. 'Pen and Emmie must be getting soaked on their walk.'

She could see Nathalie was anxious too as they set off into the downpour, calling Sim's name.

'Where were they last?' Nathalie asked, her hair already plastered to her head.

'They were over at the trampoline. I only left them for ten minutes,' said Alexandra, feeling both guilty and defensive at once.

'I'll check there and over by the horse. She loves that horse. Maybe you go closer to the hotel.'

An earthy smell rose from the ground as the rain released its heat. Alexandra moved through the gardens surrounding the house. Her top was stuck to her body, but she wasn't cold. She looked behind statues and urns, sure she was going to find Sim hiding there. Pen and Emmie joined the search, wet through after their walk. They scanned the fence line of the property, and the exterior of the hotel.

They were forced onto the hotel's porch when lightning lit the sky and thunder growled along the valley walls. Black clouds were closing in around them, bruising the afternoon light. By now, Alexandra was cold, Nathalie looked pale and Seraphine was crying again.

Emmie comforted her. 'It's okay, chook. We're going to have a look inside now.'

'Where's Macie?' Alexandra asked, her breath tight in her chest. 'She might have some ideas. It's getting pretty dark.'

'She went to pick up some more wine and supplies in the nearest town,' Caleb said. 'Would have thought she'd be back by now, but it gets pretty muddy in a downpour like this because the road's unsealed. Hope she's not bogged.'

'Okay, I'm going to stay with the kids because Sera's so upset. Maybe we'll all play Uno in the lounge room,' Emmie said. 'Light a fire. That sounds nice, doesn't it? Caleb do we have any marshmallows we could toast?'

She shepherded the kids into the lounge room, which was dark and cold. Alexandra wished suddenly they were anywhere but here in this bleak old house, with a storm upon them.

'The rooms aren't locked, so you can just go in. Check the bathrooms too,' Caleb said, heading to the kitchen to find snacks.

They split up, Pen and Alexandra taking the top level. They searched the long halls, walls lined with framed artworks. It felt strange opening each door, as though she were somehow intruding upon imaginary guests. Each room had a similar layout and had been decorated just like theirs, with lovely vintage furniture. A gorgeous timber dresser here, a mirrored vanity table there. And everywhere Macie's unique touches – a beaded scarf draped over a chair, a little vase full of dried flowers. Alexandra wondered if anyone actually used these rooms and why you'd bother to decorate them all given so few people visited. Perhaps there were times the hotel was completely full. She just couldn't imagine it. There was an abandoned air to all these beautiful empty rooms, ready for guests who would never come.

CHAPTER 25

Nathalie

Bright ribbons of light illuminated the dark hallway as lightning cracked outside. Nathalie's breath caught in her throat with each new strike and her head pounded. She was trembling. Her wet clothes stuck to her body, but she didn't feel cold, she felt numb. Her poor baby would be terrified. Sim's tear-stained face at the breakfast table returned to her – she'd been genuinely scared of this place, and now this. Eyes from paintings on the walls stared down at her as she looked behind furniture and called Sim's name. The only reply was the lashing rain on the windowpanes. Nathalie's heart squeezed and she wrapped her arms around herself, willing herself to stay calm.

She checked each door off the hallway. Some held bedrooms, much like her own, but these rooms were darker, colder than the upstairs bedrooms. The smell of mould mingled with a sharper scent of furniture polish. She came to the end of the hall and noticed a slice of light. The door on the left was ajar. She pushed it open. Inside was an office, lit by a small ornate lamp on a heavy oak desk that took up much of the room.

'Hello?' she called.

The wall behind the desk was covered with photographs. She moved closer in the dimness. They were all of a boy, a toddler. He was sitting in a little sailor's suit in the sunshine. On the front porch of the hotel, in the sand at the beach.

She started at a movement under the desk and bent down, her blood rushing in her ears. Relief crashed through her as she crawled under the desk and pulled Sim into her arms. She was wet and her hair was stuck to her face. Nathalie couldn't tell if it was wet with tears or rain.

'Oh, my baby,' she said, wrapping Sim in her arms. 'What are you doing under here? Mummy was so worried.'

Sim's bony little body was icy. 'I was hiding. We were playing.'

'But the others were all hiding outside.'

'There was thunder and I was scared so I came inside and went all the way to the end of the hall so no one would find me. And the thunder couldn't find me.'

Nathalie laughed, wiping tears of relief from her cheeks. 'Well, no one did find you.'

'Did I win?'

'Yep, you definitely won.' Nathalie kissed her hair.

'Mummy, why are there so many pictures of that boy?' she asked as they crawled out from under the desk.

'I don't know, honey. Sometimes parents like to put up pictures of our kids. Like I have one of all our family on my desk at home.'

'But there are lots,' Sim said. She was shaking with cold now.

'Yes, there are a lot. Someone must love him very much,' Nathalie said, taking in the photos. Were they of Macie's son? She'd said that her ex had custody of him. But this looked more like a shrine. Maybe she didn't get to see him anymore. Compassion moved through her. She'd felt unnerved by Macie's strange behaviour at the river this afternoon, pretending that she hadn't put her to bed and Nathalie hadn't spilled her darkest secrets, but maybe Macie had secrets of her own.

Caleb appeared at the door. 'Oh, you're in here,' he said, shock colouring his voice.

'I found her,' Nathalie said. 'Under the desk.'

Caleb came and squatted beside them. He smelled like damp earth and smouldering wood. 'You gave us all quite a scare,' he said, smiling at Sim. 'How did you even get in here?'

'I could see light shining and I wanted to hide from the scary thunder,' said Sim, pointing to the door.

'That's strange. This door is usually locked. It's Macie's office. Not even I have a key.'

'Who's the little boy?' Nathalie asked, indicating to the photos.

'Can you please not mention this room to the others. Macie is very private about it. I'm not supposed to let guests in here. It's supposed to be locked.'

'Is that her son?'

'Please don't tell the others.'

Nathalie scanned Caleb's face. His dark eyes were worried. 'It's okay, I won't tell them. Sim, we won't tell anyone about the room with the photos of the little boy, okay? I think it will make Macie sad. You understand? And we don't want to make someone sad.'

Sim nodded. 'This is a sad room,' she said, sticking her bottom lip out.

Nathalie's skin tingled at her daughter's words. Nathalie's eyes met Caleb's and she reached out and placed her hand over his. It was surprisingly warm. 'Caleb, is everything okay?'

He looked back at the door. 'We should get out of here.' He paused before removing his hand from hers. He stood and helped her up. 'Can I show you something later?'

Nathalie nodded. 'Of course.' She trusted Caleb. She sensed he needed something from her, but she had no idea what. He was a man of few words, but she liked that about him. She felt a connection there that she hadn't yet been able to properly articulate. But she knew now that she hadn't been imagining it.

She scooped Sim up and they left the room, closing the door behind them. A feeling of unease settled over her, as fine and invisible as dust. It was the same feeling she'd had driving into this valley, the same feeling she'd had at the ruins and in the river. It wasn't going away the longer they were here – it was getting stronger.

Jean
1948

She stood on the balcony overlooking the choppy blue water of Sydney Harbour. Her lungs and hair were full of the salty air and when she licked her lips, she could taste it. How had she survived so long without this feeling? Feeling free. Feeling alive. She watched the slow movement of the ferry as it crossed the heaving water. The gulls wheeled above a small fishing boat, the smell of fish on the breeze. And across the bay the city basked in the warm glow of early evening sunshine.

The housekeeper had directed them to their rooms in the guest wing of the magnificent home, explaining that Mr and Mrs Parker would see them for dinner in the dining hall shortly. Jean was glad of the brief repose to gather herself. Her heart was racing as she threw open the balcony doors to take in the air. Now she could feel the ocean calming her, steadying her.

She stepped over the landing and admired her room. She had never stayed in such a luxurious abode. Even at the height of her dancing, she had never experienced this level of opulence. The timber of her four-poster bed gleamed as though newly polished and the sheets were crisp and thick under her fingers. The lush pile was soft beneath her bare feet. From where she sat on the edge of the bed, she could still see the water. There was a knock on the door and Jean froze. She hoped it would not be Magnus. His presence electrified her, but she needed a break from the intensity, from the nerves. She opened the door to find a maid carrying a tray with a full silver tea service. The woman arranged the afternoon tea on a small table just inside the balcony doors.

If only Liv were here, she thought. Her daughter would have loved the fluffy still-warm scones with jam and cream. She would have picked up a cube of sugar and popped it into her mouth and smiled her beautiful, gap-toothed smile. The ache of missing her daughter thrummed below her sternum and she pressed her hand to her heart. She did not miss Robert. Poor Robert. He was such a simple man. She wondered if he had a depth that she'd failed as a wife to plumb, to find, or whether the depth just wasn't there. After so many years together, she knew the answer, deep inside her, but it didn't stop her from feeling bad. In some ways they were a good match. She like a balloon flying high, light and wafty, he a brick anchoring her to the ground.

She thanked the maid profusely and poured herself a cup of tea, savouring the fragrant brew, so different from the thick sludge they drank in the valley. She laid the blue dress on the bed. Again, the memories rose in her mind, again she pressed them down. There was no point dwelling on the past. But the future. Could she really have one with Magnus? Was that what this was? She knew he was wooing her, but how on earth could she ever enter this world again for more than just a moment? She imagined bringing Liv into this world. She longed to. Would there be a way to fuse Jean with Serpentine Rose? To live the life she truly desired? To escape the valley?

She sat down at the ornate dressing table. There were perfumes smelling of flowers mixed with exotic spices, face powder as fine as silk, a beautiful silver-backed hairbrush. She powdered her shiny skin, relishing the sweet smell of the make-up, dabbed perfume on her wrists and behind her ears. She slipped into the silk dress – it felt like slipping into water.

She was ready when she heard the tap on the door. Magnus was dressed in a fine black suit, with a bow tie at his neck, his dark hair slicked back, his skin glowing from the sun. She couldn't help the feeling stirring inside her. Desire. How long had it been since she'd desired a man? He offered her his arm and she took it.

'You look stunning,' he said, as they walked together down the carpeted hall lined with painting after beautiful painting.

'You look rather handsome yourself,' she said, allowing a glimmer into her eye, a frisson to pass between them. She used to be comfortable flirting with men. She used to instigate it. But that seemed like another lifetime. Another woman. This woman in the gown wasn't Serpentine, but she wasn't Jean either. Who was she? All she knew was that she was the woman who needed to be by the sea to feel alive.

Chandeliers were strung from the ceiling of the dining room and the centre table was laid with a feast, but nothing could compete with the view of the setting sun illuminating the Harbour Bridge from behind. A white-gloved waiter offered them a glass of champagne and they took it and made a toast to Sydney Harbour. A few other guests were standing by the doors opening onto the balcony, glasses in hands, breeze in their hair.

'Let me introduce you to my friends, our hosts,' Magnus said, steering Jean towards an older man with a pair of small spectacles on his nose and a stomach that spoke of a propensity for fine food and wine. But before Magnus could speak the man cried out.

'Ah, the exquisite Serpentine Rose! Is that really you?'

Jean's heartbeat accelerated and she felt sweat bead her brow. Surely this man had not recognised her after all these years.

She offered her hand, stealing a look at Magnus, whose face was dark with confusion. Her gut churned. She should have thought she might be recognised but she assumed she had changed. That the valley had robbed her of everything she used to be – her beauty, her spirit. And it had been so many years.

'May I present my friend, Miss Rose,' Magnus said, his voice steady, not betraying the confusion she'd just seen cross his face.

'Oh yes, we know who she is. I see time has not faded you. What a vision you are,' Mr Parker said. 'Welcome to my home. I trust Mrs Wembley has looked after you?' Despite her nerves and all the eyes she could feel sliding towards her, Jean felt herself slipping back into the game she used to play so adeptly, like pulling on a familiar piece of clothing you thought you'd grown out of and finding it still fitted. 'And you must be Mr Parker, thank you for your hospitality. What a beautiful home you have. This view!'

'Magnus, where on earth did you find this creature?'

Magnus smiled and nodded, again concealing any doubt. 'Miss Rose is the school ballet mistress in Glen Davis, west of the Blue Mountains, where my work takes me routinely.'

'Oh, you've come from the mining settlement. I imagine after being in that valley the water is a sight for sore eyes. What possessed the famous Serpentine Rose to go and live in the middle of the hot, unforgiving bush? And a woman is missing out there, no less? Goodness, the news is all over Sydney. One wonders what on earth could have befallen her. The harshness of the Australian bush, eh?'

Jean felt her skin flush, the redness creeping up her neck. She remembered Clara Black's face, luminous in the moonlight, so full of hope, her bare feet walking into the night. Guilt besieged her when she thought of that pillowcase stuffed with Clara's things and she tried to push the panic away.

'The valley is no place for an elegant woman, I can assure you,' said Magnus. 'We've just been reacquainting ourselves with civilisation and I think Miss Rose is finding it to her liking.'

Jean's face was burning, but she nodded. She wished she could step outside onto the balcony to feel the salt air on her skin. Instead she took a gulp of the cool champagne.

'Well, I certainly hope so. Because Sydney would be truly honoured to have you back. Now, tell me, have you danced since the incident at the State Theatre? Because I was in the audience at the performance and believe me when I say it was dramatic.'

Jean's heartbeat rose into her throat and sweat slid under the cloying silk of her dress. She wished she had never come to Sydney. Never met Magnus. Why had she snuck out of the house that night to see the hotel ball? If only she'd sat down and darned Robert's socks and read Liv another bedtime story, she'd be back there safe. Where she was meant to be. All her earlier bravado had abandoned her. How could she think this Mr Parker, who moved in the world she once had, wouldn't know about that last disastrous performance? Of course, he had been there.

A woman with soft grey hair and heavy pearl earrings that dragged at her earlobes took Jean's arm. 'Oh dear, I was there, too. We all felt for you, poor darling. Such a terrible fall. We all heard your ankle snap, I'm sure of it. We were all so shocked. We'd never seen a dancer take such a fall onstage.'

Jean swallowed down the dread, pushed back at the memories that threatened to flood her. The hot stage lights bearing down, the music swelling for her final act, leaving her behind, and she was immobilised on the ground, the pain gripping her leg, making her cry out, tears squeezing out of her eyes even as she urged them away.

So many months in hospital as her broken ankle healed. Some of the dancers had visited her, suitors had brought her flowers at the beginning, but she had watched her dreams fade like the wilt of those flowers in glass jars. They disappeared with the negative reviews in newspapers, with the loss of muscle tone in her body as she gained weight from being incapacitated for so long.

And when she went to live at her father's house, she knew everything was over. She was sad and fat and felt abandoned by everything and everyone. But there had been a man who'd been doing repair work on the house. Robert Peters was quietly spoken. Solid. He was deaf in one ear, which made him ineligible to go to war. It had also endeared him to her.

She'd always had a soft spot for vulnerability. He didn't care about her ruined reputation, or her thick middle, or the days she struggled to dress herself and get out of bed. He had sat with her in the tiny back garden in the sun as he ate his lunch. And when she'd become pregnant with Liv, Serpentine Rose and her glamorous life was finally laid to rest and her new life as Jean Peters had begun.

'None of that matters now,' Mr Parker said, shooting his wife a pointed look. 'People love a comeback. A triumph over adversity. And look at you now. There were rumours, I must admit, that you grew as big as a house. But look at you. More stunning than ever.'

Jean blushed deeply and waved away the attention, grateful to be guided by waiters to her place at an elaborate table, set with burning candles, fragrant blooms and rich food. She tried to enjoy the delicacies laid before her – roast lamb so succulent it fell off the bone, wine that tasted like cherries and spice, and fresh salads with exotic cheese and herbs. She felt she'd eaten more in this one day than she had in a month of rationing in the valley. She had to fight the instinct to wrap chunks of the soft bread in the thick serviettes to take back to Liv and Robert.

'This terrible business with Clara Black,' said Mrs Parker, leaning over to whisper in her ear. 'Tell me, are the other women in the valley nervous? Do you have any news I can pass on to my Sydney friends? A big mystery, isn't it? It's like something out of a novel.'

'Not really. No one knows anything. We're still hoping she'll be found of course,' said Jean, struggling to keep her voice level.

'A terrible business, her poor husband,' Mrs Parker said.

Jean caught Magnus's eye across the table. A shadow passed over his face. She had once been so adept at reading men like him, but now she felt overwhelmed, out of her depth. She wondered what he made of this gossip about her past. Of her spectacular fall from grace, from high society into ruin and oblivion. She felt like a fraud in her silk dress. She didn't know how long she could continue this ruse. She wondered how she had ever operated comfortably in this world. Why she had missed it so much. She wished suddenly that she was in her little house in the valley. The safe simplicity of it. The way the sun hit the back steps in the afternoon, where they would sit as Liv chatted about her school day, the light fading to gold on the escarpment.

As coffee and dessert were served, Mr Parker turned the conversation once more back to her dancing.

'So, I've been thinking during our meal and I have a little proposition for you, Miss Rose, if you'll hear me out. I own a picture palace on George Street and it's doing quite well but things are getting rather competitive. New cinemas opening all over the place. It seems all of Australia is in Hollywood's thrall. I wonder if you'd consider performing again, perhaps just a little routine accompanied by piano before the film begins. I just need something novel, an extra attraction. A beauty dancing before the show each night is just the ticket to get some extra patrons in. Of course, many will remember the famous Serpentine Rose. And we have plenty of room here at the house. You're welcome to stay right in the room you're in now. Magnus will have to fight off all the suitors, though.' He winked.

Her whole body tingled at Mr Parker's words and she pressed her cool hands to her hot cheeks. 'Oh my goodness, I'm so flattered, thank you, Mr Parker. Of course, I'd need to think about it,' she said, looking to Magnus. He pressed a smile onto his lips.

'Do think about it,' urged Mr Parker. 'It's such a waste to have a talent like yours squirrelled away at the end of the earth.'

She imagined living here on the water and catching the train into George Street every evening. Performing a little, making up new routines of her own design, the music, the dancing part of her everyday life. Being paid to do what she loved again. What she was born to do. And dropping casually into the Black and White Milk Bar where the lovely servers would know her name. Know Liv's name. Buying Liv one of the chocolate milkshakes and watching the delight on her face when she saw, when she tasted, a hamburger.

Now was the time to bring up Liv. That she had a daughter. She was in the position to bargain. Mr Parker wanted her. They could make money from what she could bring to the table. She was selling not only her dancing but her story. A triumph over adversity. She thought of Robert, dear Robert who had stuck by her through all her failures. Guilt closed over her, heavy, stifling. The words wouldn't form on her tongue. What Mr Parker was proposing was a figment, a dream girl. Who was she kidding? A mother did not fit the image of Serpentine Rose, she knew that. And how would Magnus feel to know she'd deceived him all along? That she was married and had a child. No, she couldn't tell him in this way, not publicly.

I will tell him later, she told herself, looking out onto the darkening water, the city lights reflected and shifting, like a mercurial dream.

CHAPTER 26

Emmie

Emmie snuggled into Seraphine's warm little body as lightning lit their room. The rain flicked at the windows like insistent fingers. The storm thundered and thrashed against the valley walls, but Sera didn't stir. Her daughter's lashes twitched; she was lost deep in her dreams.

Emmie had fallen into sleep easily. She had drunk too much red wine with dinner, they all had, full of relief that Sim had been found. But this wild storm felt like the brewing of something ancient inside her. She had never liked storms. And this valley flashed and roiled with it.

She prised herself from Sera's clasp and reached out for the comforting light of her iPhone. It was 3.13 am. She opened the screen and found the photo. The dread was still heavy inside her. She never should have posted the picture to Instagram in the first place. She had no idea things would go the way they had.

She had seen the likes and comments first. Hundreds of them. Her heart was beating fast and her mind raced. What was it about this picture? The kids were lined up in front of a crumbling façade in the mines. It was true, it was a nice shot because the children were all caught in motion, like birds mid-flight; not one of them looking at the camera. And the light was otherworldly, beautiful. And then she saw it. A face. Hollow-eyed and vague, but still, the shape of a human visage in the left-hand corner of the window at the top of the photo. She gasped and adrenaline spiked her system.

She was being so careful to post something where the kids were not overtly identified that she never saw it. It looked different the more you stared at it, like an optical illusion, shifting, oily. Was it just the reflection on the dirty glass of the window? She scrolled through the comments. Some people thought it was the face of a woman, others a child. Others had a scientific explanation about what could have caused light to refract in such a way. What everyone seemed to agree upon was that it was there. People had messaged her asking where the photo was taken so that they could research who the ghost might be. Thank God she'd never identified where they were staying and that where they were staying was so remote and little known.

She had ignored everything, all the questions and comments. Her immediate instinct had been to share the news with Pen, to tell the others that this photo had gone viral, but it had started raining and then she and Pen were running back over the bridge, soaking wet. Sim was missing and everyone was panicked, and then, when she was finally found, they were all numb with cold and relief. They'd crowded around the fire in the lounge to dry out and drink wine and hot cocoa, cowering against the elements raging outside. The kids had toasted marshmallows, and Caleb had brought them bowls of porridge with brown sugar and sliced cheese on long baguettes because he hadn't had a chance to finish cooking.

Mostly she had wanted to tell Nathalie. If she was honest, her friend with her photogenic face and easy grace was the star of the Instagram account. Emmie had never intended it to be this way. She was not inclined to take selfies alone, and Nathalie was just always there, with her way of lighting up the world. Some of the commenters had remarked that the ghostly face looked sad and beautiful 'like you'. Emmie knew the photo that people were referring to. A frame of Nathalie taken in the gardens on the first day they had arrived in the valley. She'd been standing under the willow tree drinking wine. Emmie had been taking photos of Macie's spectacular afternoon tea and one image had included Nathalie, leaning against the tree's trunk, a faraway look in her eye.

But what was she going to tell Nathalie? That it had all just been done on a whim and for the fun of it? That people had started to follow her and that she'd kept posting photos of them all, and followers had kept growing? And that now her ghost photo had gone viral, and people assumed the account belonged to the beautiful woman in many of the shots and she just hadn't corrected them? Maybe she would be flattered. Hadn't Nathalie said she'd wanted Emmie to help her set up an Instagram account, because she didn't know how?

Now she studied the ghostly face in her original picture. A woman? A child? She wasn't sure. Was this place haunted? She didn't believe in ghosts. If she'd been looking at this picture online, she would have thought it had been photoshopped. But what of the woman Will said he kept seeing? Seraphine stirred as thunder growled so deeply she felt it in her belly. Emmie drew her daughter to her and smoothed her hair, bright, even in the gloom. It wasn't ghostly spectres that were haunting her right now. Why had she made this whole thing so complicated by starting an Instagram account? Why hadn't she asked the others before posting photos of them? Why the hell was it now that things were just taking off for her? She had dreamt of weekends away with girlfriends like this. She had dreamt of this kind of exposure online. Now it was all happening, and her stupid Instagram posts threatened to upset everyone. Perhaps she should just delete it and pretend it never happened. Maybe they would never find out.

She went into her Instagram account now. There was no reception, so it was impossible to know where things stood. She was going to have to come clean in the morning. At the very least, everyone would probably be thoroughly spooked and go home. She'd ruined everything.

CHAPTER 27

Pen

Water beat hard against the window and Pen sat up in bed. Will was still sprawled out, fast asleep despite the loud thrum of rain. It was so gloomy that it was hard to tell if it was morning. Clouds hung like angry brows above the escarpment and dawn had peeled away the night to reveal a flat, watery, landscape. The world looked like a former version of itself, a sepia photograph, colourless, lost in time. Thunder in the distance was like old men grumbling to one another. The ominous mood matched her own. The thump in her head elicited a small groan. She'd had way too much wine last night. It had been so much more enjoyable without Macie there with her judgemental comments. She'd gone to stock up on provisions and got stuck in the storm. Was it awful to hope that she never came back? She looked over at Will. Macie had shown Will her studio behind the outhouses on the property and Will was totally into it. Pen wondered at how she'd missed this apparent overwhelming artistic flair her son had. She was a photographer. She was a creative. How had she not seen this potential for connection? She felt hurt and confused. And guilty. Yes, mostly guilty. Sure, she'd known he enjoyed art and was good at it but being out here and around Macie with her huge canvases and dozens of paint pots and tools had obviously inspired something in him. A pad of paper and a pen lay next to him on the floor. He'd been sketching God knows what until he fell asleep last night. She didn't dare look lest it was another ghost. *Bloody hell.* A stack of books sat beside his bed on the floor. She picked one up and thumbed through its tea-coloured pages. The valley's history. Why couldn't she be happy she had an inquisitive, intelligent child, rather than have these stirrings of dread?

Breakfast was later than usual, and everyone was subdued. The rain continued to sheet down the long windows in the dining room. The gutters gushed. The thunder had gone, the warring old men retired, replaced by a deluge. Macie was back, setting out another perfect breakfast of poached eggs with sourdough and telling them about her drama getting caught in the storm.

Thank God for the strong black coffee. Pen took a sip and enjoyed its burn in the back of her throat.

'I've never seen a storm in the valley like it,' Macie said, putting a fresh batch of toast and a new coffee pot on the table. 'The lightning was like a light show. I came in very late. The river was already high then, and Caleb's just been out there early this morning and it's broken the bank. If this continues, we'll be flooded in. Of course, there's a history of floods in the area. More than 30 when the township was here.

I'm afraid we're at the mercy of the elements for however long this rain keeps up,' she said, placing a tray of steaming eggs with hollandaise sauce in the centre of the table.

'Did you get a look at the forecast?' asked Pen. 'Is it expected to ease up?'

Macie shook her head. 'I had a look when I was in range and it looks like rain for days. How heavy that is, I don't know. God knows we need the rain, but this is something else. Thank goodness I got lots of supplies yesterday. Caleb should be able to ration things out a bit in case we're here for a while.'

Pen shared a look with Emmie, who was smearing marmalade onto her toast.

'Anyway, I've got some work to do this morning. You ladies let me know if you need anything else.'

'Thanks, Macie. The toast and jam is absolutely delicious, and I can't wait to try the eggs,' said Emmie.

It was true, breakfast looked amazing, but Pen's stomach was churning. She took a small bite of her toast. She couldn't bring herself to thank Macie.

'You're wet. Did you go outside?' Pen asked Emmie. She'd assumed her hair was wet from a shower, but now she noticed beads of moisture clinging to her cardigan.

Emmie laughed and brushed at her shoulders. 'Yeah, I didn't realise quite how hard it was raining. I had an umbrella, but I still got a little wet.'

'Where were you off to in this weather? I know we were talking about getting more exercise with all this rich food, but not in this downpour.'

Emmie flushed and she put down her toast. 'I think I just needed to get out of the hotel for a minute. Seraphine was playing Uno with Sim and Findlay in Nathalie's room. I was feeling, I don't know, a bit claustrophobic.'

Pen nodded and pressed a hand against her chest. She lowered her voice. 'Thank God. It's not just me.'

'The river was running very high early this morning. You do realise it's the only way out of here, over that bridge, and it's nearly flooded over.'

'You're doing wonders for my claustrophobia,' said Pen, draining her coffee.

'Sorry. I know. Let's talk about something different. Like what we're going to do today stuck inside with the kids.'

Pen laughed at her false brightness. 'Oh, I thought you were all inspired to be out here,' she said, elbowing Emmie. 'And you'd be the queen of crafting with the kids on rainy days.'

Emmie rolled her eyes. 'Yes, I must admit I do have some ideas.'

'Just as long as they don't involve Macie squirrelling Will off into her studio for hours.'

'Oh, has she been?'

Pen shrugged. 'I must just have PMS this week. Overthinking everything. You know what it's like.'

'Will does seem to be very good at art. You should let Macie show him some stuff. I think she's quite talented you know.'

'I know, I know. I'm overthinking everything.'

Emmie poured herself tea from the pot. 'Oh my God. Welcome to the party. I hate being a woman sometimes. Maybe I just need to make my special punch today. It has half a bottle of gin in it.'

'Where's the recipe? We all just need a little hair of the dog. Speaking of ...'

Alexandra sat down at the table next to Emmie and shook her head. 'I feel like complete crap today. How much wine did we even drink last night?'

'Too much,' said Emmie. 'Where's Nathalie?'

'She's gone with Caleb to check on the river situation. She tried to ring Mike on the landline this morning and couldn't reach him. I think she wants to see if she can get reception to text. Of course, she drank the most of any of us and looks fresh as a daisy this morning.'

'She didn't seem too fresh earlier when the girls were all playing in her room,' said Emmie. 'She and Caleb seem to be getting on very well, don't they?'

'She's been strangely quiet since Sim went missing. Even last night after all the wine. I hope she's okay. It must have been pretty distressing for her,' said Pen.

'I know,' said Alexandra, reaching for some toast. 'It's all been highly dramatic. I'm sorry I dragged us all out here. I honestly had no idea it was so ... remote.'

'Don't be silly, you were just trying to salvage our holiday. We were all desperate to get away,' said Pen. 'And we're certainly *away*. And the food has been excellent.'

'It's been an adventure,' said Emmie, reaching out and squeezing Alexandra's arm. 'And it's been really nice to get to know each other more.'

'I feel like we're *really* going to get to know each other if this rain keeps up,' Alexandra said. She put down the toast. 'I can't even stomach dry toast. But this lot are fed,' she indicated to the kids on the table next to them, most of whom had graduated to the floor. Jasper and Thomas were under the table launching toy cars along the floorboards and Sim and Findlay were on all fours meowing like cats. 'Soooo, what was the plan for a whole day indoors without any screens?'

'Punch,' Pen and Emmie said at the same time.

CHAPTER 28

Nathalie

'No reception,' said Nathalie, studying her phone as the rain spat at the car windscreen. The weather thrashed outside, as though the car was a boat being heaved and tipped in a sea storm. A sheet of nausea washed through her, and she fought the urge to crack open the window. She had such a strong need to check on Richie. What had happened with Sim yesterday and the storm last night had left her feeling emotional, bereft. She needed to know her little boy was okay. She couldn't actually believe she'd left him to come here. Mike wasn't picking up his mobile and she couldn't get hold of her mother-in-law either. He was so self-absorbed. She hadn't let her mind go there, but some small part of her worried that he might be seeing that woman. She felt the familiar resentment unfurl inside her like an animal wanting to be stroked.

'Didn't think there'd be any bars,' said Caleb. 'Yep, the river's flooded all right. There'll be no going over that bridge for the next 24 hours.'

'Really? There's no other way out?' she asked.

'The property's bounded by the river on either side. We'll go and have a look at the other end. That doesn't flood as easily. It's near where I wanted to show you anyhow.'

'Sorry, yeah, you mentioned yesterday you wanted to show me something.' Their eyes caught and something unspoken moved between them in the humid cabin. His eyes were dark and deep-set and looking into them felt like looking into a chasm where she couldn't see the bottom. It gave her vertigo. She looked away first. He put the car into reverse, the muscles in his forearm flexing. He was so confident talking about the valley's history, and yet there was a sensitivity, some vulnerability there that she couldn't quite put her finger on. When he'd asked her to come to see the river, her answer was pure instinct, like cold skin seeking out sunshine. She'd wanted to escape the house, even if just for a moment. She'd left the girls happy and in the care of Emmie. She'd sensed something quite desperate in him last night. After what she'd seen in that room, she needed to know what it was.

They drove in silence except for the pound of water on the SUV's roof. The hot, dry landscape had been turned lush and liquid. The smell of it seeped in. Sodden earth overlaid with the scent of freshly washed leaves – lemon, pine and eucalyptus. Caleb drove slowly over the muddy unsealed roads.

The river was running high on the other side of the property.

'We can still get over it,' said Caleb, as he eased the car through the shallow crossing, water surging around the tops of the tyres, almost reaching the body of the car.

'Will we be able to get over again on the way back?' asked Nathalie, looking behind her as they left the swollen river behind. Fear of being trapped away from her girls and exhilaration at this strange adventure mixed, making blood rush to her head. She laughed nervously.

'Should be fine. We're higher up. This part of the river doesn't tend to flood as readily. The place I wanted to show you is just up ahead.'

They turned off onto a narrow track that wound up into the bush. The road was bumpy and treacherous, and she had to hang on to the handle above her head.

Nathalie glanced at Caleb. The way he handled the car was self-assured, as though he knew these roads like the lines in his own skin. He was tanned from working outside on the land and he had a rugged air that contrasted with his intelligence. She'd always found contradictions alluring. His brow was slick with rain, his hair curlier than usual. It softened the angular features of his face, giving him a boyish look. He glanced at her with a flick of a smile.

'You okay there?'

She nodded, smiling despite her fast heartbeat. She couldn't deny that she was attracted to him. It felt like the same spell the rain had cast over the dry landscape – tumultuous, yet exciting.

'There are some amazing Aboriginal paintings around here. This is the home of the Wiradjuri nation and there are sacred sites still left. This cave painting I'm about to show you is one. You'll feel it. The art provides a physical and spiritual link to their culture, their stories. The more we learn about their history and culture, the more we learn about the truth, and the more we feel this country doesn't claim us, nor do we have ownership of it.'

'I know that feeling. I had it as I drove into the valley. I felt like an impostor.'

Caleb nodded. 'Exactly. We don't have enough reverence for the natural world.'

'It sounds like you're pretty passionate about this stuff.'

'I find history really fascinating, especially Black history. The fact that it isn't taught and is never truly shared in schools is really tragic. It's as if they've tried to make us forget. But this land ... this land doesn't forget,' he said, his eyes never leaving the wet road. 'It's why I started taking the tours of the mines, as an excuse to educate people on the Aboriginal culture of the area.'

'I for one had no idea any of this history existed, the Indigenous history, or the mines and the township.'

'I guess that's why I love it. It feels like exhuming secrets.'

She smiled. 'I love that.'

'It's also truth-telling. One history taught is whitewashed, to paint a victorious foundation, which also belittles and reduces the real harm done, while another half of history that is never truly taught, reflects the truth and real pain of how "Australia" was birthed.'

Caleb's words, the passion with which he spoke, touched Nathalie deeply and she wondered why it had taken this young man in this valley to make her reassess the truths about the country she had grown up in. They drove in silence for a while, lulled by the drum of rain.

He pulled off the track into a small clearing. It was still raining hard. 'Are we getting out?' Nathalie asked.

He reached into the back and handed her a waterproof jacket. 'Here, wear this. There's shelter not far from here.'

The rain drilled down and she ducked under the jacket's hood as they followed a narrow walking track into the bush. A knot of trepidation pulled through her. No one knew where they were. They walked for a few minutes until they came upon a sheer rock wall, soaring above them.

'Look here. You see these handprints? They're very old.'

Small hand imprints outlined in white paint, glided over a stretch of rock, like luminous moths.

'They're beautiful.'

'This is what I was telling you about. This part of the world is sacred.'

Nathalie felt a tremor, part awe, part fear, the same feeling she'd had as soon as she'd seen the walls of the valley rise around her for the first time.

Caleb motioned for her to follow him. They walked for what felt like quite a while and icy rain dripped down the back of her neck. Nathalie was about to ask where they were going when a wall of rock arched up into a huge open cave. It was like stepping into a cathedral, but one made of sandstone.

Suddenly the hammering rain was gone. She smelled wood fire and wet earth.

'Oh my God,' said Nathalie. 'What is this place? It's incredible.'

'It's amazing, isn't it?'

'You've obviously been here before.'

Nathalie walked deeper into the space, which was like a towering tunnel through the rock, fringed on either side with eucalypts and tree ferns. They had walked higher up than she'd realised because when she looked back through the entrance, she could see the wet treetops stretching out beyond the bracken. The space was big, probably the size of a tennis court. A metal fire pit sat at the heart of the cave, with two hammocks strung up like swings. A small wooden table with two chairs sat against the left wall. Candles pooled melted wax on the table alongside a bottle of red wine and a glass. A low, canvas bell tent crouched in a corner, strung with fairy lights, and surrounded by metal lanterns. It would be magical here at night. A small pile of what looked like camping supplies sat near the tent.

'You asked how I taught myself French. I lit a fire here and sat in my hammock for hours and, yes, I may have smoked some weed on occasion during all those conjugations.'

Nathalie laughed. 'You could do anything out here. How did you even find this place?'

'I know all the tracks. I've explored every nook and cranny of this valley.'

'This is so cool, Caleb. Does anyone else know it's here?'

He shrugged. 'Some bushwalkers might come across it from time to time. No one's ever stolen anything.'

'Your own private cave. It's like something out of a boy's own adventure book.'

'Yeah, it's pretty special, huh. I've thought about kitting it out a bit better and turning it into an Airbnb experience or something, but then I think, nah.'

'It's actually quite homely. And you've got your tent all kitted out and your table and chairs.'

'Something's got to keep me occupied out here.'

It was the first time he'd acknowledged that it was kind of unusual for a young guy to be living in the middle of nowhere.

'Does Macie know about it?'

Caleb shook his head and moved towards the fire pit. 'She's pretty busy with her art whenever she's out here. I'll light a fire so we can dry out a bit.'

'It's your man cave. I get it. God, I wish I had somewhere like this to go when I get sick of my kids. And my husband.'

'That happen a lot?' he asked, laughing softly.

Their eyes met. A warmth curled in her stomach.

Caleb went about setting up some newspaper and kindling and lighting the fire. He moved with a deftness that spoke of doing this a thousand times before. He was clearly so comfortable in nature and knowledgeable about history. His passion was infectious. It made him seem older than his years. He had taken off his rain jacket and his T-shirt was wet. She found herself staring at his body under the thin fabric. She flicked her eyes away as he looked up.

Nathalie took a tentative seat in one of the hammocks. 'I haven't been in one of these since I was a kid. How fun.' She warmed her hands by the fire. 'How often do you come out here? I can't imagine you get loads of visitors at the hotel.'

'Yeah, it comes in waves. You'd be surprised. Those bird watchers love it out here. I like to come and commune with nature sometimes after I've had a particularly busy week. A break from cooking. I make damper, fry sausages, read. It's just so beautiful. Nature's church. You should see the light in here first thing in the morning.'

The comment lingered in the air, loaded like the rain-heavy ferns outside. Her cheeks warmed.

'Would you like a tea?' He smiled and moved over to the table. 'Or something stronger to warm the cockles. There's a bottle of red here. Want some?'

She laughed. 'What time is it? 10 am?'

'You're on holidays, aren't you?'

Nathalie took a deep breath. The thought of a warming glass of red made her body tingle, that familiar pull. She felt adrenaline race through her. She was in a beautiful cave in the middle of a rainstorm with an intriguing man. 'Why not?'

He rinsed the glass with a bottle of water and poured the wine. 'We're going to have to share. That okay?'

There was that glint in his eye. That thing between them again.

'I can cope if you can.'

He took a sip and passed her the wine, taking a seat in the other hammock.

'Why two hammocks and only one glass?' she asked, enjoying the softness of the wine in her mouth, the growing warmth of the fire on her damp skin. She peeled off her own raincoat. She thought she felt his eyes glide over her.

'I string them together to make one huge one for when I really want to stretch out. Or maybe I was waiting to bring someone here.'

A long beat of silence echoed around them. Nathalie felt the meaning of his words shimmy through her like the bright sparks issuing from the fire. She took another sip of wine but didn't reply.

'I feel honoured,' she finally said and passed him back the glass, avoiding his eyes. 'This is going to sound weird, but I feel like we've known each other for more than only a couple of days. I have no idea why. Or why I'm even telling you this.' She laughed nervously.

Caleb stood and topped up the glass of wine. 'It's a pretty big deal for someone with agoraphobia to show someone else their safe space.'

'Agoraphobia?'

Caleb crouched down to stoke the fire. 'Yeah.'

'So, that's fear of open spaces or–?'

'Not really open spaces. I'm fine anywhere in the valley, and that's pretty open. And I love the bush. It's just leaving it that's hard.'

'Leaving the valley?'

'Yeah.'

'Can I ask what happens?'

'It's hard to describe. I've had panic attacks. It sounds stupid to say out loud.'

'No. It's not stupid. I had one of those myself, actually. Not that long ago. When I found out my husband cheated on me. It's horrible. It comes out of nowhere and your body betrays you.'

Caleb shot her a sympathetic look. 'That's it.'

'That's something no one else knows, by the way.' *Except Macie*, she thought. 'That my darling husband cheated on me.' She gave him a pointed look and took a large sip of wine. 'I self-medicate.' She shook her head. 'I can't even refuse wine in the morning.'

'Nor should you,' he said, his voice full of warmth.

She returned the emotion with a smile. A strange levity had come over her. Maybe it was the alcohol on an empty stomach but maybe it was telling Caleb what she just had. 'So, you come here. And you obviously enjoy your own company?'

He shrugged. 'Yeah, it's a lot easier than being around people. But that doesn't mean I don't crave … connection.'

'Is that what we're having here?' She laughed and so did he. She passed him the wine.

'Yep, think it might be.'

He had such a cheeky smile. It was so unexpected.

'You're trapped in a valley. I'm trapped in a marriage. That it?'

He shrugged and laughed. 'Doesn't sound unreasonable.'

'Let me analyse you. Young man. Incredibly smart, very good at everything he does — cooking, learning language, building fires, stringing hammocks from impossibly tall cave walls … but not so great around people and prefers his own company.'

He nodded. 'Accurate. Especially the smart bit.'

She laughed. 'And I can see a guitar over there. I'm guessing you play it incredibly well. And let me guess, self-taught also.'

His eyes flashed. 'Might be.'

'Oh, I've got you pinned.'

'Not quite, you forgot, "Likes older women."'

She felt her face colour and she pressed her hands to her hot cheeks. The red wine and the fire were loosening her body and her tongue. 'Oh, I just hadn't got to that bit yet.'

'Uh-huh. Okay, my turn.' He paused and she felt him studying her. It wasn't an unpleasant feeling but she squirmed nonetheless. 'You're sad. Anyone can see it, but you're so beautiful that it only adds to your allure. Like the *Lady of Shalott* painting in the hotel foyer. The beauty trapped in her tower who could only see the world through a reflection in a mirror. People ignore your pain. They focus on your outside. You feel invisible even though everyone is looking at you.'

A lump formed in her throat, tears pricking her eyes. She was quiet while she swallowed back her emotion. 'Okay, that's too much. I need more wine.'

'Sorry.' He looked at her with such emotion that she felt her body react to him. 'Too soon?'

Nathalie smiled and shook her head, avoided his gaze but desire tugged at her. 'No,' she whispered.

'I'm too intense for most people. Scare them off.' He paused. 'Especially women.'

She met his eye then. 'You don't scare me.'

He smiled and nodded, got up. 'Good.' He put more kindling on the fire and it crackled and hissed as the damp burned off. 'Thank you for not mentioning that stuff in the room to the others.'

'You mean the photos of the little boy? Are they Macie's son?'

Caleb nodded. 'I've never actually seen inside that room. I was wondering what was in there, actually. That's why I was freaking out a bit. I know she won't want anyone to know. God knows how Sim got in there. Macie must have left it open. She was in a hurry to get into town for supplies before the storm struck.'

'Are all those photos because she doesn't see her little boy anymore? Did she lose custody to the father?'

'I think she used to see him in Sydney. But she doesn't anymore. She doesn't like talking about it.'

Sympathy for Macie welled up. Maybe she was judging her too harshly. 'That's sad. That would drive any mother mad. Macie's a bit of an enigma though. I don't quite know how to take her. I can't get a read on her. How is it having her as your boss?'

Caleb didn't reply. He moved over to the guitar and picked it up, sat down cross-legged in front of the fire and started plucking out a tune.

'Yep, I was right. You're good,' said Nathalie, draining the glass and reclining in the hammock. The wine's warmth lulled her and she closed her eyes.

'Why, thank you.'

The music filled the small space, echoing around them, moving through her core. She felt as though she could stay here forever.

'She's in Sydney a lot. She just comes out here to do her art and check in on everything. She helps out with the bigger bookings.'

'So, you've got the run of this place, except for the occasional guest who wants a gourmet meal and a tour of the mines. It doesn't sound too bad.'

His fingers paused, the music stopping abruptly. 'So, I've pretty much told you my story, why I'm trapped here. Why do you stay?'

The impact of his question was like a slap. He'd seen right through her. It felt as though she was naked. How to explain the fear to someone like him? Of being alone with three kids. The judgement from others. The responsibility. The weight of it all. That she couldn't do it. She wasn't strong enough. She didn't respond. Instead she moved towards him and took the guitar from his hands. The wood was warm where he'd been holding it. She could see the power she had over him and it felt good. She sat down next to him, crossed her legs on a small cushion. She could feel the heat emanating from his body. She only knew one simple tune and she let her fingers move over the strings, free from her rational mind, pure muscle memory.

'I stay because where on earth would I go?'

CHAPTER 29

Emmie

The rain was a constant chorus, monsoonal now, and shrouding the cliffs in mist. The garden was lush, wet, its leaves shining like dark jewels in the downpour. It would have been the perfect day for reading, curled up by the fire in the lounge room, if not for the unease stretching through her.

Emmie picked up an old book and smoothed the dust from its cover. The pages were thin and yellowing with age and the faces of the past peered back at her. So many people had once lived in this valley. Families, children. The conditions were awful. She studied their eyes. These had been real people. It was so easy to look at these faces and believe that somehow your story, your life was immune from slipping between the pages of a book to be left on coffee tables in old houses and forgotten. A shiver ran through her and she drew a throw over her knees and took a sip of tea. The room's cold felt bone-deep, closing around her icy flesh despite the fire she'd lit in the grate. She switched on another lamp, but the corners of the room remained in shadow. What was she even looking for? There were several books about the history of the valley and its mine operation in the bookshelves and on the coffee table.

The words echoed through her head. *You do realise women have gone missing in that valley?*

There had been thousands of comments on her spectre in the window when she checked her phone this morning, heart pounding in the pouring rain. She had managed to find a few bars of reception standing perilously close to the roaring river.

She'd found lots of new comments and messages. Some were abusive, accusing her of photoshopping the photo. Others were from journalists requesting an interview. But some were from ghost hunters quizzing her about her location, which a history buff had figured out. Someone claiming to be a local historian had recognised the old mine and knew all about the history of the valley. *You do realise women have gone missing in Capertee Valley. One in the 1940s by the name of Clara Black (there is plenty of historical detail on this case) and another woman in the '90s, which is more speculation and local folklore, but equally unnerving.* A cold shiver had passed over her then, and it wasn't from the rain dripping down the back of her neck.

There had also been another message waiting for her.

Hi Days of Innocence,
We are loving your Instagram posts. They are so full of whimsy and something quite intangible — gorgeous but also dark. Your captions are beautifully poetic, and your photographs are stunning. That woman in the window. Wow. We'd be keen to have a chat about working together. We're a niche publishing brand always on the lookout for a fresh voice and perspective.
Thanks, Elsie
Beguilers Book Publishing

A publisher was interested in talking to her. Her heart was still swollen with hope. Damn the rain. She'd had no time to reply or to Google Clara Black and this second missing woman.

She could quiz Macie or Caleb more about the history of the valley, but then there might be questions and she'd have to tell everyone about the photo going viral. She didn't want to. With everything going on and now being trapped by the river, she couldn't bear to bring more drama to the table. This idyllic holiday with friends felt like it was sliding away from her, collapsing like the banks of the river. And now the publishing inquiry. She wasn't ready to take the account down if the others got upset with her.

She picked up a thin magazine. It looked as though it had been self-published. *A History of Australia's Last Shale Oil Town*. It opened with an overview of the township, all details that Caleb had explained on their tour of the mines. She scanned the names under the photos for a Clara Black. She wondered who this woman was. Lost in the haze of history and only now coming to light after a viral Instagram image. She scanned the faces of the women. They all wore hats and simple sun dresses, their hair in the same short, pin curl style. The men were dressed in overalls and the children all wore white bobby socks, the little girls with rag ribbons in their hair. She read some of the text.

> *Conditions in the valley were deplorable when the mines were first opened. Many families lived in makeshift tents while waiting for promised government housing. Conditions improved over the years and, eventually, there was a school, movie theatre, several churches, a post office, bank, pharmacy, newsagency and a cafe. At its height, 2500 people lived in the valley until it was closed in 1952, the last oil-shale operation in Australia until the 1990s.*

What would it have been like to live back then? Emmie thought. History was so easy to ignore, gloss over. But really, it was everything. It was perspective. It was all that made up where we were now. It was the progression of time that we chose so often to conveniently ignore.

Perhaps she could find out more about these missing women and write something for this publisher. It would tie perfectly into the spectre she'd gone viral with. She felt her head rush with excitement. If only she had internet access. Damn this rain. She heard the hotel's front doors open and the squeak of footsteps on the tiled entranceway. Nathalie and Caleb came into the lounge. They were laughing, their hair and faces wet.

'Oh, hi Emmie, you've got the best spot here by the fire. It's still teeming outside,' Nathalie said, breathless, moving towards the fireplace.

Emmie put down the magazine in her lap. 'Yep, escaped the crafting madness for a few moments. Just looking for some magazines for the kids to cut up.'

'Thanks so much for entertaining them. We've just done a lap of the whole property and the river's running high,' Nathalie said, rubbing her hands to warm them. 'We only just made it back across. It was pretty exhilarating. I felt like I was in a nature documentary with David Attenborough. Or David mixed with Bear Grylls.'

Caleb laughed and shook his head. 'Yep, by the looks of it there's going to be a lot of crafting going on,' he said taking Nathalie's jacket from her shoulder with a tenderness that didn't escape Emmie's attention. She wondered where they'd really been for the past two hours. No one else might have noticed but Emmie did. It was so clear that Caleb was smitten with Nathalie. She wondered if Nathalie would acknowledge it. There was an air of innocence about her, but really Emmie suspected she was much more knowing than she made out.

How would Nathalie react if Emmie's Instagram account was discovered? She had a lot of other stuff going on in her life. Perhaps she'd be fine with it. Emmie resolved to brave the deluge again shortly to see if she could get internet access and remove some of the photos she'd posted of Nathalie. Maybe she could also do a quick search on Clara Black.

Macie appeared. 'I thought I heard you two come in. We've been busy entertaining the kids while you've been gallivanting about in the rain.'

'More like getting drenched,' said Caleb, his eyes shifting between Macie and Nathalie.

'Well? What's the prognosis? How's the river looking?' Macie asked.

Caleb rubbed at the stubble on his jaw. 'Even the crossing at the far end of the property is pretty high. Unless the rain eases in the next few hours we won't be able to get out that end either. It's lucky you got more supplies yesterday.'

Macie turned to leave. 'Anyone want tea? Well, it's probably just as well no one can get in. I'd say we're going to be inundated very soon. It seems our little establishment has gone viral.'

Emmie's stomach dropped. Her eyes met Macie's.

'Really? Here? What kind of viral? Good viral?' asked Caleb.

'National news actually. A friend sent me an online paper that's covering it.'

'Covering what, exactly?' asked Caleb. 'The grass growing?'

'Nathalie, you've been very quiet. I daresay you're the culprit,' said Macie.

Nathalie looked bemused. 'What? Me? I don't know the first thing about technology, or going viral, or whatever.'

'The Days of Innocence. That's your Instagram account, isn't it?' Macie asked.

Nathalie's face was blank. 'I don't have an Instagram account.'

Macie's eyes met Emmie's and Emmie could hear her blood rushing in her ears. 'Well, one of you ladies does, but there are an awful lot of pictures of Nathalie on there. I just assumed it was hers. And all the kids. And the ghost.'

'Our kids? Ghost?' echoed Nathalie, confusion shadowing her face.

'Yes, a picture of the kids at the mines has gone viral thanks to what looks like a woman in one of the old buildings behind them. And people have quickly worked out about our little tour and the abandoned oil mine and … the only hotel in the valley.' Macie reached into her pant pocket and took out her phone. 'Here, I took a screenshot when I was in town. My friend sent me the article.'

Emmie knew she had to say something, but she couldn't. She was glued to the spot, her skin clammy. She bit the inside of her lip and tasted blood. She couldn't believe she'd done this to Nathalie. Why had she put so many pictures of her friend up there? The kids. Without asking. She wanted to run to her car and escape.

Caleb took Macie's phone and nodded. 'It does look a little like a ghost. It's a cool picture.'

'But not mine,' said Nathalie, her brows drawn together.

Macie flicked through the pictures on her phone. 'And this is a screenshot of the Instagram account the picture was on. You can see why I just assumed it was Nathalie's.'

Emmie felt as though all the blood in her body was boiling now. 'I can explain,' she said, her voice sounding small, pathetic. 'I took the photo.'

Nathalie was holding the screen close to her face and looked up. 'It does look like it's my account. It's all pictures of me.' Their eyes met and Emmie saw hurt in Nathalie's eyes. 'Really? You made this account?'

Emmie couldn't find her words.

'There are no photos of you. They're all me,' she said.

'There are some of me,' said Emmie, her skin crawling.

'Yeah, selfies with me,' said Nathalie, hugging her arms close, edging away from Emmie. 'It's just a bit weird,' she said, and Emmie felt the words slice her. *A bit weird, a bit strange, a bit lame.* They were words that were etched into her. All those names she'd been called at school. Always trying to fit in and she never did. And now here she thought she was finally part of something, only to find herself back where she began. On the outer.

'I'm sorry, I never meant–' she said, scrambling for a way to make it better, to make it right.

'Did you know about this? This viral photo?' Nathalie's arms were crossed in front of her, her face hard now.

Caleb was silent, his eyes trained on the fire.

'I saw that it had a lot of attention but ...'

'And you didn't tell anyone? You didn't think we might all like to know a photo of our kids was going viral?'

'I, I only just found out.'

'It sounds like it's been there for a while if newspapers are covering it.' There was an awful coldness in Nathalie's voice now.

'I think these things get picked up very quickly, things go viral fast now,' Emmie said, despising how defensive she sounded.

'Well, I guess it's quite flattering for a friend to make an account as a sort of shrine to your beauty,' said Macie.

'That's not what it is,' said Emmie. She felt annoyance buzz along her shoulders and she straightened.

'What is it then?' Nathalie asked, arms still crossed, eyes still cold.

'It's like, I don't know, a creative outlet.'

'At my expense.'

'Not at your expense. I honestly … I didn't mean for it to hurt you, I'm sorry. I didn't really think about what I was putting up, I just put up the best photos of our holiday.' Her voice sounded measly and pathetic and she hated herself for it.

'You have no idea what's gone on in my life. I don't want pictures of me splashed all over the internet without me knowing, like I'm some kind of attention-seeker.'

These words cut Emmie deep. She knew she wasn't that close to Nathalie; they'd only known each other a few months but it had felt like they had an unspoken connection since first meeting in the school hall. Their late-night McDonald's trip. Is that all Emmie was? A weird attention-seeker? Had she imagined their connection? 'I'll take it down,' she said, feeling tears spike her eyes, shame rushing through her.

Sim, Findlay and Seraphine came running into the room then. 'Alexandra and Pen said we had to ask if we could have more cake,' said Seraphine. 'Please Mummy?'

Emmie took a deep breath, grateful for a break in the tension. 'How much have you girls had?'

'Five pieces,' said Sim, holding up the fingers on her hands.

'Five pieces?' echoed Emmie, trying to find a laugh.

'She's fibbing. It was two,' said Findlay shaking her head at her sister. 'Silly. Don't say we've had *more*, say we've had *less*.'

Pen came in behind them. 'Truly, I think they've had enough cake. Kids inside all day with no screens on a sugar high is not what we need right now.'

Emmie felt cold mortification glide through her once again. The ghost. Pen was going to be triggered by the ghost in the picture. She hadn't even thought about that. Pen had confided in Emmie that she was already incredibly baffled and embarrassed by Will's random ghost comments freaking everyone out.

Macie's voice was loud behind her. 'So, it looks like Will was onto something after all, Pen. Here, let me introduce you to our resident ghost.'

Jean
1948

She had drunk far too much of the fragrant wine at dinner. It had been the only way to get through all the attention, all the eyes on her. She felt at once elated at the proposition Mr Parker had laid out for her, but also nervous at how Magnus would react to the evening's events. And now he took her arm and helped her ascend the stairs to their rooms. She wobbled and he steadied her.

His hand tightened its grip around her elbow, and she stifled the urge to cry out. His voice was a hot whisper in her ear. 'Was I the only fool in the room who had no idea about your dancing career or how it ended?' His eyes flashed with annoyance and something else that she couldn't read before he concealed it.

She felt her skin burn, and dread washed through her, the taste of bile rising in her throat. Yes, it was just as she'd expected, she had embarrassed him in front of his friends. She must placate him. Build up his ego again.

'I'm so sorry Magnus. I had no idea anyone would still remember. It was so long ago. I was in the papers for a while as the fat showgirl. Hilarious. I was totally humiliated by it all to be honest. I just wanted to forget.'

He smiled tightly. 'Well, don't make a habit of springing things on me like that. I can't be introducing you to my powerful friends without knowing these crucial details. It's humiliating and puts my reputation on the line.'

Doubt wormed deep inside her, but she pressed it down. She knew she must apologise, appease him. She knew this game. It was the game you agreed to play when you moved in this sphere. She had been here before. It was a body memory. 'I'm truly sorry Magnus, I really had no idea anyone would remember me.' She implored him with her eyes.

His face, the set of his jaw, softened. 'Well, it is all making a bit more sense now, why you were hiding in the valley teaching children. But that's just not necessary anymore. You can stop hiding now. You're beautiful and your place is clearly on the stage. I saw it as soon as you took to the dance floor at the hotel. You have that magic. People want to watch you, Serpentine Rose. And you're almost completely unaware of it, which makes it all the more charming.' His blue eyes bored into her, like the high sky on a hot day.

The way Magnus was looking at her made her want to surrender. It felt like a fight inside her heart and, right now, the chaste part of her was losing. Maybe this was what had drawn her to the hotel that night. Not just the lure of the music, but the lure of feeling something again, meaning something. Something more than someone to make food and wash clothing. Some magic. Some fire. His fingers brushed her cheek and desire blazed inside her. She'd had too much wine to resist when he ran his hands down her bare arms, traced her spine. She could feel herself dissolving.

He took her hand and led her into his room. The doors to the veranda were flung wide and the harbour was smooth in the moonlight, the breeze a soft whisper in the curtains. The night was dream-like, shadowy and warm, like the feeling of not wanting to wake. She pulled his body to her, hungry suddenly for his mouth, his skin, his warmth. She wanted to let go. She wanted to feel everything.

He tasted salty like the sea and his movements were fluid, assured. He had her naked, the dress a pool around her feet. As she stepped out of it, she could see the city glimmering in the distance, she could hear the water breathing below and she didn't care who saw her. His mouth was at her neck, closed over her breasts, kissing her belly, his tongue finding her pleasure. She cried out but it was drowned by the sounds of the breeze, the water. She felt the rush of it run through her, like foam around toes, like the arc of a wave just before it breaks. He took her with his face buried in her neck, hard, up against the wall until he broke into her.

She slid down the wall and he picked her up and carried her to the bed. They eased between the cool sheets and she couldn't help it. She thought of Robert. The wooden movements, the way he would roll on and off her. She had known pleasure before him, but never like this.

Magnus thumbed a strand of hair from her cheek. His arm tightened around her, pushing the air out of her chest. But she didn't resist. She took small, shallow breaths to compensate. 'Remember I'm the one who rediscovered you, Serpentine

Rose. Don't you forget that.' But his gaze was warm, tender and it pulled her in. She put her arms around him.

Her body relaxed, softened by pleasure, but the churn of her feelings was like a rip-tide dragging under the surface. There was so much she hadn't disclosed. She was living a lie. But it was so intoxicating, this dream. She didn't want to wake.

* * *

The day was hot and even the new hat Magnus had bought her couldn't fend off the relentless sun. She peeled off her gloves as they stepped out of his car. There wasn't much need for decorum where they were headed.

The boarding house was on a leafy street in the back of Mosman behind the main road. The worst house in the suburb, probably. It looked grottier than she remembered it. Perhaps it was the presence of Magnus beside her that made it so. She imagined him seeing the peeling white paint, the overgrown front lawn and the torn blanket hung at the front window. It had an air of abandonment; the only sign of life was a thin black cat that snaked around her ankles as they walked up the path. She'd implored Magnus to take a drink at the pub just up the road, but he'd insisted he wanted to meet her father. While it was a sweet gesture, the prospect made her wring her gloves as they walked.

Though she didn't want Magnus to come with her, she had no worry of her dad being confused about this man who wasn't Robert. Her father had not been sound of mind for years and she only imagined he'd be worse still now. The one time he'd met Liv he had mistaken her for Jean as a child. It was heartbreaking and confusing for Liv. And he'd called her Betty, which wasn't even her mother's name. Jean could only imagine it was some past love bubbling up in his poor confused mind. And as for Robert, he'd just simply ignored him altogether.

Jean knocked at the door and felt nerves crawl beneath her sweaty skin. She owed her father this, even if he may not even know she'd visited. Jean's mother had died of cancer when she was only just coming into womanhood and her poor father had had to raise her alone. But he did his best and he paid for her ballet classes. She knew dance had become her life because her real life, their real life, was sad, with an enormous mother-shaped hole at its heart.

A woman she didn't recognise opened the door. It may or may not have been the boarding house owner, who she recalled was named Molly. It had been so long.

'Hello. We're here to see Bill Fischer, please. I'm his daughter.' She hesitated a moment, aware of Magnus behind her. 'Miss Rose.'

The woman grunted and led them into the gloomy hall. It smelled of boiled vegetables and tobacco. She took them past several rooms, all of them dark despite the bright day outside. Jean felt tears prick behind her eyes. This was no life.

'He's in the lounge. He just sits and looks out the window. There's not even much to look at, poor bloke,' the woman said as they entered a bigger communal room. She saw him by the large window at the front of the house. The sight of his head, bald and vulnerable, his skinny shoulders, made her heart ache.

'Hasn't paid me in months and months, but I can hardly turn him away. He's no trouble, not really. Doesn't even eat much.'

'Oh, I'm awfully sorry. I've been away from Sydney. I thought he had enough from his pension.'

The woman shrugged and Magnus put a hand on Jean's arm, nodding. 'Here, let's let Miss Rose have some time with her father and I'll write you a cheque.'

'No, Magnus, you don't have to–'

The woman shot her a disgruntled look and Jean thanked him silently with her eyes.

She watched them leave the room and stood for a moment observing her father. Time had made him shrink and cower. His back was hunched in a way she hadn't remembered.

There was a seat next to him by the window and she sat down slowly, not wishing to startle him.

'Dad?'

He looked at her and she remembered those eyes in some deep, elemental way. A long-ago memory that would never fade. They were known eyes. She would never forget them for they were the same eyes she had looked into her whole life. They were still blue under the heavy folds of skin.

'Patty,' he said, and she pressed her hand to her mouth. Her mother's name. 'I thought you were dead.'

Jean shook her head and fought back tears. 'I just came for a visit.' She reached out and took his hand, the bones gnarly under his thin skin.

His eyes lit up and she laughed, feeling a tear slip down her face. 'I hope you're okay here,' she said.

'Jean and I are just fine.' He squeezed her hand. 'We miss you, Patty, but she's a strong girl. You'd be so proud of her. Her dancing. She has a gift. I wish you could see her onstage. Such a beauty, too. Like you. I miss your dear face, my Patty.'

Jean was silent. She held her father's hand, letting his words wash over her, like a caress. She brushed the tears from her cheeks. 'I miss you too, Dad,' she said. 'I'm sorry I haven't visited. I've been far away in a valley. We don't have any money to come visit.'

'Love is more important than money. Isn't that what we always used to say?' He nodded, smiling into the middle distance, his mind lost in his memories.

She looked towards the door, checking that Magnus hadn't returned. Her voice was a whisper. 'Dad, I don't know what to do. I miss my dancing so much. It's like it's my spirit. It's who I am. But I have a husband, and a daughter I adore. I have responsibilities. I'm not sure I can have both.'

He let go of her hand and pressed both palms to his ears. He began to rock and speak softly. 'I don't want to hear that she's dead. My Patty. The cancer took her. My poor Patty.'

'Oh Dad. I'm sorry for confusing you.' She patted his arm, trying to still his distress.

The woman entered with a tray of tea and a plate of biscuits. She set it down next to them on a small table.

'Your father will be looked after handsomely thanks to your friend,' she said. 'New clothes and bedding and better food. I'll make sure of it.'

Jean looked into the woman's eyes and believed her. She placed her hand on the woman's arm. 'Thank you.'

'It's not me you should be thanking, love.'

She looked up to see Magnus enter the room. She smiled and he returned it. Maybe she had underestimated his ability to be a good man. Maybe he was going to be the best thing that had ever happened to her.

CHAPTER 30

Pen

Pen studied the photo on the phone. There was a face in the window of the old building. It looked like a woman. It felt as though someone had traced her spine with a shard of glass.

'I don't want Will to see this,' she said, straightening her shoulders and handing back the phone. Thank goodness Nathalie had taken the kids into the dining room for more cake.

'He's tapped into something, that kid,' said Macie.

Pen pressed her mouth into a line. She wanted to scream at Macie to leave Will the hell alone and stop making him seem like even more of a freak. She could feel the muscles in her jaw working hard. 'It's probably a trick of the light. These things always are. Ridiculous it's got so much attention. I'm sure it's nothing.'

'People love their ghost stories. And don't you think it's a little fascinating that Will has been seeing a woman around the place and here is photographic evidence?' asked Macie.

Pen struggled to keep her voice even, to keep the bite out of it. 'Well, it's not really evidence, is it? It's just a grainy shadow in a photo. And as for Will, I really don't think he's some kind of ghost whisperer or something crazy like that. Ghosts ... what a load of rubbish.'

Macie raised her eyebrows. Pen felt like slapping her. She was so superior. God.

'Maybe if you showed him the picture it might build up his confidence a bit,' Macie said.

'How dare you,' said Pen, the vitriol running in her veins finding her voice. 'How dare you presume all these things about Will. I'm his mother,' she said. Immediately she regretted her words.

Macie squared her shoulders in subtle defiance but said nothing.

'I'm so sorry. I had no idea a simple picture of the kids ... what I thought was a simple picture of the kids would cause such a fuss,' said Emmie, inching closer to Pen.

Emmie had tears in her eyes. Pen wished Macie would leave them alone so she could have a proper conversation with Emmie. This woman did not take normal social cues. She'd just been chastised for God's sake.

'I should have asked for permission. I don't know, I just did it without thinking,' said Emmie, her eyes imploring Pen.

Pen sighed. She was pissed off the photo was out there, and that Will would probably see it, but she couldn't be angry with Emmie. 'It's not your fault. How were you to know there was a weird shadow and how did anyone even notice it there in the first place?'

'I have no idea. I just got such a shock when I checked on it and it had hundreds of likes and comments. I had to read them to see what they were about. And then the next time there were thousands.'

'And what were they about? Why is everyone making such a fuss about it anyway? I mean, yes, it does look like a face in the window but making the news? Is so little going on in the world?'

'Apparently people love a ghost mystery. There was a famous case of a woman going missing in the valley in the 1940s, Clara Black was her name, and so everyone's convinced it's this woman's ghost,' Emmie said.

'Sounds like fairy tales,' said Pen.

'Yes, the Clara Black story is well known,' said Macie. 'Poor woman was never seen again after disappearing from a lavish ball at the hotel in 1948. At the time people were probably more superstitious than they are now about the valley being haunted. The area has seen its share of atrocities, like the massacres Caleb mentioned. This valley has always been haunted by its past.'

'God, I don't want to hear anymore,' said Pen, pressing her hands to her cheeks. 'I don't want Will to hear a word of any of this.'

'No, of course not. I'm so sorry to have dredged all this up,' said Emmie.

'Shall I make us all some tea?' asked Macie, as though this would solve everything.

'Yes, please,' said Pen. Her words were clipped, rude even, but she didn't care. She just wanted Macie to leave them alone. When Macie had picked up the empty cups strewn around the lounge and left the room, Pen let out a sigh and turned to Emmie. 'I tell you, if it wasn't for this weather, we'd be out of here.'

Emmie gave her a look filled with remorse. 'I'm so sorry, Pen. I think it's time I made that punch for us all.'

CHAPTER 31

Nathalie

Everything felt warm and there was no tension in her body. She took another sip of the rich, fruity shiraz in her glass. From the kitchen she could see the kids through the serving hole, crowded around an old TV in the corner of the dining room. Macie had performed a miracle and produced the dusty old thing from somewhere, along with a DVD player and a stack of classic old fairy tales. *Snow White and the Seven Dwarfs*, *Peter Pan* and *Sleeping Beauty*, much to the children's – and adults' – delight. An entire day of being cooped up inside had started to take its toll. The squealing and yelling were getting a bit too much to bear.

Now they were watching cartoons, their little heads trained towards the small screen like starved saplings seeking sun. Outside the rain had stopped and night was creeping into the valley, like an animal shaking moisture from its back. The clouds were black and low, the edges tinged with yellow, like bruises, turning the air purple. There was an eerie silence outside and in, as though all the creatures were still in hiding from the storm. The children hadn't even fought over which movie to watch. They were all just relieved to be in front of a screen. Findlay was plaiting Sim's hair and Nathalie felt a rush of love. Why was it the simple moments — the flutter of their eyelids in sleep, the soft skin as they slipped their hands into yours — that triggered the strongest emotions? Sometimes Nathalie felt like the only time she could really feel properly was when she was drinking. But then it could also make her numb, which wasn't a bad thing either.

They'd already been drinking all day after Emmie concocted a strong alcoholic punch. She hadn't realised quite how strong it was until she noticed how tactile she was becoming with Caleb as he rolled pastry for a *tarte au chocolat* and stuffed chickens with garlic butter and thyme. Everyone had migrated there to help out. Alexandra was peeling potatoes, Pen was cutting vegetables, she was cutting herbs, and Emmie was in with the kids.

They had been avoiding each other since this morning. Nathalie poured herself another glass of wine and offered more to the others. They all declined, saying the punch had already had an effect. She could feel their eyes on her as she took a sip. Part of her didn't care. She felt so exposed already after Emmie's Instagram account. So, she needed wine. What mother of three didn't?

She wished she and Caleb were in that cave again, drinking wine, cocooned against the world, talking about whatever. He understood her. He didn't judge her. God, women were so much more judgemental than men.

She supposed she had probably overreacted a bit to Emmie's account. She should try to make amends by taking her some wine. She fetched a fresh glass out of the cupboard and filled it. She went into the dining room. Emmie was seated with Seraphine in her lap, her arms around her. Nathalie knew that feeling. When things weren't going well in life there was nothing like taking your child close to your body, smelling the sweetness of their hair, feeling the soft fullness of their skin. The comfort was almost instantaneous. It was a soothing drug.

Emmie looked up at her, her eyes slightly wary. Nathalie was about to offer her the wine when she felt herself tripping. She caught herself but stumbled and the red wine spilled out all over Emmie and Seraphine. The glass flew from her hands and smashed on the floorboards beside them. For a second her eyes met Emmie's and shock passed between them.

'Shit,' screamed Emmie, pulling Seraphine away from the broken glass and shaking wine from her wet arms. 'What the hell? Don't go near the glass, kids.'

'Oh my God, I'm so sorry,' said Nathalie, feeling her hands start to shake, the room start to spin. 'I tripped.'

'I can see that,' said Emmie, shaking her head.

'God, I don't know what happened.'

'Well, you're clearly very drunk, so there's that,' said Emmie, moving Sera and the other children away, her voice low and angry.

Nathalie tried to laugh it off, but her words felt slow in her mouth. 'I think we've all had a bit too much of your punch.'

'Yes, but there's a difference between being tipsy like the rest of us, and being wasted. You're wasted,' she hissed under her breath.

Nathalie felt words of response forming on her lips, but they were numb. Emmie was right. She was drunk. Very drunk. A rush of shame burned through her.

Emmie had settled the kids across the room and was now carefully picking up the shards of glass.

'I'll do that,' Nathalie said, bending down, feeling nausea rise through her, that familiar underwater slowness engulfing her.

'No, I'll do it,' said Emmie. 'God, are you going to be sick?'

Nathalie shook her head, pushing down the acid bile that had risen in her throat. 'No, I'm fine.'

'You're not fine, Nathalie. We can all see it.' Emmie's voice was a whisper, but it cut through Nathalie like a shout. Emmie paused, her hand above Nathalie's as though she was about to touch her, to comfort her. But then she turned away, her voice still quiet. 'You're drunk all the time. During the day. What about the girls?'

Nathalie felt her shame spike with a rush of something hotter. 'You're judging me? Really? After what you did? You're accusing me of being an alcoholic? Well, at least I'm not pretending to be someone else, at least I'm not some kind of stalker.' Even as she said it, she knew it sounded mean, absurd, but she couldn't stop herself. 'Maybe you should keep that Instagram account open. Alexandra said I could probably get loads of freebies, seeing as everyone thinks it's my account. Go on free holidays, free clothes. The whole bit. I should be thanking you.'

Emmie stopped picking up the glass from the carpet and looked her straight in the eye. She stood and took Nathalie's arm, dragging her into the hall. Nathalie felt like a child being reprimanded and she wrenched her arm free and stumbled backwards. 'Don't touch me,' she hissed.

'If you've got an issue with me, fine, but spare the kids the screaming,' said Emmie. 'And fine. Fine. Take it all. I'll give you the password. But it's not just your beauty that's made that account go viral. It's my writing as well. And just in case anyone's actually interested and can take their heads out of the sand for a second, there have been women who have gone missing in this valley. Massacres. Some weird stuff has gone down here. We've all felt it. It's like this place is haunted by women's voices. We can all feel it but I'm the only one who gives a damn. A publisher has contacted me and yes, I'm going to explore that and that means not taking the account down just because you think it's all about you. Not everything is about you, Nathalie.'

Nathalie was momentarily stunned by the force of Emmie's words. She was usually so softly, softly, such a people pleaser. For a second her opinion of her shifted, very slightly. She found herself lost for words.

'And also, while I'm being truthful, you clearly have a big problem with alcohol, Nathalie. No one's going to tell you because we all tiptoe around you, but bugger it. You clearly need help. You can't keep going like this. How do you even function for your kids? And yes fine, we all drink but not like you and, yes, we all want to look like you, but no one wants to be you. You're drowning and frankly, it's heartbreaking to watch.'

Nathalie recoiled as though she'd been slapped. She felt wetness in her palm and glanced down. It was blood. Her skin glimmered with a shard of glass embedded there. But she couldn't feel it. She couldn't feel anything. She had to get out of here.

She turned from Emmie and walked numbly, into the kitchen. 'Sorry, I spilled a glass of wine,' she said. 'We need paper towels. There's glass on the floor.'

She watched the other women swing into action. Macie, Alexandra, Pen. Grabbing napkins and tea towels, dustpans and brooms and rush into the dining room. Like normal people who could function and react properly to things in life. What was wrong with her? She realised how far from these other women she'd become. How? Only Caleb remained. He was by her side, holding her hand in his, wiping away the blood.

'You've got glass in your hand,' he said. 'It's gone in quite deep. Come on, we need to get the medical kit.'

She followed him out of the kitchen through the dining room where the women were cleaning up her mess and down the hall into a small office. No, it was a room. *His room*. It was sparse, almost monastic. A single bed, bedside table stacked with old books. Homer's *The Odyssey*, several *National Geographic* hardcovers, and *Magic and the Occult*. The small window looked out onto the less glamorous view of the crumbling back wall ringing the rear of the hotel. But above it the dark shoulders of the valley could still be seen. There was a vintage record player on a desk in the corner, with piles of vinyl. He must have seen her staring at it.

'I collect jazz and blues records.' He opened a cupboard and took out a medical kit from the top shelf. He took her hand so gently that she felt a tear slip down her face.

'Take me to the cave,' she said.

He looked up from her wound. In his eyes she saw concern mixed with desire. 'Can I fix this first?'

She knew he wouldn't refuse her. She knew he'd leave the dinner in the oven if she asked him to.

Her palm stung as he extracted the glass with tweezers. 'I used to want to be an ambo. Before I realised I couldn't leave this place.'

'You're very gentle,' she said.

'It looked like it was only a sliver, but it was big,' he said, holding it up to the light. 'Under the surface. You're lucky there wasn't more blood.'

'Am I a joke?' Her voice was tiny.

'What?'

'Is everybody laughing at me?'

He shook his head as he unravelled a bandage and began winding it around her hand. 'Do you think I care about the judgement of others? I don't know your friends and I don't want to. I only want to know you.'

She took his chin and raised his face to hers. 'I only want to know you, too.'

CHAPTER 32

Pen

She found him buried in the bedclothes, his little mouth wide open. Her heart ached. It had been a hard day. Outside the cliff faces were masked behind low cloud, white and ghostly. She thought she could hear the swollen river, encircling them, hissing like a snake. Pen cracked the window above her bed and the smell of wet earth and eucalyptus filled the room. She undressed and put on her pyjamas. As she eased into bed Will stirred.

'I need to go to the toilet.'

'Okay. Want me to come?' It was down the long dark hall.

'Can you just watch me walk down the hall?'

Pen's heart ached again. Kids always wanted you to watch. As though the knowledge of your presence was all that was needed to keep them safe. She realised with a jolt that she didn't actually want that to ever change. Perhaps it never did. Perhaps we always needed the safety that came with the knowledge that our parents were there, even when we were adults. 'Of course, bud.'

Will pulled the covers off and a small bound leather book slid onto the floor. He hurriedly picked it up and stuffed it under the bedclothes.

'What's that?' Pen asked, her pulse elevating very slightly. If only children knew how obvious they looked when they were being deceitful. It almost broke her, their lack of self-awareness.

'Nothing,' Will said, rearranging the bed covers and heading for the door.

'It's not nothing. Is it a book? Have you been reading it?'

'No. I'm busting,' he said, crossing his legs and scrunching up his face.

Pen's fingers found the book under the covers. Its leather cover was worn with age, like a face.

'What is this?' she asked.

'It's nothing. Just something I found, and Macie said I could read it.'

'Macie?' Pen tried to keep the high emotion out of her voice.

'Macie let me read the books in the lounge room. They're on the history of the valley.'

'You've been keeping it in your bed and reading it with a torch?' She found the torch deeper under the covers. She sat down on the bed and opened the pages carefully. The paper was thin and blotchy with age spots, like skin. It was filled with a beautiful cursive script. 'What is this? A diary? Why didn't you show this to me?'

'I thought you'd be mad,' Will said, concern etching shadows into his face. 'Mum, I think she wanted me to find this diary.' He pointed to the corner of the room. 'I was hiding behind the cupboard in hide-and-seek and there was some wobbly wood near my foot, and I pulled it and found it underneath. It's like a hidden treasure map.'

Pen stiffened and an involuntary shiver crept up her spine. 'Who wanted you to find it?' she asked, a surge of upset rising through her, constricting her throat.

'The lady.'

'Will.' The force and loudness of her voice had a physical impact on him. 'You have to stop this nonsense.' She felt guilt crush her as soon as the words left her mouth and she moved towards him.

Will stifled a sob. 'I knew you'd be mad. You never understand.' He covered his face with his hands and backed towards the door.

'There's nothing to understand.' Her voice was more controlled now. 'You're a child and I'm an adult and I'm telling you that none of this is real. I don't know why you get obsessed with these strange things. I'm at my wit's end with you, Will.'

'I hate you,' he screamed, his eyes flashing with anger. He opened the door and fled down the dark hall.

'Will,' she cried out, following him. She grabbed his little body in the dark. A switch flicked in the hall and the passageway was illuminated. They both blinked as their eyes adjusted.

Macie was standing there in her robe and slippers, a mug in her hand.

Pen wrapped her arms around Will, whose face was white with fright.

'Will, are you okay? I heard shouting,' said Macie, moving towards them.

Pen couldn't dampen down her feelings any longer. She stormed back into their room and picked up the diary.

'What the hell is this? How dare you give my son this. Just because you don't have your own son, doesn't mean you can commandeer others' children.' Macie's face was impassive, calm and it maddened Pen further.

'Will just asked me if he could take an old book that he found. He's been reading books on the history of the valley.'

Pen laughed darkly. 'It's a grown woman's diary. It's not something for a young boy to read.'

'Well, I didn't know any of that. I just know he's interested in history and loves books, which is to be encouraged.'

Pen shook her head and her arms tightened around her son. 'No, that's where you're wrong. Encouraging other people's children when you're a stranger is not normal, Macie. Stay away from Will and stay away from me.'

Macie's face registered emotion then. Sorrow filled her features. 'If you happened to take a look at your son right now, Pen, you'll see that he's wet himself.'

Shame enclosed her, gripping at her gut as she watched the wet patch spreading down Will's leg. *I am a terrible mother.*

'Maybe if you started to really see your son instead of criticising him, things would improve for you,' Macie said, wrapping her gown tighter around her waist and leaving them standing in the hall, the sound of Will's quiet sobs echoing in the dim light.

CHAPTER 33

Nathalie

The night glistened as they drove. The rain had gone now but the air was heavy with the moisture the earth could not absorb. It gathered in ghostly banks and drifted coldly past them like fingers. The bush was strangely quiet as though the mist had bewitched it. Nathalie could still feel the wine moving in her veins. They'd eaten dinner and she'd drunk more. Emmie wouldn't look at her. The red wine stain on the carpet bled like an open wound.

She knew she shouldn't be doing this. Running. Leaving her children asleep in their beds. But after what Emmie had said, it felt like an awful self-fulfilling prophecy. She was a bad mother. A drunk. It was true. This only proved it. She knew she and Caleb would have sex. She could feel it oozing out of her own pores, out of his. It was an intoxicating haze in the close cabin. Her sensuality had been switched back on after years of being too numb, too tired, to feel. Sleeping through life. Partly sleep deprivation, partly the wound of Mike's betrayal. What would it feel like to have another man inside her? To have this stranger pleasure her. She needed to know. She longed to be startled, to be woken.

Caleb stopped the truck. She looked into the trees, wet and illuminated by the headlights.

'We're here,' he said, cutting the engine.

She felt a flicker of something run over her skin. Were they here already? She didn't remember the trip being so fast last time. She pushed her hair back from her face and unbuckled her seatbelt. She could feel his eyes on her body. Her skin felt damp. Excitement mingled with something else, something older and more ancient.

'That was quick,' she said. 'Are we in the same place?'

'Yeah. Easier driving without the downpour and the river level held for us.'

He must have sensed her hesitation because he reached out for her. 'Here, how's that hand feeling?'

'Oh, it's fine,' she said, getting out of the car, the wine allowing her to push down her doubts and the throb of the wound.

A fine mist enveloped them. A torch beam criss-crossed the dark and she felt for his hand beside her and took it. He led her along the narrow track, wet branches brushing her bare arms and legs. Yes, they were at the cave, she remembered now.

Her heart was beating fast as she watched Caleb put down some cushions by a fledgling fire. She took a swig from the bottle of wine they'd brought and handed it to him. He motioned for her to sit. He'd lit lanterns and candles and their soft light cast long shadows up the cave walls. The air was dry and cool, and she felt goose bumps prick along her arms. He reached for her, his body warm. His skin smelled like fire and his lips tasted like wine. It was so strange kissing another. It had been so long. His tongue, his lips, not her husband's. So foreign, frightening yet freeing in their difference. She wondered what other women he had been with, so alone in this valley. His hand touched her neck, ran down her chest, between her breasts. She quivered with the shock of it.

'Are you cold?'

'A little,' she said.

He stood and pulled her into him. She felt protected, safe. He led her to the tent, crouching to let her enter first. Candlelight had created a warm cocoon inside. There was a low bed with a quilt. She sat down next to him. It smelled like smoke and dust, but she didn't care. She pulled off her top, unfastened her bra. The cool air made her gasp and then she gasped again at the warmth of his mouth covering her breasts. She felt her body let go then and all the rage – the hurt, the pain of Mike's betrayal filled her. Heat consumed her and she pulled at the rest of her clothes until she was naked. When she looked into Caleb's eyes, she felt beautiful.

She gave her body to this other man. She heard sounds come out of her mouth that did not sound like her own. This was different. There was no map. She felt him harden between her hands, felt the power of controlling his breath, which quickened at her touch. She let him worship her. Pleasure her. She wanted to take everything. She imagined she could see the fire flaring behind the white canvas walls, the flames licking high into the cold night. Beads of sweat turned to rivers on her skin. Their bodies were slippery with it. She braced for the moment he entered her, waiting for how he would feel.

For the difference. For the newness. He was harder, younger, better and she didn't care if that made her brutal. She was brutal. Her hunger for him was startling and it shocked her, as though her body was not her own. Her cries echoed around the cave walls, raw, shameless. She had left her babies for this. She was selfish, awful and she wanted to be punished for it. She wanted him to break her. To banish the numbness. But he didn't break her, he wouldn't. His tenderness brought tears to her eyes and she sensed that he needed her to dominate him, too. And so she did. She watched his face contort as he cried out, half man, half boy.

The only sound was the beat of Caleb's heart as she lay pressed against him. She felt light-headed. She didn't dare move. Didn't know if she could.

'You okay?' he asked, kissing the top of her head.

She nodded and gave him a small smile. She *was* okay. She had slept with a man who wasn't her husband and the world hadn't ended. They lay in comfortable silence, their eyes drawn to the fire smouldering, the flickering lights through the slit in the tent.

'I grew up in this valley, you know.'

Nathalie sat up, with some difficulty, pulling the covers over her and looked at him.

'Oh? I just sort of assumed you'd grown up in Lithgow, or a big local town and got work here.'

'No.' Caleb pulled on his underwear and his jeans and took a bag of tobacco out of his back pocket.

'So, what does that mean, Caleb?' There was a vulnerability in his voice. She could tell what he was telling her was imbued with importance.

'I guess you could say that I've never really been able to get away from this place.' He sat on the bed and rolled a cigarette while she dressed.

'That's full on.'

'Want some?' He passed her the cigarette.

'Nicotine is my weakness.' She caught his eye. 'Along with younger men and alcohol.'

'All things that are good for you.'

She laughed. 'That was pretty good for me.'

'I couldn't tell.'

She shook her head and kissed him. He tasted so good. She took the cigarette between her fingers and let the smoke enter her lungs slowly. Her head buzzed with the familiar rush of it. 'Are your parents still here? In the valley? I saw there were a few farmhouses dotted here and there when we first came in.'

'I never knew my mother. Never knew my dad, either.'

'Oh Caleb, I'm so sorry.' Suddenly, he seemed very young. She resisted the rush of guilt mixed with shame that came at her.

'It's okay, I don't like to talk about it. Being abandoned by your parents isn't generally something one likes to tell other people. Macie's been like a mother to me, really.'

'Macie?'

'No, she actually is. I don't talk about it much.'

Nathalie placed her hand on his arm. 'You can talk to me, you know.'

'I know, it's strange. I've never really wanted to dwell on all the stuff with my past but there's something about you that makes me want to tell you everything.'

She touched his face, the soft stubble of his beard. 'I feel it too. I've never been very good at showing myself to people.

I mean, the more vulnerable parts of me. I haven't been able to tell any of my friends about my husband's affair.'

He nodded and took her hand, kissed her fingers.

'Can I ask what happened to her? Your mum?'

He shrugged. 'Not much to tell. She left me here. Macie found me in the gardens of the hotel. They think maybe she was a drug addict from Lithgow who couldn't look after me anymore.'

'Oh, I'm so sorry Caleb. That's awful.'

'It's so shameful to even say out loud. That as a child even my own mother didn't want me.'

'What mother does that? Sorry, as a mother it's just difficult to imagine. Sure, we all think about running away from it all when they're driving us crazy, but to really leave them forever?'

'I don't know, but if it wasn't for Macie I'd probably have been dead.'

'How old were you?'

'Small. Too small to remember. A baby.'

'And what? Macie raised you? Here?'

'And Annabel, Macie's mother, until she died of cancer a few years back. She was very kind. Like a grandmother.'

'But who do you think she was? Your mother?'

Caleb shrugged. 'Someone who couldn't deal with having a kid. Someone selfish.'

'You've never tried to find her?'

Caleb let out a defeated laugh. 'She didn't want me. Why would she want to know who I am now?'

'You never know. Maybe she regrets it. It's very rare for a mother not to love her kid. I mean, it's ancient. It's the survival of our species.'

'She's probably dead.'

Caleb got up and left the tent and she pulled on her shoes and followed him. He bent to stoke the fire.

'I can see why you don't like talking about it. I'm sorry.' She put a hand on his shoulder.

'It's not exactly dinner party conversation. Not that I go to dinner parties. Well, I cook for them and I do meet people. Interesting people. Not your usual type.'

'So, where did you go to school?'

'Annabel home-schooled me. She used to be a teacher. Then I did high school and uni by correspondence. Essays written on my typewriter and posted to Sydney University. I still managed first-class honours in History, nailed Philosophy, too. Obviously all things I've needed living in the sticks.' He laughed and shook his head. 'They wanted me to be an academic, but I couldn't bear the thought of getting up in front of a lecture hall full of people. I've never much needed people. Especially people my own age. They always called me "gifted", but I always took that as another word for different. Strange. There was a while there when I just wanted to be normal, not a 16-year-old doing uni subjects and falling in love with his female literature lecturers.'

'Did you?'

'I might have done.' His eyes flashed.

'And did they ever happen to come for a road trip into a far-flung valley?'

'Macie was pretty protective like that. She would have sussed out if anything inappropriate was happening. When I was that young.'

Nathalie pursed her lips. 'I see. And what about now?'

'What?' He gestured between them. 'She knows I'm a grown man.'

Nathalie wanted to ask him if Macie felt like his mother. If he loved her like one. Why had Macie never mentioned that Caleb was like a son? Why had she spoken instead of the child whose picture was all over the walls of her study, but nowhere in her life? And how did Caleb feel about this disparity?

But she sensed it would be too much, too soon. Caleb had already opened up so much more than she'd thought him capable of. It had felt like they'd been in a silent confessional box and now the screen had been pulled across. She got up and stretched her legs, arranged herself in the hammock. She could feel the beginnings of a headache stretch across her skull as she began to sober up.

'Do you have tea?'

'Sure. Ever had billy tea?'

'No, but I have a feeling you're going to make it for me.' She hesitated. 'And then we should get back.' She was about to say she didn't want to be away from the girls too long but resisted. Caleb wasn't part of that world. He was an escape, a guilty pleasure. A madness. Perhaps this was what she needed to do to heal after what Mike had done to her. Perhaps it had been inevitable. Perhaps now they were even, her and Mike could continue on with their lives.

She watched as Caleb set about putting tea leaves and water into a tin can and placing it into the fire. There was something about the way he did small things. Roll a cigarette, spoon out tea leaves – it was deliberate, careful. It made him seem like he was from another era, a time when there was space to breathe. She thought about his record collections, his books, his lack of technology. His small monk-like bedroom. He was a person from another era.

'It's hot,' he said, handing her a tin cup.

She blew and took a sip. It was good. Sweetened. She drank too quickly, scalding her mouth.

'Don't you ever want to escape? I mean, go and live your life? Meet someone?' she asked.

She saw hurt flash over his face. 'I mean apart from a crazy mother of three whose life is falling apart.'

'You're perfect to me.' He said it with such earnestness that Nathalie's chest ached and he seemed young again. So young. He reached for her and she knew that if she didn't shut this down, they'd have sex again. She let him kiss her neck, her lips but she pushed him away gently.

'I'd like to, believe me. But I have to go back. In case the girls wake.'

He nodded and shifted his eyes away. He poured water on the fire and it hissed and crackled. 'We'll come back tomorrow then.'

She said nothing. She didn't know how to tell him what this was for her. A fling, an aberration, a ripple, a moment; something to think back on when she was back in her normal life. When she was being the mother she was meant to be.

CHAPTER 34

Alexandra

She'd slept late. Her eyes ached as they adjusted to the sunlight spilling over her bed. She sat up and looked out the window. The rain was a shadow of dark cloud in the distance as though the deluge had been merely a dream. A flock of sulphur-crested cockatoos rose from a bank of trees like a sudden sunrise, their screeches echoing across the cliff walls. The garden below looked new, dew-strung. She cracked the window open and smelled sweet jasmine. It smelled like summer again. She felt relief loosen a tightness in her chest and she stretched and stood up. The boys had woken at dawn and announced they were going downstairs to watch TV. She'd shooed them away and turned over. Sleep had come again, heavy like the smell of rain still in the air. Now she heard voices downstairs. Jasper rushed in and jumped on the bed.

'Mum, get up. We're hungry and the only cereal Macie has is cornflakes. We want Coco Pops. Can we go home now? It's sunny.'

'Thank God,' she said, feeling a lightness at the prospect of going home.

Jasper pulled at her sleeve. 'Pleeease Mum. I'm starving. I want Coco Pops.'

'We don't have Coco Pops,' she said, feeling frustration buzz through her. 'Just let me wake up. Off you go. I'll be down in a sec. Ask Macie for toast then.'

'She said she's busy.'

'Ask Caleb.'

'He's not there.'

Alexandra sighed. 'Ask Emmie.' Emmie was the only reliable one.

'She's looking for Pen.'

'Okay, well, watch cartoons for five minutes, I told you, I'm coming. I just have to get dressed.'

Her body felt stiff and heavy as she dressed. Too many days of eating and drinking too much. Everyone would want to go home. Between the Nathalie and Emmie tension and being stuck indoors, it was time. They'd been meant to stay another few days, but she doubted anyone would want to. God, what had she been thinking bringing everyone out here? She splashed her face with water and put on some tinted moisturiser, mascara, lipstick and ran a brush through her hair. Just because everything felt like it had fallen apart didn't mean she had to look like it had. She wondered if Maxwell had even noticed they were gone.

She heard a child crying as she walked down the stairs towards the dining room. Jasper was probably having a meltdown about the bloody Coco Pops.

Emmie was crouching with her arm around Will, who was sitting apart from the other kids at one of the dining tables.

'What's happened?' she asked, noticing Will's red-rimmed eyes.

He sniffed and wiped an arm across his face. Emmie handed him a tissue.

'Will's feeling a bit worried because Pen must've gone on a walk this morning but she's not back yet.'

Emmie gave her a pointed look, silently asking her to play along. Alexandra smiled reassuringly despite a knot of worry forming in her belly.

'Oh honey, it's okay, she'll be back. She's just stretching her legs. I was just thinking of doing the same thing. We've all been stuck inside for what's felt like days, haven't we, but the sun's out now.' She was using her most comforting, motherly voice.

'Here, have some water,' said Emmie, rubbing Will's back. He drank in large gulps. 'It's okay. It's been a bit of a funny time, hasn't it? But now that the sun's out, why don't we all go and feed the horse?'

Will swallowed hard, trying to get control of his emotions. 'I took her breakfast in bed.'

Alexandra pressed a hand to her heart and shared a look with Emmie. Kids were so incredible. One minute they were acting like crazy criminals and you were ready to throttle them, the next they were doing the sweetest thing for you.

'Mate, that's so lovely of you,' she said. Will was a bit different from the others but he was obviously just a sensitive little soul.

'It was only a cup of tea and cornflakes with not much milk. She was sad last night, and I wanted to make her happy.'

Emmie and Alexandra exchanged a look. 'I'm sure you did make her happy, Will. That's so grown-up of you to do that,'

Emmie said. 'Come on, I'll grab some apples for the horse, and we'll go for a wander. Come on kids, turn off that TV,' she called out to the others.

Alexandra handed Jasper an apple. 'Here. This is breakfast.'

'I'm not eating horse food,' he said, handing it to his brother.

'Come on, everyone up. Grab an apple for the horse from the fruit bowl,' said Emmie. 'Seraphine, TV off now.'

'But we're still in our jammies,' Sim said.

'Horses don't care about that,' said Emmie.

'Where do you think she is?' Alexandra whispered to Emmie as the kids started to stretch like lazy cats and slowly get up from the TV.

Emmie shook her head. 'I didn't see her this morning. I've texted her. Fat lot of good that'll do. Did a quick scout-around outside. She's probably doing the route I walked with her the other day. She's a runner. She's probably just gone further than she realised.'

'Have you seen Nathalie?' Alexandra asked as the kids made choosing horse apples into a serious competition.

'I want that one,' said Findlay, pointing to the apple in Jasper's hand, who ripped it away dramatically.

'The girls said she was still asleep,' Emmie said, her tone cooling.

'I'm going to go and get her up to help. It's nearly ten.'

Emmie made a noncommittal noise and wrestled an apple out of Seraphine's hand. 'Come on you guys, share. They're all the same apples.'

Alexandra alighted the stairs to Nathalie's room, which was a few doors down from her own. She found it empty.

She walked to the communal showers and pushed opened the heavy door. The sound of running water greeted her.

Alexandra stuck her head in. 'Are you in here, Nathalie?'

'Hi, yes,' Nathalie called back. 'I'll be out in a sec.'

'Okay. No rush.'

The shower switched off and moments later Nathalie emerged in a towel with wet hair. 'Is everything okay? Sorry, I overslept this morning and I knew the girls were watching TV.'

'Oh, don't worry, I've just got up myself. I felt about a million years old this morning. You haven't seen Pen, have you? Will's upset. He took her breakfast in bed, bless him, and now we're not sure where she is. Emmie thinks she's gone on a walk, or a run. The kids were watching cartoons while we were all sleeping. Great mums that we are.'

'I think we're all exhausted.'

'Yes, it's been an interesting few days,' said Alexandra, shooting her a wry smile.

'I'm sure Pen's just going for a walk or something. It was pretty full on being holed up here. She's probably needed to stretch her legs.'

'Exactly. Sorry, I'll let you get dressed. I just wanted to let you know we're all going over to feed the horse. Distract Will a bit. Get the kids into the sunshine.'

'Good idea.' Nathalie rubbed her hair with a towel.

'Are you okay? There's been a bit of tension between you and Emmie. The spilled wine last night. I feel partly responsible. I'm the one who dragged us all out here when we've really only got the kids in common.'

Nathalie's face twitched as though Alexandra had hit a nerve, but she smiled. 'Oh, don't feel bad. It's been a bit of a strange time but God, it's been better than being stuck at home with bored kids.'

'True.'

'Let me get dressed and I'll come over. I'm dying for coffee, too.'

'Okay,' said Alexandra, heading back down the hall.

Emmie had assembled the kids like some sort of Maria-miracle out of *The Sound of Music*. They were all carrying apples and carrots and had shoes on. 'Come on, let's go,' she said as she saw Alexandra.

They walked outside, Alexandra enjoying the warmth of the sunshine on her shoulders. The garden looked refreshed; the foliage thicker, greener. Lavender spilled from pots like long purple hair, scenting the air, and the grass licked the children's legs, seemingly having grown overnight. Even the cliff faces shone golden in the morning light, washed clean by the rain. The sky was an obnoxious shade of blue, as though the grey heaviness was a blanket that had been kicked off in the night.

Alexandra noticed Pen's car was still in the car park. She'd be back soon. They'd all dropped the parenting ball over the past few days. That was the beauty of going away with other mothers; you kind of knew everyone had one eye on the kids at all times and there was an intuitive picking up of any slack without having to even ask. So unlike life with Maxwell, who had to be asked and instructed on everything to do with the kids and then he didn't listen anyway. She realised that despite how imperfect this time away had been, going home held its own small stab of pain.

'Are you okay to take them? I'm just going to have a quick look in Pen's car,' said Alexandra.

Emmie nodded. 'Maybe we'll call her mobile again, too.'

Alexandra made her way over to where the cars were parked. She looked into the small Honda. She could see some camera equipment in the back and a pushbike helmet. She tried the door and it was locked.

Macie approached her wearing a chic straw hat and a linen dress. Her easy style made Alexandra acutely aware of her crushed clothing and lack of polish. It was unlike her to let these things go but somehow, she had. 'Emmie said Pen's gone on a long walk. Poor Will. I saw he was crying. Can I get anyone anything?'

'Strong coffee? No, you've done enough. Sorry, I feel like your hospitality has been extended way beyond what was expected.' Alexandra allowed herself a little exasperated laugh.

Macie made a waving motion. 'Hospitality is what I do. I love making people comfortable. I've got a cake in the oven for Will. He told me his favourite is banana.'

Alexandra shook her head. 'You didn't have to do that. You've been too good to us. Anyway, I think we'll get out of your hair today.'

'Oh no, you're not meant to be going yet. Stay one more night, at least. I've got more than enough supplies and Caleb hasn't even made his pièce de résistance. We'll have a big farewell dinner. Enjoy another day of sunshine.'

'Oh no, we couldn't. You've already done so much.'

'It's my pleasure. It's been so nice having the hotel full again. Like old times. I don't really want you all to go, if I'm honest.'

Alexandra shot Macie a warm smile. She came across a little aloof but really Macie was sensitive, Alexandra knew that more than anyone. She wanted to do more. Apologise for more. For all those years of awfulness. The bullying. Why couldn't they breach it? Talk about it? Get it out into the open? Why was it this nub that remained between them, rubbing raw under the surface like a blister? Instead she said: 'I'll talk to the others. See what the consensus is.'

'I'll set up some brunch over on the tables. They'll need a wipe down.'

'You don't have to do that, either.'

'No, it's fine. I've got the cake and some scones in the oven. I'll just cut up some fresh fruit. None of you mums have had breakfast yet. And coffee.'

Alexandra found herself giving Macie's arm a squeeze. 'Thank you.'

For a moment their eyes met, and Alexandra felt herself hover over everything unsaid, untouched, like a cloud over a sheer cliff wall.

She broke away with a quick smile. She could feel Macie's eyes on her as she headed over to the horse paddock. The kids were completely overwhelming the poor animals.

'Mum, there's another horse. We don't even know where it came from. There was only one before,' said Thomas, eyes wide.

'Two horses, wow,' said Alexandra. 'Maybe feed them one at a time. Thomas – be gentle!'

'Can we go on the trampoline now?' asked Seraphine.

Like a school of fish distracted by a bigger meal, their little bodies moved as one towards the trampoline, the horses forgotten.

'One at a time jumping,' Emmie called after them. 'The last thing we need is a sprained ankle.'

Alexandra waved to Nathalie who was approaching wearing a sun dress, her hair still damp.

'I might go and walk the route I did with Pen. Are you okay to keep an eye on the kids?' asked Emmie, watching Nathalie's approach and clearly keen to avoid her.

'Good idea. Yep, we'll keep them outside for as long as possible. Macie was going to bring out some morning tea.'

'Okay, great.' Emmie headed off towards the gate.

'Still no Pen?' asked Nathalie. 'And I can see Emmie doesn't want to be around me.'

'Oh, she's just going to walk the route she did with Pen the other day.'

'Uh-huh,' said Nathalie, biting her lip.

They walked over to the trampoline to find Seraphine in tears.

'Oh God, what now?' asked Alexandra under her breath. 'You okay, honey? Are you not all sharing and taking turns?'

Seraphine wiped her face on her nightie top. 'Will told me his mum has disappeared and isn't coming back. And now my mum has gone, too.'

Alexandra shook her head. 'Oh sweetheart, it's all okay. Pen has just gone for a walk and Will's just feeling a bit worried. Your mum's just gone to meet her. No one is not coming back. Everyone will be back.'

'My boys wouldn't even notice if I'd been gone 48 hours,' Alexandra said under her breath to Nathalie.

'Yeah, same with my girls,' said Nathalie, who was rubbing Seraphine's back.

'Oh, thank God, food,' said Alexandra as Macie approached with a tray of cake and fruit and a pitcher of homemade lemonade. 'Come on kids, off the trampoline, Macie has brought cake.'

The children trailed after Macie to the willow tree like little birds following bread crumbs. She placed the feast on the table. The cake was glazed and shiny in the dappled light and the smell of the fruit, sweetness mixed with tart lemon, lingered in the air.

'You're a lifesaver,' Alexandra said to Macie as the kids swarmed to the food.

'I may not have my own little one around much anymore, but I know what kids need,' said Macie, handing Will a slice of banana cake.

CHAPTER 35

Emmie

The sun was overhead, bearing down on her, burning into her skin. It was so unlike her not to have applied sunscreen, but the panic that bloomed like the overripe flowers in the garden was obscuring her common sense. Their sweet smell made her feel sick. Emmie couldn't help but think of Pen outside under this ferocious white-hot sky. Had she taken water? Wouldn't she be dehydrated? Where the hell was she? Was she hurt? Emmie imagined her lying injured, alone, calling out fruitlessly, her voice lost in the sheer vastness of this place. Or worse. No, she couldn't even let her mind go there. Emmie pressed her hands to her flaming cheeks and turned to the others. They had gathered on the front steps of the hotel after searching all morning, taking it in turns to look after the kids. 'I feel so helpless. Her mobile's saying no reception. Someone should check her room to make sure it's not there. How did I not think of that? And at what point do we call the police?'

'I'll do another walk over the bridge now,' said Alexandra. 'And I Googled when I had range and you don't have to wait 24 hours to report someone missing, you know.'

Emmie shook her head and began to pace. 'God, I can't believe she's still not back. Poor Will. Thank God for that TV and all Macie's cake to distract him.'

'I'll check her room,' said Nathalie. 'And Caleb can do another drive around, this time going a bit further afield. He knows the bush out here like the back of his hand.'

'I think we need to call the police. Something's happened. She must have fallen and hurt herself or something. She wouldn't just leave Will like this. I know her,' Emmie said.

Alexandra shot her a worried look. 'How long have you known Pen?'

Emmie shook her head. It was hard to think clearly. Her thoughts were like the screeching birds in the leaves above them. 'Ah, I don't know. I mean Will and Seraphine have been in the same class two years in a row.'

'It was in her room.' Nathalie returned, breathless, holding out Pen's phone.

Emmie felt a coldness creep through her despite the heat. She took the phone and examined the photo of Pen smiling with Will and Cate at the beach. Her heart ached. 'No one goes out without their phone.'

'Except when there's shit reception anyway,' said Nathalie.

'Jesus,' said Alexandra. 'How are we going to handle this with Will?'

Emmie's eyes spiked with tears. Poor Will. He'd already had to grow up without a dad. He was going to freak out if they called the police. But what else could they do?

'Okay, she's out there somewhere without a phone. It's been what? Five, six hours? We definitely need to call the police,' said Emmie.

'I agree,' said Nathalie. 'The most likely explanation is that she's gotten lost or she's hurt herself and can't get back. We need more people searching.' They exchanged a look and Emmie felt her pulse quicken, her feelings towards Nathalie soften.

'Okay, so we're in agreement that I'll call the police?' asked Emmie, her voice wavering as she spoke.

Alexandra and Nathalie nodded. 'You should use the landline in the hall,' said Alexandra. 'I'll go tell Macie and Caleb. What shall we tell Will?'

'I think we need to tell him the truth. We can't just have the police turning up without warning him. He's an intuitive little boy,' said Nathalie.

'I'll talk to him. I know him most. I'll get Seraphine to help me,' said Emmie.

Emmie's hand was trembling when she made the call. The initial lack of interest the officer on the line took was dispiriting. But she was passed on to another person who must have been higher up. She'd have to file a missing person's report at the nearest police station, but taking into account the dense bushland in the valley the policeman told her they'd send some police out that afternoon.

She hung up and walked into the lounge, her head spinning. She had no idea how she was going to tell the little boy sitting in front of the TV that they didn't know where his mum was and that the police were on their way.

She took Seraphine aside from the others. She knew her

daughter would be upset but hoped Seraphine could be strong for her friend.

'Honey, I need to talk to you for a minute.'

Seraphine reluctantly left the glow of the screen. 'Do we need to turn off the TV?'

'No, sweetness. I just want you to help me. You know how Will has been a bit worried about his mum?'

Seraphine nodded solemnly.

'Well, now we're a little bit concerned because she still hasn't come home. But we don't want to upset Will more, do we?'

Seraphine's eyes widened. 'He can sleep in my bed tonight,' she said. 'He can have Teddy Two.'

Emmie's eyes filled with tears and she wrestled with the emotion forming in her throat. 'That's beautiful, honey. Yes, I'd like Will to come sleep in our room tonight, too.'

'He can't sleep alone,' she said.

'No, he can't. Can you go and get him, and we'll have a bit of a talk with him?'

Will's face looked paler than normal and his eyes were red. They darted around the room nervously. 'Will, I know you're worried about Mum. I'm so sorry she's not here. But Seraphine and I are going to take care of you, okay?'

'You said she'd be coming back,' he said. 'But it's lunchtime and she has no lunch.'

Emmie took his hand. 'I know, I'm so sorry, honey. But the police are going to help us, okay?'

'The police?' Will's alarmed expression broke something in Emmie, and she felt a tear slip down her face, which she quickly brushed away. She had to be strong. She couldn't cry. 'It's okay. We're going to find her.'

'We can have a sleepover in my bed tonight, and you can have Teddy Two,' said Seraphine, her eyes huge.

Emmie's heart squeezed at the sight of Will's tears. Seraphine gave him a hug.

'It's my fault,' Will sobbed.

'No. No no no, honey, it's absolutely not your fault.'

'She found me reading the diary.'

'What diary, honey?'

Will sniffed and rubbed his eyes. 'She got angry with me.'

'I have a diary too,' said Seraphine.

'It's not mine. It's Clara's,' said Will.

'Who's Clara?' asked Seraphine.

Emmie's mouth went dry. Wasn't that the name of the lady who had gone missing in the valley in the 1940s? Clara Black. The one who everyone thought was the ghost in the window of her photo. She thought back to that moment on the steps by the water fountain, when Will had been so adamant that he'd seen the woman. Fear skittered down her spine.

'She's a lady from the olden days,' said Will. 'I found it playing hide-and-seek and Macie said I could read all the books in the hotel, but Mummy didn't like me reading it. It made her angry.'

'Mums usually only get angry because they're trying to protect their kids,' said Emmie, pushing down the dread that was building inside her. She swallowed back the taste of bile rising in her throat.

'Why has she left me then?' asked Will, his eyes brimming with tears once again.

'She hasn't left you. She's probably got lost,' said Emmie, trying to steady her voice. 'And the police are coming to help us find her.'

'What if she didn't want me anymore?'

She drew Will to her, his arms thin and fragile, like a bird. 'Oh, Will, she did. She does'.

She wanted to ask him more about the diary, but his little body was shaking with fear, his face wet with tears. His was a heavy burden, too heavy for a child. Why did children always blame themselves for the actions of their parents? A new seam of panic opened inside her. She hugged her daughter close, appreciating the perfect circle of her little arms, but this time it didn't quell the dread.

CHAPTER 36

Nathalie

Police officers sat on the lounge with notepads open in their laps. Beyond the windows long afternoon shadows crept over the garden and the air was thickening towards night. The cliff faces were creamy in the dying light, which was now loud with birdsong. The earth seemed determined to fall under the spell of evening, although Nathalie wished she could somehow slow it. With every shadow growing along the hotel's front entrance came a darkening around the edges of her vision, a churning in her belly.

The room was chilly and dim. Nathalie went to warm her hands on her tea but it had grown cold. The two police were women, which gave Nathalie hope. One looked too young to be a mother but the other might be, and maybe she'd intuit just how pressing this was.

'Can I ask, do you have children?' she asked the older officer.

The woman had the sort of eyes that smile without the lips needing to move. Her pen paused over her notepad and she nodded. 'I do. Grown up now, but yes.'

'Good,' said Nathalie. 'Good. I know it shouldn't make a difference but–'

The younger officer shot her a long sidelong glance.

'I understand,' the older woman said diplomatically, her eyes reassuring.

'We're doing everything we can at this stage. We've got several officers and some volunteers from the Rural Fire Service canvassing the area now,' the younger officer said, her voice tinged with defiance.

'Thank you,' said Emmie, her hands knotting in front of her on the lounge.

The officers exchanged a look and the older one spoke slowly, as though she were a teacher addressing a class of students about to do a test. 'Now, we've searched Pen's room and it does appear that her son's belongings are still there, but some of her own appear to be gone.'

Nathalie's throat constricted. 'Really? But we found her phone.'

'Yes, we realise that, but there doesn't appear to be a handbag, or something of that nature, with a wallet and small personal items. Do you know if she carried a handbag, or something of the sort?'

Emmie nodded. 'Ah, I think maybe, yes, she had a backpack. She's practical. A photographer. Are you sure?' asked Emmie, her face flushed. 'Maybe she just wanted to take some things with her on the walk. Or maybe it's in her car.'

'We've searched her car. Yes, that's what we're just trying to figure out.'

'What does that mean? Has something happened to her or–?' Alexandra asked.

'She hasn't just packed her stuff and left,' Emmie snapped, glaring at Alexandra.

'I know but, well, these are experts. Let's see what they have to say about the situation,' Alexandra said.

'We've got a few more questions. We understand Will, her son, was the last person to see Pen.'

'Yes, he took her cornflakes in bed,' said Emmie.

'And what time was that?'

'Oh, I'm not exactly sure but I know Will gets up very early. We figured maybe 6.30 am?'

'Were any of you awake at this time?'

They all shook their heads.

'And what made you think Pen went for a walk this morning?'

'She and I went for a morning walk the other day. She likes to exercise in the morning,' Emmie said. 'It's just what we sort of assumed, especially after being cooped up with all the rain yesterday.'

'Did she take her backpack when the two of you went for your walk the other morning?'

Emmie blinked and shook her head slowly. 'No, no I don't think so. We didn't take anything.'

The police officers scribbled in their notebooks. 'Was there anything happening in her domestic life? I understand she also has a daughter who's in Sydney with her father. Anything that might cause Pen to leave suddenly?'

Nathalie exchanged a helpless look with Emmie.

'No, she would never,' said Emmie, her voice thick with emotion.

'Look, we're just trying to get a proper read on what's happened,' the younger woman said.

'We'll have more questions. I'd just ask that you postpone your return to Sydney. Until we get a bit more of a bearing on things,' the older woman said. 'And obviously, there's her little boy to look after. I understand his father isn't in the picture.'

'That's right,' said Emmie, her voice now small.

'Of course, we'll stay as long as we need to and look after Will,' Nathalie said, even though every molecule of her body wanted to leave this place. Wanted to see Richie. She imagined the softness of his chubby little fingers, the way his face would light up with a smile. It had been too long.

'We'll keep in touch this afternoon and this evening. The search will resume in the morning if we don't find her in the next few hours.' The women handed them their business cards and left. Nathalie began aggressively clearing the cups of tea from the table, but her hands were shaking. She needed to do something, anything to distract herself from the dread that was pooling inside her gut.

'I feel like I got us all into this mess,' Alexandra said, wiping her hands down her face. 'God. Why is her stuff gone?'

Nathalie put down the teacups and straightened.

'Pen wouldn't have just left him. I know you're wondering Alexandra, but I can feel it in my bones.'

'It's not that I think she just up and left Will, it's just that that is one of the possibilities. The police are considering it, we have to consider it. We could all see how much she was struggling with Will and his ... I don't know. I don't blame her. He's a lovely kid but, you've got to admit, he's a bit different.'

'Really?' Emmie was looking at Alexandra. 'You really think that she just walked because her son is a bit different?'

'I said it's not that I think that, but it's a possibility,' said Alexandra, sounding exasperated. 'I'm just being real.'

'I don't think it's a possibility,' said Nathalie, catching Emmie's eye.

'Fine. I just think it's being logical. But who am I to say?' said Alexandra, leaving the room with the tea tray and her head held high.

The silence in the room felt loaded as Nathalie looked at Emmie. They hadn't spoken since the incident with the broken glass. Since she'd spoken those harsh words. 'I'm sorry,' she said, dropping into the lounge and covering her face with her hands. It was all too much. What had happened last night with Caleb, Pen gone. She couldn't even begin to unpack the stuff with Caleb. She'd avoided seeing him all day. The guilt of it prickled, like salt drying on skin. 'For what I said about the Instagram stuff. It all seems so trivial now. It was mean.' She squeezed her eyes shut and took a deep breath.

Emmie sat beside her, her hands wringing in her lap. 'No, I'm the one who should be apologising. What I did was self-indulgent and thoughtless,' she said. 'I never meant to hurt you or steal your identity or anything like that. I didn't even think. I don't know where my head's been at.'

'I know the feeling. God.'

'And what I said about your drinking was really out of line. I mean, you have three kids. Of course, you use wine as a bit of a crutch.'

Nathalie swallowed with difficulty and felt self-loathing move inside her. 'No. No, you were right.' She couldn't look Emmie in the eyes.

Silence fell, blanketing them both.

'I think we just upset Alexandra,' said Emmie, changing the topic.

'Well, I can't believe she actually thinks Pen left Will. I mean, I think we both know something has happened to Pen, don't we? That she didn't just leave Will behind. I don't really understand about her stuff, but my gut tells me that she didn't just take her stuff and leave. And where would she go?'

Emmie looked around. 'Just checking the kids aren't around to hear. Honestly, maybe Alexandra's got her head in the sand because she's known Macie since school, and she doesn't want to offend her, but something's not right here. I mean, this place. The valley. The history. Those ruins. The stuff with the ghosts.'

Nathalie felt a ripple across her shoulders, and she looked behind her despite herself. 'Oh my God. Thank you. I wanted to say as much to the police but they're probably locals and I thought they might get offended or something.'

'We should have,' said Emmie. 'Said something.'

'But it's hard. How do you put a feeling like this into words? Something just feels … I don't know … I don't know if I can even articulate it out loud.'

'I know what you mean. And Will and the ghosts. He told me he was reading an old diary last night and Pen got upset when she saw it and he thinks that's why she's gone. What's he got into his little head?'

'Oh no, poor little thing. We should go and check in on him.'

'You go, I'll clean up the rest of this,' said Emmie.

'Thanks,' said Nathalie, relieved to feel the tension between them easing.

She stepped outside to find the escarpment blue with shadow and the afternoon light golden, softened, like butter. The harshness of the surrounding bush had been mollified by these last gentle hours of daylight. There were police cars in the car park but, apart from that stark reminder of reality, it was beautiful. The feeling she and Emmie had just spoken of was absent. It felt strangely peaceful.

But she thought of those white handprints on the cave wall, luminescent reminders of an ancient people who had suffered such loss in these parts. Of the Indigenous woman Caleb had told them about, who had fled with her baby and escaped the terrible massacre in the valley. She thought of the abandoned air of the mines and the township, of Will's face when he'd seen the mysterious woman at the hotel, of what Emmie had said about the women who had gone missing, and the feeling of walking down the dark corridors of the hotel alone. Of Pen, lost and alone somewhere, probably hurt. She thought of Caleb, trapped here by his own anxious mind. Broken by what his mother had done. So many stories lost, steeped into the soil, into the valley's soul. Was Caleb right? Could places hold memories? Her heartbeat quickened thinking back to the things she and Caleb had done last night. How drunk she'd been. She saw her children in the distance and felt the familiar rivulet of shame open up.

Macie was leading Sim around the garden on a small horse. The others played on the trampoline, their cries mixing with the laughter of kookaburras and the squawk of cockatoos going home to roost. Nathalie waved to her daughter, drinking in her delighted face. Whatever Macie was or wasn't, she was certainly good with children. Nathalie wandered over to the trampoline, giving Findlay a quick hug, smoothing her wild hair from her flushed cheeks. She couldn't think of the last time she'd brushed her girls' hair. But it didn't seem to matter.

The Valley of Lost Stories

'Where's Will?' she asked. Findlay shrugged.

'Do you know where Will is?' she called to Macie.

'He went inside for a drink.'

Nathalie gave the thumbs up. 'I'll bring out some water for everyone. And it might be time to put on some mozzie spray.'

Nathalie poked her head into the kitchen, relieved not to find Caleb there. She knew she was going to have to see him, but her emotions were so overwhelming right now, she had no idea how she'd be around him. Alexandra and Emmie were washing up. 'Did Will come in here for a drink?'

They shook their heads.

A sinking feeling wormed its way into her stomach. She alighted the staircase quickly, her heart beating hard in her chest now. His room was empty. She checked the shared bathrooms and the dim corridors, calling his name softly. He was probably in distress, she didn't want to scare him.

Downstairs a movement caught her eye. She followed the dark hallway leading towards Macie's office.

'Will,' she said, fright igniting her body. 'What are you doing here?'

He was standing in front of the closed door of the office.

'Will?' She crouched down and put a hand on his shoulder. He flinched.

'Are you okay, honey?'

He stood there for a moment without looking at her, without speaking. She could feel blood rushing in her ears, the thump of her racing pulse. *Sim had been hiding here too. What the hell was going on with this part of the house?* 'Will. Come on, come away from here,' she said. *You're scaring me.*

She tried to steer him down the hall away from the door, but he resisted.

'This is where she keeps leading me,' he said.

Nathalie stiffened and she felt her mouth go dry. 'Who?' She fought the urge to run away and, instead, pulled Will into a hug. His skin was damp and his little arm snaked around her neck. Tears pricked her eyes. 'Oh Will, I know you're scared right now. Come on, come out into the light.'

'No, please,' he said, his eyes huge and pleading in the dark. 'I have to wait here. I have to. This is where the lady is. I have to stay here until my mummy comes back to me.'

* * *

She found Caleb in his room, smoking a cigarette and reading a battered paperback, legs crossed on the bed. A jab of desire mixed with mild nausea. *What the hell am I doing?* she thought.

'I need to get into Macie's office,' she said, the words rushing out, more urgent than she'd intended. She took a shaky breath. She needed him to help her, she needed to play it cooler.

Caleb put the book down, looked at her, confused. 'What, her study? Why? It's private, we spoke about that.' He shifted on the bed, reached out for her. 'I've been trying to get you aside all day.'

Nathalie brushed her hair from her face and allowed him to draw her to him. 'Oh, sorry, it's been so busy with the police here and everything that's happened with Pen. It's so ... ugh, horrible. I've been distracted.'

'I know. Pretty upsetting about Pen,' he said, shaking his head and threading his fingers through hers. 'But I can't stop thinking about last night. When can we escape to the cave again?'

He traced her collarbone with his finger and a shiver iced through her. Her stomach turned. What the hell was she doing giving in to this? Why hadn't she been able to see how immature he was? It was the alcohol. Emmie was right. It was clouding so much. She couldn't see anything clearly. But she saw Will. She saw that he wasn't pretending. Whatever he did or didn't see in that hall, he seemed to know something the rest of them did not. And she needed to help him.

She squeezed Caleb's hands, even though her instincts were telling her not to tempt herself, entangle herself further. She sat down on the bed, feeling his body warm against hers. 'Caleb, you've lived here a long time. Have you ever felt a presence in the house? I mean, do you think it's haunted?'

Caleb shook his head and laughed darkly. 'Sure. I mean, sure, I do ghost tours of the mines. The face in the window that Emmie's picture captured … and this house is crazy old. I've had some weird experiences. Objects moving places when they shouldn't have, cold air brushing past, the sound of footsteps, but I've never actually seen a ghost, if that's what you mean.'

He looked at her with a puzzled expression on his face. 'Where's all this coming from? Is this to do with wanting to go into Macie's office?'

Nathalie desperately wished she had wine right now, to take the edge off, to soften everything out. She realised she'd been viewing the majority of her life through a camera lens slightly out of focus. The hard, sharp edges soothed away.

'Will, Pen's little boy. I found him standing outside Macie's office, staring at the door. In the dark. And I asked him why he was there, I mean, he's standing by himself in the dark hall and he says that the lady's standing there, so he has to.'

Caleb's face darkened.

'He was almost in a trance. But I'm going to assume it's stress at his mum being gone rather than the ghost of the woman he keeps seeing around the hotel. God, I can't even … It's so freaky. I don't even believe in ghosts. Can I have a puff? No, I shouldn't. No, ignore me.'

Caleb handed her the cigarette and she drew the smoke deep into her lungs, the pelt of relief settling her nerves.

'Look, I've grown up here and I've never seen the ghost of a woman in this place. I'm sure he's under huge stress 'cause his mum's gone missing. I mean, that's pretty upsetting for the little guy. And Macie said he doesn't have a dad.'

'But you've never felt, I don't know, a bit spooked by the valley, the hotel? All the history here. The stuff you've told me about the spirits in this valley? The massacres?'

Caleb stubbed his cigarette out in an ashtray shaped like a top hat and got up, took a swig from a bottle of Coke. 'I think you're freaking out because of Pen disappearing. And so is Will. She'll probably be back. Most missing people are found. You'll probably find she left of her own accord. Mental stuff usually.'

A surge of defiance rose through her. 'Yeah no, that's where you're wrong. You're not a mother so … Women don't just up and leave their kids.' She saw Caleb's face cloud with pain and realised what she'd just said. She touched his arm. 'Caleb, I'm sorry. I didn't think–'

'You think I haven't Googled women who abandon their children? Ha.' He hung his head.

Suddenly the room felt very small. She needed to get out of here. 'I'm sorry. I didn't mean to open that up for you. Of course. God. It's just that I'm trying to help a little boy–'

'And you think that somehow getting into Macie's office is going to help?'

She could tell by his tone that Caleb wasn't going to help her. His loyalty was with Macie. Of course it was. She'd been naïve to come to him. 'I have no idea,' she said. *But I'm going to find out*, she thought.

CHAPTER 37

Emmie

Heat shimmered across the shoulders of the valley and the sun bore down relentlessly. The buzz of insects thrummed in the hot air, but the birds had grown silent. The trees in the distance trembled as though lit by invisible flames. The landscape felt oppressive, as though a blanket had been thrown over it. Emmie could hardly breathe. All she could think about was how Pen would be coping out there somewhere in the bush. Was she in pain? Was she scared? Why hadn't they found her yet? She'd been gone through the cold night and now another searing day. She hoped Pen *had* taken her things with her. That she was prepared and had water and clothes. They'd searched her room and car after the police left yesterday and found her camera was also gone. Maybe she'd just gone on a whim to take some photos in the bush. A little solo expedition with a bag. She was intrepid. A photojournalist, used to carrying heavy stuff. But Emmie knew it couldn't be the case that she'd packed a bag and left without planning to return. *It just couldn't be that you left Will.*

Emmie sifted through her memories of chats with Pen over takeaway coffees, while waiting for their kids at school. There had never been any talk of mental health struggles, depression. But then Emmie had never confided in Pen about her own fertility struggles, her own sadness, not like she had to Nathalie. How much did any of us really know about the inner lives of others? Nathalie was proof that even the most luminous looking life could be an illusion.

The children's cries pierced the still, stifling air. The heat had driven them into the pool and while it felt wrong for them to be swimming while a search party was being orchestrated from the hotel car park, it was some semblance of normality and relief for poor Will, who had tossed and turned all night and awoken in tears. She had held his little body tight and tried not to let her own tears touch his skin. Now, he was floating on a giant round doughnut, his little face smooth, free of pain. The sight calmed her. The pool was like something out of a 1970s Florida road trip, with palm trees, otherworldly blue water, and vintage-style plastic sun lounges that stuck to the backs of your legs. Macie had brought the kids juice and sandwiches, which they'd devoured before jumping back in. It all felt surreal. Like an awful mirage.

They'd spent the morning at the police station, and then driving around the valley until the roads ran out. Volunteer firefighters from the local area were combing through paddocks, and into the deep bush that crept up the valley walls.

She'd been able to check on her Instagram feed when they were at the station. Her viral post of the woman in the window had become news twice-over now, with the new point of Penelope Hardy's disappearance in the valley. People had shared the image of Pen from the missing person poster. The police had asked for a picture and Emmie had sent them her Facebook page profile picture. She couldn't believe her friend had become one of those smiling, lost, ubiquitous faces that filled the news. She had become the sum total of one single moment in her life.

Emmie had finally been able to get hold of Pen's daughter, Cate, and her father. Cate had wanted to come, but Emmie had said no and promised she'd keep her up to date every few hours. The fear in the girl's voice had made Emmie sob in the close cabin of her car.

A squabble over a beach ball interrupted her thoughts. The kids still had to be entertained. Fed. Looked after. They couldn't expect Macie to be a babysitter. Apart from Will, the children seemed shielded from the growing gravity of the situation. The police appeared to be a source of excitement for Alexandra's boys. Seraphine felt things so keenly that Emmie had to play things down. Make light of everything. It was exhausting keeping up a happy face.

'I'm going to make some iced tea. Do the kids need more sunscreen?' Macie asked from under an enormous black hat.

'Thanks, more sunscreen would be great. I think I left it in the dining room,' Emmie said, shading her eyes against the glare. She was sweating and her feet were burning from all the walking she'd done, but she couldn't sit down. She couldn't sit still. It didn't feel right.

Nathalie had jumped in with the kids to cool off and was still wet as she sat down on the end of a lounge chair with a towel around her waist.

'Can we talk? While Macie's gone?' Her mouth was a worried line and her eyes were tightly squinted against the light. 'Alexandra, can you come over for a sec?'

Alexandra got up from where she was sitting with her legs in the water, her dress hiked into her underwear. She hid behind big sunglasses and when she spoke her voice was flat.

'I feel so bad sitting here by the pool,' Alexandra said, dragging another pool chair over to Emmie's. 'I feel helpless.'

Emmie shook her head. 'I know. I was just thinking that. Maybe you two can stay here with the kids – it's nice to see Will looking a bit happier, and I'll go and have another talk to the police.'

'I called Maxwell this morning and he said they should hold a press conference. We need the cops to take this more seriously,' Alexandra said.

'I need to talk to you guys about Will for a sec,' Nathalie said, blinking against the light. She pressed her hand to her chest. 'Bless him. The poor little thing. So, I found him just standing in the dark hall yesterday all by himself.'

'Which hall?' asked Emmie. 'The place is like a labyrinth.'

'You know where the reception area is at the front entrance? Just off the side there. Macie has an office down the hall. I didn't tell you this before, but I found Sim in there when she was hiding in the thunderstorm. Caleb and I found her. He said he'd never been in the office before and it was usually locked. And anyway, it's full of pictures of a little boy. All over the walls. Dozens of them.' She drew her arms to her.

'What, her son, do you think?' asked Emmie. 'I gather she doesn't see him much.'

'I don't know. Caleb didn't want me to mention it. Anyway, then I found Will just standing in front of the door. It was locked, I checked. And I asked him why he was there, and he said he had to stand there until his mum came back ... and the lady led him there.'

'Oh my God, that's just totally freaky,' said Alexandra pressing her hands to her face. 'That kid. Wow.'

Their eyes moved to the little boy bobbing on a pool noodle in the shallow end.

'I'm thinking he's just under complete stress,' Nathalie said, her forehead creased in worry.

'Okay, something else. Will mentioned a diary to me,' said Emmie, her voice dropping to a whisper. 'Someone called Clara's diary. Clara Black is the name of the woman who went missing in the valley in the 1940s. I wanted to ask more but didn't want to push him, you know? And to be honest, it kind of freaked me out. I asked if he wanted to show me the diary, but he said no. Pen got angry with him for reading it or something.'

'Jesus,' said Nathalie, wrapping her towel tighter around her body.

'That poor boy clearly isn't coping,' said Alexandra. 'Will is going through psychological trauma right now. Did you say he was standing in front of Macie's office?'

'Yes.'

'I feel bad enough that we've overstayed our welcome and there's been so much drama. I don't really want to mention this to her and put something else on her,' Alexandra said. She looked over at the pool. 'Sharing, please. Come on boys, let the girls have a turn on the pool noodles now.'

'I can't help thinking there's more to Macie than meets the eye,' said Nathalie.

'What does that mean?' Alexandra replied, her tone defensive. 'I know you've never particularly liked her, Nathalie, but she's been nothing but the perfect hostess to us. Looked after the kids while the police interview was happening, and we were driving around looking for Pen.'

A piercing wail made them crane their necks towards the pool. Jasper was on his hands and knees crying.

'Yep, that's mine. I'll be back,' said Alexandra, her voice full of exasperation.

Nathalie drew so close Emmie could see the sheen of sweat on her skin. 'Emmie, don't you think it's a bit weird? Will just standing there … all the pictures on the wall. Caleb's reaction to this room? Am I going crazy?'

'No. I feel like we're all going a bit crazy. Especially Will. My heart is breaking for him. This woman he's talking about. I don't know. And I'm not sure why Alexandra isn't seeing this. Macie is acting like nothing's happened. It's all iced tea and pony rides for the kids.'

'I can't help but wonder about that room,' said Nathalie.

Emmie nodded. 'I don't think we should say anything more to Alexandra though,' she whispered as the other woman began walking back towards them.

The sound of a phone buzzing made Emmie jump. 'Oh, my goodness. There's reception here?'

Nathalie scrambled in the beach bag she'd brought down to the pool. She picked up the phone and stared at it, as though it was a foreign object. 'It's ringing,' she said. She held the phone to her ear.

'Mike? Hi. Yes. Sorry, I'm just so shocked there's reception by the pool. Sorry, it's cutting in and out a bit. You're where? Lithgow? Oh, my goodness. Okay. Yes, we're okay. I know. It's so upsetting. Poor Will. What? You've got Richie with you! Oh, my goodness, my little man.' Nathalie's face beamed. 'We'll see you soon then.'

CHAPTER 38

Nathalie

The girls rushed up the marble staircase, their bodies still glistening with water from the pool. 'Slow down, girls, you'll slip,' she called after them. The coolness of the hotel foyer was a balm against the searing afternoon heat.

Nathalie smiled as she climbed the stairs. She was going to see her baby boy. And Mike. He'd made the effort to come all the way out here without her asking. She couldn't help how good that made her feel. Perhaps her fling with Caleb was what she'd needed to bring her and Mike back together. To free her of her vindictiveness over the affair. Maybe they could start anew. She did love him. Of course she did. And he was clearly trying. This place was forcing her mindset to expand. Perhaps she needed to let the crazy stuff with Will go and focus on her own family. God knows she'd avoided doing that recently.

She opened the door of her room and stopped. Caleb was sitting on the edge of her bed, his arms resting on his knees. The girls had flung their towels on the floor and had picked up their Barbie dolls, ignoring Caleb and conversing in high-pitched doll-speak.

'Oh, hi,' she said, pulling her towel closer around her body and trying to mask her shock.

'Sorry, I didn't want to interrupt the pool party.' He flashed her an apologetic smile.

She sat on her haunches and hugged her girls to her, smelling their chlorinated hair. 'Girls. Let's go visit Seraphine. Emmie can give you guys a bath. She makes extra big bubbles in hers.'

'Yay!' they shouted, flinging their dolls to the ground and rushing out the door.

When she returned, she closed the door behind her and fixed Caleb with a serious look.

'Sorry, I just – I needed to talk to you,' he said, looking meek. He stood and then sat back down on the bed, raking his hands through his hair. 'I'm going a little bit crazy here. I'm sorry. I mean what happened the other night. I can't stop thinking about you.' He put his head in his hands and then looked up. 'I'm sorry to just barge in here.'

She nodded, taking a deep breath. She had no one but herself to blame for Caleb sitting here. 'No, that's okay. I just didn't want the girls–'

He shook his head. 'Oh, no, no, of course.' He patted the bed beside him. 'Will you come, sit? I know we probably can't just escape with everything that's going on, but I needed to see you. Touch you.'

Nathalie's head throbbed and her mouth went dry. She really hadn't thought this through, had she? Mike would be here in an hour or so and Caleb was showing all the signs of infatuated neediness. She sat down next to him on the bed and allowed him to take her hand. His were hot and clammy. He smelled woody, like smoke and cinnamon; she couldn't deny it, he smelled good. She felt desire move through her despite the protest in her mind. How was she going to break this to him?

'I've found the key to Macie's room,' he said, threading his fingers through hers and pushing a strand of damp hair from her face.

Nathalie was mute. The room spun a little. She swallowed hard and willed herself to stay cool. 'Oh?'

'I'm not sure what you want with it exactly, but I get you're worried about Will. I want to help.' A pleading look came into his eyes. 'Can you come with me tonight? To the cave? Even if it's at 3 am?'

A mild wave of nausea washed through her. Was this the exchange she was expected to make? She couldn't look him in the eyes. Couldn't see the desperation there. She realised suddenly how real this was for him. How important, and guilt sluiced through her.

'Caleb, I can't. My husband, Mike, just called. He's on his way here. And my baby, Richie, is coming too.'

His face darkened but he put his hand in his pocket and took out a small gold key. It was cool when he pressed it into her palm.

Yes, this was the exchange. She thought about Caleb's lonely reality in this valley. Of the depth of their connection, which was real. She thought about Will's pale, haunted face outside that door. Of Pen, out there somewhere. Something deeper than her rational mind, something instinctual told her that she had to take the key.

'Okay,' she said, her voice steady. 'I'll try to get away to meet you.'

* * *

Her heart ached and tears burned behind her eyes as she watched Mike carry Richie through the garden to the hotel's entrance. She ran to them and buried her face in the chubby folds of her little boy's skin. She plucked him from Mike's arms and breathed in the warm, milky smell of him. How could it be that after days away from her he still smelled the same? He still smelled like home. She caught Mike's eye and smiled.

She could see him objectively now, after nearly a week. It was funny how little time it took away from someone for their familiarity to wash off, like a scent trail lost after rain. His tanned skin and warm brown eyes, so different from her own pale colouring, struck her.

'Wow, this place is something else,' said Mike, kissing her lips. 'The middle of nowhere and there's this huge old hotel. This little one's missed Mummy, haven't you?'

'Oh, Mummy's missed you, baby boy.'

'And how about your other boy?' asked Mike, his eyes playful. A memory returned to her, bright and clear, like the day they'd met. That same look in his eye, as though the world was an easy, safe place. It was outside a cafe in the city after he'd found her wallet and tracked her down, restoring her faith in human nature and triggering a newfound belief in fate. He'd been so charming and had insisted that she buy him a drink for his troubles. That had made her laugh and after a shitty day at work it was an offer she could hardly have refused. Their chemistry had been consuming from that first beer. He'd later joke that he fell in love with her as soon as he saw her photo – a particularly unattractive one – on her driver's licence. He'd even had it blown up at their wedding, much to everyone's delight.

It was funny how the mythology of how a couple formed somehow built itself into the very fabric of the relationship, so that sometimes it was hard to tell where the story ended, and real life began. Perhaps she hadn't been able to let go of their marriage because their fairy tale was too beguiling, the myth so strong she believed it would triumph, like serendipity, like a wallet returned by a stranger.

She laughed now, feeling herself soften and expand as his arm snaked around her waist. 'I may have missed you a little too.'

'Where are the girls?' he asked.

'They're off somewhere running with the other kids. That's the beauty of this place. Seraphine is about a thousand times more mature and responsible than Findlay. She's keeping them all in check. Probably over on the trampoline or playing fairies in the garden. Hey, how did you manage the time off work?' she asked, her nose buried in the soft white hair of Richie's head.

'I told them a friend of my wife's was missing and it was an emergency. They had no choice.'

Nathalie squeezed his arm. It was the first selfless thing he'd done in as long as she could remember. 'Thank you. I'm not sure how long we're going to be here. God, it's so stressful. I'm so glad you're here.'

He turned to her and gripped her by the shoulders. His eyes were huge in the softening afternoon light. 'I want to know all about what's happened with Pen, but I just want to say that I've had some time to think. Just having space without the kids around helped. Mum was great taking Richie. And I really missed you, Nat. I mean, I know we've had our problems. They've just intensified with every one of our kids. We've drifted further and further apart. I've had my own struggles and that's played out in a way that's been so hurtful for you. But maybe we can go home and start afresh. Really give this a good shot. Pretend I found your wallet in a valley in the middle of the bush.'

Tears spilled down her face and Nathalie swiped them away with shaking fingers. 'You hurt me,' she said, her voice tiny, the rush of emotion unexpected. 'So much.'

Mike drew her to him, and she smelled the familiar scent of his aftershave, the laundry detergent from their home. 'I know. And I'd like to spend the rest of my life trying to make it up to you.'

'Oh my God, who are you?' she blurted, laughing through her tears.

'A man who knows it's a long road ahead but who's prepared to do the work. I've missed my family.'

Nathalie thought about all the counselling sessions, all the apologies, the platitudes, but underneath his words resentment had lurked and under hers, anger. None of it had been real, but this was real. The undercurrent of negative emotion that had kept them apart had fallen away. Part of her wanted to ask him to take them all home right now. To leave everything, all their possessions and drive out of this valley. It was so tempting. But the key to Macie's office sat like a heavy stone in her pocket.

* * *

A full moon was rising by the time they met in the dining room for dinner. The children were tired and hungry but placated with juice, garlic bread and the vast collection of colouring pencils and paper.

Macie placed wine on the table, but no one opened it. Their drinking, the levity of only a few nights ago seemed like a distant dream. But Mike brought a new energy to the group, shifted it somehow. Nathalie had forgotten how confident he was. How charming he could be. They listened as Mike recounted his 'single dad' struggles trying to get Richie to sleep, to eat, to do anything. Where his ineptitude once would have created a fresh sheet in the endless book of resentment, she found now a new gratitude for his calming presence. She eyed the bottle of wine in the middle of the table. Macie and Mike poured themselves glasses. She watched Macie carefully. She was dressed in one of her elegant silk kimonos, her hair pulled back into an ornate clip. Macie seemed thoroughly charmed by her husband, just as Nathalie knew she would be. Macie skirted on the surface of things. She was easily seduced by beauty.

Nathalie twisted the empty wine glass between her fingers. Her head throbbed with longing. Every part of her was trained on chasing the feeling of surrender, the blurring of her edges that she knew would come after only a few sips. She watched Macie and she knew she must resist.

Caleb slunk on the periphery of the dinnertime gathering, bringing out salads and filling the kids' juice glasses. His eyes were like torches at once boring into and lighting up her body. She couldn't deny she felt the pull of him. But there was something wild there too, something dark that made her heart quicken and her chest tight.

They all took turns explaining the days that led up to Pen's disappearance to Mike as though somehow he would be able to piece together the strange puzzle through sheer objectivity. Through the sheer will of his unflappable confidence that everything would be okay. Emmie and Alexandra were detailing the police involvement. She looked over to see Will next to Seraphine at the kids' table. The pair were drawing together, two quiet islands amid the noise and rabble of the rest of the children.

Nathalie took a deep breath. Now was the time. If she was going to do it, it had to be now. Caleb had retreated to the kitchen and Richie was fast asleep in a sling against her chest. If anyone saw her sneaking out, they'd assume she was feeding him somewhere quiet or putting him down. No one seemed to notice her go.

Her heart was beating so hard in her chest that she feared it would wake her son. She needed him to stay asleep. She tiptoed out of the dining room and into the dark entranceway, lit only by an ornate lamp of a woman entwined with a snake. On the shadowy walls, other images – sirens, fairies, all manner of women – stared down at her. An image of Will standing in the dark, supposedly led there by a woman, returned to her and she shivered. She felt for the key in her pocket as she reached Macie's office. It was almost impossible to make out the keyhole it was so dark. She listened for a beat. The voices drifting from the dining room were faint. Macie laughed. Richie stirred, his eyelids fluttering. *Please stay asleep*, she begged. *Please*.

She eased the key into the lock and turned it. The door opened with a creak. Her mouth was dry, and she was shaking as she closed the door behind her and stepped into the room.

It was dark except for the light from a low moon shining in through the lace curtains at the window. She stepped carefully towards the large timber desk against the wall. She flicked on the lamp. Another woman, belly distended, this one reclining, holding the lit orb of the lamp in her arms. As her eyes adjusted, she took in the photos of the little boy. There was a small framed photo of the same child smiling in a much younger Macie's arms on the desk. A rivulet of cold ran through her. She had no idea what she was doing in here. What she was looking for.

She took a shaky breath and tried to calm herself. She slid open one of the drawers to find stationery, pens, a calculator. A second revealed more of the same. Richie began to whimper, and she felt a needle of panic work through her. She shushed him, sitting down in the large leather chair cradling his head in her hand. He settled and she breathed more deeply. She wasn't sure what had brought her here. Actually, she was. It was instinct. It was the same thing that had told her that Mike was having an affair. Only she'd ignored it that time. And it wasn't just about this strange hotel, this valley. Will standing outside the office with the haunted look in his eye. It was about Macie. What she saw was two different women. Like mirror sisters. Twins. The woman in her silk gowns with her lavish spreads and doting adoration of the children, and the woman she sensed here. They didn't seem like the same person. She was an illusion. A spectre in a house full of spectres. Macie had never acknowledged that shameful night when Nathalie had poured out her heart. It didn't sit right. There was some kind of mask. Some dishonesty, a feeling in which Nathalie had been well schooled. A feeling she'd always pushed down, avoided, until now.

Richie was asleep, his little body warm, his breath perfectly rhythmic against her chest. She ran her fingers over an ornate silver box on the desk. The lid was adorned with yet another woman, this one writhing in either pain or pleasure, she wasn't sure. She drew it to her. Inside she found photos. Old, jumbled. Pictures of a boy who might have been Caleb, mixed with older yellowing pictures of the little boy on the walls. An intense unease crept through her. She unfolded a piece of sketch paper. The image made her gasp. Will, with his tousled hair and piercing eyes. Had Macie sketched him? It was a beautiful drawing that captured something of Will's essence, his intelligence, his vulnerability. *Why do you have this picture of Will?* All the blood drained from her head and she thought she might faint. She slipped the piece of paper into her bra and stood on uncertain feet. She knew she couldn't linger here but what else might she find? She looked behind her at the door. Still closed.

There was very little in the room except the desk, a small bookcase and a leather reading chair by the window. A filing cabinet in the corner. She opened the top drawer of the cabinet to find financial records, receipts, papers. The second drawer contained more of the same. To get to the bottom drawer she had to kneel, slowly so as not to wake Richie. She slid the drawer out to find nothing but empty folders. She stood carefully and surveyed the room again. What did it mean? This picture of Will inside the box with these other boys? She walked over to the bookcase. The classics, some self-help. A few modern novels. One of the spines caught her eye, *Grief, A Journey to Healing*. The book was sticking out further than the rest, as though it hadn't been put back properly. She slid it out.

It opened easily, revealing folded newspaper articles tucked in its centre. Nathalie felt tears prick her eyes as she took in the headlines, yellowing, torn and stained with age. All variations of the same. A little boy. A tragic accident. A young Sydney mother, gone into another room to find a towel. She had only been gone a few minutes. Her little boy, Jacob, three, had slipped under the water in the bath. It was a tragic mistake. A terrible accident. Mother, Macetta Williams, age 22.

Nathalie heard an awful noise but realised it was coming from her own mouth. Richie stirred and began to cry. Nathalie's vision was blurred with tears. She was breathless as she hastily stuffed the book back into the bookcase. It fell and the articles fanned to the floor. Jacob's face, smiling up at her like a ghost. Macetta must be Macie. It made sense. This explained her desire to skirt over, to stay on the surface of things. Because she herself had a secret she couldn't face. But what mother wouldn't hold that secret close to her, closet it, hide it? Try to press it down. The guilt. It would eat you up.

Richie's cries echoed off the walls and she scrambled to pick up the newspaper clippings, but her vision was still blurry. She started at a noise and swung around. Was someone at the door? She shoved the articles back in the book and slammed it into the bookcase. She ran for the door, heart pumping. Her little boy wailed louder. She glanced back into the room to see a newspaper article still on the floor, like a dried petal dropped from a dead flower. She hesitated, about to run back in, but she heard footsteps and the sound of voices approaching. She ran down the dark hall, aware only of the beating of her blood and her little boy's terrible cries. When she got to her room, she realised she no longer had the office key in her pocket.

CHAPTER 39

Alexandra

She watched Macie patiently scoop ice cream into the kids' bowls with a practised fairness as each serving was carefully scrutinised lest someone got more. This woman had been nothing but hospitable to them all. And now they were stuck here in this awful situation, just waiting for what felt like bad news to come. The hours and minutes stretched out, charged with unspoken dread, so that it seemed like days and days since they'd last seen Pen, since things had been normal. Emmie was off calling the police on the landline for an update and Nathalie was putting Richie down. Nathalie was quick to express her dislike of Macie and yet here she was refilling their children's ice cream bowls and handing out more drawing paper.

It was true, Macie was a bit different. She always had been. That's what had stood her apart from their peers at school. Children had a knack for singling out difference like trained sniffer dogs. Why was it human nature to bring down the weak or different? She watched Will squeezing topping onto his ice cream. He had recovered from a bout of tears earlier in the evening and was now his usual subdued self. He was always quiet, self-contained, observing. Pen had spoken about tantrums and meltdowns but what Alexandra saw was a kid who was on the outside looking in. If she was honest, there was something about his physical appearance that also marked him. His large eyes, his pale skin. There was a vulnerability about him, an owlishness that suggested wide-eyed innocence and wonder. And children quickly ascertained that this was a kid for whom their barbed comments would strike deep. Alexandra wondered if Will had been bullied at school. He struck her as a loner. Her boys had initially included Will, but that had cooled over the days spent here and it was clear that the friendship between Seraphine and Will was the strongest.

'Well, we're all out of chocolate and strawberry,' said Macie, showing Alexandra the two empty ice cream containers. 'Want some vanilla? I've got balsamic strawberries in the fridge that would go nicely.'

'Thank you for looking after the kids so well. They've never been better fed, or more consistently. Dinnertime at our place isn't always around a table and it's certainly not at the same time each night.'

'I think children do well with consistency. Well, I know they do. I've done all the reading, of course, with my own.'

Alexandra thought of what Nathalie had told her, about the office filled with pictures of the little boy. 'Your son, how old is he now?' she asked, watching Macie closely, knowing it was a touchy subject, treading carefully. What had she said to Pen on that first night? That her son was with his father in Sydney and she didn't get to see him much.

Macie pressed her lips together and she gazed over the children at the table in front of them. 'He doesn't like vanilla ice cream very much either. He's the same age as Thomas, Findlay, Seraphine and Will. Drew gets very possessive. Doesn't like sharing him. We're not on speaking terms.'

A lump formed in Alexandra's throat. She'd assumed as much. She couldn't handle it if Maxwell took her boys. 'That's your ex, I take it. It must be very hard.'

'I've still got his room all set up in the Sydney house, of course.'

It was no wonder she had photos of her little boy all over her office. This wasn't some weird thing, it was what any mother would do if she was separated from her child. Alexandra wondered what had happened to make custody an issue.

She was about to ask whether Macie needed to return to Sydney for any art commitments when Emmie came rushing into the dining room. She took Alexandra by the elbow and led her away from the children's table.

'I've just gotten off the phone with the police.' Emmie was whispering. 'They have a lead. Someone saw the missing person signs and thought they'd seen Pen or someone who looked like her walking around the local township just outside the valley.'

'When?'

'Yesterday.'

'Really? Haven't they searched there?'

Emmie sighed. 'Yes, I think so, but maybe we should check it out tomorrow. Hopefully it's not just some bored local wanting to call Crime Stoppers.'

'What else did they say?'

'They're looking at her phone to see if they can get in and track the last few people she called, but seeing as there's no reception here, it's unlikely there'll be much to track. Anyway, they're widening the search to talk to people in townships surrounding the valley. And I thought maybe we could go out and chat to shop owners, a few locals outside the valley, that kind of thing. Put up some more missing person posters.'

'I guess there's nothing else to do. I'm tempted to get Maxwell to come and pick up the boys. Work is okay about me staying for a few more days into next week, worst-case scenario, but we've got to be realistic. We can't stay here forever,' said Alexandra.

Emmie shook her head. 'I know. But can you imagine telling Will he has to come home without his mum?' She wiped under her eyes with the heel of her hand. 'Sorry, I just can't believe what that little boy is having to go through.'

'Okay, let's widen the search tomorrow. Maybe Nathalie or Mike can look after the kids and we'll go out early. We can't ask Macie again.'

Emmie indicated over to where Macie was drawing something on butcher's paper on the ground, all the kids crowded around her. 'Somehow I don't think she'll mind.'

CHAPTER 40

Emmie

Another restless night, another dawn laced with hope and dread. The thin blue line of daybreak ached light into her tired eyes and she pulled her body from the bed and dressed quickly. She couldn't sleep, she couldn't eat, she couldn't stay still. Will and Seraphine were still curled tight like little snails. The hours before they could commence searching were torture, the seconds and minutes stretching slowly, like the arms of sunlight over the landscape.

The morning sun warmed her face and arms now but the knot in her gut refused to unfurl. The vibrant green paddocks seemed lurid, and the bright slash of blue above was like a mocking smile. They drove away from the hotel, past the volunteers and police who were assembling for another day of searching. The hope she'd felt last night after speaking to the police was gone, replaced by a heaviness that made it hard to perform the most menial of tasks. She wound down the window and the sickly sweet smell of crushed insects reached her. Mike put the radio on, but it skipped and buzzed until he switched it off.

'So, I'm planning to door knock the shops and houses on the main street and put up some posters,' said Mike, his hands resting casually on the steering wheel, the huge watch on his wrist glinting in the sun.

He had the air of someone reading a particularly intriguing crime novel that he was determined to solve first. She knew she should be grateful for his help, but Emmie couldn't help feeling annoyed. This was Pen gone, not a stranger, not a puzzle to be enthusiastically solved.

Nathalie hadn't protested at being left behind with the kids; it was clear she was loving having Richie back. Alexandra sat in the front seat, her eyes trained on the road, her mood also subdued.

At last the valley narrowed and they climbed up through dense bushland to emerge onto a sealed road and then a single-lane highway. The only sign of life were the flies that buzzed around roadkill. The sun bore down relentlessly on the asphalt and the hiss of cicadas filled the air. It smelled like rubber and oil tinged with something sweeter, like baking bread, or blood.

Walleratta was five minutes down the road and its main strip was tired. A fish and chip shop's rusted signage competed with the Chinese restaurant's faux exotic window display. There was a grocery store and a bakery, but several shopfronts lay empty. Two blocks from the shops they'd passed the police station where they'd first reported Pen missing. It was housed in a beautiful sandstone house, surrounded by an English-style garden. Emmie guessed nothing too dramatic happened around here. The police station was possibly the nicest establishment in the town.

They parked on the main strip and got out. They agreed to touch base on their phones. Alexandra checked hers. Mercifully they all had reception. 'Looks like only the bakery and grocery store are open. I'll see if I can get any local gossip out of the check-out chick. And surely the bottle shop will be open soon in a place like this.'

Emmie shot her a look. 'Remember to be nice.'

Alexandra waved her away.

'I'm going to check in at the library if it's open. It should be just near the shops. Librarians always have their noses to the ground in the community,' Emmie said. She checked her phone. It was 9.30 am. She studied the map on her screen and began to walk. The library was around the corner, next to the public school in a quiet country-town street. The houses were mainly fibro, some with a charming heritage bent, although their facades wore the same tired expression as the shopping strip. A dusty pall lay over the street. The heat was intense. The valley was verdant compared to this town, as though it had sucked all the moisture from the nearby areas. It might have been remote and mired in the past but at least it was beautiful.

The library was a blond brick structure with a ramp leading up to its entrance. Doubt wormed in her gut. She had no idea what she would ask. She just knew she was fascinated by the history of the valley. It felt like a compulsion, an itch that needed to be scratched. She needed to know more. About this Clara Black. And the other woman in the '90s that the historian had mentioned. She figured the local librarian would be a fount of knowledge about the area and its people.

To her relief the library was open. It was cooler inside, but like the rest of the town relatively deserted for a weekday morning. A few older people sat at a computer station and a mother was in the children's section with her toddler.

A woman with curly red hair and a friendly, sun-worn face stood at the front desk putting books into neat piles.

'Excuse me, sorry, do you have a minute?' Emmie asked, pulling the A4 missing person poster of Pen out of her handbag.

'Hello,' said the woman, pushing the books aside. 'What can I do you for?'

Emmie unfolded the piece of paper and placed it on the counter. 'I'm not sure whether you've heard. My friend is missing. She went missing in the valley two days ago and we're just doing a bit of a door knock of the surrounding towns.'

The woman picked up the piece of paper and put on a pair of reading glasses hanging around her neck. 'I had, yes. News travels fast in these parts, as you can imagine. Heard a Sydney woman was staying down at The Valley Hotel and went missing.'

'That's right,' said Emmie, her heartbeat accelerating slightly. This woman seemed clued-in. Emmie watched her face as she inspected the photo of Pen.

'It's a shame about your friend. Penelope, is it?'

'Yes, we were just here visiting with our kids for the week and she just wasn't there one morning when we all woke up—' she shook her head. 'It's just baffling. We're really worried.'

'Not somewhere I'd personally visit,' the woman said, her glasses slipping down her nose.

'Oh? The hotel?' replied Emmie, her breathing suddenly shallow.

'The valley. Gives me the spooks,' she said. 'Lots of local legends about that place. Aboriginal people are reluctant to discuss its past. Awful killings back in the day. The genocide of the custodians of these lands. It's truly shameful what happened during the Bathurst Wars in these parts. So much innocent blood shed. And a few women missing in the valley in more recent history. Clara Black, famously, during the mining town era. We have some books here.'

'Yes, I know. I've heard the stories. And we did the tour of the mine ruins so I know a bit about the history of the place.'

'Not much of a tour either. It's all so overgrown. Snakes and the like about. No proper tracks. Locals wouldn't be going there, I can tell you that. They do have a campsite by the river that sometimes gets busy during school holidays, but there are no amenities so it's only for your hard-core campers. Gets lots of people going in on dirt bikes.'

'We haven't seen any campers. Or people on bikes.'

'It's not somewhere people usually go out of their way to visit,' the woman said.

'The hotel's quite charming though. They get people staying.'

The woman raised her eyebrows. 'To you city folk maybe. Everyone knows Macie Laurencin, of course. Spends most of her time in Sydney these days. Strange bird. Artistic type. Quite well known in the art scene in Sydney apparently.'

'Strange how?'

'Waltzes into town with her big car and her big hats and her orders for organic beef and wine, as though she's running a health retreat in Sydney, not a run-down hotel.'

'She's not well liked then.'

'Oh, she keeps to herself enough. Doesn't deign to mingle with us ordinary town folk. Just because she has money. Her parents bought that hotel outright and spent millions, millions restoring it and for what? It's beautiful enough, for sure, but there's a reason that valley is a ghost town.'

Emmie felt a chill move through her. She willed herself to remain quiet, hoping the woman would go on, but she took a book from the top of her stack and stuck something into it with a thump.

'You mentioned some books on the history of the valley. Do you think you could point me to them? I'm quite keen to read about the missing woman from the 1940s, Clara Black.'

The woman paused in her book stamping. 'There was another woman too, it's believed. It wasn't widely publicised.' Her voice dropped to a whisper. 'She was a druggie. No one was sure if she offed herself, or ran off with some of the bikers who were notorious in the region at the time. But people around here have long memories. There's also the Lithgow correctional facility just down the road. Been some escapes there. You can imagine the types.'

'And this other woman. Who was she? When did that happen?' asked Emmie, trying to sound more casual than she felt.

The woman scrunched up her face, trying to remember. 'Gosh, the memory's not as good as it used to be. Now you're pushing it. I'd say 20 years back. More. Yes, that seems about right. Went under the radar. Not like Clara Black – she's the reason people come for the ghost tours. Here, I'll show you what we've got. Laura Blakey, retired teacher with a bit of time on her hands, wrote a bit of a potted history on the place a few years back.'

Emmie followed the woman through the stacks. The smell of old books transported her to the simple school libraries of her youth. It was like going back in time 30 years. In fact, the whole town seemed stuck somewhere in the 1980s.

'Here it is.' The woman slid the book out by its slender spine. 'This section here is where you'll find local history. Enjoy.' She began to walk away, then she turned. 'And I'm sorry about your friend. I hope you find her.'

Emmie smiled. 'Thank you. Thanks for your help.' She sat down in a faded armchair. She realised her hands were shaking as she opened the book.

Jean

1948

The valley smelled familiar, like eucalyptus and dust and the heat of the day still lingered in the night air. Conflicting feelings churned inside her as the car crunched its way through the hotel gates. It was late and only a few rooms were lit. Her heart grew warm at the thought of seeing Liv. Her darling. Her girl. But the feeling was overlaid by something dark, a shadow she could feel growing stronger. Now that they were back here in the valley her ruse felt bigger, more serious. And her desire to escape this place felt stronger, too. If only she had not seen the sea.

Exhaustion had lulled her to sleep on the descent into the valley. She had removed her shoes and curled up, her stockinged feet tucked underneath her. It felt like she'd lived a lifetime in two days and her visit with her father had torn something deep inside her. And yet there was Magnus's huge generosity. She felt even more beholden to this man. She desired him, respected him, so why did she fear him? She could feel all the threads of her life tangling, like the branches of the trees out there in the dark. She knew she must tell Magnus about Liv and Robert. She knew he wanted her to return with him to Sydney, take up Mr Parker's generous offer. And why wouldn't she? Magnus had even told Mr Parker she had accepted his proposition before they left, as though it was his decision to make. She had been too weak to protest. And she had wanted it, if she was honest with herself, she wanted the room over the harbour, the dancing every night, the smell of salt on her bedsheets.

Magnus cut the engine, the whites of his eyes flashing as they met hers in the dark.

He placed his hand on her leg. 'A nightcap in my room perhaps, after such a long drive?'

She hesitated. Still, the feeling of wanting to please him was there. He had done so much for her. The gifts, all the money for her father. Anxiety whipped through her. She couldn't keep putting this off. She had to break it. Had to be brave. She clenched her jaw and took a deep breath. 'I'm sorry, Magnus,' she whispered with more gravitas than the refusal of a drink would warrant.

An awful silence stretched out and somewhere a lone bird call echoed through the valley.

'For what?' There was still warmth in his voice, and she held onto the promise of it.

'Magnus, I wanted to be her. I wanted to be Serpentine Rose again. It was nothing more than that, I promise you.'

It was hard to read his expression in the dark, but he took her hand. 'You *are* Serpentine Rose.' He stroked her cheek, tenderly, and she could feel her resolve wavering under his touch. 'You're tired. It's been a long journey. We'll rest for a few days before returning to Sydney.'

But her father's words came to her. *She's a strong girl. You'd be so proud of her.* She remembered her mother's face. The way her smile lit her eyes. That smile that was never far away. That face so known, so dear. Always there. Her comfort. Her home. She remembered the aching pain of when she was gone. The hollow mother-shaped hole that no amount of anything good would ever fill. She could never do that to Liv.

She exhaled and closed her eyes. 'I have a child, Magnus. A little girl. Liv is her name.' She didn't dare look at him. 'So, you see, I'm not who you think I am.'

There was silence and it thickened the air, making it hard to breathe. She felt beads of sweat form on her brow. Her heart was loud in the still cabin of the car as she waited. And then there was a thump as Magnus hit the steering wheel, hard with his fist. Jean knotted her hands together in her lap to stop them from shaking.

His voice was tinged with something she'd not heard before. Menace, but disguised by a light tone. 'What's this? Another humiliation for Magnus? Did you set out to purposely make me look like a fool?'

She shook her head, swallowed hard. Her voice was weaker now. It had an awful pleading quality. She sounded like a child herself. 'Of course not. I wanted to tell you on that first night we met at the ball and then at the ballet hall. But I couldn't. I was so seduced by it all.' She paused, willing him to listen. To understand. 'By what you offered. By you. By the memory of what my life used to be. I missed it so much. But coming back here, I've missed my daughter. And I can't keep lying to you. I'm a mother. A wife.'

She could feel his eyes on her, boring through the dark. 'A wife?' His voice was strangled. 'You're married?'

Her voice was tiny. 'Yes. But–'

He made a dismissive gesture with his hand, as though it was all a joke. As though none of it really mattered. 'Well, it's obvious you don't love him. And by the looks of how I found you, he has no money. You'll leave him. Mr Parker wants you to dance for him. You can open in the autumn. It's a done deal. We'll leave in the morning.'

'But my daughter, Liv ...'

As she spoke her name Jean formed an image of her child dancing in their tiny kitchen. She could smell the sweetness of the soap on her skin, see the lift of her little chin, the easy way her feet found the steps. The way she smiled when she twirled. She longed to be there in that small kitchen watching her daughter dance.

'Serpentine, this life you've been offered is no place for a child.' His voice was a bark. 'I have no want of a child.' He ran his hands through his hair and shook his head. 'I'm already keeping your father in housing, and paying for the clothes on his back, for God's sake. What more do you want from me? You women are all the same.'

She felt his words reach her like small slaps. She swallowed, feeling everything slow. She remembered the feeling of salt air on her skin. She knew she would never feel it again. The ache of what she was giving up moved through her and she felt tears wet her face, but she met his eyes.

'I understand, Magnus. And I want nothing more from you. I'm sorry, I truly am.' She opened the car door, the warm night air, familiar, dusty, rushed in, enveloping her, calling her back

The Valley of Lost Stories

to her child. He grabbed her wrist and instinctively she drew back, panic rippling through her. His fingers burned into her skin and she yelled in pain but the more she pulled the harder he gripped.

His voice was low and there was no lightness disguising the menace now. 'You don't get to just walk away from me. Not after everything I've done for you. And I know what you'll do. You'll go around me. I know how women like you operate. You think you're the first? You're not.' He laughed and it sounded sharp and cruel. She felt it like a stab. 'You'll take your daughter and go back to Mr Parker. But that's not how this works. Parker's allegiance is to me.'

She saw then clearly that he already thought he possessed her, that she was his to trade, to own. Nothing was ever free in this life. She'd deluded herself to think it could be more than that, because of his tenderness, because of what he'd done for her father. But a man like him dealt in particulars. In ownership. And she was his now. He had bought her, and she had let him. His generosity with her father had confused her, seduced her, blinded her for a moment, made her think that what they had was bigger, grander. She realised with an ache how much she wanted that big love and how far she'd come from having it. How wrong she'd been. She saw that in his eyes now.

But she had Liv. She may not have a man she truly loved, but her love for her daughter was the sea, quiet at dawn, and the movement of her body lost in dance. It was all and it was everything. She was adored. She was needed. Something lit in her, some small spark and she wrenched hard, freeing her arm.

It felt like fire burning up from her core and she turned to him, looked him straight in the eyes and she wasn't afraid anymore. 'Men like you think you own women, but you don't. I'll do what I please with my body, with my talent. I don't belong to you. I don't belong to any man. My gift is my own and nobody else's. And you're so very mistaken if you think I'd choose the seductions you offer over my own daughter.'

She heard him growl, low like a wild animal in the dark and she knew she must run. She pictured her daughter in bed, the feeling of slipping in beside her, wrapping her body around those long, growing limbs, pushing her nose into that sweet-smelling hair. And Robert. He would protect her. Sweet Robert. Darling Liv. An image flashed into her mind as the pebbles and sticks dug into her bare feet, and she ran from the car. She glanced behind to see Magnus gaining on her as she flew towards the gate, towards her love. She remembered the figure of Clara Black, right here, walking barefoot in the moonlight, disappearing from sight, as the night claimed her forever.

CHAPTER 41

Nathalie

Under the dense, shady arms of a weeping mulberry tree Macie had laid out a white cloth. In the centre sat a tray full of delicacies – fresh fruits, tiny cakes and sugar cubes. A miniature tea set had been laid with a milk jug and teapot, and teddy bears stood as placeholders, one for each child.

It was as though Nathalie had slipped down a rabbit hole and emerged into a strange enchanted land. A fractured fairy tale. As though the darkness of the past few days was merely a dream and this idyllic garden setting was reality. It made her uneasy, this stark contrast. Didn't Macie know how stressed they all were? She had wanted to leave the valley with the others rather than be left alone with Macie, especially after what she'd seen in her office. But Richie was fussing and unsettled and the girls were tired after a night of broken sleep and before she knew it the car was pulling away in a plume of dust.

The children squealed in delight as they saw the picnic.

'It's like a magical cubbyhouse,' said Jasper, picking up a bear and hugging it to him.

'Do you think this is where the fairies live?' asked Sim, her little eyes shining.

'Maybe sweetheart,' said Nathalie with false brightness to mask the feeling of foreboding as she crawled on her hands and knees under the shadowy branches. The harsh morning sunlight diffused through the thick foliage. The children were spellbound, but under the sweet note of cake she could smell damp earth and rotting flowers.

Sim snuggled in her lap and Nathalie tried to find a place for the rising emotion in her throat. An image of that little boy's face flashed into her mind. *Jacob. How is Macie even able to do all this for our kids? Isn't it too painful?* She was reminded of the feeling she'd had in Macie's study. What she'd found buried there. How much it deviated from the perfect picture Macie presented on the surface. Like a pristine white picnic cloth laid over darker, deeper things: soil, dead insects, twisted roots, secrets.

Seraphine and Will entered the tree's shady lair last, and Nathalie noticed the girl had an arm protectively around Will. His little face lit up when he saw the picnic.

Nathalie smiled and squeezed Will's arm.

'Are those bears for us?' he asked, bending down and stroking one with a tenderness that brought tears to Nathalie's eyes.

'I think so,' said Nathalie. She ran her fingers along their soft fur. They looked new. Had Macie gone out and bought these for the kids?

Macie appeared then, ducking under the foliage and crouching to the children's height. She wore a loose white linen pant suit, better suited for a wedding than sitting on the ground in the middle of a garden.

Nathalie felt a cold tremor run though her, but she smiled brightly. 'This is an unexpected surprise,' she said, to cover the loud beat of her own heart.

'I just thought they could do with a bit of magic. It's been such a hard time.'

'It has.'

'Make sure you have some fruit as well as the cake,' Macie said to the children, who were stalking around the food on their hands and knees like hungry animals. Sim was inspecting the wide green leaves, very possibly for fairies. 'Everyone put some food on their little plate. You all have a cushion to sit on,' Macie said.

'This is so fun. The best morning tea ever,' said Seraphine. 'Thank you, Macie.'

'That's lovely manners,' said Nathalie. 'Everyone thank Macie for the picnic, please.'

'Thank you for the picnic, Macie,' their small voices chorused in singsong and Nathalie and Macie shared a smile.

'And for the adults a different kind of tea,' said Macie, indicating for Nathalie to take a seat next to a bottle of wine a little apart from the children. She handed her a pretty floral teacup, which she filled with sparkling pink rosé.

'Oh, I'm trying to cut back. I shouldn't, and Richie is inside napping,' said Nathalie, holding the sweet-smelling wine to her nose and feeling her resolve softening. It was intoxicating under here. The sunshine was a lace of light through the branches above their heads. She allowed herself a small sip from the china cup. It was sweet and cool. She took another and settled onto a cushion. She had to stop judging Macie so harshly. The poor woman had been through so much and here she was making teddy bear picnics for their children.

Macie passed her an angel sponge cake filled with whipped cream and fresh strawberries. 'Oh, I used to love these as a child. Thank you. Just as long as there's enough for the kids.' Nathalie took a bite. The cake was light and delicious, with a sticky strawberry jam centre.

'Do you like it, Will?' asked Macie, calling him over to them.

Will nodded, hugging his bear to his chest. Nathalie felt tears well in her eyes once more. This was actually a lovely thing Macie had done for Will, and given the loss of her own son, it seemed extra gracious. They watched him join the others, sitting cross-legged on their cushions in a little circle.

She glanced at Macie who was watching the children with a beatific smile on her face. Perhaps she should come clean, tell Macie she knew about Jacob. Try to connect, mother to mother. After all, Macie knew her darkest secrets.

'Macie, I just wanted to say how nice this is and I'm … I'm amazed you're able to be so gracious with our children. I know how difficult it must be with your son—'

'You couldn't bear that I knew your secrets, you had to know mine, too. Is that it?'

Nathalie froze.

'I know you paid a little visit to my office.' A smile remained on Macie's pink lips even though her tone was not friendly.

Their eyes met and Nathalie felt herself recoil. The article she'd left on the ground. The key. Her temples began to throb and she put down her cup. 'Macie, I can explain. I'm so sorry, I didn't mean to—'

'Drink. Drink. It's organic from a local vineyard. I always like to support the locals.' Macie calmly topped up Nathalie's teacup.

Nathalie watched the wine fizz and did as she was told, her head spinning a little. Her tongue felt thick in her mouth. She didn't know what to say, how to excuse her transgression. She felt ashamed that she'd gone in there, forced her way into another mother's private space, another mother's pain. She tried again.

'I shouldn't have gone in there. It's just that I saw all the photos on the wall. Of your son.'

'We're not always honest with ourselves, are we?' Macie asked, taking a sip from her own cup and brushing cake crumbs from her lap. 'But I feel like you and I are made of the same stuff. I felt that as soon as you told me about the pain of your husband's affair.'

Nathalie's heart was so loud she was sure Macie could hear it above the rustle of the leaves and the children's chatter. This was the first time Macie had acknowledged their encounter. She felt her mouth go dry.

'I was once as beautiful as you, Nathalie. But pain changes us. Distorts us. But you know this, don't you?'

Nathalie's skin felt slippery with sweat, the air under the tree too moist, too heavy. It was hard to breathe. The children were giggling as they ducked in and out of the leaves, bears clutched to their chests, their mouths smeared with cake.

'Your son. Jacob. I'm so sorry, Macie. I had no idea you'd been through that. It must have been horrible.'

Macie gave her a knowing smile and sipped from her cup. 'Well, if anyone is to know my secrets, I would choose you.

But secrets are secrets for a reason. Doors are locked for a reason.'

Nathalie pressed her hand to her heart. 'I'm so sorry. We just stumbled upon the office. Sim was hiding in there. During the thunderstorm. I have no idea why she was there, and I saw the photos of Jacob. I'm so sorry. It wasn't my place to go in there.'

'But that's not the whole story, is it? The whole story is never told. You have to dig a little to find it.'

Nathalie was lost for words. What was Macie getting at exactly? It was like she was talking in riddles. It was like she was enjoying this.

Nathalie's voice was flat, dark. 'I'm not following.' She shook her head and gestured to the picnic. 'Is this … is all this some kind of game to you, Macie?'

'Fun, isn't it?' A puff of laughter, the pink-lipped smile.

Nathalie felt sick. The cloying smell of sugar mingled with the damp soil, the rotting leaf litter.

'It's interesting you and Caleb have such a connection, don't you think?' Macie asked, reaching for a bowl of strawberries.

Nathalie's gut lurched. So, Macie knew. Had he told her everything? She took a large gulp of the wine, willing the panic stretching through her to ease.

'You're both a little trapped. I understand it perfectly,' Macie said. 'You in a marriage tainted by your husband's infidelity but with three young children to think of, and Caleb by all of his anxieties, his self-doubt. And with a mother complex. It was inevitable, really.'

Nathalie's face flushed and she shook her head. She wanted to crawl out of this place, shrug off the discomfort of what she'd done with Caleb, escape from what Macie was implying.

She could feel the knotted, gnarled tree roots under her, like fingers, like bones. She shifted, dread creeping through her. She balled her hands into fists and lowered her voice. 'It's really none of your business. Caleb is a grown man, and my marriage and what I choose to do in or out of it has absolutely nothing to do with you. Look, I'm really sorry for what you've been through, but I never meant to hurt you, or Caleb. Now, I should really check in on Richie. He's been asleep for half an hour.' She turned and began to crawl towards the edge of the foliage, towards the bright relief of daylight.

'But you see it does concern me, Nathalie. Because I know he told you everything. How he came to be with me. Abandoned by his own mother. He's never told another soul that, but he told you.'

Nathalie turned back to Macie and felt her skin prickle.

'His mother was no good.' Macie hulled the strawberries as she spoke, her nails digging into the pink flesh. 'One thing I will give you Nathalie, you *are* a good mother – you didn't abandon your children that night at the hotel. They're who you do it all for. Why you stayed with your cheating husband. And I know you won't abandon them now by destroying their lives, making them lose their father. I could be wrong, but Mike doesn't seem like the kind of man who would cope well with competition.'

She was rooted to the spot. Numb. Was Macie threatening her? Threatening to tell Mike about her and Caleb? She watched her girls putting flowers in each other's hair, soft singing issuing from their lips, and felt sick.

'Your children are who you do everything for. It's beautiful. That's why I know you and I understand each other. And we both have our secrets.'

Nathalie pressed her palms to her forehead. The wine had made her woozy. She needed to think but she felt muddled. As though she had drunk a bottle, not a cup. As though everything were the wrong way up.

'Why do you and I understand each other, Macie?' The words were too slow in her mouth.

'You understand what needs to be done to protect a child.'

The compulsion to crawl out of this place was strong, but Nathalie needed to know what strange thing was at play here. 'But you couldn't protect Jacob.' The name felt like a cuss on her tongue. Nathalie saw its physical impact on Macie. Like she'd been slapped. Macie's eyes went glassy in the dappled light. She bowed her head and sighed softly, running her hands down her pants.

'Why did you lie to us about Jacob? You told us he was alive and living with his dad.'

Macie unfolded her legs from under her. 'Will, come and show me your teddy. What have you named him?'

Will and Seraphine came over to them and Nathalie felt an intense protectiveness envelop her.

'They're both girl teddies,' said Seraphine. 'Will's is called Jean and mine is Bonnie.'

'Lovely. What charming names. And did you enjoy the cake?' Macie asked, taking Will's hand in hers. 'I made it especially for you because you told me cake with jam in the middle is your favourite, after banana cake.'

'When's my mum getting back? I feel a bit sick,' said Seraphine.

'Me too,' said Will.

'Oh, you've all had too much sugar,' said Macie, laughing. 'Here, have some strawberries. Fruit evens things out.'

Nathalie felt her own queasiness intensify. She wanted to break up this party and usher the children into the sunlight, but it felt like she'd just picked at a loose thread. It felt like the fabric of everything was unravelling, messy but joined somehow and all she had to do was follow the thread, tug a little until she could poke her finger through.

'That little boy is so special,' said Macie, watching Will. 'We can all see that. It's such a shame his mother couldn't. Maybe that's why she left. She didn't love him. Not as a mother should. She must know deep down what's best for him.'

Everything stilled. The sound of the children, Macie's voice, the birdsong from the garden. It all quietened, and all Nathalie could hear was her own blood pumping in her ears. Nathalie felt loose from the wine, sleepy. Sleepier than felt right. She could still get the words to the tip of her tongue, but they were blurry, indistinct. 'What's best for him, Macie?'

'That he's loved, of course,' Macie laughed and shook her head. 'You know that. Not all mothers do, but you do.'

'And you want to protect Will.' Her voice didn't sound right. It was slow and garbled.

Macie put her hand on Nathalie's knee and smiled as though she was a child only just catching the meaning of a particularly baffling riddle.

'It's better this way. That little boy was not loved. I could feel it in my bones. I knew that she'd abandon him, just like Teresa abandoned Caleb.'

Nathalie felt bile rise in the back of her throat and she covered her mouth, swallowed it back. 'You knew Caleb's mother?'

'Are you not feeling well?' Macie asked, smoothing a strand of stray hair off Nathalie's face.

'I think I need some air,' she said, feeling pinpricks of sweat bead on her brow. 'The wine.' Her mind was spinning, the foliage was unnaturally bright, the roots like snakes twisting in the ground beneath her. Everything felt tangled, the branches, the roots, the things Macie was telling her.

'I gave her every chance to love that boy, gave her a job in my kitchen but, no, she just kept choosing the drugs.'

Nathalie tried to push past the thick haze in her mind. Caleb's mother. Will's mother. She tried to hold on to the connection, but the blackness edged into her vision. 'What did you do, Macie?'

Macie leaned in so close Nathalie could smell the sweetness on her breath. 'Nathalie, do you think your husband and friends would like to know that you slept with a boy in his 20s? Aren't you ashamed of yourself?'

Nathalie's head swam. She summoned everything to push back the blackness, to find the words. 'Macie, have you put something in my drink?'

'You are a bit partial to wine, aren't you, Nathalie?'

The last thing Nathalie felt was Macie's hand smoothing her hair. The last thing she saw was her girls' faces smiling, happy, being led out into the sunlight. The last thing she thought was of her helpless baby sleeping, before the world tipped sideways and went black.

* * *

Nathalie was disoriented when she woke. She sat up, with difficulty, rubbing her eyes. Everything was blurry and she was covered in sweat. Where was she? Her hands found sheets.

She was on her bed. She pulled the curtain aside to look out the window. The sun lingered on the cliff face, the colour of weak tea. It was late afternoon. Or was it early morning? She couldn't tell. Birdsong chorused in the trees. Were they morning or afternoon calls? Her head thumped and her heart raced. Where were the girls? Richie? Panic gripped her. She found a note on the bedside table before she found the empty travel cot.

Didn't want to wake you. I've taken him for a drive, M x

Relief flooded through her knowing that Richie was safely with Mike, and she took a deep breath. She pressed the palms of her hands to her forehead. The picnic under the weeping mulberry tree. The wine. What Macie had told her. It all flooded back like a terrible dream. A nightmarish fairy tale. The sound of children's laughter tinkled through the open window and she scrambled over the bed to follow it. The kids were all below in the garden and on the trampoline. Emmie was with them. Another rush of relief. They were okay. The others had returned.

She sat back down on the bed and reached for a bottle of water. Drank thirstily. Was she imagining what had happened in the cool, sun-dappled space under the tree? Had she drunk too much of that delicious wine? She'd sipped only a few mouthfuls, hadn't she? And this wasn't a hangover, this was something different. Her head was spinning and an unnatural tiredness dragged at her. It was hard to keep her eyes open. But what was the alternative? That Macie had put something into the wine? Wasn't she drinking from the same bottle? Was she just imagining these things? The conversation was hazy but she couldn't ignore the feeling in her gut. She'd felt like she was in a shadowy confessional box under that tree, or some dark amusement park. Had Macie done something bad? What had she said about Caleb's mother? Nathalie ran her hands down her face and rubbed her eyes, forced her brain to work through the fog. Macie had said Caleb was better off without his mother. *Drug addict. Kitchen.* Words came back to her like fragments of a dream. *Teresa.* That had been her name. She'd been a drug addict, and she'd worked in the kitchen here. Caleb had no idea about this, she was sure. His mother was a nameless enemy who had abandoned him in the garden. So, where had Teresa gone? What had happened to her? And Pen. Macie's words came back to her. *You understand what needs to be done to protect a child.*

Her gut ached and nausea rolled through her. Something had gone on here. She could feel it even if she didn't fully understand it yet. She was so used to stilling these feelings, pushing them down. Covering them up with wine. More wine. Nathalie felt bile rise in her throat and she rushed to the hand basin and leaned over it until the nausea passed. She splashed her face with water and looked in the mirror. Her skin was pale, dark bruises under her eyes. An image came to her of the painting in the hall. The one Caleb had spoken of and later had shown her. The Lady of Shalott looking into a mirror. The woman trapped in her tower who only saw the real world as a reflection in a mirror. Is this how she had been seeing the world?

She had to tell the others about the wine under the tree and ending up on the bed with no memory of getting there. Macie's strange words. She felt dizzy and sank down next to the basin, pressing her forehead to its cool rim, her limbs like lead. Would they even believe her? Emmie already thought she was a drunk. What else had Macie said? That she'd tell Mike about her and Caleb ... if what? She told the others what had been spoken under the weeping mulberry tree? What did she know that the others did not? *Jacob's death. Caleb's mother.* Macie's words came back to her like a chilling whisper. *That little boy was not loved. I could feel it in my bones. I knew that she'd abandon him, just like Teresa abandoned Caleb.*

Nausea rose through her again and this time her body convulsed and she vomited into the basin. She wiped her face with a wet towel and squeezed her eyes shut. She must tell the others about all this, of course she had to.

But Mike couldn't know about Caleb. *He couldn't know.* She thought about how he would react to the news she'd slept with another man. What would he do? Would he abandon her and the kids? A tremor ran through her and she drew her arms close. She realised she was shaking. She looked out the window to find the escarpment in shadow. Night was coming. Pen was out there somewhere, and dread moved inside her, darkening the edges of her vision. She knew the answer. Deep inside her, she knew. She had always known. Ever since she received that email from him to his lover, she knew. It was like tiptoeing on the thinnest of ice, knowing that with any step everything could shatter. She would be left alone. With the children. With herself. She was caught in a web. She could see it shining now, glinting coldly on her skin. She shook her arms, but it clung on. She needed to get out of this place.

CHAPTER 42

Emmie

Emmie felt a buzz of annoyance as she watched Nathalie descend the stairs like some sleep-addled princess. Her hair was messy and her skin was pale, as though she'd just got out of bed. So, while everyone else was trying to help the search effort and entertain the kids Nathalie was drinking wine and napping.

'Here she is,' Emmie said, effecting an upbeat tone that she didn't feel. 'We were all wondering where you were. Mike said you were asleep, and Macie mentioned you had a little bit too much wine with lunch. She told us about the picnic. It was a nice thing to do for the kids,' she said, trying to hide the wave of resentment for the way Nathalie seemed to have forgotten that their friend was lost and another fruitless day of searching was wrapping up, another dark night edging in, bringing with it feelings of doom that stifled all the hope buoyed by the daylight.

Nathalie looked dazed rather than guilty. She shook her head, confusion clouding her features. 'I didn't think I had that much wine actually. I ...' She rubbed her arms and looked around. 'Where is everyone?'

'It's dinnertime. The kids are just coming in to wash their hands, Caleb's made quiche. Don't know how that'll go down with the kids but it's nice of him to keep cooking for us all despite everything. It's some semblance of normality for Will.' The kids trailed into the entrance hall behind her. She clapped her hands. 'Come on, it's dinnertime. You were all complaining of being hungry a second ago. Go and wash your hands in the hall bathroom.'

Nathalie crouched down to her girls and wrapped them in her arms, pressing her face into their hair. When she stood Emmie thought she saw tears in her eyes.

'Go on, go and wash your hands,' Nathalie said, ushering them towards the bathroom. 'Thanks for looking after them. I ...' her voice trailed off and she took a deep breath. 'What did you find out in town? Did you speak to some locals? What are the police saying now?'

'Mike did but I don't think there's anything much new. They've put a call out on social media, and in the local paper. They're still interviewing people in the area. None of it feels like it's enough.' She looked towards the darkening evening. 'And now it's another night.'

Nathalie swallowed hard; it was clear she was feeling emotional and despite her lingering resentment, Emmie reached out and touched Nathalie's shoulder.

'Are you okay? You seem a bit ...' She shrugged. 'Off.'

Nathalie's mouth quivered at the corners. 'I think I'm just overwhelmed with what's happened. I ...' A flicker of pain passed over her face. 'I think I must have drunk too much wine with lunch. I feel so awful to have been asleep when you were all out there looking.'

'Oh look, we're all emotionally exhausted.' Emmie sighed. 'Not that it's helped much. I did find out a potted history of the valley though, in a book written by a local history buff.' She looked behind them and up the stairs, making sure Macie wasn't around. Her voice was whispered. 'Spoke to the librarian there who knows of Macie Laurencin and had a few things to say.'

Nathalie's eyes widened. 'What did she say?'

The kids began to stream back into the hallway, and they ushered them into the dining room. Emmie lowered her voice further. 'Let's talk after dinner. Macie isn't well liked. None of the locals would dream of coming into the valley. They're spooked by it. It made me think of Will and his strange behaviour.'

'Really? Oh my God.'

'And it's true, Clara Black went missing in the 1940s – it was a huge story at the time. It's all recorded in a book on the history of the valley. The librarian let me borrow it. And there was another missing woman. In the '90s. Local drug addict. Not much of a story, hardly an effort put into looking for her. No mention of her in the books I looked at. More of a local rumour. Was involved with local bikie gangs, apparently.'

All the colour had drained from Nathalie's face. She opened her mouth as though to say something and then closed it, shook her head and closed her eyes for a moment. Emmie took her elbow. She couldn't help herself. There was something about Nathalie that made you want to look after her. She was like a frail, exotic bird. 'You look like you need something to eat.'

Caleb came into the hall and Emmie felt Nathalie stiffen beside her.

'Oh, hi,' he said, running a hand through his hair, looking awkward. 'I just wanted to check whether the kids would prefer the bacon or salmon quiche.'

'Caleb, what would we do without you? So thoughtful. Seraphine will eat anything,' Emmie said.

'Thanks, my girls will want the bacon. But I'll serve them. You've done enough. Thank you,' Nathalie said, rushing into the dining room at a speed that surprised Emmie. Something was definitely going on between the two of them. The tension was clear.

Macie and Nathalie began serving food onto the kids' plates. It felt so wrong that they were here enjoying another meal when Pen was God knows where. She looked over at Will. Nathalie had served him first. Putting food onto his plate and filling his plastic cup with water. How long was this going to go on? At some point they all needed to go home. Will needed to go home … but to where? Cate could stay with her father but he wasn't Will's father. And it was pointless to try to contact Pen's mother, Will's grandmother. Emmie knew that she was in a nursing home suffering from dementia or Alzheimer's. Pen had mentioned going to visit her several times and how sad it had made her.

Emmie's heart ached for this little boy. After yet another futile day of searching she had to face the painful truth. Maybe Pen wasn't coming back. The police couldn't keep looking forever. Her heart felt like it was being stretched across her chest and the black pit she'd been staring into for days yawned, became a cavern. *A valley*. Taking Will in for a while if the worst came about, made sense. He and Seraphine were friends. There was nowhere else for him to go right now. How would Dave react? He'd be fine. Of course he would. He was a good man. She realised that she missed him. He'd offered to come out to help in the search, to comfort her, but Emmie kept telling him she was okay. That they'd be home soon. Not to worry. Pen would be found. She'd been deluding herself. Homesickness washed through her. The librarian's words came to her as she placed a slice of quiche on Seraphine's plate and kissed her daughter's head. *Gives me the spooks. Locals wouldn't be going there.* She thought of that ghostly face in the window at the old mines. Up until now she'd thought it all just a fanciful tale, a story told to scare and fascinate in equal measure, but now she didn't know.

CHAPTER 43

Nathalie

Mike entered the hall with Richie strapped to his front, her son's little legs kicking madly. She felt a rush of love. Relief. She went to them and kissed them both on their cheeks. They were cool from walking in the evening air.

'He wouldn't sleep in the car, so we went for a long walk, didn't we buddy?' Mike looked Nathalie in the eyes. 'You okay, Nat? You were dead to the world. Richie was crying in the travel cot and you were out of it. I couldn't even wake you.'

Nathalie's cheeks burned. She felt everyone's eyes on her, and the shame lit up again deep within her. She wanted to cry out right now – *I wasn't drunk. I know, I have a drinking problem, but I swear, this time it was something else. This was Macie.*

But instead she swallowed the shame and the panic down, bowing her head and mumbling her response. 'Sorry. I'm really tired at the moment. I'll go fix Richie his bottle.'

The kitchen was empty – a small comfort. She couldn't bear to be close to either Macie or Caleb. She'd avoided both their eyes, kept her head down. The last thing she wanted was to have to be alone with Caleb. She prepped a bottle for Richie and put it in the microwave. She was testing the heat on her wrist when Caleb came in carrying an empty tray.

Their eyes met and Nathalie looked away first. Caleb was next to her before she had a chance to escape.

'I need to talk to you,' he said, his breath hot on her bare shoulder. 'You've been avoiding me. I knew you wouldn't meet me last night.'

She moved away from him, but he grabbed her arm. She disentangled herself from him and held up her hands in protest. 'Caleb, I'm sorry, my family's here. I'm not sure what you expect from me. I'm sorry. Pen is missing. It's–'

He took her by the shoulders and forced her to look him in the eye. 'We've been so honest with each other. Admit it. We have. You're hiding that part of yourself now. The real part. You're numbing yourself with alcohol again because you can't face the truth.'

Anger flared in her and she manoeuvred out of his grasp. She wanted to tell him about what had happened under the tree, what Macie had told her about his mother. But she knew she couldn't.

'The truth. Caleb, do you have any idea?' She shook her head and screwed her hands into fists, trying to steady her breath. 'Did you tell Macie you gave me the key to her office?'

Hurt flashed over Caleb's face and he was a boy again. Vulnerable and alone. Regret washed over her and she squeezed her eyes shut. He hadn't told Macie. He was a victim, too.

His gaze dropped to the floor. 'I really thought we had something special, you know? A connection. An understanding.'

His eyes met hers. 'If you knew me at all, you'd know I'd never do that.' He turned away.

She reached for him. 'I'm sorry, Caleb.' He pulled her towards him and kissed her hard, their bodies pressed together. She was stunned, immobilised. The bottle of milk slipped from her hand. She broke away from him and dropped to the floor to pick it up, gasping, her face flushed with emotion. She touched the bottle with trembling hands.

The door opened and suddenly Mike was in the room. She could hear Richie fussing. 'Where are you, Mummy? I'm hungry,' said Mike.

'Sorry, I spilled his milk,' Nathalie said, standing up too fast, dizziness overtaking her. She looked between Caleb and Mike. Caleb handed her a roll of paper towel.

'Well, we won't cry over spilled milk, will we?' said Mike, chuckling.

Nathalie felt the tears come then, unbidden. She had to get out of here. She couldn't stand it anymore.

'I'm sorry,' she said and ran towards the screen door at the side of the kitchen. As she escaped out into the night, she looked back to see both men staring at her.

* * *

The air was cool on her cheeks, the moon a slip of light in the sky. She could feel the ghosts of the valley all around her. Strange animal cries, the hum of crickets and insects still warm and buzzing from the heat of the day. The cliffs were black, foreboding, a dark curtain. She wanted to part them, go beyond this strange, haunted place. But she was trapped.

Fresh tears fell down her face and she brushed them aside. She looked back and the only light in the whole valley was coming from the hotel dining room. Everything else lay in blackness. She couldn't breathe. She forced the air into her lungs, gulped it down. What was she going to do? How could she escape this situation? She wished she had a bottle of wine. She wished for the numbness, the relief. She should have grabbed one from the kitchen. She followed the gravel path around the side of the hotel until she reached the front garden. This was where the cliffs were highest, magnificent and frightening, looming like gods, shadowed against the stars.

She moved through the dark garden, the statues luminous in the pale moonlight. Nymphs, unearthly women, horned, mythical creatures. She came to the car park. Again she felt it. The urge to flee. To get in the car and just drive.

A scuttling in a nearby bush startled her. 'Hello?' Her voice was puny against the deep hum of the night. She despised her voice. She was so weak. So pitiful. To even contemplate leaving her children, even for a second. She would never do it. Pen would never do it. She felt this chime deep inside her. She imagined Pen outside now somewhere, lost in this dark, bewitched place. Alone. Or worse. Her chest ached and she pressed her hands against it.

She thought of Macie. What Emmie had said she'd found at the library. Teresa, Caleb's mother had to be the other woman who had gone missing in the valley. There was a strange equation at work here, and on a gut level she knew she'd already worked it out. She tried to quiet her mind. Listen to something more elemental inside her. She felt painfully sober.

She looked into the deep bank of bush in front of her and took a step into its shadows. And another. Until she was entangled by dark branches. It was eerie, quiet, but the ground beneath her seemed to scuttle with life. Animals. Insects, unknown things. She thought of Clara Black, the woman who had been lost in this valley so long ago. Had she run into the bush? Had it been a night like this? Of Teresa, a woman labelled a drug addict and a neglectful mother. No one even trying to find her. Of Pen, who was gone so suddenly.

She looked up but the stars were obscured by trees. Her heart was beating fast, ricocheting through her body like a train. There was a clearing up ahead, where the moonlight lit an expanse of rock, like a silver pool. It felt cool and she lay down and looked up. She could see the stars here. The cliffs were gone. She forced herself to face what was in her heart.

Could she do it? Could she give up her life? Mike, who was just coming back to her. She imagined his face twisted in anger at her betrayal. All her security. What would she do as a single mother who hadn't worked in years? How would she survive? Where would they live? She was weak. She wasn't capable. She was an alcoholic. As she admitted this to herself an awful choke sounded from her throat. She wished she could erase the past week of her life. Go back to the innocence of that time before they came here, where everything existed silently just under the surface, able to be pushed away, ignored, skimmed over, numbed. She wished Macie had never told her what she had under that weeping mulberry tree. That she'd never discovered the truth about what was in that office. That she'd never gone to that cave with Caleb.

But as she lay bathed in moonlight, she heard the trees whisper in the wind. They did not whisper to her. She was inconsequential. She felt the strength of this old, dark place, of its past, of all the lives it had borne witness to, of all the lives that would come after she was gone. She felt her own smallness in the long thrum of life.

She was not drunk. She was clear-headed, her senses alight. The certainty of the rock beneath her back. The ancient trees, the ancient cliffs. All the lives that had been lived here before her, that she could feel, they could all feel. All those stories lost forever. Her own was tiny, part of something bigger, something unknowable and huge. It terrified her.

But she'd seen a glimpse of what freedom, what truth, what courage felt like. It was Caleb who had shown it to her. He had shown her who she used to be. Before Mike, before the kids. She'd been strong. Fearless. Free. Where had that woman gone? An image came to her bright and clear as though it were her own memory – a mother strong and fast and brave, her baby strung to her front, her feet never stopping. Running, running for her life, for her child, escaping as terrible shots rang out through the valley. Nathalie sat up and realised she was alone, surrounded by the dark bush. But she wasn't afraid. And she knew what she had to do.

CHAPTER 44

Nathalie

She heard voices calling her name. Emmie's was higher, more urgent than Alexandra's lower octave. A new energy poured into her. She called back, rushing through the bush, feeling the sting as branches bit at her bare legs, cutting her skin. But she didn't care. She was breathless by the time she found them in the garden.

'Macie. We have to find Macie. Please.' She grasped at them in the dark. 'We have to do something.' The words rushed out of her. 'I couldn't say before. I'm so sorry.'

Emmie drew her into a hug before studying her with worried eyes. 'What's going on? You've got blood on your face. Mike is so worried about you. He said you ran off into the night.'

'I don't have time to explain everything.' She looked about, the garden's nymphs and sirens, glowing in the dark like little ghosts.

Emmie led her to a marble bench next to the fountain. Alexandra sat on the other side of her, wordlessly encircling her with her arms, then taking her hand. Nathalie knew her friends thought she was just drunk.

'I'm not drunk, I promise. I've never felt so clear about anything. I know things, about Macie. I should have told you earlier, but she threatened me. She blackmailed me.'

'Blackmailed you?' Even in the dark she could see Alexandra's face was screwed up with disgust, but she pressed on.

'The picnic Macie had under the tree for the children, she drugged me. I know she did. I only had a few sips of the wine, and it knocked me out completely. I don't even know how I ended up in my room. Mike said I slept through Richie crying and I never do that. I literally can't, even when I'm drunk. And the things she told me.' Her voice broke.

Alexandra dropped her hand and stood. 'Oh my God, Nathalie, what the hell do you have against Macie? Do you hear what you're saying? That this woman, who has been nothing but kind to you and your girls, drugged you? That you weren't drunk? My God, can you hear yourself? I love you dearly but …' She shook her head. 'You're an alcoholic telling us that you passed out and blaming Macie for drugging you? Do you realise what that sounds like?'

She felt nauseous at Alexandra's words. Her head spun. What a joke she was. She'd known they wouldn't instantly believe her, help her. She felt her stomach drop, her skin bead with sweat. The night they'd all gone out for drinks at the beach flashed back to her and shame crashed over her. She'd been so drunk they'd had to carry her back to the car. She'd passed out on a school night. Why wouldn't she pass out at a kids' picnic? Who was she kidding?

She felt Emmie squeeze her arm then and she turned to face her. 'I believe you,' Emmie said. 'Tell me. I'm listening.'

Her face was suddenly wet, and she choked back tears. 'You do?'

Alexandra let out a huff and crossed her arms, but she didn't move.

Nathalie took a deep breath in and exhaled a shuddering one. 'I'm not sure where to start.'

'Just start at the beginning,' said Emmie.

'Caleb's not just a hotel manager. Macie brought him up after his mother abandoned him here as a baby.'

Emmie's body went rigid beside her. 'What? I thought he was just the cook. I mean, I didn't mean *just* the cook.'

'He told me Macie found him in the garden when he was tiny. She and her mother raised Caleb here.'

'I had no idea,' said Emmie.

'I won't pretend I'm not shocked about Caleb, but I think that's pretty amazing to take in an orphan,' said Alexandra. 'I don't see why this somehow makes Macie out to be the baddie.'

'I take it you didn't know any of this?' asked Nathalie. 'Even though you two went to school together.'

Alexandra waved her hand. 'Oh, that was years ago. I hadn't seen her in 27 years. You do realise Macie splits her time between here and a house in Sydney. She's only out here to host us.'

Nathalie nodded. 'The house in Sydney. That's where Jacob died.'

'Jacob?' asked Emmie.

'Her son. The one whose pictures were all over the walls of her office I told you about. I found newspaper articles inside a book about grief. He died in the bath when he was three.

I know. It's awful. Macie went to get a towel. It was just a terrible accident.'

Alexandra pressed her hand to her mouth. 'Oh my God. That's awful. Heartbreaking.'

'Oh gosh. Poor Macie. I'm surprised she handles hanging around with the kids so much. She's so good with them,' said Emmie.

'She's been wonderful with them,' said Alexandra.

'So, what's Macie done exactly? Why do you think she drugged you?' asked Emmie gently, her eyes searching, confused.

Nathalie swallowed hard. She tried to keep her voice steady, but it wobbled when she spoke. 'I've been having … something … with Caleb.'

She paused but there was only silence so she spoke into it. 'I'm not proud, but Mike … he cheated on me. Last year. It broke me. I suppose I was getting revenge on him in a way. And I do feel a connection with Caleb. I don't know. I have no idea. I've not been the best parent. The drinking. Sleeping with another man.'

'Why didn't you tell me?' Alexandra's voice was high, tinged with upset. 'About Mike.'

'I don't know. I didn't want it to be real. Didn't want to face what it might mean for our family. For me. I was ashamed. Scared.'

'So, you stayed with him?' Alexandra's voice held a note of contempt. Nathalie had been expecting this.

'Yes. Yes, we've been doing counselling.'

'I can see how that's working out for you,' Alexandra said. But then she squeezed Nathalie's hand and her tone softened. 'Sorry. Sorry. I just can't believe you didn't tell me.'

'I'm telling you this now, okay?' Both women were silent, so she went on. She felt the heaviness of their judgement and shame nipped at her bare skin like the cool night air, but she tried to ignore it. 'When we were having the picnic under the tree Macie was acting weird. She told me about Caleb's mother, Teresa. She was a drug addict who worked in the kitchen here. She said that Caleb was better off without her. That's a different story from what Caleb knows. He thinks his mother abandoned him here. It doesn't add up. Where did Teresa go? Was she the missing woman the librarian was talking to you about, Emmie? Didn't she call her a druggie? And then Macie started talking about Will and how Pen didn't love him and her going away was the best thing for him. Then she said if I said anything to anyone, she'd tell Mike about me and Caleb. And then I couldn't keep myself upright. And the next thing I woke up in my bed.'

'Why would she tell you all this if she had something to hide?' Alexandra asked.

'I don't know, I don't fully understand either, but I know her secrets — about Jacob, and about Caleb and his mother. Maybe she felt threatened by that. She said he'd never told anybody about his mother abandoning him before. And she knew my secrets. I got really drunk on the first night, and I told her about Mike's affair and how I was too weak to leave him. She used that against me. Maybe she didn't think I would tell. And she kept saying that she and I are the same because we do what's best for our kids. Maybe she has this warped view that, I don't know, we have some kind of bond. We've traded our terrible secrets. It's like it's some kind of sick game to her.'

Alexandra let out a loud laugh, tinged with hysteria. 'Can you hear yourself? This is a woman who lost her child. Why would she hurt another mother? And why on earth would she admit that to you Nathalie?'

'Because secrets are heavy burdens to bear,' Nathalie said. She felt light with the truth of it.

Alexandra grunted. 'And yet you're happy for her to look after your children. She's in there now scooping out ice cream flavours.'

'But don't you see? That's the whole point. She thinks she's doing the right thing. Saving these boys from their neglectful mothers.'

'Boys?' asked Alexandra.

'You think Macie's done something to Pen, don't you?' asked Emmie. Their eyes met and understanding flashed between them. Nathalie gripped Emmie's hand. Time seemed to still as they sat in the enormity of those words. Silence descended, as long and eerie as the shadows in the garden.

Alexandra broke it. 'I can't listen to this anymore. It's bullshit. All I hear is a story of a broken woman who lost her son and who has somehow had the good grace to open her home up to us and our horde of kids and look after them. And we could all see how much Pen was struggling. Will is a weird kid. All that ghost shit. It's scary as hell. It scares me. That woman walked away from her child and left him here. That's what neither of you want to admit. But that's what happened. You're just not prepared to face the awful truth.'

Alexandra turned and walked towards the hotel. Nathalie realised Emmie was still gripping her hand.

CHAPTER 45

Alexandra

Alexandra found Macie in the kitchen scraping plates into a compost bin. She was dressed in one of her signature silk robes, a deep red, rolled up at the sleeves. Under the harsh industrial lights, she could see the tideline of Macie's foundation at her jaw and this small vulnerability made Alexandra's heart squeeze with pity.

Had she misjudged Macie? Surely not. She felt defensive of her, especially given everything Macie had been through. She'd been tempted to tell the others about the bullying Macie had endured at school, that it was happening all over again, but the shame of her part in it was too great. And now to discover the poor thing had lost her son in a tragic accident. The spike of pity intensified as she watched Macie stack plates into the industrial dishwasher.

Nathalie was clearly having some kind of breakdown to accuse Macie of these things. And Emmie was just a follower. It was obvious she was in Nathalie's thrall. She should have smelled the whiff of desperation coming off her in the school hall that first day they'd all met. And posting all of those pictures without asking – she'd practically stolen Nathalie's identity.

Alexandra couldn't ignore the unease that wormed inside her. She couldn't help feeling that the friendship tables were turning. There had always been an unspoken bond between herself and Nathalie. That they were best friends. But who didn't tell their closest female friend about their husband cheating? It smarted. Alexandra would never keep such a thing from Nathalie. And the Caleb thing was just a bit off. He was a lonely young man. They could all see that. Sure, he was intelligent and attractive, but really? She couldn't believe Nathalie was the same person she'd known for years.

'Are you going to help me with these pots and pans or just stand there?' Macie's voice snapped Alexandra into the present.

'Oh, sorry. Yes, of course. What can I do? Thank you for another lovely dinner.'

'Caleb's in a mood so it looks like I'll be cleaning up tonight.' Macie pulled on a pair of washing-up gloves and handed Alexandra a tea towel. 'You can dry. I see the others aren't going to chip in. Nathalie's got the drama queen act down pat, I see.'

'Macie, I'm so sorry. You've been doing everything. Looking after the kids, cooking. Putting up with us all in circumstances no one could have anticipated–'

Macie sighed. 'So, Alexandra, are we going to talk honestly after all these years?' Macie straightened at the sink but didn't turn around.

Alexandra wrung the tea towel in her hands, her heartbeat fast. Macie turned and under the harsh light their eyes met. It felt like a bolt of electricity.

'You mean school?' She hated how desperate her voice sounded.

'Because if we are, I need a cigarette.' Macie pulled off the gloves and tossed them into the sink. She grabbed a packet of cigarettes and a lighter from a kitchen drawer and walked outside without looking back. The screen door banged behind her. Alexandra was left standing there. She felt stuck to the spot. She wanted to go back into the dining room and find her boys, take them upstairs and climb into bed with them. Smell the small comfort of their tired little bodies. Forget Macie. Forget all the drama of the past few days. Go back to how things were. Even Maxwell was a comforting thought right now. But she owed Macie this. Disquiet leaked through her.

She crossed the bright kitchen and stepped into the night. It was always a shock how dark it was in the country. She smelled the cigarette smoke before she saw her. Sitting on the low brick wall that encircled the back of the hotel, as though it could somehow, absurdly, keep out the encroaching bush. Crickets sang and a cool breeze combed the trees. The cliffs loomed behind them. Listening, bearing silent witness.

'So, are you going to finally pay me back then, after all these years?'

Alexandra stopped a few steps away from Macie. She felt glued to the spot. 'Pay you back?' she asked, hoping she didn't sound as breathless as she felt.

'I know Nathalie will have told you. I can see it on your face. And that's what the drama queen act was about earlier. That woman always has to be the centre of attention. As though being beautiful and having three gorgeous children isn't enough. Oh, and a younger lover who's smitten by her.' Macie took a long drag of her cigarette and offered it to Alexandra.

Alexandra took it but shook her head, trying to untangle her thoughts, her feelings. 'I defended you. She's talking about you putting something in her wine at the picnic for the kids, blackmailing her about Caleb.' She shook her head. 'It's absurd.'

Macie laughed. 'Hmm, yes, imagine all the things that have been *put* in Nathalie's wine over the years. Not the wine itself mind you that makes her sick. Couldn't possibly be that.'

Alexandra felt conflict wrench through her, and she bit her lip until she tasted blood. Part of her knew Macie was right, the other part wanted to defend Nathalie.

'If you're not going to smoke that I'll have it back.'

Alexandra took a drag and handed her the cigarette.

'But I think we both know that other women have never particularly liked me. It's a fact of life I've become quite used to as I've matured. It helps if you have a hotel in the middle of a valley to escape to and art to pour your soul into.'

'No, Macie. I like you.' The words were out of her mouth before she could stop them.

Macie took another long drag on her cigarette and the only sound was the high hum of crickets. 'You do? Because it's funny, I always thought you did. But then the way you treated me … It was confusing.'

Alexandra felt heat rush to her face. She was glad of the darkness and she pressed cool hands to the back of her neck. She wanted the dark to swallow her up. She wanted to run, to hide, but she couldn't. She realised everything had been leading up to this point. How had she thought that this conversation would play out?

'I was young, Macie. We both were. I'm so sorry. It's just ... it was peer pressure. Being different, you know how it is.'

'Oh, I know how it is, but do you, Alexandra? Really? Because you are different. And so am I. It's just that I can own it. You, on the other hand. Does your husband even have an inkling?'

Alexandra's mouth went dry. Her whole body was consumed by a thick dread. A bird cried mournfully into the night. She felt the wetness on her cheeks before she knew she was crying. 'No. No, he doesn't. We don't really ... things haven't been good for years. Macie, I'm sorry. I wasn't prepared to have such strong feelings. At such a young age.'

'You abandoned me. You left me to the wolves. Not only that, you led the wolves. You incited them to devour me.'

Alexandra was crying. 'I'm sorry. I'm sorry. I was too weak. I couldn't face the strength of my own feelings. I didn't understand them. I was ashamed.'

'We had something. You know we did. I remember. And then the person who really saw me destroyed me.'

'I thought it didn't mean anything. I told myself it was a schoolgirl crush. But it wasn't. I know it wasn't. I punished you for the power you had over me. I'm sorry.'

'You shaped the course of my life, Alexandra. When I met Drew, I was broken from you. Nineteen. So young. Too young to become a mother. But Jacob was the love of my life. He gave me purpose. To see that I wasn't a useless piece of shit after all. That I could make a little baby and look after him.' She laughed darkly. 'Except that I couldn't in the end.'

Alexandra stepped towards Macie. 'I'm so sorry. About what happened. I had no idea.'

'Yes, platitudes. That's all there is left. I've lived a lifetime of platitudes. What do they do? What do they change? Nothing. They just make the person saying them feel better.'

Alexandra couldn't stand up anymore. Her legs were shaking, so she sank onto the wall next to Macie. She felt strangely light-headed. She faced the other woman. 'I don't blame myself for not being able to face my sexuality. But I do blame myself for my cruelty. That was unacceptable. That has haunted me.'

'Cruelty. What is cruelty?' mused Macie, standing up, stubbing her cigarette out. 'Life is cruelty. Cruelty is life. It's all one and the same. It's survival of the fittest.'

'I'm so sorry.' Her words were a whisper.

'You keep saying that. I've forgiven you, Alexandra. Why else would I have invited you and your friends here? But I could see you were bearing a heavy burden. Now you're free of it. As free as any of us can be.'

Macie began walking back towards the kitchen door. Alexandra realised she didn't want her to go but she didn't have the strength to call out. She wanted to talk things through. Make things better in the soft, safe cocoon of night. She got up on unsteady legs and followed Macie inside. The light was an assault. Macie wasn't in the kitchen. She pushed open the swinging door to find her in the dining room. The children were gone. Nathalie and Emmie must have rounded them up for bed. Macie was at the coffee and tea station, pouring boiling water from an urn into a teapot.

'There's some leftover lemon cake in the fridge. Can you get that and some more milk, please? Mike doesn't like the light stuff we all drink,' said Macie, arranging teacups on a tray.

Alexandra's chest tightened. 'You're not going to tell him, are you? About Nathalie and Caleb? Please don't.'

'Maybe you should tell him, Alexandra. You seem to have a knack for telling people's secrets.'

Alexandra's stomach turned and she felt nausea wash over her. 'Macie, it's not up to you. They're obviously having lots of problems in their marriage. Let them work it out.'

Macie straightened and passed Alexandra the tea tray. 'You're right. You should tell him.'

Alexandra put down the tray, a cold dread running through her. 'Macie, what on earth is going on here? Is this all a game to you?'

'You should know. You know all about playing games with people.'

Macie turned and walked into the kitchen. She emerged with a plate of cake and a bottle of milk, which she poured carefully into a jug. She picked up the tray.

'Please don't.' Alexandra hated the strangled sound of her voice.

Macie fixed her with a cold stare. 'You should try the lemon cake, Alexandra. I've always had such a fondness for lemons.'

Alexandra felt her face, her neck flush. Macie had not forgotten those schoolyard lemon taunts. How could she have treated Macie so cruelly? She had no words. She followed Macie as she walked into the lounge, feeling numb, guilty, confused. Mike was sitting on the lounge flicking through a newspaper. Macie placed the tray in front of him.

'You take milk in your tea, don't you, Mike?'

He looked up. 'Thanks, yep, I do. Great service here.' He winked.

Alexandra felt the muscles in her neck relax a little as Macie poured his tea in silence. She brushed past Alexandra on her way out and Alexandra's body collapsed in relief.

Macie turned at the door. 'Oh Mike, you might want to check in on that gorgeous wife of yours. Ask her to tell you about Caleb and what happened in his cave. It sounds intriguing, doesn't it? It might go a way to explaining her dramatic behaviour of late.'

Mike's face was blank, but when his eyes met Alexandra's, a horrible understanding flashed in them.

CHAPTER 46

Nathalie

'He's a fucking child!' Mike spat the words and Nathalie felt the warm spittle hit her face.

Rage coursed through her, hot and ripe. 'That's what you're focusing on? His age?' She hissed the words, whispered them over their children's sleeping bodies. The hotel room felt too small, too close, too full of him. His sweat, his anger, his revulsion. She could smell it in the air, and she couldn't breathe.

'Oh, believe me, there are plenty of other things I could focus on. We're just getting to those.' His voice boomed and she hushed him.

'Shhh, you'll wake them.'

'Oh, and *now* you're thinking of our kids.'

The anger intensified but she wordlessly pulled him by the arm until they were outside the room. In the dark hall their footsteps echoed loudly. She made for the small second-floor balcony off the hallway. The air outside was cool, and she was glad of its effect on her skin. She drank it in. The stars burned above, and the cliffs stood silent. She took a breath and turned to face him.

'Does that somehow make it worse for you, Mike? That he's younger than me? What, it's okay for you to cheat with a younger woman, but it's not okay for me to have sex with a younger man, is that it? Well, Ruby's a fucking child, too.'

Mike ran his hands down his face, which was shiny with sweat. She could smell it. Even in the dark she could see his face was contorted with hurt and it twisted something deep inside her. She still felt something for him, even after all of this.

'I thought we were getting things back on track, Nat. All those hours with that stuck-up bloody counsellor. I thought we were better than ever. Missing you, coming here, it felt like a new start.'

'I'm a drunk, Mike. Did you happen to notice that? I haven't been coping. Not for a long time. That's what alcoholics do. They numb their pain. It broke me, what you did to me. What you did to our family. It absolutely broke me.'

'Oh, so it's my fault, your drinking?'

She let out a dark laugh. 'It sure didn't help.'

'So, you thought you'd just have a bit of revenge sex to add to the charming picture, is that it?'

'Is that what you think this is?'

'Isn't it?'

Nathalie shrugged. 'Maybe. I don't know. I've been so fricking confused, hurt, abandoned, tired. So damn tired, that I've been in a dream for months. A really shitty, bad dream.'

'Does it mean anything this thing with … what's his name?'

'Caleb. His name is Caleb.' She shook her head and covered her face with her hands. 'I don't know Mike, did yours mean anything with Ruby?'

The name hovered between them.

'It sounds to me like this was just a revenge fuck.'

Nathalie laughed. 'All you're talking about is the sex. But it's more than that, isn't it? It's feeling connected to someone else. Feeling heard and seen. It's feeling something. Anything other than hurt and rejection and numbness.'

'You didn't have to stay with me after the Ruby stuff. It was your choice to stay.'

Nathalie felt as though she'd been punched in the gut, right down low, low the way she'd carried all her babies. She gasped, a roaring intake of breath. 'It was my choice, was it?' She nodded, laughed softly, disbelieving. She wiped her hands down her face and looked up at the dark cliffs, drank in their huge, dark strength. 'What choice did I have, Mike? To leave you and be alone with a newborn baby and two small children? To have no security. No job prospects. To lose my home?'

'You paint yourself as the victim, but you haven't been innocent in all of this. We used to talk. We used to connect. What happened, Nat?'

'Children fricking happened, Mike. Sleep deprivation happened but you couldn't ride it out, could you? No, your wife wasn't putting out, wasn't as available emotionally because she was so exhausted, so spent and stretched, so you decided to go and get a bit on the side.'

'You don't get to judge me anymore. You gave that up when you left our children in a strange hotel and went to a bloody cave to screw a 20-something. Were you drunk? Oh, silly question.'

Nathalie hung her head.

'I think you know that our children aren't in the best care when they're with you.'

She snapped her head up. 'What? Don't you dare say that.'

'Did you even tell anyone where you were going?'

'The girls were here with the other mums. That's what women do. We look out for each other. We have each other's backs. We care for each other's kids. Without even having to ask.'

'You know what your problem is, Nathalie? No one ever tells you how it is. Not me, not your friends. But I'm telling you now. My children aren't safe with you. I knew the situation wasn't ideal with your drinking, but now I really know what you're capable of.'

'What I'm capable of? I'll tell you what I'm damn well capable of. Keeping three little people alive and well, day after day, even while my spirit is breaking. Even when I'm so lonely I feel like I'm in a black void. Even when I'm too tired to keep my eyes open. And yes, even after a few glasses of wine.'

'I don't think the court would see it that way.'

'The court? Don't you dare.'

'You don't get to tell me what to do anymore. You don't get to be the martyr and the victim.' Mike pushed the heavy door and disappeared into the hall. Nathalie stood there, shocked, unable to move. Then she felt adrenaline kick through her, and she ran after him. He was throwing clothes into his bag in the room.

'You'll wake them,' she hissed, touching his arm. He shrugged her off violently.

Sim and Findlay stirred. 'What's happening, Mummy?' asked Findlay, her eyes wide.

'It's okay darling, back to sleep,' she soothed.

Richie began to cry softly in the travel cot. Both girls sat up, rubbing their eyes, their hair over their faces.

Mike slung his bag over his shoulder, grabbed his keys off the dresser. 'Get dressed girls, we're going home.'

'Don't be ridiculous, Mike. It's the middle of the night.' She curled her body around her girls on the bed.

'This is happening, Nathalie. I'm taking my children. They're not safe with you.'

'Don't be ridiculous. You're scaring them, Mike. Let's talk about this tomorrow, when we're both thinking clearly.'

'Oh I'm thinking perfectly clearly. The clearest I have since I met you. Come on girls, get up. Put on some clothes.' He opened the girls' pink suitcase on the floor with his foot. 'Damn it. It doesn't matter about clothes. Here, put your shoes on.' He took Findlay by the hand softly as he placed thongs by her feet. Nathalie resisted the urge to grab her away. She could see him softening. Her daughter's face was pale, her eyes huge as she looked between the two of them. 'Come on now, don't you want to go home? Go back to your own bedrooms? Come on. Put on your thongs.'

'But it's dark outside, Daddy,' said Sim.

'Mike, please, calm down. Don't scare them. We're not going anywhere right now.'

He still had hold of Findlay's hand, but she could feel her girls' limbs grasping her flesh like tender flower stalks winding around her, seeking comfort.

'I want to go home, Daddy, but why are you and Mummy fighting?' asked Findlay, dropping his hand and nestling back into Nathalie's chest.

He grabbed both girls by the arms and pulled them away from the bed, away from Nathalie's hold on them. She cried out with the violence of it and the girls' piercing squeals made Mike let them go.

'It's okay,' she whispered into their hair, into the sweet smell of them as they huddled close to her, their bodies trembling.

'Fine,' he said.

She watched, numbly as Mike reached down for Richie and picked him out of the travel cot. She stood, in slow motion, the girls still clinging to her.

'Mike, please.' She grabbed for his arm, but he pushed her to the ground. Richie's high-pitched wails made her get back up, reach for him again, but Mike was out the door. She followed him, calling his name, the girls trailing after her, the horrible echo of her children's cries bouncing off the walls.

'Richie,' she called, running down the staircase, running out into the night, through the garden, across the gravel of the car park. Mike kept pushing her back, but she would not give up. They reached the car and Mike turned to her, his eyes shining in the dark.

'Get back or I swear I'll ...'

What? Break me? Destroy me? You already have, she thought. She summoned every last ounce of energy and courage and lurched for her son in Mike's arms. She heard the crack of his palm meeting her cheek and she fell.

She heard the car engine start, the screech of tyres, but she couldn't move. Her head felt too heavy. Her face was burning, swelling. Everything was black. She tasted blood on her lips. It felt like her heart had been ripped from her chest. *My baby.* Emmie and Alexandra were by her side. She heard their whispers. Everything hurt. She felt herself being picked up off the ground and the hair smoothed from her face.

'He took Richie. He took my boy.'

Her daughters nestled into her, one under each arm like little birds under her wings. She sobbed into their bodies.

'It's okay, Mummy,' said Findlay, her voice wobbling, her cheeks wet with tears, hands stroking Nathalie's hair. She opened her eyes and saw how scared her daughter was and how brave she was trying to be. Her heart squeezed and something inside her solidified, crystallised, a fury as cold and startling as the sudden absence of her son, and she knew what needed to be done now.

She used everything she had to pull herself to her feet, ignoring Emmie's and Alexandra's protests. Her face throbbed and her mouth felt thick. The moon had risen, and its light shone a path through the garden to the hotel. Macie was standing there on the front steps in a white nightgown, like a spectre.

Each step reverberated through to her face, her jaw, but she kept walking and then she was running, flying towards her. Nathalie expected her to flee, to run into the warren of rooms in her hotel but Macie just stood there, the breeze lifting her gown, her pale hair.

When she reached her there was no resistance. Her hands found Macie's neck. Nathalie forced her backwards, pinned her against the hotel doors. Her own words were choked.

'Is this what you wanted, Macie? Was this your plan from the start? You've taken him from me. Are you happy? I'm in as much pain as you. I'm as bad a mother as you. You've fucking won. You've taken my son.'

Macie's face contorted as Nathalie pressed against the soft flesh of her throat. She had never felt more powerful, more in control, more sure of anything. A gurgle issued from Macie's throat, but Nathalie pressed harder.

'You're a monster.'

She heard Emmie's voice, felt hands grasping at her, pulling her back, but she was in a nightmare from which she couldn't wake. It felt like time had stilled, stretched out between her and Macie as their eyes locked together. Nathalie saw that Macie was choking. She couldn't breathe. Something passed between them. She saw fear, pure and unadorned in Macie's eyes. But also, something else. Sorrow. Simple and deep. A horrible vulnerability. Brokenness. She also saw pleading and she realised Macie wasn't pleading for her life, she was pleading for death. She wanted to be free from the pain, the sorrow.

The recognition struck Nathalie at her core. She saw herself. She remembered herself that night at the hotel in the city. How close she'd been to ending it. How much she'd wanted to leave, for the pain to just go away. This woman had lost everything. She had lived with the burden of the blame, of self-hatred for what she'd done to her own son. Life had crippled and twisted her. Nathalie saw clearly her warped charge to save these children from their neglectful, imperfect mothers. Of which Nathalie was one. Shame and sorrow welled inside her, engulfed her. Of which Caleb's mother was one. Of which Pen was one. She saw that Macie truly thought she was helping these boys. She was saving them from the version of herself that she so deeply despised.

Nathalie wanted so badly to keep pressing. It would only

take seconds. She wanted Macie to die for her insanity, her cruelty. She didn't deserve to live. The words came to her lips and she spoke them aloud. She looked into Macie's eyes, glassy, the life almost gone.

'None of us is perfect.' And she let go.

Macie's eyes were closed and her lips were an awful blue. She slipped to the ground.

Alexandra was at her side and Emmie stood back, arms around her girls, who were whimpering softly. *What have I done? What on earth have I done?* she thought. Alexandra put her hand on Macie's head, touched her face with a tenderness that made tears prick Nathalie's eyes. Alexandra whispered Macie's name and bent to check she was breathing. Nathalie felt her daughters' little bodies latch to her legs. Emmie touched her shoulder, pulling her away from Macie, but she resisted, bending over until she felt warm breath on her cheek. *She's alive.*

'I'm sorry,' she said. 'I'm so, so sorry.' She pressed her face to her girls' tear-stained skin until Emmie gently prised them from her and took them inside.

She heard Caleb's voice before she saw him. Confusion contorted his features as he crouched down. Bruises were forming under Macie's skin, like a dark necklace. Her face was blanched, white and blank, but her chest was heaving air into her lungs.

'What the hell have you done to her?' he asked, his face pained. Caleb cradled Macie's head in his lap. A deep rasping was coming out of her now. Tears spilled down her face. Her words were whispered.

'Caleb.' Macie reached for him. 'I didn't mean to hurt you, Caleb. I just wanted to protect you. I didn't want anyone to suffer.'

'What are you talking about?' asked Caleb, his hand on Macie's cheek.

'Your mother. Teresa. She did love you. She didn't abandon you. Not really.'

'My mother? You know her? What are you telling me?' He shook his head.

'She overdosed on the kitchen floor. I could have helped her. But I let her die.'

'On the kitchen floor?'

'You wouldn't remember but she came here asking for a job. You were just a baby. I couldn't stand to watch it. How little she cared for you. How selfish she was. I didn't want you to become Jacob, I didn't want you to become my son, dying in a shallow bath because his mother wasn't attentive enough.' A soft howl of pain escaped her lips and she hid her face.

Caleb's face twisted in disgust. 'You lied to me about my mother leaving me?'

'Caleb, please, I only meant to protect you. She was on a mission of self-destruction.'

'Protect me? You trapped me. You took away my self-worth. You made me think I was nothing, not even someone a mother could love.'

'I love you.'

'That's not love.' He squeezed his eyes shut and his body lurched away from her. Her head rolled to the ground.

Nathalie placed her hand on Macie's shaking shoulder. She knew she had to act quickly, while she was still exposed, vulnerable. Before her hard shell grew back.

'Macie, please, please tell us if you know what happened to Pen. Please, I'm begging you.'

Alexandra was on her knees. She pressed Macie's hand between her own. 'I'm so sorry. For all the pain I caused you. For what you've been through. Please, Macie, please help us. If you know anything at all about Pen, you have to tell us.'

Macie groaned and rolled away, pulling her knees into her chest, curled into the foetal position.

Nathalie got to her feet. She found Caleb sitting on a bench, his head in his hands.

'Caleb, I know how much you're hurting right now but you're the only one who can get this out of her, if she's done something to Pen. Please.'

He looked up. His voice cracked. 'If that's the case she's a fucking psycho.'

Nathalie grabbed his hands. 'No, Caleb, she's broken. It's made her do insane things, but she loves you.'

He shook his head.

'She lost her son. She thinks she killed him. But it was a tragic accident. Can you see how that's ruled her life? Her decisions?'

'You want me to forgive her after I've just found out she let my mother die and lied to me my whole life. I can't do that.'

Nathalie put her arms around him and held him for what seemed like a long time. His body was very still. She took his hand and led him back to where Macie was curled tightly in a ball on the ground.

'I'm sorry. I can't talk to her,' Caleb said, breaking away.

Nathalie bent down and smoothed the damp hair from Macie's face. Her eyes were closed.

'Macie, please, we know you thought you were protecting Will, but we need you to tell us about Pen. What's happened to her? Please.'

Macie put her hands over her ears. Her body was trembling.

Nathalie turned to Caleb again. 'Please, you're the only one who can get through to her.'

Caleb shook his head, his face drawn in pain.

Nathalie felt a hand on her arm. She looked down to see Will. Very small, very still. Her stomach turned. *How much had he heard? How long had he been watching?*

Slowly Will got down next to Macie on the ground and folded his arms around her waist. After a long while her body stilled. He spoke to her softly.

'Thank you for looking after me, Macie. I love you. You're a very good mummy. But I miss mine.'

Macie rolled towards him. She looked at him for a long time. She brushed the tears from his cheeks. Very slowly she pulled herself off the ground. Will helped her stand and took her hand in his. Together they began to walk out into the night.

CHAPTER 47

Pen

She had been asleep, but now she was painfully awake. The sound of voices. She was sure they were voices. She sat up, feeling her arms ache, her head throb. She listened, her mind more alert than it had been in days.

'Hey. Hello. Help.' Her voice was raw, dry, weak. She listened and heard nothing. She called out again. Again nothing. She sank back down onto the hard makeshift cot. Maybe the voices had been a dream after all. She had called out so many times before. No one had come. And it had slowly, dreadfully dawned on her that she was in some kind of underground room. She could smell the earth and the roots and the damp. It was no bigger than a bathroom with dirt walls and a stack of mouldy boxes in the corner. Some of the foodstuffs dated from the 1950s. Rusted cans and bags full of salt and flour that turned to dust at the touch. But there were bottles of water and cans of baked beans and tuna. It was some kind of basement storage that they must have used when the mines were in operation.

There had been an electric light at first. It worked for about 24 hours and then spat terrifyingly and fizzed out. And now she was using single white candles that looked like they were from a time of rationing. She lit them carefully. Each match a lifeline. She resisted counting the candles, counting the matches. She was terrified of when they would run out. Of when she would be in the dark.

The last normal thing she remembered was the beautiful breakfast Will had brought her in bed. A spindly daisy picked from the garden on the tray, the cornflakes soggy and the tea mostly milk. She had felt an enormous rush of gratitude and guilt, which mingled together like that lukewarm tea. She had been so cruel to Will the night before over that diary. So unnecessarily unkind, and then he'd gone and done something so beautiful. She'd never felt such self-disgust.

She had played everything over so many times in her head. She knew, deep in her bones, that Macie must have put something in that tea. It was the only thing that made any sense. She remembered the fierce burn of Macie's eyes as she'd pointed out that Will had wet himself. The intense, crushing shame she'd felt. And the suffocating tiredness after a few sips of that tea. She remembered kissing Will's cheek, sinking back into the bed, closing her eyes. She'd woken briefly once, so delirious that she couldn't move. She'd felt frozen, her body a numb, useless thing. She'd seen through slitted eyes that she was in another room in the hotel, not her own but almost a carbon copy with the pretty bed covers and antique furniture. She'd tried to call out, mustered everything she had, but it was as though a dark hood had been pulled over her head.

And then she was here. She'd had so much time to think. Too much time. Truth and regret were her constant companions, like the cockroaches and ants, the daddy-long-legs in the corner. So much regret. She would have stopped eating and drinking – it was hardly eating. When the tuna and baked beans ran out it was tinned soup, gloopy and cold and hard dried noodles way past their expiry date. But she forced the food into her body for her children. She took tiny sips of the water for her children.

It would have been easier to find a way to die quickly. But she thought about them growing up without a mother, in the world alone. Especially Will. Where was he now? Were they looking for her? How on earth would they find her here, somewhere under the ruins, lost, like the history of the valley. These thoughts haunted her. She scratched them all on an ancient pad of paper with a pencil. It was the only thing she had to do as the intense anger cooled to despair.

Dear Will. Dear Catelyn. She wrote them letter after letter.

Dear Will, I didn't love you like you needed to be loved. I let you down. I imposed my own expectations onto you instead of seeing you for who you are. Loving you for the person you are. Accepting you for who you are. I made it about me instead of you. You are everything to me. I'm so sorry.

Now she pulled herself off the cot and crawled to the top of the metal stairs. She pushed the trapdoor above her and banged on it as she had countless times before and cried out. She listened. Nothing. The voices had been in her head. Of course they had. Every molecule of her body felt the disappointment, like thunder rolling over an already blackened sky. The thick dread settled back into her. She knew she mustn't give up.

She couldn't. But she was getting so tired. It was getting so hard to keep the darkness at bay. Maybe she shouldn't even blame Macie ... maybe Will was better off without her. That boy deserved a mother who loved him easily, accepted him and understood him. Macie seemed to be able to do that better than she'd ever managed to.

She thought back to his birth. It had been a difficult one. She'd laboured for hours, a whole day, only to have him cut out of her. She remembered the shock of his slimy body on her chest, his scrunched-up face. She remembered pasting a smile onto her lips when the doctors looked at her. But there had been no recognition. No spark. Not like with Cate. And there had been no help. Her mother had just started down the road to dementia and there was no father this time. There was no time either. She couldn't take maternity leave like she had with Cate. She had to keep going because she had to keep her job to pay the rent. And Will hadn't slept well. She remembered those early days with him in her arms heating the metal coffee pot on the stove on those cold July mornings. She must have had eight cups of coffee some days. She'd never had time to stop and consider what was going on. She had just been running. Scrambling, trying to hold everything together. But now she had time to think and the thought had bubbled up, like the thick black espresso that ran in her veins all those years, that maybe she'd had post-natal depression with Will. And it had never gone away. She had mistaken caring for a child for loving one.

She pulled herself into the corner of her cot, drawing her knees up to her chin. She wondered if she just allowed her mind to give up, her body would eventually let go too. If you decided to die, would your body obey? She closed her eyes and heard his voice. *Mummy.* Felt his breath, warm on her face, and she thought, *This is what dying feels like.* In the dim light of the candle she could make out the small shape of him.

Will.

She felt his skinny arms around her and she wished with all her heart that she had hugged him more. She was slipping away, but at least Will was here.

I'm sorry.

But then she felt someone wrapping something around her. A blanket. She was too tired to even open her eyes properly, to register the face, but it looked familiar, like a recurring dream. *Emmie.* Emmie was here. She could feel the wetness of Emmie's tears smear across her face. And she was being lifted, her arms wrapped around shoulders, her body pulled up the metal stairs and then there were stars. Millions of them. And air. So bright and cool it stung her skin, her lungs. She gulped it in.

Tears fell out of her like rain but her sobs were sandpaper dry. She held her little boy in the dark, the shadows of the mines all around them. *Will. Will. Will. I'm sorry. I'm sorry. I'm sorry.*

The others tried to get her to stand but she couldn't, she didn't want to. They tried to cover her skin in blankets, but she shrugged them off to feel the fresh air caress her skin. She didn't want their food or water. She stayed there clinging to her little boy for a long time, but time had become elastic and she realised it didn't matter anymore.

When the paramedics came the light was coming up from behind the cliffs, a pale, new pink. She let them wrap her then in crinkly foil, and she drank and drank the delicious liquid they gave her. She hadn't known how thirsty she'd been. After she had eaten a small, dense bar, as the daylight grew bright on the cliffs, she felt her mind begin to clear.

She saw a single police car arrive, its lights blue and red in the soft dawn light. The officers spoke to her in hushed tones, crouching to her level, their eyes serious and steady. Emmie took Will away for a little while.

They asked her how she'd got there and how long she'd been there. She said she didn't really know. She didn't mention Macie. It sounded absurd. She didn't know if that was true, after all. It felt like she'd just woken up and everything was indistinct. She tried to answer their questions in between small sips of water, to find her voice, but she felt so tired.

She watched Macie get into the police car flanked by two policewomen. She didn't feel anger. That had burned off days ago. She had no heat left in her for it. She didn't even need to know why Macie had done it. All she felt was gratitude.

Will returned to her and she looked into his eyes. 'I love you,' she said. 'I'm sorry I didn't see you before. I'm sorry I didn't listen to you. I think I was sick and I couldn't find a way to get better. But I'm here now. I am here, my love. I'm going to get better.'

His eyes were red from crying. Her heart squeezed to think she'd caused him so much fear, so much pain.

'I thought you left because you didn't love me anymore.'

Pen's heart ached and she drew him close. 'No, no, I would never ever leave you. Do you understand? Never.'

Will fixed her with his intense gaze. 'But you were so angry with me. Because of the lady, and the diary.'

'I'm sorry. I didn't mean to be. I was just scared because I didn't understand. But I want to understand. I want to help.'

Will curled his hand into hers. 'Mummy, I know you want to go home now but before we go, can we please help the lady?'

Pen nodded and tears spilled down her face. 'I know. That's what you were trying to tell me, wasn't it? When I got so angry.'

Will nodded.

Her heart crushed in her chest as she realised the depth of her son's empathy. How had she not seen it before? How had she only seen his difference, his strangeness. Mistaken his sensitivity for weakness, for darkness? 'Okay,' said Pen, hugging him to her. 'I'm listening.'

* * *

They stood at the end of the dark hallway in front of a closed door. Pen tried it. Locked. The weak light from an old lamp did nothing to illuminate the shadowy corners. Pen felt the familiar unease shift and move inside her, but she fought it back and crouched on her haunches so she could look into Will's eyes.

'Tell me about this place,' she said, taking his small hand in hers, pressing it between both her palms.

'This is where she keeps leading me, Mummy.'

Pen smoothed his soft cheeks with her thumbs. He was hot and flustered. She wanted to lead him outside into the light, into the sun, away from the dark corners of the world, the unknown. She wanted to protect him. She wanted to protect herself, but she knew she must face this.

'Okay,' she said.

'This is Macie's office,' said Emmie. 'Nathalie told us about it. Nathalie found you here, didn't she, Will? But the door's locked. Hang on, there's a torch at the reception. Let me grab it.'

'Why do you think the lady's leading you here?' asked Pen.

'I don't know.'

Emmie returned, shining the light along the walls, which were lined with paintings, mostly landscapes and women reclining on day beds. She hovered the light above Will's head.

'This one's a framed newspaper article. I've seen this. At the library when I was reading about the history of the valley and the missing woman, Clara Black. It was a huge scandal at the time. A woman ran off to Sydney with a man and left her family in the valley. She left her daughter. They attended parties in Sydney together and then neither of them were ever seen again. It was speculated that they left Australia, went to London.' Emmie took the frame from the wall and smoothed the dust off with her hand. The newsprint was yellow with age. She read the headline aloud.

> *Local Dance Teacher in Valley Scandal*
> *Jean Peters, the local school ballet mistress has been embroiled in a scandal of Sydney proportions after she ran off with ladies' man and oil magnate Magnus Varesso. She left behind her miner husband, Robert Peters, and small daughter, Liv Peters.*
>
> *Sources indicate that Jean was once a famous dancer named Serpentine Rose who danced at some of Sydney's most esteemed establishments. Local mothers expressed their alarm that such a person of disrepute had been schooling their children in dance and had abandoned her six-year-old child to pursue a scandalous affair*

in Sydney, where the pair were spotted, before reportedly escaping to London, where Varesso had business interests.

The scandal hit the close-knit town only weeks following the mysterious disappearance of local woman Clara Black.

'And Clara Black is the missing woman who's supposedly haunting the valley. The ghost from your Instagram post,' said Pen.

'Yes, everyone thought it was her ghost in my photo in the ruins,' said Emmie. She crouched down to Will to let him see the article. 'Will, the diary you found, was that a lady called Clara?'

Will looked at Pen, a shadow of shame passing over his face. Pen put her arms around him. 'It's okay. We can look at it. I'm sorry I didn't let you tell me about it before and I got so angry.'

Will offered her a small smile. 'That's okay, Mummy. I forgive you.'

Pen's heart ached and she pressed her hand to her chest. She and Emmie shared a look.

'Your son is all kinds of amazing,' said Emmie as they watched him run down the hall to fetch the diary.

Pen shook her head. 'I've been struggling so hard that I haven't opened my eyes to what I actually have.'

Emmie rubbed her arm. 'Are you sure you're okay to be doing this?'

Pen nodded. 'Will needs me to.'

'Do you even believe in ghosts?'

Pen smiled. 'I'm not sure. But I believe in Will.'

The diary was cracked with age, its pages flimsy and thin. On the opening page in a small, neat hand was scrawled:

Property of Clara Black. Emmie carefully found the last page of writing. The date was February 1948.

It is the night of the hotel ball. I'm upstairs in my room, in my ballgown, trying not to cry as I make up my face. I'm escaping tonight. I'm going to sneak off into the dark when the ball is at its peak and everyone is giddy and drunk, and Magnus will be flirting and distracted. Mary is going to help me. She has a car packed and ready on the edge of the settlement with a bag containing only a few precious things. I know I must leave Magnus in this way, quietly, without him knowing, or I fear I'll not live to tell the tale. He will kill me rather than lose me. His controlling nature has become unbearable, frightening. It has become physical. I've had to cover the bruises with scarves. My heart feels like it's coming out of my body as I write this. I don't know why I ended up with a man prone to violent fits of possessiveness. I know I brought it all on myself by starting up this secret affair, betraying Richard. I thought Magnus would be my escape from a tyrannical husband. But he turned out to be worse. I must get away from them both. This time tomorrow I'll be in Sydney making a new life for myself, God willing, even if it means vanishing forever from the lives of everyone I know.

'If this is the same Clara Black, she got out of the valley,' said Pen, her fingers tracing the ink. 'She intended to go missing. Will, I'm so sorry I didn't listen to you when you showed me this.'

'So, it's not Clara Black's ghost that haunts this place,' said Emmie, carefully leafing through the pages. 'She's detailed Magnus's cruelty. He was abusive. Will, I'm so sorry you had to read this.'

'It's okay. I like mysteries. I like reading and writing detective stories,' he said.

'He's actually a good writer as well as drawer,' said Pen, feeling a rush of pride overtake the usual dull thump of shame. She hugged her little boy to her and looked him in the eye. 'What do you think, Will? What does your detective brain say?'

'Maybe it's Jean.'

A shiver, like a cool fingertip, traced along Pen's spine. 'I just got tingles.'

'Me too,' said Emmie. She read the article aloud again. 'Jean supposedly left her family and ran off with Magnus to Sydney. But Will, you think she might still be here?'

Will nodded.

'We know this Magnus was a dangerous man,' said Emmie. 'And Jean was having an affair with him. Could the same thing Clara Black was afraid of, have happened to Jean? Maybe Jean wasn't as lucky as Clara Black. Maybe she didn't escape the valley.'

'She wants something, Mummy,' said Will, his little face strained with emotion.

'Oh honey.' Pen hugged him to her.

'What could she want?' asked Emmie.

Will shook his head.

'I think I might know,' said Pen, her eyes meeting Will's.

CHAPTER 48

Will

We went to the house of a lady called Liv. It was a posh house on Sydney Harbour. Liv was a little girl, maybe my age when she lived in the valley, but now she's old, like really old. Much older even than Mummy. She used to be poor because everyone who lived in the valley was poor, but she's rich now because she became a famous ballerina when she grew up. Mummy said she'd even performed at the Opera House and it's funny how she became a dancer, like Jean, her mum. And that Jean would have been proud of her, just like Mummy's proud of me.

We went and sat in an old room with a nice view of the Harbour Bridge and the Opera House, and Emmie talked a lot about a book she's writing about the valley. She's really excited about it and Liv seemed to want to talk to her lots. She told her about how she used to play a game with an old cotton reel on a string, and how she went to the movies, which were called 'the pictures' in the olden days, and how she had fond memories of the valley. That bit was kind of boring because I knew most of what they were talking about because of all the books I read when we were staying there, but at least I got a lemonade and to count the seagulls and boats. Finally Mummy said I had something I wanted to show her.

'Let's see, what have you got there, young man?' Liv asked in a kind voice. She had kind eyes, too. The ones that crinkle up in a nice way.

'It's a diary of a lady called Clara Black. I found it at the hotel we stayed at in the valley.'

She took the diary carefully, much more carefully than most other adults. She held it like it was a small, helpless animal and I liked that.

'Clara Black. The woman who went missing in the valley just before my mother left. Yes, I remember it well. How extraordinary to have found this. It's a little piece of history. Where did you come across this, Will?'

'I found it under a creaky floorboard in my room at the hotel.'

'Extraordinary.'

'Read the last entry,' said Emmie. 'It's about Magnus Varesso, the man who—'

Liv's body stiffened. 'I know who Magnus is,' she said, her voice not as friendly as before.

When she finished reading the last page, the bit where Clara escapes the mean Magnus man, she had tears in her eyes.

'Will has something he wants to say to you,' said Mummy.

I was nervous because sometimes adults don't understand stuff you say, or they don't really believe you, but Mummy gave me a look that means *I love you, it's okay.* She squeezed my hand and I held it without letting go. Everyone was looking at me and I felt stupid, but then I remembered how bad I felt for the lady at the hotel and how sad she seemed and what if she really was a lady called Jean who never got to tell her little girl she loved her, like my mum got to tell me she loved me.

'I don't think your mum meant to leave you. I thought my mum left me, but she actually didn't.'

Liv's eyes got sparkly when I said that, and she took my hand. Hers felt soft, and also rough, like paperbark.

'Tell me, why do you say that, Will?'

'I know you might not believe in ghosts. Not many adults do. But I think I saw Jean. At the hotel we stayed at in the valley. The paper said she ran away with a bad man called Magnus and left you, but she's still there.'

Liv squeezed my hand and she didn't talk for a little while. I think maybe she was crying but it was the kind of crying where you're a little bit happy as well as sad. When she did talk her voice was husky.

'I believe you're probably right, Will. Thank you for being brave enough to share that with me. It's very kind of you to be so concerned and to come and tell me this. And I knew. Deep down I think I always knew my mother never meant to leave me.'

'How did you know?'

Liv looked out the window towards the sea. The wind smelled like salt and she smiled. 'Because she never came to my performances. In Sydney, or in London. I became a ballerina because of her. And every time I danced, I danced for her. And the mother I knew would not have missed that for the world.'

EPILOGUE

Pen

She opened the doors to hear the breeze playing in the gum trees. Currawongs sang their soft song and the ocean whispered at the shoreline. She could see all the way to the horizon, to the clouds crisping to gold in the early evening light. Pen would never tire of this time of day. Of this view. Of this house.

The doorbell rang and she walked the long, bright hallway, her neck craned, seeking the skylight and the green lace of leaves above. She heard the thump of Will's running feet from the other end of the house, and he was there beside her, his hand slipping easily into hers.

Nathalie, Alexandra and the kids all poured into the hallway. Nathalie held a cheese platter in one hand and Richie in the other. Cate appeared and took the little boy from her arms, his face a picture of delight at seeing his babysitter again so soon. Alexandra proffered a bottle of wine, which she cracked open and took onto the deck. Emmie and Seraphine arrived just as they were settling in for their regular Sunday night supper together. Emmie's belly was as round as the green olives in the bowls. Nathalie rubbed it affectionately and they clinked their glasses of sparkling water in solidarity.

Their talk was easy. The week ahead, what their weekend had held. Nathalie's acrimonious divorce. But the water drew their gaze like a balm. The children came and went between their games, picking at pieces of cheese and grapes like the greedy birds in the branches above. The house was cushioned between bushland and water. Will called it their magical tree house. It was this, more than the fancy appliances, the huge floorplan or the pool, that appealed to Pen. People had said she shouldn't accept Macie's home. Or at the very least, she should sell it and take the money. And didn't she know that Macie's little boy had died there?

She'd been shocked when she'd opened the letter to find Macie had transferred the house into her name. The feeling had struck her deeply, more deeply than hearing that Macie had been sentenced to jail for Pen's kidnapping and for concealing Teresa's death, then taking her son.

But she understood that this house was not only for her. It was for Caleb when he visited Sydney. For Nathalie when she and her children needed sanctuary. It was for all of them. It was something bigger, vast, like the valley walls, like the thing that linked Will and Liv, like the small blue bear that sat in the room on the second floor. She said a prayer for Jacob every night as she hugged her own son close. She wrote a letter to Macie and told her simply that. And that she was no longer afraid of ghosts.

AUTHOR'S NOTE

This book is inspired by a real place: the beautiful Capertee Valley in NSW. The Traditional Owners of the land are the Wiradjuri people, whom I would like to acknowledge and pay respect to their Elders past, present and emerging.

When I stumbled across this remote place online, filled with little-known fragments of Australian history, I knew I had to visit. My mum, daughter and I embarked on a road trip; we drove across the Blue Mountains and into the valley, unaware of what we were about to find.

There's little more than a long-abandoned town – a virtual ghost town – with the crumbling facades of buildings and an old pharmacy, with medicines dating from the 1950s still in the window. The ruins of the shale oil mines shimmer in the distance. Only a beautifully restored Art Deco hotel, built in 1939, remains in business. I immediately knew this was where I wanted to set my story. Thank you to the owners of the Glen Davis Hotel who hosted us.

As well as its rich history as a shale oil town, the valley is a place of unparalleled natural beauty. The sandstone escarpment drops into a deep chasm that forms one of the largest canyons in the world. The landscape has an extraordinary atmosphere, at once magnificent and haunting.

As I researched the Indigenous history of the area, I learned what had happened to the Aboriginal Wiradjuri people in this region in 1824, during the Bathurst Wars. Reading the devastating accounts, I began to understand the atrocities that had taken place in these parts. To present details in my book thoughtfully and appropriately, I consulted an Indigenous sensitivity reader, and honouring the importance of 'truth-telling', I want to acknowledge this tragic past.

I found Leonie Knapman's book *Glen Davis: A Shale Oil Ghost Town and its People 1938–1954* helpful in informing the background of the region during its mining years, as well as illuminating some of the area's Indigenous history.

All my characters are fictitious, and I have used creative licence with the mystery surrounding Clara Black and Jean Peters. Many of the details about the town are drawn from real life. And the brutal stories of what happened to the Wiradjuri people are real – a reality that bears illuminating, remembering and telling the truth about.

For those readers who may have been triggered by the depictions of historical violence, domestic violence, post-natal depression and alcoholism, help can be found at lifeline.org.au, whiteribbon.org.au, blackdoginstitute.org.au and cope.org.au.

ACKNOWLEDGEMENTS

Thank you Soph and Jeanette. If you hadn't come with me on a random adventure to a far-flung valley, I never would have written this book.

And to Kirstin Bokor and Georgina Penney, your early feedback gave me the courage to submit my story to my wonderful publisher, Anna Valdinger. Thank you, Anna, for your insights into the manuscript and the much-needed chuckles. Thanks to my agent, Jeanne Ryckmans, for the excellent homeschooling debriefs.

Huge thanks to Catherine Milne, Barbara McClenahan, Lucy Inglis, Di Blacklock, Alex Craig, Pam Dunne, Amy Daoud and the whole wonderful team at HarperCollins. Thank you to all the passionate booksellers who are riding out such a hard year.

Danielle Townsend, your early edits were invaluable. Alexandra Joel, your messages and chats helped keep me sane. Karina Ware, thank you for the inspiring book suggestion texts. Abi Lewis, thank you for lending me your knowledge about gardens. Thanks to Ali Lowe and Judith Mendoza-White for the writing talks over coffee at Rosebery St. Thanks to Faye

James for the beach walks, Emma Jane Hogan for the beautiful messages of support, Janneke Thurlow for all the playdate swapsies and support, and Joanna Wolfe for the luscious platters.

A big thanks to Diggers for his knowledge of police procedure and criminal law.

Bec McSherry, your unwavering belief in me means more than you know.

And to Ben, thank you for ... everything.

To all the women in my life – this book is for you.

In Range

Ven'Thyl Saga Part I

Fables of J